MW01503927

THE CULTURE

CHAMBER

a novel by

Jeffrey D. Stalk

Copyright © 2012 Jeffrey D. Stalk

All rights reserved.

ISBN: 148193385X
ISBN-13: 978-1481933858

DEDICATION

To my lovely wife whose stories about the Dutch resistance set me on my journey of discovery.

This book is a work of fiction. References to real people, events, establishments, organizations, or locales are intended only to provide a sense of authenticity, and are used fictitiously. All other characters, incidents, and dialogues are drawn from the author's imagination.

The Culture Chamber. Copyright © 2012 by Jeffrey D. Stalk. No part of this book may be used or reproduced in any manner without the written permission of the author, except in the case of brief quotations embodied in articles and reviews.

Cover design by Robin Hill.

Truth will come to light; murder cannot be hid long.

Shakespeare, The Merchant of Venice

Chapter 1

Amsterdam Police Department
    Report no: 43-8241
    Precinct: 35
    Subject: Found Body

I, the undersigned Theodore Bakker, a police constable with the city of Amsterdam assigned to the 35th precinct on the Stadionweg, declare the following:

At or about 9 p.m. on April 21, 1943, while assigned to duties at the station, I received a telephone report of a found body. The body had been found in a clothing chest that had been pulled from the Boerenwetering Canal.

I immediately went to the location and spoke to the informant, Cornelius Kooij, 46, a plumber, who lives at 43 Hobbemastraat. He said that at or about 7:45 p.m., he and his 15-year-old son, Hendrik, had been walking his dog when they saw the chest in the water near the wall of the canal. Curious as to what was inside, they pulled the chest from the water but could not open it because the lid was secured by a small padlock. The informant stayed with the chest and sent his son to his home to get a hacksaw, which they used to saw through the lock. When the informant lifted the lid, he discovered the body of a man inside. The informant did not get a good look at the victim because he was in shock by what he found. He said, however, that he does not know who he is. His son also was unable to identify the body.

The chest, with the lid closed, was on a strip of grass at the side of the canal when I arrived. I opened the lid and saw what appeared to be the fully nude body of a man. The body was wedged tightly into the chest with the legs and head contorted in unnatural positions in order to fit inside. I could clearly see evidence of severe trauma to the back of the head. The victim appeared to be about 30 years old; the body was in the early stages of decomposition.

The chest was made of wood and sturdily built, measuring 125 centimeters long, 60 centimeters wide and 70 centimeters high. Iron handles were affixed to the sides.

I checked with the neighbors who had gathered at the scene but none of them knew who the victim was....

Origins can be elusive, difficult to identify, the more so in this case, given the passage of so many years. If one is scrupulous about it, if one seeks a circumstance about which there is no dispute, the story must begin in Amsterdam with the first meeting between an earthy, near-destitute young woman looking for work and a prominent artist looking for a model.

Saskia Hoogeboom had spent a miserable hour in the dingy anteroom of the artist's canalside studio, feeling as out of place as she had ever been in her life. She sat amid a dozen other young women, all of whom -- to her self-conscious eye -- looked like finalists from a beauty pageant. Demure, stylishly dressed, they sat patiently with their beautiful figures and sapient smiles, striking elegant poses as they smoked and chatted amiably among themselves. No one spoke to Saskia.

Like the others, Saskia had answered a newspaper advertisement for an artist's model, though where she got the nerve to do it, she never figured out. She had no modeling experience whatsoever and there was nothing about her physical appearance to suggest she ever would. Skinny, flat chested, a bit gawky, with shoulder-length, dirty-blond hair and a spattering of freckles on a blade-thin nose. Her woolen pullover and skirt were clean but obviously homespun. Taken together with her waifish appearance, she looked more like a runaway from juvenile hall than an aspiring model.

More than once, Saskia considered standing up and walking out the door; it was her desperate need of a job, coupled with her dread of running the gantlet of knowing eyes that kept her glued to her seat.

The artist was interviewing the applicants one by one in his atelier, which was partitioned from the waiting room by a grimy, paint-flecked blue curtain. From time to time, Saskia could hear giggling coming from the other side. She watched morosely as the artist emerged with first one girl, then another, laughing, familiar, exchanging kisses on the cheek. They were all part of a big, wonderful club, she thought. So elegant, so la-dee-dah. Walking around as if their shit didn't stink. What the hell was she doing there, she fumed.

Finally her name was called and with her nose in the air, she strode quickly across the room and went behind the curtain that the artist politely held open for her. She expected the interview to be short and unpleasant and to be back on the street in five minutes. What the young woman didn't know was that she had at least one point in her favor. What Dutch painter could fail to be touched by a woman who answered to Saskia, the praenomen of Rembrandt's treasured wife and model?

Maarten Dijkstra peered at her face, her chest, her legs, from the left and from the right, an inspection that Saskia found unnerving. Like he was staring right through her clothes, seeing her as she was. Skinny as a broom handle with less breasts than most men. Flat tush, small bush.

"How old are you?" he asked.

"Twenty-three."

"I asked how old are you?"

"I'm twenty-three," she said defiantly. "Do you want to see my identity card?"

Dijkstra smiled. "That won't be necessary." He continued to walk around her like he was inspecting a new automobile. "Have you ever done any modeling?"

"No."

"The work may be more rigorous than you think," he continued. "You may have to sit a certain way for long periods. Do you suffer from muscle cramps?"

"No."

"Any physical problems? Back problems? Leg problems?"

"No."

"Any objection to posing undressed?"

"No."

"The pay is adequate but not enormous. Three guilders a day to start. Any objections?"

"No."

"Good. When can you start?"

"Right now."

In fact, she began modeling for Dijkstra the next day. That was in November 1939 -- two months after the German invasion of Poland but six months before Nazi troops stormed into Holland.

It did not take long for her job to evolve into something beyond what was advertised in the newspaper. Within a month, she had moved into Dijkstra's Amsterdam home, becoming his fulltime cook and housekeeper, a part-time model and occasional bed partner. Materially, it proved to be a symbiotic relationship. She received free room and board and a generous salary, most of which she was able to save. She had two rooms to herself and the run of Dijkstra's gabled, three-story townhouse overlooking the Keizers Canal. It was quite a step up for an unemployed seamstress living with two other women in a squalid apartment on the fringe of the red light district.

And Dijkstra suddenly found himself in the alien environment of a tidy, well scrubbed home, eating nourishing meals on a regular basis. He was enchanted with this new wrinkle in his life.

But on an emotional level, their relationship was not in balance: she adored him; he was fond of her.

Saskia Hoogeboom had fallen head-over-heels in love with the dashing painter whose work brought fat fees and rave reviews. She was dazzled by his sophistication and in awe of his smart friends. She admired the way he enjoyed his wealth, spending money lavishly on his pleasures: big parties, first-class travel, women.

5

She knew about his other relationships -- after all, she lived in the house and usually managed at least a glimpse of the visitors he brought home. These were expensive women -- cool, glamorous, beautiful, the kind who turned heads in restaurants. She would burn with jealousy when he led them up the narrow staircase to the bedroom she knew so well.

From the beginning, Dijkstra made it clear to Saskia that he was not interested in a serious relationship with her. They would come together from time to time, but on his terms. There were no commitments, no plans, no promises to stop seeing other women.

Their relationship drove her crazy. In bed he was a fervent lover, making her feel like the only woman in the world. But the passion disappeared in the morning like a wisp of smoke. He would become her employer again -- friendly, attentive and as distant as the moon. Worse, he seemed perfectly content with the status quo, oblivious to her despair.

Over the months, Saskia came to know quite a bit about Maarten Dijkstra. He was in his early 40s, had studied engineering in Delft and had worked for an oil company for ten years in the Far East. Transferred back to the Netherlands in 1930, he suddenly quit his well-paying job and started to seriously pursue what heretofore had been a hobby: painting. And practically overnight, he had become a success. His lush landscapes of Indonesia were snapped up by wealthy buyers. That led to even more lucrative commissions to do portraits of bankers and their fat wives.

In 1936, Dijkstra added another title to his resume: professor. The University of Amsterdam hired him to teach art and art history and he soon became one of the university's most popular faculty members. Students battled for the limited spaces in his class, while others forked over hefty fees for private lessons at his studio.

Saskia knew that Dijkstra had a wide circle of friends: artists, professors, writers, actors and musicians. His life seemed so perfect.

For his part, Dijkstra asked few questions about Saskia's past which was just as well. It was not something she was eager to talk about. She had fled a broken home at fifteen and had been on her own ever since. She had tried her hand at a number of jobs: packing tulip bulbs, answering telephones, sewing dresses. From time to time, when the money ran short, she had rented out her body.

Her life did not begin to acquire meaning until she met Maarten Dijkstra. And in a skewed way, it was she who had triumphed over her well-heeled rivals. The others came and went but she was the one who had found a niche in his life.

Saskia remained under Dijkstra's roof even after the Germans took over Holland. The occupation had little impact on their lives at first; Saskia continued to cook and clean as before and Dijkstra continued to paint and to teach at the university. The streets were full of German troops but so what? Apart from the odd whistle or two when she shopped, they left her alone. Those were still the early days of the occupation and the Germans were on their best behavior.

But slowly, almost imperceptibly at first, the couple's living pattern began to change. Saskia was startled one day when she suddenly realized that at some point -- she was not clear when -- Dijkstra had stopped bringing other women home. There were still plenty of visitors to the house, but invariably they were men. They would huddle for hours around the dining room table.

Once, as she brought tea for the visitors, the shy young woman screwed up the courage to ask what they were talking about.

"We're convening our own Culture Chamber," Dijkstra had said and everybody laughed. She hadn't the faintest idea what he was talking about. Seeing her puzzled look, Dijkstra had winked and said. "You really don't want to get involved in the schemes of madmen."

Saskia knew in a vague way that Dijkstra was involved in Resistance work but she had no idea how deeply. He sometimes left the house in the middle of the night. Sometimes he disappeared for several days, leaving her to churn with worry. He never offered an explanation for his absences and again she didn't ask. Theirs remained a strange relationship. She was now sharing his bed almost every night but he still treated her like an employee.

On the surface, Dijkstra was the same suave, charming man he had been before the war. But there were changes there, too, and Saskia -- who was not particularly perceptive -- noted them. The spider web of lines around his eyes had grown and deepened and his sardonic smile -- so much in evidence early in their relationship -- was rarely seen. And there was something else, something she couldn't define, an edge, a keenness about him that frightened her. Part of his attraction, what made him different from other men she had known, was his gentleness. She had once believed him incapable of violence. And though he never so much as raised his voice to her, she now discerned a ruthlessness in him she never knew existed.

One day in April 1942, he said to her, "We have to move."

"Why?"

"Because the Germans want to kill me."

She thought he was kidding and searched for the ironic twist at the corners of his mouth. But he was deadly serious. They had moved in with a friend that night and two weeks later, moved again.

By March 1943, Dijkstra had moved a dozen times, staying with relatives, friends, colleagues. Each time he warned her about the dangers of remaining at his side and asked if she wanted to leave. And each time she pleaded to stay with him.

"Where can I go?" she would ask. "Who would take me in?"

"You're right. You're safest with me."

Then one night, as they lay in bed in the loft of a building on the Vijzelstraat that belonged to Dijkstra's uncle, he said to her, "Would you do a favor for me?"

"I'll do anything you ask."

"Anything?" he asked playfully.

"Anything."

He paused. "What I am going to ask you to do is distasteful. It's distasteful for me to ask and it will be even more distasteful for you to do it. Are you still willing to do anything?"

"Yes," she said without hesitation. She yearned to be part of his secret life but never dared ask.

He said what he wanted, and his request indeed stunned her. At first, she was hurt. She wanted to yell, "How can you ask me to do that? How can you?" But as she lay silently with her head in the crook of his arm, the realist in her asserted itself. She had done worse in her life, for less noble reasons. It wouldn't be the end of the world. A few unpleasant moments and that would be it. Like waiting for a streetcar near a *pissoir*. In war, everyone makes sacrifices.

She did not verbalize her thoughts but after considering the matter carefully, she asked, "Why don't you hire a prostitute?"

"This has got to be done quietly," he said. "I don't trust the whores to keep their mouths shut. Some of them are drunks. Some of them have *moffen*" -- krauts -- "for boyfriends. I can't take a chance on this getting out."

His frankness surprised her. It was the closest he ever came to taking her into his confidence.

She rolled onto her side, her face away from him, and brought her knees up into a fetal position. Tears welled in her eyes. Not for herself. Not for what he asked her to do. But for how vile life in Holland had become.

She swallowed hard, not wanting him to know she was crying. And when she recovered her voice, she said simply, "Okay."

He stroked her hair and kissed her forehead.

"It'll be all right," he finally said, but she didn't answer. She lay silently beside her lover for more than an hour before she finally fell asleep.

Chapter 2

Leo Wolters was edgy -- and scared -- so much so that he hardly touched the excellent lunch his sister had prepared for him. The meal was a treat, obtained through black market connections at considerable cost. Mashed potatoes crowned with a dab of precious butter, a mound of fresh string beans and a cut of pork almost as tender as veal. And to top it off, coffee -- real coffee -- with a heaping teaspoon of sugar.

"Why aren't you eating, Leo?" Monique asked, reproachfully eyeing Leo's full plate. "I worked hard to get these things for you."

It was Saturday afternoon, March 20, 1943 -- his twenty-first birthday -- but Leo did not feel much like celebrating. Still, he cut a piece of pork, speared a string bean, pushed some potatoes on top and popped the whole thing into his mouth.

"This is really, good, Mon," he said, chewing loudly. "Delicious."

Monique, who had already polished off her own meal, was not impressed.

"What's going on, Leo? How come you're not eating?"

Leo looked closely at his sister. Brother or no brother, there was no denying how beautiful she was: creamy, sensuous, ash-blond with legs that could rival Betty Grable's. He didn't have to ask how his 19-year-old sister obtained the ingredients for the meal. For the past several months, to the disgust and anger of their banker father, Monique had been carrying on a reckless affair with one of the most notorious figures in the *penose* -- the Amsterdam underworld -- a swarthy, muscular gangster named Dries Riphagen. Dubbed by the press the "Dutch Al Capone," Riphagen controlled gambling and prostitution for most of Amsterdam. He ran his flagitious empire from a swank gambling club on the Rembrandtsplein that before the war had been a popular hangout for Holland's fast set. In addition to his other illegal enterprises, Riphagen had become a major dealer in the wartime black market and it was to him, no doubt, that Monique had turned for the lavish lunch.

Leo took another forkful of pork and mashed potatoes and said, "I'm seeing Maarten Dijkstra later."

"Oh." Monique said.

She watched her brother eat for a couple of moments before asking, "Are you going to go?"

"I have to."

"You don't *have* to. You don't have to keep doing work for him if you don't want to."

"You don't understand, Monique. I can't back out now. Not now."

"Why not?"

Leo didn't answer.

"Why not?" she demanded.

"I can't tell you."

"Well, all I know is that if it's making you miserable, you can tell him to go to hell." And having disposed of the matter in one sentence, she stood up and began clearing the table.

Leo, who was not a courageous man, secretly admired his younger sister's insouciance. *Tell him to go to hell.* If only he could.

What Leo didn't tell Monique was that Dijkstra was well into an elaborate plan to pull off the most audacious raid of his career and woe to the man who got in his way. Leo knew what was in the works; indeed, he had been involved -- marginally -- in the preparations. His role to date had been miniscule. When called upon, he had hopped on his creaking bicycle to take messages from Dijkstra to one or the other of his subordinates.

But the unexpected arrival that morning of a message from Dijkstra had signaled an alarming turn of events. The Resistance leader "urgently" needed to see him at 2 p.m. in the Admiraal de Ruyter bar on the Vijzelstraat. The thought of becoming more enmeshed in Dijkstra's schemes frightened the devil out of him.

It's extremely doubtful that Leo Wolters ever killed a German soldier, as he repeatedly boasted later in life. In fact, very little about his alleged wartime deeds can stand up to healthy cross-examination. Leo was not a war hero, nor a hardcore Resistance fighter. He fluttered around the relatively safe periphery of Resistance work, an enthusiastic wannabe without wanting to be too badly. He ran errands and delivered messages, activities that allowed him to swagger a bit in front of his friends without great danger of getting shot.

But lately even such duties as he performed had become dangerous. After nearly three years of occupation, the Gestapo had established an omnipresent network of informers in Amsterdam. Armed with accurate intelligence, Gestapo agents had been carrying out late-night raids throughout the city in an effort to stamp out Resistance activity once and for all.

Leo knew what to expect if he was ever picked up. It was almost a given that he would spend at least one night of indescribable pain in the cellar of the three-story, red-brick building on the Euterpestraat in South Amsterdam that housed the Gestapo (before the war, the building with its graceful clock tower had been a girl's school, of all things).

Once there, specially trained interrogators, officially referred to as "examiners," or even more benignly, as "secretaries," would be sent down to interrogate him.

Anybody picked up by the Gestapo was assumed to have some knowledge of subversive activity and therefore likely to be tortured. The most common form of interrogation was a beating, with the examiners using rubber truncheons on the most sensitive areas of a prisoner's body. If the prisoner refused to talk, more severe measures were used. He might have his head pushed into a barrel of ice-cold water until he was asphyxiated, then revived and subjected to the same process again. And again. Or sharp pointed matches might be jammed under his fingernails and wads of cotton wrapped around his wrists. The matches were then lighted. Or electrodes might be placed on his penis and the juice turned on. One favorite technique used by the Gestapo throughout Europe was to crush a prisoner's testicles with a terror-inspiring apparatus designed just for that purpose.

The interrogation might last an hour or several hours, or even to the next day, with teams of examiners taking turns inflicting the punishment. And when it was over, the prisoner could expect one of three things to happen. The Germans might let him go. That happened occasionally. But if the Gestapo believed that he was holding back, that he had not disclosed all of his secrets, the prisoner would be taken by truck to a special wing of the security service prison in the coastal town of Scheveningen near The Hague, a facility the inmates referred to with gallows humor as the *Oranje Hotel*. There further examinations would be conducted in a room that resembled a medieval torture chamber. Prisoners were left to hang by their thumbs or had barbed wire cinched tightly around their heads. Or they were burned with solder irons, or shocked with cattle prods, or had swastikas branded into their cheeks.

When the Gestapo was satisfied that it had wrung from the prisoner every last drop of useful information, they would have him taken in the middle of the night to the dunes beyond the town and shot.

The third possibility was equally feared: sent to the transit camp at Westerbork on the Dutch side of the border, and from there, shipped east by sealed cattle car to die in places like Sobibor and Auschwitz.

These terrible thoughts were going through Leo's mind as he buttoned his worn sailor's pea jacket and pulled a dark woolen cap over his head.

"I am taking the bicycle," he shouted to his sister, who was washing dishes in the kitchen.

He carried the bike down two flights of stairs and out to the street where he was immediately slammed by a gust of the icy, bone-numbing wind that had been raking the city for two days. It had stopped raining but the cobblestone streets were slick from several days of thundershowers. Not a crack of sunshine broke through the leaden skies.

Leo got on his bicycle and began pedaling into the teeth of the wind, feeling very alone. Hardly a soul was on the street. Even the handful of German soldiers who usually patrolled the neighborhood were absent, probably drying out in a nearby bar.

Head bent, a scarf wrapped around his neck, he pumped doggedly forward, following the Boerenwetering canal to the Stadhouderskade, then crossing the bridge at the Singelgracht and riding down the long, straight Vijzelstraat.

Dijkstra had asked to meet him at the Admiraal de Ruyter bar, which stood at the far end of the Vijzelstraat, across the street from the old Mint tower where for centuries, the specie used around the globe by the Dutch East India Company was struck and issued.

It was an exhausting ride and Leo was sweating when he reached the De Ruyter. He took several deep breaths before hoisting the bike and carrying it into the bar. In those days of shortages, nobody was foolish enough to leave a bicycle outside.

There were three people in the taproom when Leo walked in: the barman, who was also the owner, and two men whom Leo didn't know. They were sitting by the window playing cards.

14

At the sight of the two strangers, Leo was about to turn around and walk out when he caught a nod from Piet, the barman. Piet moved his head, indicating the bar's back room but Leo still hesitated. Finally, after another look at the two strangers, Leo took a deep breath and darted into the other room. One of the most wanted men in the Netherlands rose to greet him.

"There are a couple of guys out in the bar," Leo blurted out.

"They're with me," Maarten Dijkstra said, and he clapped his former student reassuringly on the arm.

Leo had last seen Maarten Dijkstra about a month before but in the interim, the Resistance leader's appearance had taken a turn for the worse. Dijkstra had always been lean as a whip, but now he looked like a walking skeleton. The skin around his jaw line was so taut that it appeared the bone might tear through at any moment. What was left of the brown in his close-cropped hair had turned white. He was wearing workman's overalls and a faded leather jacket.

"Sit down. Sit down," Dijkstra said. "Do you want a beer?"

Leo had worked up quite a thirst during the ride and he nodded. As the older man drew two beers from the tap, Leo caught Dijkstra's cool, appraising look and grew uncomfortable. He knew the meaning only too well. Weighed and found wanting. How often had he seen the same expression in his father's eyes?

Dijkstra seemed to hesitate a moment, then smiled.

"I hope I didn't alarm you by asking for this meeting," he said, sitting down and pushing a foamy brew toward Leo. The younger man shook his head.

"Good. There's nothing to be alarmed about." Dijkstra paused and again looked at Leo intently. "Everything okay with you?"

"Can't complain," said Leo, trying to appear calm and failing. "And with you?"

"Not so good. There's been a hitch."

"Yeah?"

"Meijer was picked up."

Leo was startled by the news. Herman Meijer was an important member of Dijkstra's group, an expert forger whose skills were critical to the upcoming raid.

"When? How?"

"Yesterday. He was visiting his girlfriend on the Jodenbreestraat when the *moffen* raided the neighborhood. They were picked up -- along with a lot of other Jews."

"Shit." said Wolters.

"That doesn't begin to describe it."

The Germans were carrying out their *razzias* -- roundups -- at night when they knew the Jews, living under a strict 8 p.m. curfew, would be home.

"Where did they take him?" asked Leo.

"The Schouwburg," Dijkstra answered, meaning the Hollandsche Schouwburg, a large theatre in the eastern part of the city, smack in the heart of the Jewish quarter, that the Germans had converted into a holding center for Jews awaiting deportation.

"The *moffen* aren't keeping them there very long," Dijkstra continued. "A couple of days at the most. Just time enough to complete the paperwork. Then they are shipping them out to Westerbork. We have to get Meijer out of there. Fast."

The comment sent another chill down Leo's spine. A jailbreak from the Schouwburg? He *can't* mean it. The place was crawling with guards. What does he want *me* to do? I'm no gunman.

"I don't want to trespass on your hospitality, Leo," Dijkstra said quietly. "But would you mind putting Meijer up for a little while. Just until we find another place for him. I know your sister has moved in with you and it may be a bit crowded, but it's only temporary. It shouldn't cause you too much inconvenience."

Leo practically sighed with relief. Is *that* all he wanted? "Uh, yeah, sure. Sure I can. But how are you going to get Meijer out of the Schouwburg? The place is like a fortress."

"There are ways," Dijkstra said. He didn't elaborate.

"I really appreciate your help, Leo. As I said, it's very temporary. Just to give us a little time to arrange something more permanent."

"Sure. Sure," said Leo. But he was already beginning to have doubts. "Only, I was just thinking. What about the neighbors. None of them can be trusted to keep their mouths shut."

"The neighbors are not to know about it," Dijkstra said. The quietness of his voice italicized the menace in his words. "We'll bring Meijer to you at night. We'll brief him on the 'house rules'. No going out. No loud talking. No using the toilet when you're not home. He's a reliable man. I'm sure he won't cause you any problems."

Dijkstra stood up and clapped Leo on the shoulder. As he did, his jacket fell open and Leo saw the dull-black butt of a semiautomatic pistol shoved in his belt.

"Come on, Leo. Don't worry so much. You'll give yourself a rash. It's strictly routine. You shouldn't have any problems."

Dijkstra drained his beer and added: "You've been doing a fine job for us, Leo. Everybody knows it. Don't get itchy now. Not when victory is so near. We're getting closer every day."

Leo gave a wan smile but he really didn't see things that way. Every day, existence became tougher, not easier. Less food, less fuel for the stove and the furnace, more Draconian laws, more arrests, more friends and acquaintances gone and -- it hardly seemed possible -- more *moffen* on the streets.

"I know. I know, Maarten," Leo said. "Don't worry. I'll get the job done. I always have, haven't I?"

"You haven't failed me yet," Dijkstra said.

"And I won't fail you this time," he said.

"I know you won't."

The two men stood up and shook hands and Dijkstra said: "I think you should leave first." Dijkstra said.

"Oh, Leo," he called, as Wolters headed for the door. "Happy birthday!"

Despite his *angst*, Leo managed a smile. "Thanks."

"You'll be hearing from us," Dijkstra said.

Chapter 3

Three blocks away, in a comfortable apartment near the Waterlooplein, a courtly, gray-haired attorney named Rudolphus C.J. Vanderwal slowly put down the telephone after a short conversation.

"It was that gangster -- Riphagen," he told his wife.

"Riphagen? Calling *us?* What did he want?" But with a sinking heart, Heddy Vanderwal had already guessed the answer.

"He knows about the *onderduiker*," her husband said limply. "He's coming over here for a talk."

"Oh my God," said Mrs. Vanderwal.

For eight months, the Vanderwals had been sheltering a Jewish man from the Nazis.

Arie Cohen, a balding, 35-year-old bachelor and Vanderwal's law partner, had secretly moved in with the Vanderwals in the summer of 1942, shortly after the Germans instituted a welter of bizarre anti-Jewish measures, measures that banned Jews from sitting in parks or cafes, prohibited them from riding trams, stipulated that they could not own cars or bicycles or radios, could not fish, could not use the telephone, could not attend university, could not swim in public pools, could not buy vegetables at non-Jewish shops, were not allowed outside after 8 p.m., were not allowed to visit non-Jews, were not allowed to enter hotels, theatres or restaurants unless the establishment was owned by Jews. Jewish women were even barred from going to the hairdresser.

And there were more laws. Marriage between Jews and non-Jews was strictly forbidden as was sexual intercourse. Jews were banned from participating in sports, not allowed to travel outside the country, could not step out of their homes without wearing a large yellow star sewn to their clothing and could not change address without notifying the authorities.

The measures convinced more than a few that the country was in the hands of lunatics. Why would Nazi Germany -- fighting a world war and maintaining huge armies from the English Channel to North Africa -- worry whether a Jewish woman went to the hairdresser or not. It was incredible.

Then came notices warning that all Jews who did not immediately report for work in Germany would be arrested and deported to the Mauthausen concentration camp. The "work in Germany" business was a ruse meant to disguise the Nazis' ultimate plans for Dutch Jews, but the possibility of forced labor in Germany was fearsome enough to drive many Jews underground.

Cohen and Vanderwal had been law partners for more than ten years and during that time, they had become close friends. Cohen did not have to ask for help -- Vanderwal offered it.

Cohen had been living in the so-called *Joodsche Wijk* (Jewish Neighborhood) in the eastern part of the city. Though the roundups had not yet started in earnest, clearly the Germans had some terrible things in mind for the Jews.

"You can't stay in the *Joodsche Wijk*," Vanderwal said. "It's only going to get worse. God knows what the *moffen* have in mind. Come live with us."

And so he did. Cohen abandoned his furniture, most of his clothes, most of his cherished collection of rare books, and became an *onderduiker* -- a person in hiding -- taking only two suitcases with him to the Vanderwals. Ruud Vanderwal knew that one of the suitcases contained some jewelry, stock certificates and a considerable amount of cash. He knew because Cohen had immediately given most of the cash and some of the jewelry to the Vanderwals to help meet household expenses.

Sheltering a Jew involved more than a little strain on the host family; if caught, the penalty was usually deportation to a concentration camp. Cohen's presence in the apartment had to be kept a strict a secret. Mrs. Vanderwal's brother was told because he could be trusted and because he commuted regularly between Amsterdam and Haarlem. He took occasional messages from Cohen to his widowed mother who was in hiding in Haarlem.

But nobody on Mr. Vanderwal's side of the family was told for the simple reason that Vanderwal's brother was an early joiner of the Dutch Nazi Party and a nephew was fighting with an SS unit in the Soviet Union.

The biggest concern was keeping the *onderduiker's* presence a secret from the neighbors. There were plenty of people willing to turn in a Jew for the 7.50-guilder fee (roughly three dollars) that the Nazis paid per head.

The Vanderwals had handled the pressure with grace and dignity and hardly a single cross word had been exchanged between them and their guest in the eight months Cohen had been under their roof. Indeed, they had come to think of him as a member of the family, a son they never had, and joked about allowing him to stay even after the Germans were ejected from their country (and they were sure that day was not long in coming). For his part, Cohen proved to be a model *onderduiker*, strictly adhering to the "house rules." He had learned to control his somewhat stentorian voice. He never used the toilet when the Vanderwals were not home. And he had been outside only a half-dozen times in the eight months, and then only to stand for a few minutes on the front porch during the deadest hours of a sub-freezing winter morning.

"What are we going to do?" Mrs. Vanderwal asked, trying to keep her voice calm.

"We'll hear what he has to say," said her husband. "What else can we do?"

The Vanderwals had never met Riphagen and had no desire to, but they were getting the opportunity anyway -- he was due at their doorstep any minute.

At that moment, Arie Cohen padded into the living room, the smile on his face dying the moment he saw the Vanderwals.

"What's the matter?" he asked, his own alarm going off.

"Have you heard of a hoodlum named Riphagen?" asked his former law partner.

"Sure."

"That was him on the phone. He knows about you and he's coming over here."

It seemed impossible for Cohen -- who had not felt the sun on his skin for eight months -- to become paler, but he did. He suddenly looked as if all of the blood had been siphoned from his body.

"What does he want?" Cohen said.

"He didn't say but my guess is money."

Cohen slumped down on the couch and put his head in his hands. "God!"

"I am going to make some tea," said Mrs. Vanderwal who vanished into the kitchen.

"How much do you think he's going to want?" asked Cohen.

"All he can get," answered his partner. "From you -- and from me."

Cohen shook his head. "I am sorry about about this, Ruud. So sorry. I didn't mean --." He broke off, tears filling his eyes.

Vanderwal put an arm around his shoulder and said, "Come on, Arie. Pull yourself together. Let's hear what the man has to say."

"Yes, but --"

"But nothing. You're not to blame for anything. We knew the risks. And we would do it again. In a minute. Good law partners don't grow on trees, you know." It was trite but Cohen knew that Vanderwal, who was not an emotional man, was sincere.

There was a knock at the door and Vanderwal went to answer it. Two men stood in the hallway: one compact, swarthy, sporting an expensive overcoat and felt hat; the other larger, meatier, wearing a scum-green raincoat.

"Are you Vanderwal?" asked the shorter of the two.

"Yes."

"Riphagen."

They stood there for a moment staring at each other, Riphagen waiting to be invited in, Vanderwal weighing whether to slam the door in his face. The gangster looked balefully at the lawyer, who finally stepped aside and allowed the two men in.

Dries (rhymes with grease) Riphagen took everything in with a glance: no silver on the coffee table, nothing valuable on the walls, nice furniture but of little value these days -- except as firewood. The guy on the couch must be the Jew. And that was Vanderwal's wife coming out of the kitchen. Riphagen nodded to her and ignored the Jew.

Vanderwal had met with criminals before during his long career, plenty of them, and he had a number of proven ways in dealing with them. With an ambitious punk like Riphagen, he decided to take the high-handed approach.

"I would make introductions, Mijnheer Riphagen, but I know you won't be staying long," he said. "Please state your business and leave."

"My business is simple," said Riphagen. "I want five thousand guilders from you and five thousand from 'im." And he pointed carelessly at Cohen. "In cash. Now."

"Or?" Vanderwal asked softly.

"You don't need an answer to that."

"I do. Just for the record."

Toying with the gangster was risky. He was well-connected in the underworld and had a reputation for violence. But Vanderwal wanted to plant the idea, gently, that Riphagen just might have to answer for his crimes one day.

"Or I make one phone call and you and 'im and the woman are on the next train to Auschwitz," said Riphagen.

"That seems clear enough. And how long must we keep paying you to keep this little business to yourself."

"It's a one-time deal. Pay up and live happily ever after."

"And how do I know we can trust you?"

Riphagen drew his thin lips back to reveal two rows of tartar-encrusted teeth. "You don't," he said, the mirthless smile on his face growing larger. "But if you know anything about me, you know that I don't go back on my word. It's bad for business."

"I see. That's very reassuring but I must tell you that there's nowhere near that much cash around this place. I don't even know if I can raise it," Vanderwal said calmly.

"What do you have here?" asked the gangster.

"A few hundred guilders. Some food ration coupons. That's about it."

"Get it."

Vanderwal went to the kitchen and returned with the money and coupons.

"And 'im," said Riphagen, pointing a contemptuous finger at Cohen.

"You will have to ask him."

"I don't have much," said Cohen. "It's been a long war. Most of what I had is gone."

"Bring it out here," Riphagen ordered. "Everything."

Cohen got up and went to his room, followed by Riphagen's enforcer, a hulking, evil-looking ex-longshoreman named Rutger. They returned a moment later, Cohen carrying a leather suitcase. He opened it and extracted a wad of bills -- about two hundred guilders -- and a brown paper bag holding a couple of gold rings, a gold chain and his parents' wedding rings.

Rutger scooped up the cash and the jewelry and passed it to Riphagen, who deposited the meager booty in his overcoat. At a gesture from his boss, the enforcer took out a large folding knife and slashed to ribbons the lining of the suitcase, finding another five hundred guilders.

Spurred on by that success, Rutger went through the house, cutting into upholstery, shredding pillows, eviscerating clothing, but finding nothing more. Mrs. Vanderwal watched the scene in horror, a hand over her mouth. Vanderwal looked grim but said nothing.

"Well, you got what you came for," he finally said, when the exhausted thug closed his knife and put it back in his coat. "Now leave."

"Not so fast," said Riphagen. "I said I wanted five thousand guilders from you. You barely gave me a tenth of that. When can you get the rest?"

"I said I didn't know if I could raise that much money."

"You've got three days," said Riphagen. "Three days."

When the men left, Mrs. Vanderwal collapsed on the couch and began to sob. Cohen looked like he had been struck by lightning. Vanderwal looked at the shambles in his living room and then walked over and put an arm around his wife. "That tea is probably cold by now. I'll make some more."

Riphagen could not suppress a grin as he got into the plush back seat of his dark-blue Cadillac town car. He pulled out a small, leather-bound notebook and a mechanical pencil from a jacket pocket and began putting down facts and figures in a neat column on the page, whistling quietly to himself as he did so.

"You want me to come back here in three days to get the rest?" asked his enforcer, who got into the driver's seat and started the motor.

"No. I think we squeezed all that we're goin' to out of them," Riphagen said.

"Where to?" asked Rutger.

"The club." By that he meant his gambling club on the Rembrandtsplein. Riphagen owned a string of businesses in Amsterdam -- two bars on the Damrak, a tobacco shop, a brothel and an Indonesian restaurant elsewhere in the city -- but it was from the gambling club on the Rembrandtsplein that he ran his little empire.

The distance from the Waterlooplein, where the Vanderwals lived, to the Rembrandtsplein could be covered in under ten minutes at average walking speed but Riphagen chose to be driven there in his gas-guzzling, unbelievably expensive, American-made town car that had rolled off a Detroit assembly line in 1935. It was the ultimate symbol of his power and prestige in the Amsterdam *penose.* Had the weather been better, he would have pulled the top down and rode like a dignitary in a presidential motorcade.

Everyone in the neighborhood, from the humblest shopkeeper to the crusty dowager who lived as a virtual recluse in a top-floor suite of the Doelen Hotel, knew the car and knew who its owner was. And all breathed a sigh of relief when he gave a curt nod and kept on going.

 The chauffeur-thug dropped Riphagen off at his club, then continued on a couple of blocks to the garage -- another luxury -- where the car was kept warm and ready when not in use. Riphagen did not own this garage, but neither did he pay rent for it. Its fiftyish owner had run up a substantial gambling debt in Riphagen's club and was slowly -- very slowly -- paying it off by providing a garage with a locking door for the car.

Upon entering the club, Riphagen gave a quick nod to his bar manager, then ensconced himself in his office where he immediately took out the money, jewelry and even the ration coupons and put them in the safe. He did not like carrying around more than a hundred guilders at a time, a prudent habit acquired from his childhood days working for a bookie.

With the money in the safe, he took off his hat and coat and sat down at his desk to tackle the paperwork from his various businesses. The managers of his bars, bordello, tobacco shop and restaurant were under orders to keep thorough records of the day's transactions and have them on his desk by the following morning. He wanted to know about every drink poured, every trick turned, every package of cigarettes sold. The same applied for his illegal businesses. His bookies faced a severe beating if they were less than assiduous in their record-keeping. From what well this compulsion for strict bookkeeping came is impossible to say. What's beyond doubt is that Riphagen left a gold mine of information behind for the investigators who would one day try to plumb the depths of his murky criminal career.

He totaled the previous nights' receipts with the precision of an adding machine, every now and again giving a grunt of satisfaction. Nothing he saw in the records brought the much-feared scowl to his face. Later he would send Rutger and another thug to collect the money.

Satisfied that the bookkeeping was in order, he poured himself a slug of *vieux*, took a cigar from the humidor on his desk and leaned back in his chair. There was one last piece of business left to do. He picked up the phone and placed a call to the Euterpestraat, to a contact of his at *Judenreferat* IV-B-4, the section of the Gestapo responsible for tracking down Jews.

"Ja?" boomed a voice at the other end.

"This is Frankie," Riphagen said, giving his code name to his contact, a captain in the SD (*Sicherheitsdienst* -- Security Service) named Karl Schmidt. "I think I have found a girl for you."

"A girl? Excellent. Where does she live?"

"Oude Schans 14. Third floor. She's just your type."

"Oh, ja? Does she live alone?"

"No. But the landlord's a pushover. You shouldn't have any problems."

"Sounds exciting."

"Oh, she's a lot of fun," Riphagen said, taking a sip of the fiery, copper-colored *vieux*, "but she may be leaving town soon."

"I'll get right over there. Thanks. I will send you your usual fee."

Riphagen's "usual fee" was seven guilders and fifty cents for every Jew arrested as a result of his tip, five guilders for every non-Jew in the house and a small kickback from sale of the furnishings after the SD plundered the apartment.

The Dutch Al Capone put down the receiver, lighted his cigar and puffed contentedly for a few moments. Of his many criminal enterprises, his sideline of informing on Jews was the one that gave him the most job satisfaction. That night, with Monique Wolters at his side, he would dine expensively and well at a restaurant on the Leidseplein that catered to German officers. His good mood would continue after dinner at a small club near the Central train station, where he danced with Monique and joked with fellow gangsters to past midnight.

And the next morning, relaxed and refreshed, he awoke about 9 o'clock and, without disturbing the naked young woman in his bed, washed and shaved, ate a first-class breakfast of orange juice, real coffee, real marmalade and toast, then went to his office.

His exuberant late night romp between Monique's silky thighs was already a distant memory as he sat down in his office to tackle the new day's business. With the door locked, he took out his small, leather notebook and placed a call to the home of a grocer who was living on the Overtoom. Though he had never met the man, Riphagen already knew quite a bit about him, thanks to an underworld snoop. The call was brief and businesslike. Riphagen began the conversation with these words: "I know about the Jew."

Chapter 4

Herman Meijer looked dazed. He looked as if someone had taken a two-by-four and beaten him about the head with it. He still couldn't make sense of it all as he sat in relative safety at a splintery table in the back office of a plumbing supply shop on the Ceintuurbaan.

"You're safe, Herman," Maarten Dijkstra said. "You're with friends. Just keep telling yourself that."

Meijer nodded weakly. Dijkstra went over to where a kettle was hissing on a small stove and turned off the fire. He placed a little cylinder packed with soggy tea leaves in a glass and poured hot water over it. There was no sugar, no lemon and the tea leaves -- after five previous leachings -- would never produce a strong brew, no matter how long they steeped. But at least it was warm. Dijkstra brought the tea to Meijer.

"What about Esther?" Meijer asked, his fingers curling around the glass.

Dijkstra shook his head. "I'm sorry, Herman. I couldn't swing it."

Meijer, impervious to the burning sensation, gripped the glass so hard that it was a wonder it didn't break.

"Easy, Herman. Take some tea. It'll settle you down." Dijkstra was indeed fearful that the glass would shatter and injure Meijer's hand, which would have been disastrous.

Meijer brought the glass to his mouth and took a shaky sip. He took another sip and shut his eyes. The dizzying series of events of the last 24 hours had left him numb, exhausted. During that time, he had experienced a lifetime of emotion and feelings -- contentment, terror, anguish, shock, relief, sadness, confusion.

Friday, March 19, had begun routinely enough. He had gotten up at 9 a.m. in his Ferdinand Bolstraat apartment, after putting in long hours of work for Maarten Dijkstra the night before. Meijer was a forger and counterfeiter, a first-rate craftsman who earned a substantial living before the war fabricating everything from passports to currency. He gave up most of his criminal activities following the onset of the occupation, working fulltime for the Resistance forging birth certificates, residency permits, identification cards and food and fuel coupons -- most of that work done at the behest of Maarten Dijkstra.

For the past two weeks, he had been involved in a particularly delicate assignment -- forging Green Police identity cards. The work had been going slowly, very slowly, because of the precision necessary to replicate items that the Germans tried hard to make fake-proof. One thorny problem had been copying the florid signature of the Green Police commander in Amsterdam, Sturmbannfuhrer Rolf Guensche. Guensche wrote in an obsolete Gothic script that was hard to read and even more difficult to copy. Another problem had been duplicating the small seal on each identity card, but Meijer had found a simple solution to that one. Using a stolen identity card as a model, he had made his own seal by carving the necessary configuration into the end of a section of broom handle. When carefully inked, the homemade stamp left an imprint good enough to pass all but the closest inspection.

At the time he was doing this work, Meijer was living openly as a non-Jew in a working class neighborhood of Amsterdam, shielded from persecution by an identity card and a residency permit that he forged himself. His papers identified him as Boudewijn Humma, a 30-year-old janitor and handyman who was born in Utrecht but who had lived in Amsterdam for the last five years. His parents were not Jewish, nor were their parents -- or so his self-made "Aryan Declaration" stated.

Still groggy from only four hours sleep, Meijer had washed and shaved that Friday morning, had eaten a skimpy breakfast of crackers and tea and then had gone out to visit his girlfriend, Esther Goldburg, who lived on the Jodenbreestraat in the Jewish Neighborhood.

To get to her home, he had to pass under a large, crude, wooden sign with the words JEWISH NEIGHBORHOOD painted on it in bold letters in both German and Dutch -- *JUDEN VIERTEL/JOODSCHE WIJK*. It was a grim reminder that Meijer was entering another world, a sinister, dangerous place from which he might not return.

Sometimes there were guards near the sign checking papers, sometimes people came and went as they pleased. Had anyone questioned Meijer, he would have displayed another self-made document, an official-looking pass that declared him to be the landlord of the building in which Esther lived. The pass gave him permission to go into the area to collect the rent. In fact, the pass was the product of breathtaking *chutzpah*, because as far as Meijer knew, no such document existed. He had invented it, adorning it with a variety of seals and stamps. Meijer theorized that the best way to get along in a world as bureaucratic as Nazi-occupied Holland was with more paperwork. He would not have to show the pass to any official, just to the bored-looking conscripts on duty at the Jodenbreestraat checkpoint. And they never raised an eyebrow.

Twenty minutes later, he was hugging and kissing Esther and talking about how he "fooled those apes again."

Despite the horrible conditions in the Jewish Neighborhood, and a daily food intake of less than 800 calories, red-haired Esther still managed to look attractive. There was an alluring blush in her cheeks and still some padding around her hips.

"When are you going to lose that?" Herman said, giving her a playful squeeze. "All that dieting and you still have a roll."

"You said you liked big girls," retorted Esther, who had lost 25 pounds in the last four months and in no way could be described as a "big girl." But it had become a favorite fantasy to talk about her as if she were. It gave them an excuse to salivate over all of the luscious food they yearned to eat.

"No more pastrami sandwiches for you," said Herman. "No more potato *latkes*. No more cheese cake. Not until you slink down to Hollywood size."

"Watch it, buster, or you won't be getting any cake, either," said Esther, and she put her hands on her hips.

"Okay. Okay. You can have all the *latkes* you want, only don't blame me if you swell up like a blimp."

They made love on her tattered, cardboard-thin mattress, and later giggled over the complaints Esther's downstairs' neighbor had made following Meijer's last visit.

"Old dry-cunt," Meijer said.

"Sssssh," said Esther. "You shouldn't say such things. The poor lady is all alone. Her husband died last year."

"Well, invite her up here," said Meijer. "It's only the people not at the party that complain about the music."

Esther punched him in the arm. "Enough of that talk. I mean it."

Afterwards, they went shopping. Not that there was much to buy: a few over-ripe tomatoes, a spongy, unappetizing cucumber, a half-loaf of rye bread and a jar of cooked peppers.

"I will make you a wonderful meal tonight," Esther promised, and she did her best. With a scrawny clove of garlic and half an onion, she came up with a rich-looking tomato sauce that she spread over slices of toasted bread and served with cooked peppers on the side.

Herman ate in silence, feeling a twinge of guilt that he was consuming food that she needed to survive. He usually tried to bring something with him when he visited -- a small bag of candy, some tea, whatever produce he could find -- but this time he couldn't come up with anything. His own cupboards were bare, save for a box of crackers, and there was hardly anything available on the street.

The Germans controlled the food supply in the city and periodically stopped its distribution to punish the population for some Resistance attack or other. Food had become scarcer anyway, due to the fact that the Germans were diverting more of it to feed their own troops on the Eastern Front. God, when will it all end?

Meijer looked at his girlfriend and marveled at her good spirits. She had not seen her parents since they were picked up by the dreaded *Ordnungspolizei* (referred to locally as the Green Police) three months ago. She had heard that they were in a transit camp on Dutch territory but she had no way of confirming that.

"If I think about them too much, I'll go nuts," Esther once told him. "I can't do anything for them except to stay alive myself."

Meijer had spent the rest of the afternoon and early evening in the apartment and the two of them had engaged in another favorite fantasy: formulating plans to flee Holland and go to Palestine. Meijer knew people who knew people who were actually arranging such journeys for a chosen few but it was an adventure fraught with danger, even if they did manage to get out of the country alive and even if Meijer could forge the necessary documents.

It was getting close to 6 p.m. -- two hours before the strictly enforced curfew when any Jew found outside his home could be shot -- and Esther was becoming worried. "It's getting late, Herman. You have to go."

"I know. I know." They were lying fully clothed in her bed, looking at a well-worn map of Europe and the Near East but Meijer was unable to tear himself away from her arms. The hours he spent once a week in Esther's company were the highlight of his week.

"You have to go," she said, nudging him and he said okay. But then he began kissing her and they never heard the arrival of a half-dozen police trucks on the street or the thump of boots on the stairs. The first sign of trouble was when Esther's front door flew open and a squad of Green Police stormed into the apartment.

Esther screamed.

"Up! Up!" one of the policeman shouted, and to make his pointed, he jammed the barrel of his machine pistol into Meijer's ribs.

Esther, who was screaming, was yanked to her feet by her hair.

The German who seemed to be in charge was barking orders but Esther was beyond reason. Meijer, who was nearly out of his mind with fright himself, went over to her and shook her. "Esther! Esther! He says we have a minute to get our coats and get out. We have to listen to him. Get your coat." But she stood there trembling and sobbing until Meijer yelled at the top of his lungs, "Get your coat!"

Meijer was so consumed by what was going on in Esther's apartment that for the moment he did not realize that the entire apartment building resounded with shouts and screams. Green Police swarmed over every floor, rousting residents and herding them to the street.

He became aware of that fact when he, too, was prodded out the door, down the stairs and outside into the stinging cold. When he paused on the porch a moment to take in what was happening, a policeman kicked him viciously in the leg and shouted, "Keep moving, you dirty kike."

Meijer saw that Esther was being led to another truck and tried to get over to her, but he was kicked again. "That way! That way!"

During past *razzias* in the Jewish neighborhood, the Germans gave residents a few moments to pack some personal belongings before they were hauled away, but not this time. Everywhere, half-dressed men and women were being loaded into trucks at double-time speed. It had been no more than fifteen minutes from the time Esther's door was kicked open to the time the driver started the motor of the truck Meijer was in.

He took a look at his traveling companions -- about a dozen men, none of whom he had seen before. Most were sullen, subdued but one fellow -- a rugged-looking, gray-haired man -- had a few things to say.

"Sons of bitches. Didn't even give me time to grab my cigarettes. Just `Move, move.' What's the damn hurry? Nobody's chasing them. They own the whole damn country. Bastards. Look at this," and he pointed to the mouse under his eye. "A Gestapo swine says `move, move.' So I'm moving, but not fast enough so he hits me in the face. I tried to put some clothes in a bag -- a shirt, some clean socks -- but he kicks the bag out of my hands. What's it to them if I take some clothes. Sons of bitches." And he kept up the monologue through most of the short ride. The man, like a lot of his fellow citizens, mistakenly believed that the Green Police and the Gestapo were one and the same and, considering the circumstances, it's unlikely he would have cared a damn had he known that the green-uniformed *Ordnungspolizei* was a separate unit from the Gestapo, whose personnel wore black uniforms. The Gestapo often used the more-thuggish Green Police to do its dirty work and it was the "Greens" -- not the Gestapo -- who became the symbol of Nazi terror in Holland.

As the truck bounced along the cobbles, Meijer briefly considered jumping from the back. He had known of people who had done it and escaped. He also knew of others who had been shot dead. If the ride had been longer he might have tried to escape but as it was, it seemed the truck had only been going about five minutes before it stopped at the Hollandsche Schouwburg on the Plantage Middenlaan.

The welcoming committee consisted of troopers from another branch of the Nazi terror apparatus: the SS. A line of SS men, some with German shepherds at their side, others armed with MP-38 sub-machineguns, stood ready to take charge of the prisoners. There were thousands of SS troops in Holland at the time, many of them Eastern Front veterans who were no longer fit for combat duty. They were assigned as guards to the huge transit camps in Westerbork and Vught or to detention centers such as the Schouwburg, or they were used against the Resistance.

The SS men were as ruthless as the Gestapo or the Green Police, but with a difference. They were combat veterans who had seen enough bloodshed for ten lifetimes. Many had seen comrades die because their superiors had stupidly squandered men and supplies chasing Jews, instead of employing them where they were most needed: in the life-and-death struggle at Stalingrad. Those SS troops sent to Holland after service in the East often arrived broken in both body and spirit. Some were no more than drunks in uniform. Some were only interested in satisfying their own gluttonous appetites to offset the great debt they believed society owed them. Resistance leaders soon discovered that these SS men -- some of them, anyway -- were not unwilling to bending the rules, if the price was right.

But these cracks in the armor of authority were not visible when Meijer and the other arrestees were brought to the Schouwburg that evening. Instead, the rules were rigidly enforced. No talking. No moving unless ordered to move. At a command, the subdued prisoners were led into the once-grand, 19th-century building through a pair of huge double doors, and herded into a room that had once served as the costume department. There identification papers were checked and they were shorn of money and jewelry. For one wild moment, Meijer was about to plead that he was not a Jew, that he was on the Jodenbreestraat merely to collect his rent. But he knew his invented background could not stand up to the most cursory inspection. He figured his best chance at survival was not to stand out at all and to that end, tried to melt in with the residents of the Jodenbreestraat. His most serious moment came when he handed his forged, i.d. card -- affirming his Aryan status -- to a guard. His card was very different from the i.d. cards that Jews carried, which were stamped with a large "J" and a star of David. The guard might have asked some pointed questions as to what he was doing on the street in the first place. But the SS man showed more interest in the expensive-looking watch that Meijer surrendered and which the guard casually flipped into a wire basket. And with a jerk of his thumb, he sent Meijer on his way to the next station -- the so-called "booking desk." Meijer nervously gave his name as Boudewijn Humma and his address on the Ferdinand Bolstraat. Under no circumstances did he want the Germans to find out his real name. That would have been disastrous, considering the thick dossier that already existed on him at the Amsterdam Police Department.

Though no one would have guessed it to look at the slight, bespectacled, serious-looking man, Meijer had earned his living on the wrong side of the law most of his adult life. He had been a crook and a forger and his extensive rap sheet attested to his revolving door relationship with the penal system in pre-war Holland.

He had been arrested three times: in 1931 for petty theft (a charge that was later dropped); in 1934 for forgery (he served six months), and in 1936 when he was arrested with three other men for counterfeiting French money. He was sentenced to six years but only served two. In 1938, he was paroled for hardship reasons (his father had died) but instead of staying at the side of his widowed mother, he moved to England to begin his criminal career anew. His mother's death in 1940 brought him back to Amsterdam and that's where he was living when the Germans invaded in May of that year.

All of that information was on file with the Amsterdam Police Department, which meant that the *Sicherheitsdienst* also had access to it. The arrest of a forger is an important catch in time of war and there was no doubt in Meijer's mind that he would be in for rough handling if the Germans ever identified him. On top of those worries was concern for his girlfriend. He had not seen her exit from a truck and didn't even know if she had been brought to the Schouwburg.

"Keep moving! Keep moving!" A guard yelled. The prisoners were ordered to walk down one corridor, then another and suddenly, they were outside in the sub-freezing cold again. Meijer found himself standing in a large courtyard where about 200 people of all ages and both sexes, collected in tight knots, rubbing their hands and shoulders to keep warm.

Meijer tried to pick out Esther's face but it was nearly impossible. Most of the people stood with their heads bowed, not in supplication, but against the icy wind that whipped through the courtyard. Night had fallen and the only illumination came from search lights on the roof that leaped from one huddled figure to another.

The arrestees were left outside all night. They weren't fed. They weren't allowed water. Bodily wastes were expelled in a vapory hiss against a wall. More people were crowded into the courtyard until their number swelled to 300. There was barely room enough to sit down.

With his prison experience, Meijer should have adjusted to confinement as well as anybody. But the hours of suppressed fear, the fact that he had so much to hide, the cold, the hunger, the stench -- all had taken a toll. And suddenly it hit him with the violence of seasickness. He swayed as his world made dizzying orbits in front of his eyes. He tried to fight down the nausea as he lurched toward a wall but he never made it. He was shaken by one spasm, then another. He gasped, retched. Nothing came up. There was nothing inside to bring up. "Yaaaaggh." He dropped to his knees in the darkness, awaiting the next spasm but it didn't come. Instead, as he struggled for air, he felt a hand on his shoulder. "Easy, son, easy," a man's voice said. He could not see the speaker's face but he could smell the stale breath and another wave of nausea hit him.

"Leave me alone." Meijer said weakly. "Leave me alone. I'll be okay."

"I know you will," said the man, and the hand vanished in the darkness. Meijer began to shiver uncontrollably as the wind raked his clammy skin. "God," he whispered. "God."

The worst was over. The icy gusts revived him, helped him recover his equilibrium. In a little while, he managed to regain his feet. The dizziness was gone, replaced by a hole in the pit of his stomach. How he got through the hours before dawn, he never knew. Sometimes he stood, sometimes he sat. And the minutes just crept by.

In the grayness of first light, he heard a woman shout, "Herman! Herman!" He was relieved to hear the voice, but almost too exhausted to look up.

"Hello, Esther," he said, barely raising his head. She threw her arms around him and sobbed, "Oh, Herman." Her distress gave him the strength to put his arm around her. He stroked her hair and kissed her neck. "Sssssh. Don't worry. Ssssh. It's not going to help anything."

With more light, Herman looked around, trying to identify the man who had come to his aid the night before. But all he saw were drawn, haggard faces. Nobody so much as glanced at him.

At about noon, they were led at gunpoint into the building and into theatre area itself. The Germans gave no reason for the shift but Herman heard from a Jewish orderly that they would soon be shipped out -- probably to Westerbork. Herman also learned the reason why they were forced to stand outside all night. The theatre had been filled with other prisoners. It had nothing to do with preferential treatment. When the theatre was filled, the Germans simply put the rest of the arrestees outside. Those who had spent the night in relative warmth inside the building had been forced into boxcars that morning and shipped out. Herman's group was next.

Meijer had only a vague idea of what was in store for him. He figured he probably would be forced to work long hours in a German factory, making weapons for Nazi troops. He knew there would be little food but he had no idea how little. And he knew nothing of the gas chambers and crematoria of Auschwitz or the bestial conditions under which the Jews were interned.

At about 2 p.m., Jewish orderlies brought in the first nourishment the prisoners had received since their arrest: some coarse black bread and a few of barrels of water. The Germans provided no dippers and the water was soon befouled by dozens of dirty hands. Frantic pushing and shoving erupted as the inmates fought to slake their thirst. Esther didn't dare venture into the muddy melee. Meijer almost made it to the front, but then was pushed aside. He didn't have the energy to try again. He managed to grab a chunk of bread, which he shared with Esther, but their mouths were so dry they could barely chew it.

Night fell. Meijer was sprawled on a once-plush velvet theatre seat with Esther by his side when he suddenly heard his name -- that is, his alias -- shouted by an SS guard.

"Humma! Boudewijn Humma! Step forward. Immediately!"

Herman recoiled in horror. They had discovered who he was! He was going to pay for his lies in the basement of the Euterpestraat!

"Humma! Humma!" The guard shouted again. It sounded so terrifying coming from German lips. "Who-MAH! Who-MAH! Identify yourself!"

"That's you, Herman!" Esther whispered fiercely. "What do they want with you?"

Meijer was so frightened, he couldn't answer. He shook his head.

"Humma! Step forward! Immediately" Meijer struggled to his feet.

"Don't go, Herman," Esther pleaded, grabbing his arm.

"It's okay, Esther," he said absently, and he walked over to the guard, a pudgy SS sergeant, and said, "I'm Humma."

"This way!"

Meijer followed the guard through the lobby to the huge front doors. At a nod from the sergeant, the guard at the entranceway opened the door. Meijer just stood there, confused, not daring to move.

"Out!" said the sergeant. "Out!"

Meijer stepped outside, to be greeted -- not by the Gestapo -- but by the grinning face of Cees Spanjaard. Spanjaard grabbed him and hugged him. "You don't look any the worse for wear," he said, poking him playfully in the stomach. "They must be feeding you pretty well in there. Looks like you put on a little weight."

Meijer was too stunned to speak. Seeing that his friend was in shock, Cees led him gently to where a taxi was parked at the curb. He guided Meijer into the back seat and nodded to the driver who sped off. Ten minutes later, Meijer found himself sitting at the splintery table in the plumbing supply shop, drinking tea and trying to calm his frazzled nerves.

"Esther," he said weakly. Maarten Dijkstra could only look grim and say, "I'm sorry."

Esther Goldburg was shipped out early the next morning with 476 other Jews. Records show that she spent two months in the transit camp of Westerbork before being transferred to Auschwitz. Sometime in January 1944 -- the exact date is not known -- Esther died there of starvation and disease. She was 23 years old.

Chapter 5

Maarten Dijkstra knew about Meijer's arrest three hours after it happened. Dijkstra was supposed to meet the little forger at 8 p.m. at Meijer's Ferdinand Bolstraat apartment to pick up a German police identification card that Meijer had forged.

When no one answered his knock, Dijkstra let himself in with a fine wire and an even finer touch. The place was tidy, like Meijer always kept it. He found the I.D. card behind a piece of wallpaper in the kitchen, a favorite hiding place. But where was Meijer? It was not like him to miss an appointment.

Dijkstra quickly assembled a likely scenario. Despite his warnings, he knew that Meijer was in the habit of visiting his girlfriend in the Jewish Neighborhood at least once a week. He also knew that the Germans had stepped up their *razzias* there, arresting thousands of Jews in the last couple of months alone. It was not a large leap to posit that Meijer had been arrested by the Germans in one of the raids.

Dijkstra had ways of finding out. With his fisherman's cap pulled low on his head and a shawl coiled around his neck, he went to a nearby tavern and called Cees Spanjaard. In guarded language, he conveyed his suspicions about Meijer's arrest and told Spanjaard to "visit the lion."

"Visiting the lion" meant going to the Red Lion, a bar that, aptly enough, was located across the street from Artis, the Amsterdam zoo. It was also a stone's throw from the Hollandsche Schouwburg and a favorite hangout with off-duty SS men.

Like Leo Wolters, Cees (pronounced Case) Spanjaard was a former student of Dijkstra's, but there the similarity ended. Where Leo was held in low esteem by the Resistance leader, Spanjaard had become a trusted confidant. Over the past year, Spanjaard had displayed a level-headedness, an emotional maturity, beyond his 22 years. Dijkstra had come to refer to him as his right arm and often turned to him when an assignment required particular skill and delicacy.

The visit to the Red Lion was a case in point. Dijkstra's group maintained sporadic contact with several disgruntled SS guards who -- for the right price -- would simply "look away" from time to time, allowing a small number of Jews to escape the Schouwburg. Not many, of course. The guards were not willing to bring the wrath of their superiors down on their own heads by letting too many Jews fall through the cracks. Of the 60,000 Dutch Jews who passed through the Hollandsche Schouwburg between 1942 and 1944 en route to almost certain death in the concentration camps, Dijkstra's group secured the release of about two dozen.

Spanjaard, a friendly young man with sleepy blue eyes and a wispy goatee, entered the smoky pub and made his way to the bar. He ordered a beer and as he waited for it, discreetly surveyed the tables for a familiar face.

The Red Lion was what is known in Amsterdam as a "brown cafe", a drinking establishment of ancient vintage whose low ceiling had been stained dark brown by centuries of tobacco smoke. There were several high-backed benches and wooden tables, a handful of stools and a long wooden counter, nicked and pitted, stained almost the same color as the ceiling that ran the length of the bar. Spanjaard had been a regular in the days before the war when it had been a cozy neighborhood bar. Now he only came on business.

As he nursed his beer and flirted with a waitress, he spotted a "friendly" at a nearby table, a corpulent, low-slung SS *unterscharfuhrer* (sergeant) named Alfons Misch. With his tunic unbuttoned and his peaked cap pushed back on his sweaty head, Misch was engaged in a boisterous debate with several other SS troopers. The table around which they sat was a war zone of peanut shells, cigarette ash and spilled beer. At some point, Misch looked up, caught Spanjaard's eye and gave a slight nod.

Spanjaard already knew quite a bit about the SS sergeant, who had turned out to be a talkative drunk. Like many SS men in Holland, Misch was a veteran of the Eastern Front. He had lost a lung at Stalingrad and after hospitalization in Warsaw, had been assigned to a non-combat unit in the Netherlands. Misch had a wife and two children back in Germany whom he had not seen in more than a year and to whom he did not seem terribly attached. From time to time, possibly to assuage his guilty conscience, he sent money and food home, receiving in return a hand-knit sweater or a couple of pairs of socks.

Misch grew up in the strange, feudal-looking Rhineland town of Worms. Though he had quit school at an early age to become an apprentice baker, he knew quite a bit about the town's early history and liked to boast of a particularly sanguinary incident from the First Crusade when the peasant-soldiers of Peter the Hermit passed through Worms on their way to Jerusalem. During their brief stay, the Hermit's men massacred every Jew in the district and looted and burned their homes. Misch always ended the story with a knee-slapping guffaw when he told it to the barmaids. "Now that's the kind of town where an SS man should live, *nicht wahr?*"

Spanjaard had been sitting in the Red Lion for about fifteen minutes when Misch got up and lumbered over to the bar for a refill. He swayed a little as he stood next to Spanjaard's stool, watching the barman fill a pitcher with the golden brew. The death's head insignia on his cap glinted even in the pub's dim light.

"We think a friend of ours is in the Schouwburg," Spanjaard said quietly in German. "We want him out."

"Ja? You want him out and I want to fuck a Dutch girl. A nice Dutch girl."

The German's breath could have felled an ox.

"That won't be difficult to arrange," said Spanjaard, sipping his beer and looking around the bar.

"I don't want a whore!" Misch said loudly. He's drunk, Spanjaard thought. Tread softly.

"We won't get you a whore. It'll be a nice Dutch girl." He made the promise not knowing where he was going to find a volunteer.

"The prisoner's name is Humma," Spanjaard said, giving the alias Meijer used. "Boudewijn Humma."

"She had better not be a whore," the beery German said. "I don't want a whore."

"She won't be. Do you remember the name?"

"Do you think I'm stupid? Do you think all of us Germans are stupid?"

Great! A quarrelsome *mof.* That's all he needed right now. Calm. Calm. "No, I don't think you're stupid. But Humma is a Dutch name. I just want to make sure you remember it."

"Humma is a German name!" Misch said. "German names I can remember. How stupid do you think I am?"

Oh, the virtue of silence, Spanjaard muttered under his breath, turning his head away from the swaying German.

"I asked a question." Misch demanded belligerently. "How stupid do you think I am?"

"You are not stupid," Spanjaard said quietly. "Nobody thinks you're stupid."

The pitcher was full and Misch hoisted it with a pudgy fist and headed unsteadily back to his table. As he was walking away, he turned and said, "It'd better not be a whore! *Verstehen*? No whores."

Spanjaard left the bar a few moments later and bicycled over to Dijkstra's hideout on the Vijzelstraat.

"I made contact with one of the *moffen*," he reported. "Misch. He's willing to check around for Meijer at the Schouwburg and if he's there, to let him go. But he wants a woman. A nice Dutch girl. No whores."

"No whores, this time, eh," Dijkstra said scornfully. "He's too good for whores. He wants a *nice* Dutch girl." The Resistance leader was silent for a moment. "The problem is what nice Dutch girl would want *him*?"

That night in bed, Dijkstra had asked his favor of Saskia and she had agreed.

The Resistance leader met with Leo Wolters the next day and arranged temporary shelter for Meijer. At 4 p.m. that afternoon -- March 20 -- Saskia was taken to the Schouwburg in a taxi driven by Jan Middelburg, another of Dijkstra's men. Dijkstra had instructed her to tell the guard at the door that she wanted to speak to Sgt. Alfons Misch and she had done so. Five minutes later, she watched as a short, stout SS man approached her.

"Spanjaard sent me," she said, as she had been instructed.

Misch inspected her with cold, watery eyes, looking for telltale signs of meretricious activity. Too much makeup, too much lipstick, a hard mouth, hard eyes. But, no. She's no slut, he thought. Too plain.

He led her up the tatty staircase to a room on the top floor that the NCOs used as a rec room. There was a billiard table and some chairs and a makeshift bar. Several SS men were lounging about when they walked in but left quickly amid crude jests.

When the door closed, Misch went behind the bar and got a bottle. He offered her a drink but she declined. He poured himself one and gulped it down. He walked over to her, put an arm around her waist and pulled her to him. He sniffed for perfume but all he smelled was lye soap. He kissed her cheek, neck and clenched mouth. To that point, Saskia had not resisted but she had not participated either. Everything about this man revolted her: the uniform he wore, the pleats under his chin, the cloying stench of his unwashed body. His rough hands were like sandpaper on her delicate skin. When he kissed her, she could taste the beer and burnt tobacco on his breath.

He continued to nuzzle her neck and to squeeze her buttocks and to say things to her in German, a language she did not understand and didn't want to.

She was staring stoically at the ceiling, trying to avoid the wet, thickish mouth, when it suddenly occurred to her that if she didn't perform well, the fat SS man might renege on the deal, and then Maarten would be angry. She would have let him down and he would be upset and angry with her. In all their years together, Dijkstra had never raised his voice to her nor made a mean-spirited remark. But it was her greatest fear that one day he would, that one day he would be so angry with her that he would finally see her the way she saw herself: plain, unsophisticated, unattractive. And then he would kick her out and she would loose the only happiness she had ever known. The fear of arousing Dijkstra's ire was greater than her loathing of the German. And so, as Misch groped at the buttons on her blouse, she gently stopped him and began undoing the buttons herself. Off came the blouse, then the brassiere, as the SS man stood gaping at her.

For just an instant Misch was disappointed. He wanted a girl like those back home, a girl with plump, jiggly, milk-white breasts, not a bony specimen like Saskia.

But his disappointment was short-lived; clearly this was a nice Dutch girl. No woman could earn a living selling her body with a chest like that. It was practically unexplored territory.

Misch pulled Saskia to him again and planted another rubbery kiss on her mouth, and to his shock and surprise, she kissed back. She did rather more than that. His flabby body was suddenly jolted out of its boozy stupor when her tongue darted into his mouth and skipped about inside for an all-to-brief moment. He hadn't expected that. In his wildest imagination, he hadn't expected it. Despite an afternoon of heavy drinking, he was suddenly on fire with lust and he went after Saskia like a barbarian attacking a vestal virgin. Misch took her on the billiard table in a sweaty, noisy, porcine tumble that left him exhausted and happy, but left the soft white skin on her back bruised and rug-burned. When he finally rolled off of her, Saskia got up slowly and painfully and put her brassiere and blouse back on. She kept telling herself that she had been through worse in her life. At least she didn't feel like throwing up. As she dressed, she stole a glance at Misch who seemed to be walking on air as he tucked in his shirt and buttoned his fly. He was talking to her and smirking but she blissfully could not understand a word.

Misch took out his bottle and again offered her a drink. She declined. Shrugging, he tilted the bottle back and took a hefty pull. Again he held out the bottle and again she shook her head.

"I have to go," she said. "It's getting late."

"Ja. Ja. Ja."

The corpulent SS sergeant could barely suppress a whistle when -- ten minutes later -- he led her down the stairs. At the front door of the Hollandsche Schouwburg, he gave her a whack on her bottom and told her that she was welcome anytime. Saskia walked slowly out to the street where Jan Middelburg waited by his taxi to pick her up. She did not look at him as she got in and he did not speak to her on the ride back home.

Dijkstra was not there when she walked in the front door of their Vijzelstraat hideout. She cleaned herself at the kitchen sink, then made some tea and an hour later, crawled into bed and closed her eyes. She wanted to blot out the afternoon as quickly as possible. She was sound asleep by the time Herman Meijer was released from the Schouwburg later that night.

Chapter 6

Leo Wolters and his sister, Monique, were unnervingly similar in some ways and total opposites in others. Both endured difficult relationships with their father, both looked upon their childhoods, privileged though they were, as unhappy, and both had tastes and interests that might be considered self-destructive. Had Maarten Dijkstra known the siblings better, it's doubtful that he would have sheltered Herman Meijer under their roof, for Chez Wolters was an unstable environment, rife with potential trouble.

As far as his banker father was concerned, Leo had been a disappointment from very early on. As a boy, he lacked ambition and discipline, did poorly in school and showed no aptitude for anything practical. He was a dreamer and a loafer, unfocused, unmotivated. He preferred to spend hours drawing pictures of the birds in the garden than studying mathematics or learning other useful skills. Leo would never become the banker or lawyer his father wanted him to be. If the boy had any talent at all, it was in art. To the annoyance of the senior Wolters, who looked upon most art as frivolous, Leo was always drawing. During his teen-age years, he turned out hundreds of drawings of his home, his family, his friends, his pets, anything that caught his fancy. It took awhile but Michiel Wolters eventually gave up the idea that his son would ever enter a respectable profession. With a heavy sigh, he agreed to pay Leo's way through art school.

In March 1943, Leo was 21 years old and living in a moderately expensive, two-bedroom flat on the Schubertstraat in South Amsterdam, thanks to an allowance from his father. He was no longer studying art. The art department had been disbanded at the University of Amsterdam a year before amid insults and recriminations over whether faculty members should join the Culture Chamber.

Leo had little independent income, and much of what cash he did have was spent on his vices and pleasures, including but not limited to frequenting whorehouses, drinking with friends and gambling at the clubs (his father did not know that Leo had fallen three months behind in his rent because his allowance went to cover losses from a newly found passion for blackjack).

Apart from his father's monthly checks, Leo's only source of income was some part-time handyman work he did at the City Theatre on the Leidseplein. It was through his work there that the skinny, awkward, long-haired young man finally found his calling in life. Leo discovered that he liked being around actors and directors and started going to the theatre on his days off. He made friends with the cast and crew and filled in at rehearsals when an actor was absent for one reason or another. Leo decided that when the war was over, he was going to become an actor or a director, maybe even get into the motion picture business.

Until three months ago, Leo had been living slothfully but contentedly alone in the Schubertstraat apartment -- and then his sister had come to live with him. If Leo had been a disappointment to his father, the rash, lovely, headstrong Monique had turned out to be a downright disaster.

Two years younger than her brother, Monique was basically a warm-hearted girl but she had a wild streak a mile wide. She had been in and out of hot water since age 14 when she took the key to their father's study and had a duplicate made in order to steal sherry for her girlfriends and herself.

Michiel Wolters had packed his wayward daughter off to a finishing school in Switzerland in the hope that she would straighten out in the company of the well-bred daughters of bankers, diplomats and aristocrats. It was wishful thinking, of course, but at least for the first year and a half, Monique seemed to settle down. She excelled in English, French and German and accrued no serious conduct demerits, but that's only because the stern headmistress had not yet found out about the French teacher. One night, after requesting a private tutoring lesson, she offered herself body and soul to the startled young man. She was two weeks shy of 16 and he was 27 and married. At first the teacher demurred but she was -- despite her tender years -- too temptingly beautiful to resist for long. Soon Monique and the instructor were sneaking away to the nearby town to spend nights in sexual riot at a back street *pension.*

Her career at the school came to an abrupt end for an entirely unrelated reason: she was caught pawning a piece of jewelry belonging to a classmate. Her staid father was appalled when he heard the news and his shock turned to mortification when he learned that, not only had she been expelled, but she was also three months pregnant. The thick walls of the family mansion could not contain the uproar as father and daughter screamed at each other into the night.

Against his daughter's wishes, the senior Wolters bribed a prominent local surgeon who performed an abortion but, because of the relatively late stage of pregnancy, the operation did not go well. Monique's convalescence was slow and painful and she spent weeks bedridden, sometimes in so much pain that she wanted to die. She demanded morphine to lessen her suffering but her father would not allow it. The thought of his daughter going straight from an abortionist's table to an asylum for drug addicts was too grim to visualize. Eventually her young body healed but she never forgave her father for the agony she endured.

Monique continued to live on the family estate outside of Amsterdam while attending a private school in the city that her father had found for her. For a time, she again seemed to settle down, attending school regularly, getting good grades, shunning her more precocious friends. She even expressed an interest in studying at a university abroad, possibly the Sorbonne, or going to law school. Then about six months ago, Monique brought more noisy discord into the Wolters home when she took up with "that hood" -- as her father always referred to him -- Dries Riphagen.

"Are you trying to be the death of me?" the senior Wolter railed. "Stealing from me, stealing from your classmates, getting knocked up by that bastard of a teacher, for God's sake, and now this. Going out with that hood. What's the matter with you?"

"There's nothing that's the matter with me," Monique had said defiantly. "I love him."

The elder Wolters was astounded. "You love him?!"

"Yes! I love him."

Despite his initial shock, Michiel Wolters took the news with equanimity. He knew his daughter well enough to know that she would tire of Riphagen as soon as the novelty wore off. It was just a matter of time. But when she was still dating him three months later, another loud row ensued that ended with Wolters slapping his daughter. She left home the next day and moved into her brother's apartment. It was supposed to be temporary until she could find her own apartment but three months later she was still there.

Leo still hadn't adjusted to having Monique under foot when he was saddled with another "guest" -- Herman Meijer.

Leo had met the little forger a number of times before (they both worked as part-time repairmen at the City Theatre) and found him "annoying." Like a lot of Jews, Meijer was *kapsones* -- stuck up, arrogant -- Leo later told a police detective.

Meijer was still in shock when he was brought by Cees Spanjaard to Leo's apartment shortly before midnight March 20. He mumbled a hello to Leo and Monique but refused to make eye contact with anybody. The only thing he asked was, "Is my room ready?"

The room business was another sore point with Leo. There were only two bedrooms in the apartment -- his and Monique's. But Meijer needed a place where he could work without being disturbed, so Leo gave up his bedroom. Leo would sleep on the couch during (what he hoped would be) Meijer's brief stay.

"How long is he going to be here?" Leo asked after Meijer had gone into his room and shut the door.

"Not long," said Spanjaard. "We're looking for a place to move him to. Somewhere in the country. The important thing now is that he finishes his work."

"What a sad little man," Monique said.

"He's in shock," said Spanjaard. "Yesterday at this time, he was at the Schouwburg awaiting deportation to a camp. His girlfriend was with him."

"Oh, oh. You couldn't get her out, too?" asked Monique.

"No way. It was hard enough just getting him out."

"What's going to happen to her?"

Spanjaard didn't answer.

"So, just a few days, right?" said Leo

"He'll be here as long as it takes to get the job done, Leo," said Spanjaard. "He won't give you any trouble. He knows he's got to obey the house rules."

Leo looked dubious.

"One other thing, Leo," Cees said sternly. "Don't attempt to contact Maarten or anybody in the group unless it's an absolute emergency. That's the word from Maarten. He doesn't want to run the risk of you leading the *moffen* back to Meijer. We're putting Meijer in with you because you have not been closely tied to us.

Hopefully the *moffen* don't even know you exist and Maarten wants to keep it that way."

Leo nodded slowly but he did not look happy. Spanjaard studied him for a moment. Spanjaard had known Leo a long time. They had practically grown up together. Spanjaard's father had been Wolters' father's attorney. Over the years, Spanjaard had plenty of opportunity to observe Leo Wolters at work and at play -- mostly play -- and was not favorably impressed by what he saw. Long after the war, Spanjaard told a reporter that "Leo was a fool on the best day he ever lived."

But it was Monique, not Leo, who concerned Spanjaard the most. Spanjaard had known for months about Monique's affair with Dries Riphagen but had kept the matter to himself. He did not want to bring trouble to the Wolters family, a family that he had known virtually all of his life. Though Spanjaard was unaware of Riphagen's work for the Gestapo -- that information did not come out until the end of the war -- the mere fact that the sister of a Resistance member, even one as tangential as Leo Wolters, was dating an unsavory character like Riphagen represented a serious breach of security.

Spanjaard wanted very badly to tell Dijkstra about it but didn't.

What a pair, he thought, after parting company with Leo and his sister that night. He wondered how it came to be that a savvy, respected banker like Michiel Wolters raised a couple of lamebrains like Monique and Leo.

"Shit fuck," he said, as he climbed into Hugo de Jong's taxi. It was a favorite curse. He started the engine and drove away, swearing quietly to himself all the way home.

Chapter 7

To call Dries Riphagen an anti-Semite is to underrate him. Practically from the cradle, his animus toward Jews was fierce and relentless. There was, of course, no shortage of anti-Semitism in the neighborhood where he grew up, but it was of a relatively benign nature when compared to Riphagen's violent bigotry.

He was born Bernardus Andreas Riphagen on Sept. 7, 1909, in a seedy, working class neighborhood of South Amsterdam known as The Pipe.

His was a classic story: mother dying young, father a drunk, the boy hitting the streets early, running bets for a bookie by the time he was ten and becoming an underworld enforcer at sixteen.

Thus, his criminal beginnings are easy to trace. The origins of his titanic hatred of Jews are harder to identify. As a teen-ager, he and fellow thugs beat up younger Jewish boys "just for the hell of it. It was fun," he once confided to a reporter. When he was 20, he was arrested for trying to burn down a Jewish-owned bakery, but the arson charge was subsequently dropped, thanks to the work of a sharp attorney hired by his gangland bosses.

For by that time, Riphagen was a young man on the rise in the Amsterdam underworld. He was the leader of a goon squad for the numbers and protection rackets in South Amsterdam. How many arms he broke and kneecaps he smashed is not known but a former colleague later told an investigator, "Dries loved his work."

And apparently he was good at it. His bosses were so satisfied that they rewarded him with the manager's job at a gambling club on the Rembrandtsplein. Riphagen later bought the club, and then another club and a couple of bars, and a brothel, all of which he ran at a profit under the beaming guidance of the syndicate overlords.

By the time he was in his late 20s, Riphagen had become a celebrity in the Netherlands. Dutch luminaries who liked an edge to their nightlife began hanging around his club on the Rembrandtsplein and Riphagen was soon seen squiring actresses and models to swank restaurants and nightclubs in town. It was then that the press started to refer to him as the Dutch Al Capone, a comparison he delighted in but one which would not have flattered the real Scarface, who in all likelihood, never heard of this upstart Dutch hoodlum.

Oddly, it was after another American gangster that Riphagen patterned himself: the Jewish mobster Bugsy Siegel.

Siegel had "style," Riphagen told friends, "lots of style." So, he started wearing the sleek, expensive suits favored by Siegel, worked some American gangster slang into his vocabulary and took care to be photographed at fancy clubs with a beautiful woman on his arm.

Riphagen's standing with Amsterdam's fast set was not injured when he was arrested in 1938 in connection with the brutal killings of two gangland rivals (the charges were later dropped). Nor did his reputation suffer very much when -- later that year -- he told reporters that he had joined the Dutch National Socialist Workers Party, a small group of anti-Semitic extremists who busied themselves smuggling Nazi pamphlets from Germany into the Netherlands.

When asked by a journalist why he joined, Riphagen smiled broadly and replied, "*Een jood en een luis, zijn de pest in je huis --* a Jew and a louse are the plagues of your house."

The arrival of the Germans in May 1940 did not seriously impact Riphagen's operations. Quite the contrary. Through his membership in the Dutch National Socialist Workers Party, he made contact with a wide assortment of mid-level Nazi bureaucrats and soon Germans began to visit his clubs in droves, spending money on his girls and losing money at his card tables. The kickbacks he was paying to the Gestapo to remain in business was peanuts compared to the money his clubs were taking in. Riphagen also used his Nazi contacts to expand his empire. It did not take him long to gain a lucrative foothold in the wartime black market, and he was soon dealing in everything from coffee to petrol to stolen art. Dutch investigators believe that millions of dollars worth of stolen paintings and other objets d'art passed through his hands on their way to the villas of Nazi bureaucrats and generals.

Sometime in September 1942, a beautiful 18-year-old woman with long, ash-blond hair walked into Riphagen's club. Monique Wolters, disgraced student from a Swiss boarding school and on the lookout for new thrills, arrived on the arm of a rich brat a couple of years her senior.

Riphagen noticed her. Everybody in the club noticed the leggy, well-dressed blonde who filled out her clothes like a movie star. Riphagen had no difficulty separating Monique from her date, who was bounced from the club by one of his goons.

The Dutch Al Capone bought the beautiful teen-ager a drink, gave her a few pointers on poker then led her into his office for a private chat. They were not seen again until a bouncer knocked discreetly on the door to announce that the night's take was ready for counting.

Monique began to hang out at the club and it was soon clear to Riphagen's pals that she was included among the smallish bevy of women to whom the Dutch Al Capone laid claim -- thus off limits and to be treated with respect.

But Riphagen, himself, was under no obligation to treat her with respect and he didn't. Her beauty did not stop him from shuffling women in and out of his life as deftly as he shuffled a deck of cards. Once, when Monique objected to the attention he was paying to a particularly stunning girl, Riphagen ended the quarrel with a sharp right to the eye. Monique had learned the hard way never to make a scene in his club. Still she kept coming around.

And through Monique, Leo Wolters began to frequent the gambling club, buying drinks at exorbitant prices, renting hookers at even steeper rates and betting heavily at the card tables. Leo's game was blackjack at which -- to put it tactfully -- he did not excel. Learning such basic rules as when to double down (and when not to) was something he was too indolent to do. Consequently he dropped a tidy sum, not all of which he was able to pay off.

In late 1942, Riphagen's criminal career reached its nadir for malevolence: he became a *Vertrauensmann* (or *V-mann,* informant) for the Gestapo. Making use of his network of underworld contacts, the Dutch Al Capone began to deliver Jews into the hands of *Judenreferat IV-B-4,* for which he was paid 7.50 guilders per head. Records at the National Center for War Documentation in Amsterdan show that Riphagen informed on more than 200 Jews during the war, most of whom were arrested and sent to their deaths in Nazi concentration camps. He also shared in the spoils when their homes were looted and their possessions sold off by the *Sicherheitsdienst.*

Despite a mountain of sworn affidavits that corroborated the allegations, war crimes investigators found it hard to believe that a man as profit-driven as Riphagen would waste his time on such an unremunerative pursuit as turning in Jews. That is, until they discovered that not only was the Dutch Al Capone informing on *onderduikers*, he was extorting money from them as well. A lot of money. During the course of the war, Riphagen extorted hundreds of thousands of guilders from dozens of hapless victims before gleefully turning them over to the Gestapo.

Among the many whom he blackmailed and later sold out was David Boerosa, a well-known Amsterdam gambler and brothel owner. Through his own underworld sources, Boerosa learned that Riphagen had good contacts in the Gestapo. He asked the Dutch Al Capone to help him obtain the freedom of his Jewish girlfriend who had been arrested by the Green Police and was incarcerated in the Hollandsche Schouwburg, awaiting deportation.

Riphagen said that he could arrange the release but that it would cost 10,000 guilders. Boerosa, who was not Jewish, raised the money which he turned over to Riphagen in a bar on the corner of the Herengracht and the Vijzelstraat. The following day, Gestapo agents materialized at Boerosa's apartment and arrested him. But Riphagen and his Gestapo contacts were not finished with the man. Riphagen told Boerosa that he could recover his own freedom by agreeing to turn in other *onderduikers.* In fear of his life, Boerosa informed on several acquaintances but when he ran out of names and address to give the Germans, he was deported to Bergen Belsen where he died of overwork and starvation. His girlfriend was also deported to Bergen Belsen but she survived the war and later published a book about her experiences.

On a cold, rainy night in late March 1943, Riphagen was at his usual place in his club -- on a raised wooden platform near the roulette from which he could survey his domain -- when two German officers walked in. They stood for a moment inside the doorway, slapping the water out of their caps and removing their wet overcoats. Riphagen immediately recognized one of the men, who was wearing the coal-black uniform of the SD. It was his principal contact within the security service, Capt. Karl Schmidt. The other man, who was an SS officer, he didn't know.

Schmidt spotted the gangster seated at his usual perch and grinned broadly.

"Ah, Riphagen. I have brought you a new customer. Come join us for a drink. One moment, *Fraulein*," Schmidt said, grabbing the arm of a passing waitress. "Bring us some schnapps."

As the Germans headed for a table in the corner, the three men who were already seated around it made a hasty exit.

"Riphagen. Come. Come. Join us," the SD man boomed again.

Riphagen descended from his little platform and walked across the smoky club to where the two Germans were sitting.

"Capt. Schmidt, it's a pleasure to see you here again," he said in passable German. "It's been a little while. Don't tell me you've found a place more congenial than this?"

Schmidt, a small but powerfully built man with a growing paunch, laughed loudly.

"We cannot allow ourselves to lose all our money here, Riphagen, as charming as your little place is. We Germans have to prove that we are fair and even-handed. Other owners might complain if we only lost money here."

Riphagen smiled in an unconvincing effort to hide his annoyance. He didn't like Schmidt over-playing his hand. Gestapo officers never lost money in his club. The racketeer who extorted others during his long criminal career now had to pay protection to Schmidt and several of his colleagues to be allowed to stay in business.

"Riphagen, I want to present a friend of mine. He has just come to Holland from Berlin. May I introduce you to Sturmbannfuhrer Werner Naumann. He's a good man to know," Schmidt said with a leer and a wink.

"Herr Sturmbannfuhrer," Riphagen said with a greasy smile, proffering his hand. Major Naumann nodded but declined the handshake.

Riphagen slowly withdrew his hand and looked shrewdly at Naumann. What he saw did not impress him. Naumann was a serious-looking, dark-haired young man, neither handsome nor ugly. Strip away the uniform and he's just another street punk, Riphagen thought. Perhaps a little smarter than some, but still a punk.

Then Riphagen caught sight of the Knight's Cross on Naumann's tunic and that gave him pause. So a war hero, too. Probably saw action on the Eastern Front. Still he didn't look so tough. A couple of rabbit punches with a knuckle duster would cut him down to size. And if that didn't work, there was always the ham-fisted Rutger and his knife.

"As I was saying, Riphagen, the major is a good man to know," Schmidt said, ignoring the play between the gangster and the SS man. "He's just come from Berlin to be the senior aide to General Rauter.

SS-General Hanns Rauter sat at the pinnacle of the Nazi enforcement structure in the Netherlands. Hand-picked by Hitler himself to "clean up" Holland, Rauter was the overall commander of the SS, the SD and the *Ordnungspolizei*. It was sheer lunacy to run afoul of him or any of his subordinates.

"Congratulations, Herr Sturmbannfuhrer," Riphagen said with another unctuous smile. "I wish you only success with your new assignment."

"Thank you," Naumann said.

"Sit. Sit, Riphagen," said Schmidt. "There is a little business to discuss. Ah, the schnapps."

The Gestapo man leered as the waitress put a bottle of the liquor on the table with three glasses. He pinched her rump and she gave a little squeal, so he pinched it again and she gave a yelp of pain. Schmidt laughed. "You will have to send this girl around to my apartment sometime next week, Riphagen. I like her."

"Of course. Anything for the Gestapo."

Schmidt filled the glasses with the expensive liquor that he had no intention of paying for and raised his glass in a toast.

"To the Fatherland," he said, knocking back the drink before anyone could join in. He poured himself another and raised his glass to Naumann. "And to my new colleague, Major Naumann. *Prosit.*"

"*Prosit,*" said Naumann and all three men drank.

Schmidt wagged a finger playfully at the Dutch Al Capone. "It used to be better here, Riphagen. I hope you are not watering down the schnapps, ja? That would be an insult to the German people."

"I would never do such a thing, Herr Captain," Riphagen said. "I will have a word with my supplier."

"Do that, Riphagen. We do not only come here for the pretty girls. We like to enjoy a drink sometimes and we can't enjoy our drink when someone has been playing with the schnapps."

Riphagen glanced at Naumann who was listening to the conversation with a look of disdain, but saying nothing.

"But I said that I wanted to discuss a little business with you, Riphagen and I will do that now," said Schmidt. A red blotch had appeared on his pale cheek like blood on snow.

"Your tip the other day was outstanding, Riphagen," Schmidt continued. "We had been looking for this kike lawyer, this Arie Cohen, for some time. I just wish you could have been there to see it. What an old woman. Crying his brains out and begging us not to send him away. It was quite a sight, I can tell you that."

"And the people who were hiding him," Riphagen asked. "What happened to them?"

"Ja, ja. What were their names? Ah, yes. Vanderwal. Fine upstanding Dutch citizens. Hiding a fugitive criminal in their home, can you believe it? And such behavior going on practically under our noses. Yes, we are very happy that you did your duty as a good citizen, Riphagen. The sooner we can clean out scum like this, the better it will be for the Dutch people."

"So what happened to 'em," Riphagen asked, ready to enjoy the juicy details.

"Nothing extraordinary, Riphagen," said the SD man. "Contrary to what you think, we are not butchers but we must follow the law." Schmidt glanced at his watch. "Right about now, the Vanderwals and the Jew are probably having their dinner at Westerbork." Westerbork was a transit camp on the Dutch side of the border. Jewish prisoners would be kept there an average of a few weeks, before being sent to places like Auschwitz and Sobibor. A typical "dinner" at Westerbork consisted of a bowl of turnip water and a chunk or two of coarse bread. But that meal would seem like a feast when compared to the slow starvation that awaited the prisoners at Auschwitz.

"And the apartment," Riphagen asked.

"Don't be greedy, Riphagen," Schmidt said, slapping the hood on the back. "You will get your share. We found some nice jewelry in the mattress. Very nice, indeed. It made everything worthwhile." And the SD man winked.

The *mof*, Riphagen thought, was as wearying as always. Riphagen finished his drink and stood up. "If I sit too long in one place, the boys will steal me blind," he said. "Enjoy yourselves."

"We intend to do just that, Riphagen," Schmidt called after him.

The Dutch Al Capone took a leisurely stroll around the club, pausing at the roulette wheel, the dice table and the card games going on near the bar.

"How's business tonight, Wubbo?" he said to one of his dealers. Wubbo, a jovial ex-taxi driver who went to work for Riphagen shortly after the German invasion, said, "Business is good tonight, Dries," he said. "Real good and fat. We're about five thousand ahead."

Riphagen grunted approvingly.

Business was indeed good. The club was filled to capacity, with many of the players pimply faced German conscripts begging to be trimmed. They're getting younger and younger, Riphagen thought. Next they'll be sending 10-year-olds to the Eastern Front.

Not that Riphagen cared about the slaughter going on in the Soviet Union. In fact, the greener the soldiers who stopped in his club, the better it was for business.

"You know what happens if you short-count me," Riphagen grinned. "I'll cut your fingers off."

Riphagen said the same thing to Wubbo at least once a week and the dealer always grinned back. But he never doubted for a second the truth of those words.

As the gangster headed back toward his platform, a hand touched him lightly on the arm and the scent of something nice reached his nostrils.

"Hi, darling," Monique said, kissing him softly on the cheek.

Riphagen pushed her away.

"I told you before not to do that out here," he said gruffly. "Can't you keep your ovaries from rattling until we get off the floor?"

Monique looked crestfallen but the Dutch Al Capone didn't care.

"I'm hungry," she said.

"You're hungry," he sneered. "Everybody's hungry. There's a war going on, or haven't you heard."

"You promised to take me out to dinner."

"I can't. I'm busy."

"You promised," she pouted

"Shit." Riphagen pulled fifty guilders from his pocket. "Here. Take yourself to dinner. And don't skimp on the tip. I can't have people thinking that Dries Riphagen is a piker."

"Dries," she said. "You promised."

"I'm warning you, Monique. Knock off the bellyaching. I told you I can't leave. I have important guests in the club."

"Dries," she said. "You always are saying how you keep your promises. I got all dressed up to go out to someplace nice. Please, Dries," she cooed.

Riphagen sighed and looked around. The few heads that had been turned in his direction quickly looked away.

He turned back and ran his eyes over Monique, taking in the high, pointy breasts and the magnificent legs. Yeah, she had been fun once, Riphagen thought almost wistfully, but he had lost his appetite for her months ago. He was fed up with her airs, her jealousy, her bossiness, her nagging, everything. For six months, she had been in and out of his life. Six months! Longer than any woman he knew. Once it had been exciting to despoil the rich man's daughter, to use her like he used a crisp silk handkerchief to blow his nose.

But now he no longer saw her as a great piece of ass. Now she was just a pain in the ass. More than once he considered throwing her out but always changed his mind. And it had nothing to do with any affection for the girl. Just business. An instinct, a gut feeling, something told him that there must be a way to turn her into a profit. Kidnapping was a possibility. So was blackmail. He had photographs in his safe at that very moment that could be used to squeeze her old fart of a father for a mint.

So Riphagen kept her around, waiting for the right moment, the right plan.

"Where's your goddamn brother?" he growled.

"I don't know. Why?"

"He still owes me money. I ain't running a charity. You tell that son of a bitch to get his ass in here and pay what he owes or I'm going to smash every bone in his body."

"You wouldn't do that to *my* brother, would you, Dries?"

"Oh, wouldn't I," he sneered. "I would and I will if he doesn't cough up what he owes. You tell him that. Now get out of here. I've got work to do."

Riphagen went to his office and shut the door. Bitch, he thought. Dumb, soft, rich bitch.

He spent the next hour going over his accounts, tidying up his bookkeeping. It was getting time to make another deposit in his already bulging bank account and that meant that he would have to see the corrupt Red Cross official who carried the money to Switzerland. The official was known to bankers and gangsters alike as a reliable courier with good connections in the Nazi bureaucracy. He made dozens of trips between Nazi-occupied countries and neutral Switzerland during the war without once failing to deliver the goods (the gangster didn't know it but Monique's father also used the same courier to ferry *his* funds in and out of the country). The problem was that he was expensive -- cutting himself in for 15 percent of whatever he carried. Riphagen planned to renegotiate He didn't mind him turning a dishonest guilder, but he didn't like to be gouged.

After he finished with the accounts, he put his books in the safe and went into the small washroom adjoining his office to splash some cologne on his face. He did have a date that night but it was not with Monique. A voluptuous German file clerk that he met at the Gestapo headquarters was due at the club in a few minutes. He inspected himself in the mirror. There was a little shadow under his chin but he had no intention of shaving again. He liked the look; it made his swarthy face look more menacing than usual.

Riphagen rubbed some scented pomade into his thick black hair, put on his coat and went back to the casino. The German woman was just coming in the door when Riphagen came out of his office and she waved at him. He was watching her hang up her coat when Monique stomped over to him.

"I thought I told you to take yourself out to dinner," he said.

"So that's why you're breaking our date. You're going out with that slut."

The German woman had finished hanging up her coat and was walking toward them. What a dress she was wearing. He couldn't wait to tear it off her.

"Take a hike, Monique. I mean it. Blow."

"You bastard," said Monique. "You lousy bastard."

She began hitting him in the shoulder. Angrily Riphagen grabbed her arms and made a signal to the bull-necked Rutger who was standing nearby.

"Throw her out of here!" Riphagen almost shouted, and he shoved Monique into the arms of the hulking thug. Monique, her arms immobilized by the bodyguard, lashed out with the only weapon left to her. She tried to kick Riphagen's leg. With a laugh, he avoided the kick, but in doing so, he bumped into a customer who was just lifting a mug of beer. The beer splashed on Riphagen's expensive suit and dark silk shirt.

"Shit," he said.

Monique laughed. "Serves your right." The words were already out of her mouth before she caught the murderous gleam in his eye and shrank back. Practically on fire with anger, Riphagen gave her a sharp backhanded slap across the face.

"Bitch!" he barked. "Throw her out of here! Now!"

The Dutch Al Capone was so absorbed in the commotion with Monique that he did not see danger approaching. Suddenly he was spun violently around. A Knight's Cross was in his field of vision, and above the medal, a pair of cold brown eyes, eyes that he recognized as belonging to Major Werner Naumann.

An irrelevant thought crossed Riphagen's mind: he's taller than I thought. The next thing he knew, all of the air whooshed from his body as Naumann's fist plowed into his solar plexus.

"Aaaggh," the gangster grunted, stumbling backward, but Naumann wasn't finished. He grabbed Riphagen by the hair, yanked his head down and sideways and socked him squarely in his swarthy face. The sound of bunched knuckles hitting cheekbone was sickening. The hoodlum crashed to the floor in front of a knot of startled customers, bringing down a table as he went.

Seeing his boss go down, Rutger let go of Monique and took a few steps forward, but then stopped. Rutger was not an intelligent man but even he could see that assaulting an SS officer was tantamount to suicide. As he stood near his fallen boss, confused, hesitating, Naumann walked over to *him*.

"Do you have something to say about this?" he asked in a quiet, steely voice. Rutger did not understand German, but it would not have made any difference if he had. His mind, less than nimble under the best of circumstances, was at that moment frozen, inoperative, incapable of answering a simple question, let alone resolving the ticklish problem of whether to pull the big knife in his pocket.

In any event, the SS officer did not wait long for an answer. There was a blur of movement, a thwack and suddenly Rutger felt as if his private parts had imploded. As Naumann withdrew his fist, Rutger grabbed his crotch and let out a bellow that reverberated through the club.

What happened next was frightening in its machinelike ruthlessness. Naumann grabbed a handful of the bodyguard's shirt with his left hand -- to steady him -- smashed him under the nose with the flattened heel of his right, then brought the rigid edge of the hand down in a vicious chop that broke Rutger's collarbone.

The hulking gangster staggered backward, dazed, nauseous, hurting in so many places he didn't know where to rub first.

"Enough, enough!" he blurted out as blood poured from his splintered nose.

But it was not enough for the adrenalin-charged Naumann. In Russia you didn't leave the enemy standing. The German cross-hatched Rutger to the floor, twisted his head to the side and cracked him soundly on the mastoid bone just behind the ear. Rutger went out like a light.

And as quickly as it started, it was over; the entire episode had lasted less than a minute.

With the blood of battle still rushing around his ears, Naumann stood up slowly and took a deep breath. It was only then that he noticed the semi-circle of customers and employees who stood gaping at him in stunned silence. The ferocity of the attack had frightened the devil out of them. One or two wanted to help the fallen gangsters but didn't dare, petrified the SS man would turn on them next.

Blood continued to spew from Rutger's broken nose and there was a bronchial rattle as he reflexively tried to clear fluid from the back of his throat. He just might choke on his own blood, thought Naumann, feeling a momentary flicker of sympathy for the man he beat nearly to death. He had seen men die that way before. It was a horrible death.

Ignoring the two sprawled figures and the roomful of stupefied customers, Naumann walked over to where Monique stood with her eyes wide and a hand at her mouth.

"Are you all right, *Fraulein*?" he asked.

Monique nodded slowly.

"I am delighted to hear that." Naumann paused for a moment, then said, "It may not be my place to say so but this is not a suitable environment for a young lady such as yourself. I would consider it an honor if you allowed me to drive you home. You needn't be afraid of me. My intentions are completely honorable. As you can see, I am an officer and a gentleman."

Still stunned by what she had just witnessed, Monique allowed the German to take her arm and lead her from the club.

Chapter 8

On the raw, damp afternoon following Herman Meijer's release from the Hollandsche Schouwburg, five men sat around the rickety table in the office of the plumbing supply shop on the Ceintuurbaan.

From the outside, the shop was indistinguishable from the plethora of vaporous, rundown businesses that lined the street. The windows were grimy, the porch dusty, the iron railing in need of a paint job. A passer-by would guess that the owner was making a living but not getting rich. The few customers who ventured into Van Cuiper's Plumbing Supply that day were helped by Van Cuiper himself, who pretended no knowledge of what was going on in his back office. Which was wise, because at least two of the men in the office ranked near the top of the Nazis' Most Wanted list.

Presiding at the table was Maarten Dijkstra, the former oil engineer-turned-painter who was the leader of a small but industrious clandestine organization known as the Artists Resistance Movement.

Dijkstra was 44 years old but looked ten years older. His closed-cropped hair had gone from brown to bone-white in less than a year and his once-wiry, five-foot-nine-inch frame looked shrunken, emaciated, as if it belonged to a concentration camp survivor. Yet there was a keenness about him, an aura of authority that stamped him as a leader, the kind men follow with something akin to blind devotion.

Dijkstra's was an elusive personality. He was smart, tough, charming and charismatic -- but not necessarily a nice man. Even his friends had to concede that he was more than a little arrogant, an admitted prick when it came to women and prone to fits of melancholy, even before the war. Some who knew him during the occupation described him as ruthless. He certainly displayed a determination and single-mindedness that was rare in Dutch Resistance circles.

Whatever his shortcomings, Dijkstra inspired intense loyalty, not only among his followers, but among scores of friends and acquaintances who loaned him money, offered him shelter, ran errands for him and in other ways lent support to him and the Artists Resistance Movement. Many risked their lives sheltering Jews for a few weeks or months or even years; some would pay a heavy price for their loyalty.

Since forming the group, Dijkstra had insisted on keeping it as independent as possible from other Resistance organizations, which he knew to be riddled with informers. That was perhaps the principal reason why ARM was still operational after a year while other partisan groups had been infiltrated and smashed.

(Indeed, so successful were the Nazis in penetrating the Dutch Underground that at the height of the war, the most important Resistance network in the country was totally under German control. The story is quickly told.

(In early 1942, German counter-intelligence agents in Holland captured a British-trained Dutch radio operator and persuaded him to send messages back to London under their supervision. The Dutchman thought he could warn his London bosses about his capture by omitting a pre-arranged security check from his transmissions, but the British never twigged. Other agents who parachuted into Holland to rendezvous with the radio operator found the Gestapo waiting for them on the ground, and they, too, were forced to transmit for the Germans. At the peak of the operation, the Germans controlled seventeen transmitters, which they used to get the British to deliver an arsenal of weapons, explosives, money, food, clothing and radio equipment. On the other side of the Channel, the British were delighted. They thought they had built an effective Resistance organization in the Netherlands. They were receiving reports of railroad bridges being blown up and ammunition depots destroyed. In fact, the Germans did blow up a couple of worthless structures in case anyone in London was checking aerial reconnaissance photographs, but they needn't have bothered. Nobody in London was that alert.

(The ruse -- if such an innocuous word can be used -- went on for two years, despite the fact that more RAF planes were shot down on supply runs over Holland than anywhere else in Europe. Two partisans actually managed to escape from a Gestapo prison and -- at great risk -- make it back to England, via Spain, but when they told their story to British Intelligence, they weren't believed. To add injury to insult, the British threw them in jail on suspicion of being double agents. It was not until another agent escaped and told the same story that the British finally caught on. But by that time, the Germans had executed more than a hundred brave men and women, captured tons of supplies, shot down dozens of RAF aircraft and crippled Resistance efforts in Holland for the rest of the war. The fiasco ranks with SS Major Otto Skorzeny's rescue of Mussolini as Germany's greatest cloak-and-dagger successes of the war).

Among his other qualities as a leader, Dijkstra also had a talent for recruitment. The disparate personalities he brought together had bonded into an effective fighting force. On a mission, each man knew his job and each did it well. So effective had Dijkstra's group been over the past year that the Gestapo was offering a ten-thousand-guilder reward for his capture.

Sitting clockwise from Dijkstra's left were his four closest associates: Cees Spanjaard, Hugo de Jong, Jan Middelburg and Jeroen van Duin. Before the war, each had made a peaceful, law-abiding living from the arts. Among the five, only Middelburg had so much as fired a gun before the war.

Hugo de Jong, 31, was a novelist and screenwriter who had penned a string of sea yarns loosely based on his adventures in the Dutch merchant marine. He moved to Hollywood in 1937 to write a screenplay from one of his books and remained there for the next three years, a well-paid slave in the Tinseltown script factories. With his leftist politics and professional facade as a mocker of institutions, the Dutch writer cut quite a swath in Hollywood. He lived in a swank home in Coldwater Canyon, dated a chorus line of actresses and partied with the likes of Dashiell Hammett, F. Scott Fitzgerald and John O'Hara. A photograph published in *Life* magazine in 1938 showed a wolfish De Jong gnawing on the obligatory pipe as he schmoozed with Hammett and novelist Nathaniel West.

De Jong was in the Netherlands visiting his family in Utrecht when the Germans invaded. Unable to return to California, he began writing for an Underground newspaper, a job that eventually brought him in contact with Maarten Dijkstra. When Dijkstra started his group, De Jong was one of his first recruits.

Every man at the table noticed but did not comment on the fact that De Jong kept his left hand in his pocket. Three months earlier, a couple of days before Christmas, De Jong had been picked up by the Gestapo and put through two days of hell on earth. Two of his fingernails were torn out and his hand smashed by a hammer blow. The pain and terror of those 48 hours would be forever etched in his glassy, blood-rimmed green eyes. Miraculously De Jong had not talked, and even more stunning, the Gestapo let him go -- probably as a living warning to others who even contemplated resisting Nazi authority.

In the months since his arrest, De Jong's hand, shattered beyond repair, had stiffened into a claw, and in deference to others, he usually wore a glove or kept the appendage in a pocket. Dijkstra had tried in vain to get De Jong to "retire," to quit the group but De Jong would not hear of it. Centuries of Dutch stubbornness was very much a part of his character.

"What do you want me to do, Maarten, sit home and die of boredom? No thanks." And so he remained. Unable to work as a writer because of his refusal to join the Culture Chamber, he drove a taxi, passing along whatever intelligence he picked up from his German fares to Dijkstra. The cab itself had been absorbed by the Resistance. It provided excellent cover for moving around town and whenever De Jong did not need it for work, he made it available to his colleagues.

Sitting quietly next to De Jong was undoubtedly the handsomest member of the group, a blond, blue-eyed, angelic-looking former seminary student named Jan Middelburg. At 19, Middelburg quit his studies to drive an ambulance for the loyalist forces in Spain and was wounded during fighting in the Jarama Valley. While convalescing in a Madrid hospital, he began to draw seriously for the first time in his life, putting down on paper some of the horrific sights he witnessed on the battlefield. It was not long before his latent artistic talent started to attract attention. A number of his drawings eventually were published to critical acclaim in a Dutch magazine -- one drawing in particular became famous throughout Europe and the United States when it was featured on a fund-raising poster.

Middelburg briefly considered re-entering the seminary after his return from Spain, but decided instead to go to Paris where he studied art. He later worked for a small Left Bank gallery. The Nazi invasion brought him back to Amsterdam where, through another Spanish Civil War veteran, he came into contact with Maarten Dijkstra. As the only member of the group with combat experience (even if most of that experience had been in a non-combat capacity), Middelburg found himself teaching the others what he knew about infantry tactics, weapons, field first aid, etc.

He, too, had nearly been captured when a squad of "Greens" suddenly showed up at his Jordaan apartment the month before. But the saints had been smiling upon him that day. As the Germans smashed their way in, the story goes, Middelburg drew a pistol from under his mattress and peppered the wood with gunfire, then climbed out a window and jumped two floors to the street. There he exchanged shots with more policemen, ducked into an alley and escaped in the rabbit's warren of narrow lanes. Since then, he had been living the life of a hunted criminal, rarely venturing into public. The reward for him had reached five thousand guilders.

Jeroen van Duin, a violinist by profession and a former member of the Amsterdam Philharmonic, was one of the few members of Dijkstra's group not thought to be on a German wanted list, which was extremely ironic. He, too, lived in the bohemian Jordaan -- known as the Greenwich Village of Amsterdam -- and it was at his apartment that Middelburg had first sought refuge after his shootout with German police.

Van Duin was in his late 30s, a tall, patrician-looking man with a pencil-thin mustache that put people in mind of David Niven. Dijkstra and Van Duin had been friends for twenty years -- the Resistance leader had been godfather to Van Duin's only child, who had died of pneumonia (and the scarcity of medicine) the previous year at age nine.

The boy's death had changed Van Duin. Gone were the wisecracks and the sparkle in his eyes. Now he lived only to kill. Everybody in the group knew that Van Duin was slipping out of his apartment late at night to pick off German soldiers. His favorite targets were the drunken servicemen who staggered from the bars at one in the morning. And his favorite method of attack was to push them into a canal. Once in the chilly water, it was virtually impossible to climb the high, slippery-smooth canal walls to safety. The heavy overcoats the Germans wore did not improve their chances of survival. Their only hope was to scream for help as they floundered in the scummy water and hope someone had a rope to pull them out.

A thin but sturdy thread bound these five men together, a thread that ran deeper than their work for the Resistance. Each was known to the others as one who refused to join *De Kultuurkamer* -- the Culture Chamber -- the hated bureau that represented the Nazis' attempt to control the arts in Holland. Each had paid the penalty for his anti-fascist stance. They were banned from working in their professions. Even to be seen holding a paint brush or sitting behind a typewriter was now a serious crime for them, a crime punishable by deportation -- or worse. The name of their organization proudly proclaimed their opposition to Nazi tyranny -- the Artists Resistance Movement.

Over the past couple of months, Dijkstra and the others had met at least at least 20 times at various locations around town as they plotted and prepared for a daring raid that had at least a fifty percent chance of getting them all killed.

Dijkstra, suave and self-assured, usually kept the tone light at these meetings but he was brisk and businesslike as he worked his way through that day's agenda. Everyone noticed the change in his demeanor and it made them all a little edgy.

"For those of you who haven't already heard the good news," Dijkstra said, lighting a cigarette, "Herman Meijer's back among the living."

"Hear, hear," said Spanjaard, and the others clapped and whistled, but not too loudly.

"He'll stay temporarily with friends while he works on the identification cards," the Resistance leader said. "He should be safe there for the time being. We'll move him to the country later."

Spanjaard pulled on his wispy goatee but didn't say anything.

Dijkstra looked at the saturnine Van Duin. "When can we expect the uniforms, Jeroen?" He asked the question for the others' benefit. He already knew the answer.

"Tomorrow," Van Duin mumbled. "They'll be brought to my place." Dijkstra's men had been busy for months trying to assemble three Green Police uniforms. They had managed to steal things like helmets, caps, overcoats, insignia and even a couple of holsters from bars frequented by the *Ordnungspolizei*. But the rest of the uniforms had to be sewn from scratch. The job had been given to two tailors -- brothers -- who had a shop about two blocks from where Dijkstra and his men were now sitting. They were reliable men who had done work for other Resistance groups. Working from photographs, the tailors had fabricated Green Police pants, tunics, collars and scarves. They had even customized the uniforms to fit Dijkstra and two of his men -- Jan Middelburg and Cees Spanjaard. Spanjaard knew that the day was approaching when he would have to shave off his treasured mustache and goatee.

"Let's see the plans again," Dijkstra said.

Jan Middelburg pulled several large, well-creased sheets of yellow paper from his pocket and unfolded them on the desk.

Dijkstra picked them up. Though he had long since committed everything on them to memory, he scrutinized each one as if seeing it for the first time.

What is he looking at? Spanjaard wondered. Christ we've been over them a hundred times. Spanjaard was as familiar with the documents as Dijkstra was, as every man at the table was. For weeks, those smudgy yellow pages had been at the center of their existence. Everything they did seemed, in one way or another, connected to them. It was the focus of their thoughts during the day and their dreams at night. For security reasons, there was only one copy and that had been entrusted to Middelburg for safekeeping. When not needed at a meeting, they were kept stashed somewhere. Only Middelburg and Dijkstra knew where.

In all, there were just three pages. Carefully drawn on each sheet was the layout of a floor of a seemingly unlikely Resistance target: the so-called *Bevolkingsregister* -- the municipal Hall of Records -- on the Plantage Kerklaan in Amsterdam. Such was the nature of the brutal occupation that this block-long, nondescript edifice, which before the war housed several innocuous municipal agencies, had become an important pillar in the Nazi terror apparatus in the Netherlands. Dijkstra and his colleagues planned to set fire to the building and to destroy as many files inside as possible.

To understand why the *Bevolkingsregister* was targeted, one has to know something of the bureaucratic side of the Dutch character. The Dutch are inveterate record-keepers. For centuries, the average Dutchman's journey through life has been a well-documented affair from cradle to grave. Bureaucrats working at a time when doublets were still in fashion were kept busy recording when and where a person was born, where he lived, what guild he belonged to, how much tax he paid, what his marital status was, what his religion was, etc.

This diligence in record-keeping continued through the 20th century and clear to the present.

In 1943, the *Bevolkingsregister* in Amsterdam was filled from floor to ceiling with steel filing cabinets holding hundreds of thousands of meticulously kept records on the good *burgers* -- everything alphabetized, labeled and cross-indexed. A few minutes with those records and one could acquire an enormous amount of information on just about anybody.

Naturally the Germans were ecstatic when they discovered this trove of information. They plundered the *Bevolkingsregister* for information about Jews with the zeal of a mongoose plundering a hen house for fresh eggs. The building soon became home to offices of the Gestapo, the *Ordnungspolizei* and a sinister organization known in German as *Zentralstelle fur Judische Auswanderung* -- the Central Office of Jewish Emigration. This bureau processed the paperwork that sent millions to their deaths.

Three-quarters of Holland's Jewish population lived in Amsterdam. From those voluminous municipal files, the Gestapo obtained names, addresses, work places, everything they needed to round up and arrest Jews.

It's not clear when Dijkstra first decided to destroy the *Bevolkingsregister.* There is some evidence that he was already considering it as early as May 1942. Whatever the case, once he decided to do it, he devoted practically every waking hour to accomplishing that single goal.

The drawings he held in his hands represented a masterpiece of stealth and detective work. Middelburg, the best draftsman in the group, had prepared them, based on information gathered painstakingly and at considerable risk. Middelburg, Spanjaard and another member of the group, Rob Groen, had discreetly struck up acquaintances with more than a dozen Dutch civilians who worked in the building, finally settling on three who could be trusted to keep their mouths shut. From them, they obtained the critical data they needed for the raid -- where the guards were posted, when the shifts changed, in what rooms the Nazis kept records pertaining to the Jews, and other details.

Equally important, Dijkstra's men discovered that the *Bevolkingsregister* -- which was usually staffed with German personnel, day and night -- was virtually deserted on weekends. There would be a few guards, of course, both inside and outside the building, but it was rare to find anyone else working there from Friday night to Monday morning. Even the Gestapo needed time off.

With the phony uniforms and I.D. cards, the partisans could bluff their way into the building, overpower the guards, torch the file rooms and be out of the neighborhood before the alarm could be raised. If everything went according to plan.

Putting down the drawings, Dijkstra asked, "What about the *lucifers*?"

"They're ready," Spanjaard said. "All of the Clown's surprises are ready. All I have to do is pick them up."

It's worth noting that until a couple of weeks before, neither Dijkstra nor his colleagues knew anything about arson, an awkward problem for people planning to set fire to a large office building. So Spanjaard was dispatched to the home of the legendary Wim Witteman, better known by his Resistance *nom de guerre* -- the Clown, for some pointers. What Witteman did not know about explosives and arson was not worth knowing.

Like his codename recklessly indicated, Witteman was a former circus clown who, during his long career under the big top, became an expert in pyrotechnics. For more than a decade, he rigged the elaborate fireworks displays for the City Circus Amsterdam that dazzled huge crowds throughout Europe. When war came, Witteman turned his talents to bomb-making, furnishing various Resistance groups with a variety of explosive devices that seldom failed to get the job done.

Resistance lore has it that he used to make his bombs while sitting in his bathtub in his apartment above a grocery store on the Albert Cuypstraat. It was an efficient way of rinsing away the residue of his labor. His neighbors, of course, would not have been pleased to know what he was up to, but they didn't find out until after the war.

Tragically, Witteman was killed during the last moments of the Nazi occupation, and not by one of his devices. He was part of a large crowd in the Dam Square celebrating the end of the war when a group of panicky German marines in a nearby building opened fire on the revelers. More than a dozen people were killed, including Witteman.

But in March 1943, the Clown was very much alive and in good health and he gave Spanjaard a crash course in the science of arson. He said that the best incendiary triggers were simple devices, easily made and easily carried.

"Don't get fancy," he stressed. "People get hurt when they get fancy."

The Clown explained how "to rig the room" to create the all-important "flashover," that point in a blaze when the room gets so hot that everything starts to burn: furnishings, the floor, even the walls. And Witteman stressed importance of care when handling accelerants like gasoline or kerosene; more than one amateur had set himself alight through inattentive handling of highly flammable fuel.

Like the good student he had always been, Spanjaard learned the lessons well and passed on what he found out to Dijkstra and the other members of the strike team.

With a satisfied look on his face, Dijkstra folded the plans and gave them back to Middelburg.

"We're close," he said quietly. "Very close."

No one spoke for a moment. It was Spanjaard who finally asked the question that was on everyone's mind.

"When?"

Dijkstra shrugged. "All we're waiting for are the i.d. cards. If Herman gets his work finished in the next day or so, we can go this weekend." The nonchalant way he said it did not lessen the impact of his words. *We can go this weekend.* The statement hit them like an electric shock. As De Jong later described it in a book about the raid, "I felt a surge of adrenalin as I suddenly realized that this was for real. After so much planning, we were actually going to do it. It was thrilling stuff, but also pretty scary."

"Are there any arguments against going this weekend?" Dijkstra asked. It was like him to involve his closest associates in the decision-making. It tightened the bonds even more.

No one spoke for a moment, then De Jong said, "You won't get an argument from me."

"Now that *is* good news," Dijkstra said. "Hugo is not going to argue with me." A grin lit up his tired face and his eyes twinkled with inner amusement, and just for a moment, he looked like the insouciant, fun-loving Dijkstra of old. Then it was back to business.

"If there are no objections," he said, "let's agree to keep this weekend free for a little of the Queen's work."

The meeting was over but no one was ready to leave. Each man sat in his own little world, smoking and thinking, until Dijkstra dismissed them ten minutes later. They agreed to meet in two days' time at the Admiraal de Ruyter bar on the Vijzelstraat to finalize their plans.

Chapter 9

Rudolphus Vanderwal had never felt so filthy, so scrofulous, in his entire life. It had been six days since he'd last washed. His hands were slick with grime and after three days of sleeping on a soiled burlap sack stuffed with straw, his skin was mottled with more than a hundred insect bites. His once well-groomed head of silvery hair now resembled the stringy ends of a wet mop. His scalp itched all the time and it was all he could do not to scratch. While in his sleep, he had scratched so hard that he had drawn blood, which attracted more insects.

Westerbork.

It was only in the last hour that his nose had grown immune to the stench around him -- the nauseating smell of vomit and soiled clothes, of unwashed bodies, diarrhea and disease.

How many people were living within the confines of the guard towers and barbed wire? Three thousand? Four thousand? Five thousand? He didn't know. He had heard that during "busy" periods, fifteen thousand people would be crammed into the camp. There was running water at Westerbork and he was supposed to be allotted five minutes at a basin in the wash room, but the Germans had suspended water privileges for the entire camp the day before as punishment for a fight involving two prisoners.

As he stood in front of the camp infirmary, sipping the muddy ersatz coffee that was his breakfast, Vanderwal again allowed himself the luxury of mentally raging against the man who was the source of his current predicament: Dries Riphagen, the so-called Dutch Al Capone. With a disgusted shake of his head, Vanderwal had to admit that he badly misjudged the gangster. He thought Riphagen would greedily try to extort every last guilder out of him before going to the Gestapo. And like a chess master, Vanderwal had planned a series of counter-moves based on that theory, moves that would have bought him time to arrange the disappearance of his wife, Arie Cohen and himself. He planned to make false promises to the gangster, to string him along, but when the moment came to hand over more money, he would already have disappeared into the woodwork.

Yes, he had been wrong to underestimate the hoodlum. But he just didn't think Riphagen was smart enough to be satisfied with what little he got.

Vanderwal surveyed his new surroundings -- the guard towers, the barracks, the haggard, pitiful-looking prisoners, the squalor -- and again he grew enraged. If he ever got out of Westerbork, he would kill Dries Riphagen. Never mind that he never had fired a gun before. He was going to procure a pistol and put a bullet in the gangster's swarthy face. That was one promise he intended to keep. But first he had to survive and that was not going to be easy.

Westerbork.

It was a transit camp and people were coming and going all the time. During the early morning hours, trains pulled up right to the gates to disgorge the latest batch of victims of Nazi madness. At night prisoners who had been in the camp a while were herded into box cars and shipped out -- their destination not revealed but it was widely assumed it would be a concentration camp in Germany or Poland.

Vanderwal had no idea how long he would be confined at Westerbork. A few weeks, a few months. It depended on when and where the Germans had to replenish their supply of slave labor. Just that morning an orderly had given him the less-than-happy news that "it's going to be worse at the next camp."

Vanderwal closed his eyes as he sipped his coffee, sorting out the blurry images of the last six days -- the unmitigated fright when a half-dozen hard cases from the Green Police stormed into his home; the two days at the Hollandsche Schouwburg during which time he and his wife and Cohen had been given only bouillon and stale bread to eat; the nighttime train ride to the camp. They rode in a regular passenger car, not a box car, but it was jammed with people and they could not sit down. On the train, Vanderwal witnessed the only act of kindness he had ever seen rendered by a uniformed German. A well-scrubbed, curly-haired boy of about six had begun to cry. His father picked him up and talked to him in soothingly tones but the child continued to sob.

A Green Policeman sitting on a stool by the door -- a heavy-jowled man in his 30s with a rifle on his lap -- witnessed the tears and called to the child: "*Hast du Angst?*"

"He's asking if you are afraid," the father told the child. The bewildered little boy looked at the German and slowly nodded his head.

"*Du brauchst doch keine Angst zu haben,*" the German said, and he winked reassuringly. "He says that you don't have to be afraid," the father translated and the child stopped crying.

The prisoners arrived at Westerbork cold, hungry and exhausted, only to be forced to stand for hours in the freezing pre-dawn cold outside the registration hall waiting for their turn to answer a lot of pointless questions. The Vanderwals and Cohen had been among the lucky ones who had sweaters and coats with them. One old man -- clad in a pale-blue sweater but no coat -- had dropped dead from exhaustion and cold as he waited in line to be processed.

After registration, the inmates were sent on to the next room to be examined by a doctor. The purpose of the medical examination was not clear to Vanderwal. People complained of a variety of ailments but they were not given any medicine. The doctor would tell them that "there's nothing wrong" or that they "would soon feel better."

The doctors would not touch the prisoners at all. The so-called examination consisted of asking a few pointed questions. "Have you been treated for lice?" "When was the last time?" "Have you ever had tuberculosis?" "When?" "Has anybody in your family had the disease?"

The answers were scrupulously noted down but no attempt was made to segregate prisoners who admitted having had the disease or being treated for lice.

Once the "medical exam" was completed, the prisoners were led to one of the empty barracks. By that time, it was light enough to see that the barracks were painted olive green and each building had a large white number on it.

Vanderwal was brought to barracks 45, a long, low building containing five rows of three-high metal bunks. There was barely a foot of space between the rows. On each bunk rested a dirty, straw-stuffed burlap sack that was the mattress. The sickly sweet odor of puke clung to the sack on which Vanderwal was assigned but he was too exhausted to care. He made a pillow out of a sweater, used his overcoat as a blanket and was asleep almost the second he lay down.

After the processing and medical examination, the trio had gone three separate ways. Vanderwal had been taken to a barracks for male prisoners; Mrs. Vanderwal had been sent to a women's barracks; Arie Cohen was led away by two SS guards. A Jewish orderly later explained that Cohen had been taken to a special isolation section of the camp. It was a camp within a camp, fenced off with barbed wire, where prisoners were sent for punishment. Their heads were shaved, they were given very little food and they worked 12-hour days digging trenches and building bunkers outside the camp, constantly under the glare of trigger-happy guards.

"Cohen had an 'S' stamped on his travel document," the orderly explained. "The S stands for *Straffe* -- punishment. You're friend must have done something wrong."

In the eyes of the Germans, Cohen had done something very wrong. He secretly had lived eight months outside the long reach of Nazi law. That was enough to get an "S" on your travel papers. But the Vanderwals had broken the law, too. Hiding him was a crime. Why didn't they get a similar stamp? Vanderwal had asked.

"Your punishment is being sent here," said the orderly. "You're not Jews but you hid one in your home, so you will be treated like Jews. That's your punishment. The *moffen* may be crazy but there's always a bit of logic to everything they do."

It was not an unusual occurrence for a prisoner or two from the *Straffe* section to be shot every week, with or without cause. Their corpses would be brought back in a wheel barrel by other prisoners and left on display for a day or two before they were buried.

The Vanderwals grieved for Arie Cohen but there was nothing they could do to help him. They could not even talk to him. As regular prisoners, they were not allowed within 25 yards of the *Straffe* area.

Vanderwal couldn't stomach any more of the foul coffee and threw the rest of the viscous liquid on the ground. He looked around for his wife. Heddy Vanderwal was supposed to meet him in front of the infirmary 15 minutes ago, but since very few of the prisoners still had watches, being punctual for an appointment was difficult.

As camps went, Westerbork was something of an anomaly in that it was not built by the Germans, but by the Dutch. In the late 1930s, the Dutch government ordered the camp to be built to temporarily house the thousands of German refugees who were streaming over the border to escape Hitler's murderous regime.

After the invasion in 1940, Nazi officials were delighted to find a camp already in place and what's more, filled with Jews. The Germans, of course, made some modifications, putting in guard towers, search lights, barbed wire, barracks for the SS troops, etc. The status of the Jews was immediately changed from refugees to prisoners and the dormitories, which were built to sleep one hundred people, now held about four hundred. The comfortable mattresses were taken out and dispersed among German troops and the burlap bags were brought in as replacements.

Some of the German Jews were immediately transferred to concentration camps but others were kept at Westerbork and put to work as clerks, orderlies, nurses, cooks and even camp policemen. As far as possible, the Germans let them run the camp, happy to have as little contact with the Jews as they could manage. The German Jews handled most of the registration chores and decided to which barracks the prisoners would be assigned. They staffed the infirmary, worked in the kitchen, sorted out disputes among the prisoners and acted as a liaison between the Dutch Jews and the Nazi officials. They also made sure that the Dutch Jews followed Nazi regulations. Because of the authority they were given, the German Jews came to be detested by the Dutch Jews perhaps even more than the Dutch Jews detested the Nazis.

Week after week, the German Jews remained in place at the camp, keeping the bureaucracy running, while the Dutch Jews were transferred out. Consequently many of the German Jews survived the war on Dutch soil in the relative safety of Westerbork while the Dutch Jews perished in the extermination camps of Auschwitz or Sobibor or were worked to death at Bergen Belsen.

"Ruud! Ruud!"

Vanderwal turned to see his wife walking toward him.

"Where have you been?" he asked, as if they were standing in their old apartment and she had been tardy returning from the beauty parlor. Despite the squalid conditions, Heddy Vanderwal managed to look well made up. Her gray hair was neatly beehived on her head and her clothes looked clean.

She clutched his arm and whispered, "Come. Come quickly."

"Where?"

"Follow me and don't ask questions."

She hooked her arm under his and casually led him past the infirmary as if they were on a stroll in the park. They walked past several rows of barracks and a locked shed where the ditch-digging tools and other equipment were kept. When they reached the kitchen, Mrs. Vanderwal led her husband around a corner and along the building to a smaller wooden structure that stood about 20 yards from the kitchen. Several German trucks had been parked and left unattended behind the smaller building.

"They're full of food," said Mrs. Vanderwal.

"How do you know?"

"Because I looked."

"*You* looked? Are you crazy, Heddy? They might have shot you for going near those trucks."

"Who would shoot me? There's nobody around. Come."

She pulled back the canvas flap on a truck and pointed. There were cartons and cartons of tinned beets, sauerkraut, beans and hash.

"I can't climb up. I need you to give me a boost," she said.

"*What*? I'm not letting you go in there. If the Germans see it, they will shoot you dead."

"Rudolphus Vanderwal. I don't see any Germans. Do you? We're wasting time. I haven't had enough to eat in a week and if you don't help me get into that truck, I am going to do it by myself!"

And she made a move as if to climb up.

"Okay. Okay," Vanderwal said, taking hold of his wife's arm. "I'll go up."

He sighed and took a furtive look around. Amazingly in the crowded camp, they stood alone behind the trucks. Nobody was in view.

Vanderwal was past sixty but he was in fairly good shape. Without much effort, he was able to hoist his lean frame into the truck. Once inside, he slowly made his way to where the boxes were stacked as if he expected to be shot any moment.

"Hurry!" his wife hissed.

"I am hurrying," he hissed back.

Vanderwal was not one to act rashly. In both his personal and professional life, he used logic and common sense as his guides and took considerable pride in his usually well-reasoned decisions. But now as he rummaged among the boxes in the German army truck, he didn't know what he feared more: being shot or dying like a fool. With nervous fingers, he started to open one of the boxes.

"Not the beets," his wife whispered. "I hate beets. Go for the hash. Over there."

With a sigh and a suppressed oath, Vanderwal went to the other side of the truck and opened a box containing tins of hash. He put a few in his pocket and brought a few more back to his wife.

"Get some of the beans," she said. "And the sauerkraut."

"Let's not get killed for being greedy," he retorted, starting to get out of the truck.

"Don't be such a scared cat, Ruud Vanderwal. Get the beans. Quickly."

Vanderwal knew how stubborn his wife could be and he never doubted that she would find a way to climb in the truck if he did not do what she said.

With another muttered oath, he went back to the boxes and extracted some tins of beans and sauerkraut and brought them to his wife, then nimbly jumped out of the truck and put the canvas flap in place. Without further conversation, they stuffed the precious booty into their coat pockets and down their shirts and walked quickly away from the trucks.

They were barely able to suppress grins when they parted at the women's barracks. They agreed to meet later in the day at the infirmary.

"*Bon appetit*," Mrs. Vanderwal said before walking into the barracks, and she blew her husband a kiss.

Vanderwal walked back to barracks 45 and stashed the loot under his mattress. He would share the food with every other prisoner in the building and he later found out that his wife had done the same thing at her barracks.

"You're a stubborn old woman," he said to his wife when they met that afternoon in front of the infirmary.

"I had to be," she said, giving her husband a hug. "How else does the wife of a lawyer survive the marriage?"

Vanderwal embraced his wife, clasping her head to his chest. "We are going to get out of here," he thought to himself. "She's too fine a woman to die in a place like this."

Chapter 10

Throughout March 1943, the trains rolled from the Dutch transit camps at Westerbork and Vught to their final destination: the death camps of Sobibor and Auschwitz in Poland.

Captured German records show that on March 2, 1,105 people were packed into wood-framed cattle cars and shipped east. Eight days later, another 1,105 people were transported to Sobibor, followed by 964 people on March 17, 1,250 people on March 23 and 1,255 people on March 30.

The deportations continued in April and May, reaching its zenith on June 18 when 3,000 condemned souls were shipped east to die.

In the meantime, the *razzias* continued on the streets of Amsterdam and throughout the Netherlands as the Germans continued their efforts to liquidate the country's entire Jewish population. The dirty straw mattresses at Westerbork were still warm from their last temporary tenants when they were assigned to a new batch of inmates.

The Final Solution in the Netherlands was moving inexorably forward.

"How long is he going to be here?" asked Monique, her hands on her hips.

"Sssssh. He'll hear you," answered her brother.

"I don't care if he does. He's an *engerd* (creep) and I want him out of here."

"Ssssh! Keep your voice down, Monique. I mean it."

It was Thursday evening, March 25, and Leo was crouched over his radio, trying to tune in the Dutch broadcast from London. He listened to the optimistic messages from the government-in-exile with something close to religious intensity. He wanted desperately to believe that Liberation Day was nearing. That there was a light at the end of the tunnel. That one day the goose-stepping Nazi troops would be swept from the streets of Amsterdam and he would be rid of the bottled-up, gnawing fear that was part of everyday life in the occupied country.

"Leo, you're not listening to me," she hissed.

"I am listening to you, Mon. I heard everything you said. For crying out loud, he's been here less than a week. Dijkstra will move him out soon. Just be patient."

"*Just be patient*? Aren't you the tolerant one all of the sudden. *Just be patient.* I want him out of here! I mean it, Leo."

Leo stopped fiddling with the knob. He spoke to his sister in a weary voice, keeping his eyes fixed on the radio. "I can't kick him out now. Maarten would have my head. Just be patient for a couple of more days. Then he will be gone."

Monique glared angrily at her brother, then turned and went to her room, slamming the door behind her.

Leo fully expected Herman Meijer to be moved to another home soon. Two days earlier, the little forger had finished his work and the German identity cards had been handed over to Cees Spanjaard to bring to Maarten Dijkstra.

Spanjaard said Meijer would be moved to another safe house, but not immediately. Dijkstra wanted Meijer to remain under Leo's roof until the raid on the *Bevolkingsregister* was over.

Leo took the news phlegmatically, hoping that a day or two longer would not make a difference. But Monique had thrown a fit.

When Meijer first arrived, Monique had felt sorry for him. She had called him "a sad little man" and tried to cheer him up with a smile and a flirtatious wink. But the little forger shied away from her. He would mumble his thanks when she brought a meal to his room and then hastily close the door.

It did not take Monique long to sour on her new houseguest. The first night after Meijer arrived, there occurred the first of the "bathroom episodes." Monique, wearing only a slip, had come out of the bathroom to find a sheepish Meijer at the door. He had stammered out something about not knowing she was in there and had darted back into his room. Monique was inclined to believe him but then it happened again the following morning. After that, Monique stuffed paper in the keyhole every time she used the bathroom.

She had told her brother about the incidents, calling Meijer an *engerd* -- a creep -- who was spying on her in the bathroom.

Leo had sighed.

Perhaps if Meijer had been a better looking young man, some of the friction might have been avoided. Monique -- poor, callow Monique -- vain about her own looks, was undoubtedly attracted to the physical beauty of others.

The truth was that Herman Meijer was not a man to whom nature had been particularly kind. His short black hair curled tightly (too tightly) against his scalp. His thin face was unevenly parted by a scimitar of a nose. With his horned-rimmed glasses, protruding ears and skimpy mustache, he looked like the eternal victim, someone bullies would have sought out from across a crowded schoolyard. He was, as Saki once described one of his characters, a man whom wolves had sniffed at. Consorting with criminals and serving time in prison had not imparted the slightest edge to his features.

It had not helped that Meijer was in shock when he was brought to Leo's apartment. His normally gloomy visage was even more downcast, more lugubrious. He had gone straight to his room and that was where he spent most of his time ever since.

Once when Monique came home, she found Leo and Meijer having a quiet chat in the living room. But the second she walked in, Meijer had excused himself and gone to his own room -- i.e. Leo's room.

"What's the matter with him?" Monqiue asked.

"I don't know."

"What were you talking about?"

"Oh, just the good old days before the war."

Monique had let it pass, but she soon noticed that Meijer *always* avoided her. When she would walk into a room, he would leave. The only time they were ever together was at meals -- that is, the few meals that Meijer didn't eat in his room. And even then, he kept his eyes averted and didn't engage in conversation with Monique.

Every now and again, however, she caught him looking at her surreptitiously from across the table. His eyes would dart away immediately but not before she saw something in that look. It was a sad look but there was something more, something that took her a while to nail down. And when she did, she was startled. It was a look of reproach. No, it was more than reproach. It was more like -- revulsion. *Revulsion?* It was unbelievable. How could *she* be revolting to *him.*

One day she demanded of her brother: "Have you been talking to that guy about me?"

"What guy?"

"You know who I mean. Our *guest.*"

"No, of course not. What put that idea in your head?"

"You haven't told him about Dries?"

"No. I haven't told him about Dries. I haven't told anyone about Dries. It's not something I go around telling people. What's all this about?"

Monique didn't answer.

"What's all this about, Mon?"

"When is he leaving?" she asked.

"Soon."

"When is that?"

"Soon. That's the best I can tell you."

Monique knew little about why Meijer was placed under their roof and Leo left it that way. He did not often discuss Resistance business with his sister. The two enjoyed a close relationship but Leo was no more happy than their father that Monique was dating a gangster. The less she knew about the Resistance, the better it was for him.

Monique had complained several times to her brother about "the way" Meijer looked at her.

One occasion made Leo chuckle. "Do you think he's after your hot little body?"

"That's not what I mean. He looks at me like -- like it's my fault the *moffen* took his girlfriend away."

"Come on, Mon. The man's in shock. It has nothing to do with you."

"I'm telling you that I don't like the way he looks at me."

"I think you just have a guilty conscience. Why don't you stop seeing Riphagen?"

"I don't have a guilty conscience!" Monique practically screamed. "But I want him out of here."

"Well, he'll be gone soon."

For her part, Monique could not understand her brother's sudden benevolent attitude toward Meijer. Leo certainly had not been happy about the fact that the Jew would be staying under their roof. He had moaned and complained about it and it was *she* who had told him that it would only be for a short time.

But now Leo was behaving as if Meijer was a long lost friend. He sometimes acted as if he *didn't* want Meijer to leave. Where did all of this charitable tolerance come from all of the sudden? What were they talking about the day she walked in on them?

Monique mulled the matter over as she pouted in her room. Her brother was up to something but what? She didn't know. Leo liked his little secrets. Even as kids, he had been secretive, hiding his money in places where he did not think she would find it. Well, secretiveness was a family trait. Their father could hardly be described as an open book, nor could Monique who had any number of skeletons in her own closet. With a shrug, she dismissed it all from her mind. Leo was right about one thing. Meijer would be gone soon. And anyway, she had more important things to worry about. She went to her closet and sorted through her extensive wardrobe. She had a date that evening, a very interesting date, and she wanted to look her best.

Chapter 11

Arthur Seyss-Inquart, the Nazi *Reichskommisar* for the Netherlands and one of Hitler's most loyal disciples, sat alone in his office in The Hague. It was nearing 7 p.m. on Friday, March 26, 1943. Seyss-Inquart expected a visitor at 7 and to pass the time, he re-checked the typewritten document that lay before him. It read:

-- *1 suitcase or rucksack*
-- *1 pair of work boots*
-- *2 pairs of underpants*
-- *2 pairs of socks*
-- *2 shirts*
-- *1 sweater*
-- *2 woolen blankets*
-- *2 sets of sheets*
-- *1 bowl*
-- *1 mug*
-- *1 spoon*

The rucksack or suitcase is to be clearly marked with the first name, family name, date of birth and the word "Holland." Also take enough victuals for three days and all of your food coupons.

It was typical of Seyss-Inquart, the highest-ranking German official in the Netherlands, to concern himself with such details as what property Jews could take with them when rounded up for deportation. The trim, bespectacled *Reichskommisar* was very much a hands-on administrator when it came to carrying out the Final Solution, right down to fretting over the number of socks Jews could take with them.

As he waited for his visitor on that March night in 1943, Seyss-Inquart could look back on his work in the Netherlands with justifiable pride. Perhaps nowhere else in Occupied Europe was a nation so thoroughly under the Nazis' thumb. The Germans used and abused the Netherlands as if the nation were their own personal toy, raiding and plundering at will, taking over Dutch oil reserves, refineries, factories, ships, harbors, airports, the entire industrial strength of the country.

Priceless works of art were stolen and shipped back to Germany -- statues, paintings, rare books, religious artifacts just disappeared.

The Nazis took control of the food supply and heating fuel, supplies which they cut off from time to time to punish the population for Resistance activities. (The most brutal reprisals came during the last winter of the occupation when the Germans -- at the brink of defeat -- cut off all shipments of food into Northern Holland, including Amsterdam. Starvation followed. It was probably the only time in the city's history that rats were in short supply. Not only was there no food, there was no heating fuel. Virtually every tree in Amsterdam was cut down as the *burgers* tried to fend off weeks of sub-freezing temperatures. More than 15,000 people starved to death or died of the cold during that last winter of the war, which the Dutch refer to with stoic understatement as the Hunger Winter.)

Not content with seizing the Netherlands lock, stock and canal, Seyss-Inquart wanted the hearts and minds of the population, too, and to do that, he had to control the press, arts, radio, theatre, film industry and music -- everything the people saw, read or heard. But instituting massive censorship in a traditionally freedom-loving country like the Netherlands was no easy matter. A way had to be found to get artists and journalist to toe the line without triggering massive civil unrest. It was Seyss-Inquart who came up with the solution. The Culture Chamber.

The Culture Chamber was not a single entity, but rather, an amalgamation of labor unions and guilds covering every artistic, literary, theatrical, musical and journalistic and broadcast profession in the country. In short, the Germans decreed that anyone connected with those vocations "voluntarily" join the appropriate Culture Chamber guild or be banned from working under penalty of arrest and deportation.

Ostensibly, the organization was established to ensure that writers and artists conformed to Nazi ideas of what was "appropriate culture" and what was not. It was a clumsy and heavy-handed attempt at censorship, or more accurately, at self-censorship, but the sinister undertones of the organization soon became apparent. In effect, the Germans wanted Dutch writers and artists not only to censor their own work, but also to legitimize the Nazi-run government in the Netherlands. By joining the Culture Chamber, artists were in fact saying that they supported the ideological dogma of the enemy, however repellent it was.

Jews, naturally, were barred from the Culture Chamber. Jews were degenerates. Their art debased society. Every Culture Chamber member had to sign an Aryan Declaration swearing that he or she did not practice that vile religion. The ever-thorough Seyss-Inquart even had notices distributed to Dutch artists, explaining why Jews were not allowed to join.

"The Jew is a great danger," he wrote, "not only to the German culture, but to the Dutch [culture] as well. Only artists who share our own Aryan nature can help build the new cultural world of the future."

The Culture Chamber turned out to be another success for Seyss-Inquart. Thousands of artists, writers, actors and journalists -

- frightened of losing their livelihoods -- joined the hated organization and obeyed its rules. But there were still wrinkles to be ironed out, and that was the reason Seyss-Inquart had set up a meeting for that night.

At precisely 7 p.m., there was a knock at the door and Seyss-Inquart said, "Come." The door opened and SS General Hans Rauter, Seyss-Inquart's chief enforcement officer, entered the office and saluted.

"Good of you to come on such short notice, *Gruppenfuhrer*," Seyss-Inquart said cordially. "Please sit down."

"Thank you."

"It's late, and I won't detain you longer than necessary," said Seyss-Inquart. "What do you think of this?" And he handed the list to Rauter.

The saturnine Rauter was a bloodthirsty psychopath who once boasted, "*Ich wil gerne mit meiner Seele im Himmel bussen fur was ich hier gegen die Juden verbrochen haben.*" My soul will gladly answer in heaven for what I did to the Jews here on earth.

The general took one look at the list and said, "If it were up to me, I would shoot the damn Jews in their homes and save the railroads for more important work."

"We are a nation of laws, *Gruppenfuhrer*," Seyss-Inquart said sternly. "We have our orders and the best way to carry them out is in a lawful and orderly fashion."

Taking the list back, Seyss-Inquart opened a file on his desk.

"The list is not why I called you here tonight, *Gruppenfuhrer*," he said. "I have been reading the report you sent me from the Gestapo commander in Amsterdam. As usual, his work is very thorough."

"It seems this renegade group of artists led by Maarten Dijkstra is undermining all of our good work. With each success these criminals have, the credibility of the Culture Chamber suffers. Morale sags. The members are less willing to obey the rules."

Seyss-Inquart tapped the file with an index finger. What he had read convinced him that Dijkstra was among "the most dangerous criminals in the Netherlands."

Dijkstra's group sprang from a raucous emergency meeting of artists and writers at the City Theatre in Amsterdam in early 1942, a meeting called after the Germans instituted the Culture Chamber.

By all accounts, it was a noisy, rowdy assembly, with the usual vices and virtues one sees whenever frightened people gather under one roof. Tempers flared. Angry words were said. There was some name-calling, some pushing and shoving. At the point where the whole room threatened to erupt into violence, Maarten Dijkstra stood up and calmly walked to the stage.

There were about a hundred people in the room and Dijkstra knew most of them. The Dutch cultural world was small and incestuous and if there was some scandal going on in an artist's life, it was not likely to remain a secret for long.

Dijkstra gave a brief speech that night that was taken down verbatim. In part, he said:

"You may think that joining the Culture Chamber is a very minor act. You sign a piece of paper and then you can go about your business. ... By signing that paper, you are giving a nod to the most evil regime in the history of the world. ... If you think you can pacify these sadists by turning in your neighbors and colleagues, then you deserve exactly what you're going to get.

"... When I walk out of the door here tonight, I am going to disappear and some of you will not see me again for awhile. So I bid you good-bye and hope that all of you can hold your heads high on Liberation Day."

When Dijkstra left the stage, he walked over to where the treasurer of the Artist Guilds sat with a little iron strongbox containing the membership dues.

"How much is in there?" he asked.

"About five thousand guilders (roughly $2,000)," said the treasurer.

With every eye in the room on him, Dijkstra picked up the chest and walked out of the theatre, followed by about a dozen of his friends: Cees Spanjaard, Hugo de Jong, Wim Langelaan, Jan Middelburg, Jeroen van Duin and others. Nobody tried to stop them. He later used the money to aid the families of artists who refused to join the detested Culture Chamber.

All of this information, obtained from well-placed informers, was in the report Seyss-Inquart had before him. What the Germans didn't know at that time was that Dijkstra and his friends had set up a clandestine printing plant to manufacture the welter of documents needed to live in Nazi Holland.

To mass produce personal identity cards, ration coupons, residency permits, birth certificates, business licenses, etc., required an expert printer, so Dijkstra recruited an old friend, an amusing scoundrel named Romke Dietvorst.

Dietvorst's checkered career included a term in prison for embezzling some of his father-in-law's money to start his first printing business. His untidy business dealings aside, Dietvorst was a first-rate printer and a rabid anti-Fascist who was delighted to have a chance at striking a blow for freedom. He didn't dare use his own printing company in South Amsterdam for Resistance work because the Germans kept a close eye on such businesses.

So together with Dijkstra and other members of ARM, he started another printing company, this one to be used solely for Resistance work. Using cast-off equipment he repaired himself, Dietvorst set up a shop in an abandoned warehouse in a rundown neighborhood near the harbor. The sign he hung outside the business proclaimed it to be a salvage yard and he adorned the front of the premises with an array of rusted equipment he found along the waterfront. Dietvorst partitioned the warehouse in two, filling the front part with more junk and doing the printing work in the back.

He and Dijkstra had no trouble bringing in a number of skilled workers to do the printing, including another of Dijkstra's pre-war friends, the forger and counterfeiter, Herman Meijer.

For nearly two years, Dietvorst and his printers worked unmolested in the harbor, practically under the noses of the Germans. ARM printed and distributed 80,000 phony documents, thereby helping to save the lives of thousands of Jews and others wanted by the Nazis.

"This Maarten Dijkstra is clearly a leader," Seyss-Inquart said. "The kind of leader who can cause serious problems for us. I see in this report there is a large reward offered for him."

Rauter nodded slowly. The truth of the matter was that the general had not read the report. He merely forwarded it to Seyss-Inquart as a matter of routine. As head of the security services in the Netherlands, Rauter was responsible for the SS, Gestapo, Green Police, Military Security Service and other organizations. It was a lot to oversee. Rauter had devoted most of his energies to rounding up Jews, and had let the Gestapo worry about the Resistance.

"And the reward has not flushed him out," Seyss-Inquart continued. "Why do you suppose that is, *Gruppenfuhrer*, given all the funds we are spending on informants?"

The stone-faced general cleared his throat and recited what little he knew about Dijkstra.

"Maarten Dijkstra has kept his group independent of the main Resistance networks, *Reichskommisar*, which, as you know, we have under control. His group is small and very close-knit. And there seems to be a lot of people who are fiercely loyal to him and are willing to help him."

"All the more reason to arrest him as soon as possible, wouldn't you say *Gruppenfuhrer*?"

Rauter said nothing.

Seyss-Inquart picked up a pen and began to write. "I want you to make the capture of Maarten Dijkstra and his band a top priority. I want these criminals caught and dealt with. Use whatever manpower you need. I am putting this in writing, which you will receive tomorrow morning."

Rauter was not happy with this turn of events. He was getting orders from several different quarters at the time, orders that often conflicted with each other. Everyone wanted their pet project to have "top priority."

His SS bosses in Berlin, for example, had recently ordered Rauter to "intensify your efforts" in arresting Jews, because they were needed at Auschwitz to rebuild a factory destroyed by RAF bombers. Then there was the directive that originated with the under-minister for armaments who wanted thousands of non-Jewish Dutch civilians rounded up for work in German factories.

As it was, Rauter barely had the manpower to carry out the routine SS work in Holland, like staffing the huge transit camps, guarding railroad bridges and transporting prisoners. Now, to add to his worries, the paper-shuffling *Reichskommisar* wanted him to divert precious resources to look for this artist and his band of thugs.

The general was feeling harassed, which meant that his subordinates would soon be getting an earful.

"I'll want a progress report in three days," Seyss-Inquart said, without looking up from his paperwork. "In triplicate. The other copies are going to Berlin. That will be all, *Gruppenfuhrer*. Thank you again for coming on such short notice."

The general stood up, saluted and left the office, looking even gloomier than usual.

Chapter 12

The subject of the meeting between Seyss-Inquart and General Rauter was at that very moment in a Resistance safe house on the Prinsengracht, several blocks from the *Bevolkingsregister.* The raid was set for that Friday night, a time when -- save for a few guards -- no one was likely to be working in the Hall of Records.

By 7:15 p.m., Maarten Dijkstra's six-man team was in position. Dijkstra, Jan Middelburg and Cees Spanjaard were dressed in Green Police uniforms, and each carried in his pocket one of Herman Meijer's forged police identification cards, the key to getting into the facility. The trio had been joined a few minutes earlier by a fourth man who was not wearing a uniform.

Twenty-five-year-old Rob Groen was a last-minute addition to the strike team, brought on board after Dijkstra calculated that an extra man was needed to help ransack the offices and destroy files. A strapping six-footer, Groen was a writer for a small Resistance newspaper called *Rattenkruid* (Rat Poison). He was dressed in a borrowed raincoat and his only suit. Dijkstra hoped to pass him off as a plainclothes policeman. As the time slowly ticked down to zero hour, Groen fingered the small automatic pistol that was in his raincoat pocket. This was his first major raid and he was nervous, as even the veterans were.

Parked in front of the safe house was a black German sedan that Middelburg had stolen two days previously and had garaged in the barn of a Resistance sympathizer on the outskirts of Amsterdam. It would be used to take Dijkstra and his men to and from the *Bevolkingsregister* and then abandoned.

The other two members of the team, Jeroen van Duin and Hugo de Jong, were at that moment sitting in the group's much-used taxi, which was parked down the block from the Hall of Records. De Jong sat in the driver's seat and Van Duin -- as the fare -- sat in the back. His story, if questioned, was that he was waiting for his girlfriend to leave the nearby pub so he could see if she was two-timing him.

Their assignment was to create a diversion should Germans arrive unexpectedly at the building. A hand grenade lobbed down the block would create a very effective diversion, and De Jong had one, British-made, cavalierly stowed in his overcoat pocket.

Van Duin and De Jong had a secondary task -- to make sure Dijkstra and the others were not followed after they left the building.

The six raiders were checking their watches and counting down the last few moments to zero hour when they suddenly heard an all-too-familiar noise: the window-rattling rumble of large army trucks.

Dijkstra, who was about to walk out the front door, stopped in his tracks.

"Shit!" he said, as he looked out the window. "*Moffen*!"

A half-dozen trucks passed by the safe house. The partisans heard the faint squeal of brakes. Dijkstra was swearing under his breath.

"*Greens,*" he hissed. "An army of them. There's a *razzia* going on."

On the very night Dijkstra planned to hit the Hall of Records, the green-clad troopers of the *Ordnungspolizei* had descended on the neighborhood to arrest more Jews. Green Police were everywhere. Cars and trucks zoomed up and down the street. Dijkstra and his men could hear the shouts of the Germans and the crying of children as the policemen stormed into homes and rousted the residents. The Green Police remained in the neighborhood for nearly two hours, forcing Dijkstra to abort the mission that night.

At 9:30 p.m., Jan Middelburg darted out of the safe house and made his way to the taxi. There he found Jeroen van Duin and Hugo de Jong hunkered down inside the vehicle.

"It's scrubbed for tonight," he said.

Though it was extremely risky, Dijkstra and his men spent the night in the safe house, leaving the taxi and the stolen German sedan parked on the street.

And so it came to pass that at 7:40 the following night, Saturday, March 27, the black German sedan pulled up in front of the *Bevolkingsregister* and baby-faced Jan Middelburg, dapper in his police uniform, stepped out on the driver's side. He went around the car to open the door for Maarten Dijkstra and Cees Spanjaard, while Rob Groen got out from the front passenger's seat. Middelburg took hold of two heavy-looking leather document cases, the kind the red tape-laden German bureaucrats were seen carrying around in the city.

As far as the partisans were concerned, the weather was near-perfect: overcast and very cold. The darkened street was virtually deserted.

With Middelburg trailing behind them, Dijkstra, Spanjaard and Groen marched up the steps of the Hall of Records to where two Green policemen stood in the fuzzy yellow glare of a single light. Dijkstra and Spanjaard flashed their i.d. cards and the guards let them by with hardly a glance.

Dijkstra opened the door and walked in, closely followed by the other three. The raiders took a few moments to orient themselves. They were standing in the marble-floored foyer of the 19th century building. A spiral staircase leading to the file rooms on the second and third floors was about fifteen feet directly in front of them. To their left was a small office that presumably was the guards' office. No one came out of the office when they walked in and they could not hear any sounds emanating from inside.

Dijkstra nodded to Middelburg and Groen to stay at the front door, then he and Spanjaard went into the office. There was one man there, a fortyish Green policeman with a ruddy face and short gray hair, who sat with his feet on the desk, smoking a cigar and reading a German army newspaper. He clearly was not expecting visitors.

At the sight of the two "officers," he scrambled to his feet and dropped the cigar into his empty teacup.

"Where is everybody," Dijkstra said in excellent German. "Are you here alone?"

"No, sir," said the guard. "Bauer is upstairs. Making his rounds."

Dijkstra gave a curt nod and step forward to show the German his pass. As the guard's eyes swiveled down, Spanjaard whipped out a sap and walloped him just above the left eye. The police trooper fell backward and Spanjaard followed him down, clouting him twice more.

Breathing hard, the former art student stood up and stared at a shiny drop of blood on the sap. Before the war, he had never harmed another human being and still had not adjusted to the violent side of his new life.

"He'll be in the arms of Morpheus for awhile," Dijkstra said. "Come on."

They left the guard behind the desk and went into the foyer where the second guard was just coming down the stairs. The German held a flashlight in one hand and his other hand rested on the butt of a holstered pistol. He, too, was not expecting visitors. The German waited at the foot of the stairs as the two "officers" approached.

Dijkstra proffered his pass and when the guard bent to read it, Middelburg stepped from the hollow of the staircase, looped a piece of piano wire around his neck and yanked backwards, nearly pulling the German off his feet. The policeman's hands flew up to his neck as the wire bit deeper into his flesh but the struggle was short-lived. Spanjaard stepped forward and coshed him into insensibility.

For a few tense moments, the Dutchmen held their breaths, expecting the guards outside to investigate the noise. When nothing happened, they dragged the second policeman into the office and dumped him beside his unconscious colleague. Then Dijkstra, Spanjaard and Groen took the document cases and went upstairs, leaving Middelburg to tie up the Germans and confiscate their sidearms. He would remain downstairs to deal with anybody who came into the building.

Dijkstra knew that most of the vital files pertaining to the Jews were kept in a large room on the second floor that had been turned into an operations center for the notorious *Zentralstelle fur Judische Auswanderung* -- the Central Office of Jewish Emigration.

Having found the room, he and his men worked quickly. They opened drawers and threw handful after handful of documents to the floor. The slush pile grew into a massive mound as cabinets and closets were emptied and desks swept clean. The raiders were blessed with a piece of good luck in that most of the filing cabinets were not locked. Those that were locked were pried open with crowbars that Dijkstra and Spanjaard had brought into the building taped to their legs.

"Okay! Enough," Dijkstra hissed. "We don't have all the time in the world."

Spanjaard and Groen opened the rectangular flaps of the documents cases. Each case held three whiskey bottles, some filled with gasoline, some with kerosene. The bottles had been wrapped in rags to prevent them clanking and breaking.

The Dutchmen, sweating from their labors, doused the sloping paper heap with the liquid, then scattered the rest around the office. They left a large patch of flooring near the door dry.

Dijkstra opened the windows a crack. He didn't want the fumes to build to a level that would cause a premature explosion when he struck a match.

Spanjaard removed a box from his overcoat pocket and slid back the lid. There were four incendiary triggers inside. The devices were simplicity itself, the old arsonist's standby of matchsticks and cigarettes. Three matchsticks fastened by a rubber band to each cigarette; each cigarette deposited in its own paper bindle with the ends twisted closed. Crude but effective. The triggers gave the men ample opportunity to start the fire and get out of the building before the blaze really got going.

As Spanjaard removed the bindles, Dijkstra and Groen made several trails of crumpled paper leading from the kerosene-soaked pile in the center of the office to the dry area near the door. At the terminus of every trail, they placed a bindle. When everything was ready there, Dijkstra went into an adjoining office that was used by the Gestapo. In it he placed another of the Clown's "surprises" -- nearly eight pounds of scarce TNT, tightly packaged, with a detonator and a goodly length of fuse attached. "It's not enough to destroy the office," the Clown had said, "but it'll certainly do a job on the furniture."

With a hand that trembled only slightly, Dijkstra lit the fuse and made sure that it took, then went back to the other office. At the sight of him, Spanjaard and Groen struck matches. There was a soft hiss as Spanjaard's two bindles caught fire. Groen got one going but the second wouldn't take.

"Forget it! Come on!" Dijkstra said and the three men ran out of the room, along the hallway and down the stairs. At the foot of the staircase, they picked up Middelburg.

"Fire's started," Dijkstra whispered fiercely. The four Dutchmen raced for the entranceway, taking just a heartbeat to compose themselves before Dijkstra opened the door and led the way outside. With a masterful piece of self control, he returned the salute of a guard, then walked purposefully toward the waiting sedan.

Middelburg ran around car to open the door for him and he and Spanjaard climbed inside. Groen got into the front passenger's seat and Middelburg started the engine. He sped away with more of a squeal of rubber than he wanted to make.

As the car pulled away from the curb, Dijkstra and Spanjaard looked up at the second-floor window.

"See anything?" Middelburg asked.

"Not yet," said Spanjaard.

They made a right turn and then another and headed toward the city center.

Van Duin and De Jong had seen their friends come out of the building but their job was to remain at the scene until they saw that the building was on fire. That happened six minutes later when an explosion blew out a row of second-floor windows, sending a shower of sparks and broken glass to the street. Tongues of flame could be seen near the splintered window frames.

"I've seen enough," Van Duin said. "Let's go."

"You won't get an argument from me," said De Jong, gunning the engine.

For all of that, the files did not burn very well. It's said that paper burns at 451 degrees Fahrenheit, which means that it should have been hot enough in that file room to turn every page to ash. But setting a huge pile of documents on fire is always a chancy business. Some will burn, some won't. As any arson investigator will affirm, documents have been known to survive residential fires in which the structures themselves burned to the ground.

And so while some of the files were indeed destroyed in the blaze at the Hall of Records, others were only lightly singed or untouched altogether. What the fire did do was generate a lot of smoke.

At about 8:30 that night, the phone rang at the Keizerslaan station of the Amsterdam Fire Brigade and was answered by Senior Engineer Willem Gouwens.

Gouwens, a lanky, taciturn firefighting veteran, had dealt with every type of informant during his twelve years with the department, from the ice-cold calm to the panic-stricken. The caller on that particular night was reasonably calm, though he was speaking quickly and in a loud voice. The problem was that he was speaking German. Gouwens did not understand most of it but he did pick up a few key words: *fire, Plantage Kerklaan, building.* The senior engineer's knowledge of the city was encyclopedic. He knew that the most likely building on the Plantage Kerklaan about which a German would be reporting a fire was the *Bevolkingsregister*, the municipal Hall of Records.

"Calm yourself, mijnheer," Gouwens said in his level professional voice. "Help is on the way."

When he hung up, he pushed a button on his desk that started bells ringing throughout the firehouse. The firemen quickly assembled in the garage where a ladder truck and two pump-and-hose trucks stood ready. There was a full complement of twenty-five men in the fire station, thanks to the fact that the German authorities had exempted firefighters from forced labor in Germany.

By time-honored custom and to save repeating his message a dozen times, Senior Engineer Gouwens did not relate the cause of the alarm until the station captain, Cornelius van der Laan, walked into the garage.

"What's all the excitement about, Wil?" asked the gray-bearded captain who had an unlit pipe in his mouth.

"A building on the Plantage Kerklaan is on fire, sir. I think it's the *Bevolkingsregister.* The call just came in."

"Who's the informant?"

"A *mof.*"

"The *Bevolkingsregister,* eh? All right. Let's go." Van der Laan climbed into the cab of the ladder truck and Gouwens got in beside him and started the motor. With sirens blaring and bells ringing, the three fire trucks rolled out of the station and headed in single file for the burning Hall of Records.

Smoke was billowing from the second floor of the building as the fire trucks pulled up at the curb. About a hundred Germans, wearing every manner of uniform, were milling around, watching the structure burn.

With agility that belied his fifty-two years, Van der Laan hopped down from the cab and walked over to a German officer who was at that moment yelling at a Green Policeman.

"Are you in charge here," the fire captain asked in Dutch, since he didn't speak German. The German began shouting at him and gesticulating toward the burning building.

"All right, all right," Van der Laan said, realizing that any sort of dialogue was hopeless.

"Keep your men back. Back away from the building," and the fire captain made a sweeping motion with his arm.

The German officer understood and began yelling for everyone to step back.

Wearing gas masks, Van der Laan and Gouwens went into the smoky building to make an inspection. They made their way up the staircase and followed the wall of the second-floor hallway. It was hot in the building, but not blistering hot, indicating there was more smoke than fire. Dropping to their knees, they crawled into the file room that had been vacated about 30 minutes before by Maarten Dijkstra, Cees Spanjaard and Rob Groen.

Smoke had collected against the high ceiling but at floor level, visibility was relatively good. The firefighters could readily see that the blaze had been deliberately set. The place reeked of gasoline and there was a huge mound of papers in the center of the room. The top layers of the pile had been blackened to ash, like the slopes of a recently active volcano, but underneath, the documents had hardly been touched.

As he crawled along the ground, Van der Laan found one of the bindles, slightly charred on the outside but otherwise intact. He had seen that kind of device before. He untwisted one of the ends and emptied the contents into his hand: a single cigarette bound with three matchsticks. Suppressing a grin, he dropped the cigarette back into the bindle and shoved the thing into a jacket pocket.

The firefighters found little in the way of fire, a few struggling patches of flames here and there and some smoldering furniture, and that was it.

The men returned to the street.

"Hell, it's no great job," said Gouwens. "We can haul a few buckets of sand up there and have the thing out in a few minutes."

Van der Laan did not answer at once. He was staring at the second-floor windows from where smoke continued to rise into the night sky. Van der Laan was a sixth-generation Amsterdammer. His father had been a firefighter and his eldest son was now an engineer at another station.

"Captain. Should I order the men to take some sand up there?"

Van der Laan remained silent. No one could say that he had not been a dedicated public servant. He had the injuries to prove it: damaged lungs, a broken arm that never healed properly, a disfiguring patchwork of scars on his back from an explosion at a chemical factory. He was very proud of his three decades of service. There was a shelf full of medals and commendations at home that his wife treated as if it were a shrine, dusting it every day.

"Captain?"

But the great pride Van der Laan once felt for his work was long gone, replaced by feelings of guilt and shame. It was the shame that comes with witnessing an automobile wreck and doing nothing to aid the victims. Only in this case, it was like being confronted with a new wreck every day -- wrecks in which people burned to death while he went on about his business as if nothing had happened. What could he do to stop the *razzias*, he kept asking himself. He was but one man, a man with a wife and family to support. He wanted to help but what could he do? It did nothing to ease his stricken conscience to know that many of his fellow Amsterdammers were troubled in the same way.

"Captain?"

"Huh?"

"Shall we get some sand up there?"

"No."

"No?"

The captain fixed his eyes on Gouwens and issued his orders. "Tell the men to break out the ladders and hoses. I think we can handle this from the outside. Get ladders into position there and there and get a couple of men to rig up a pump. We will run hoses into the canal just to make sure we have enough water."

The senior engineer was looking at his captain with his mouth wide open. "Captain?"

"Do you have something to say, Wil?" Van der Laan asked.

The senior engineer hesitated, then said, "The *moffen*, Captain. Do you know what they do here?"

Van der Laan took a moment to re-frame the question. What Gouwens was really asking was, "Do you know what the krauts will do to us if they find out we've been screwing with them?"

"You have your orders, Wil. Let's get started. Remember, I want lots of water. I don't want a valuable old building like this going down because we didn't do our job."

"Yes, sir," said Gouwens. He turned around and began to bawl orders to the other firefighters.

Chapter 13

The German response to the raid was no less brutal for being predictable. Ten people were arrested at random and publicly executed near the Victoria Hotel, across the street from the Centraal Station. The Green Police rounded up two hundred people on the street, brought them to the hotel and forced them to witness the executions. One of the witnesses was a 12-year-old boy who, fifty years later, vividly recalled the sound of machinegun shells bouncing on the sidewalk.

"It sounded like somebody dumping a bucket of marbles from a great height on a big glass plate below," he told a reporter.

Another witness was a woman who watched in disbelief and horror as her husband of three years was shot dead in front of her eyes. A half-hour earlier they had been taking a Sunday stroll in the Vondel Park when they were set upon and arrested by the thugs of the Green Police and brought to the hotel: one to die and one to watch.

The death toll would have been higher, but for the fact that no Germans were killed in the attack on the Hall of Records. The two Green Policemen who had been overpowered and tied up during the raid were rescued from the burning building by guards at the front door.

Following the raid, the *Sicherheitsdienst* and Green Police swung into action with a vengeance, arresting scores of innocent people on the pretext of Resistance activity and torturing them in the cellars of the red-brick building on the Euterpestraat. The interrogators wanted the names and whereabouts of those involved in the raid and to that end inflicted the most excruciating punishment they could devise on the hapless prisoners. The fact that none of the arrestees knew anything about the attack only increased the Germans' anger and frustration.

The SD launched midnight raids in every quarter of the city -- the Jordaan, the Pipe, East Amsterdam, downtown Amsterdam, finding new victims to feed to the "examiners" at the Euterpestraat, but all of their efforts came to naught. At the end of a week, they knew little more about the culprits than when they started their investigation.

The daring raid had finally given the long-suffering Dutch something to cheer about. People began to gather near the charred *Bevolkingsregister* even before the firefighters finished mopping up. By eight o'clock the following morning, the crowd had grown so large that the Germans used dogs and gunfire to break it up. The SD cordoned off the site for two blocks in all directions and posted signs warning that anyone caught in the restricted area would be shot.

But nothing they did dampened the pride Amsterdammers took in this unprecedented attack on Nazi authority. In homes, pubs, restaurants, the workplace, they toasted and cheered the anonymous Resistance fighters who had pulled off such a feat. Resistance newspapers like *Het Parool* (The Password) and *Rat Poison* spread the news from one end of the country to the other. Word of the raid even made it across the Channel to the newsroom of the BBC in Broadcasting House. The Dutch who still had radios gathered around to hear the well-modulated voice of a news reader speak of the "skill and daring of the Dutch partisans" and the "blow they struck for freedom in Occupied Europe."

From her home in exile in England, Queen Wilhelmina took to the airwaves to describe the raiders as "national heroes about whom all Dutch men, women and children can be proud."

On Thursday, April Fool's Day 1943, SS General Hanns Rauter, the commander of the SS and the SD in the Netherlands, called a meeting of senior staff at his office in the Binnenhof in The Hague. Minutes of the meeting show that for a half-hour, Rauter subjected officers of the SS, the SD, the Gestapo and the Green Police to a searing harangue that left them in no doubt that their careers were on the line.

The general's near-sighted eyes were set in a perennial squint, like a sniper getting ready to fire, a gaze that had an unsettling effect on his staff (at Rauter's trial after the war, one ex-subordinate testified that "the general had a way of looking at you as if you were dead already.")

Over and over again, the dour, hawk-nosed general ranted about the seriousness of the delays caused by the loss of "the Jewish files" and how it upset "a carefully calculated timetable."

"Berlin is screaming for more Jews," Rauter raved. He impatiently snapped his fingers and an aide, SS Major Werner Naumann, handed him a memorandum.

"From Berlin," Rauter said, waving the paper. "From Dr. Harster." Dr. Wilhelm Harster held the rank of major general of police and was Rauter's immediate superior.

Rauter cleared his throat and in his nasally speech-making voice, began to read.

"To *Gruppenfuhrer* Rauter, commander of the SS and the SD for the Netherlands Territories, the following steps must be taken in the coming months concerning the treatment of Jews:

"In the months of May and June a large number of Jews from the West will be necessary in Auschwitz, where a new Buna factory must be built because the one in the West was destroyed by air raids. By May we must try to attain our goal of 8,000. We are in agreement here that by combining trains, the transit camps of Westerbork and Vught can be emptied quickly. But because the Office of Reich Security demands another 15,000 Jews in June, you are directed to intensify your efforts to locate and arrest Dutch Jews. This aim accords very well with our plans to evacuate all Jews from Amsterdam by the end of the year."

It was an enormous quota of Jews that Harster had set for the coming weeks, and Rauter needed those files at the Hall of Records, files that were now a pulpy, unreadable mess following the fire and water damage in the building

"This cowardly attack could not have come at a worse time," Rauter stormed. "I want these criminals. I want them punished so severely that no one will dare commit such an act against the Third Reich again."

The *Gruppenfuhrer* ordered one hundred additional SS troops to Amsterdam to aid the Gestapo and the Green Police in their search for the perpetrators. He also sent ten trucks equipped with the latest radio-finding equipment and technicians to run them, and he approved a ten-thousand-guilder reward to anyone who furnished information leading to the arrest of the culprits. And he assigned one of his aides, Maj. Naumann, to act as a liaison between himself and Willi Lages, the senior Gestapo official in Amsterdam.

Sturmbannfuhrer Rolf Guensche's Green Police would be used around the clock to arrest and transport Jews. Files or no files, the general intended to carry out his orders, if he had to offer a thousand guilders for every Jew who was turned in. Even the judges at his subsequent war crimes trial had to concede that when it came to carrying out orders, Rauter had an unblemished record.

Dries Riphagen had kept a low profile since his thrashing at the hands of the SS officer. His visits to his club had been so infrequent since the incident that some of the regulars believed that he was in the hospital.

In terms of injuries, Riphagen had been fortunate. Except for his bruised face, which made sleeping on his left side too painful to contemplate, the gangster had not been badly hurt. The same could not be said for his chief enforcer, Rutger Smit. The brutish ex-longshoreman had been carried to his mother's home where he remained virtually bedridden since the beating. His fractured collarbone made the slightest movement unbearably painful; his smashed nose was packed with cotton wadding, forcing him to breath through his mouth; he was tormented day and night by a fierce earache and he was often nauseous.

Riphagen had not visited his bodyguard but he had sent several bottles of grape juice, Rutger's favorite beverage. Rutger's mother had sent back a note thanking him and saying that she hoped her son would still have a job when he was well enough to return to work.

The Dutch Al Capone was not sure about that part. The pasting he had taken in front of a club full of customers was more than personally humiliating; it had, in fact, put him in disfavor with his gangland bosses for the first time in his long criminal career. Each of the four men who sat at the top of the most powerful crime syndicate in Amsterdam had made a point of visiting their fallen centurion. Each had been polite and solicitous about his health. But each had also made it clear that such a public thrashing was bad for morale, bad for business, bad all the way around.

"Black" Piet Verhoeve, the gambling overlord for Amsterdam who also had developed a lucrative sideline selling stolen artwork to the Germans, had been particularly blunt.

"This ... this incident in your club, Dries, it's gotten to be the talk of the town," said Verhoeve, who, in his three-piece suit, looked more like a stockbroker than a mobster. In the tone of a scolding father, he said, "It's been bad for business, especially protection. Our collectors are taking lip from people who never dared open their mouths before. Word on the street is --" and Verhoeve tried to keep the sneer out of his voice "-- the Dutch Al

Capone isn't so tough. They don't fear our muscle like they used to, Dries, but that's small potatoes. We'll put things right in that department soon enough. More important is that you upset the apple cart with respect to our dealings with our German friends. It was a very delicate balance. 'Til now, we've been dealing with them from a position of strength. That's the only reason we're still in business. They wanted to make money, not waste their efforts fighting us for control of the streets. It was easier to work with us than against us. That was the status quo. But now it looks like some change is in the wind. They canceled a meeting with Joop (Joop Haasdijk ran the protection racket in Amsterdam. For a thick slice of the action, Gestapo commander Willi Lages had allowed Haasdijk to stay in business).

"Lages later sent one of his flunkies to Joop's office to tell him to expect some new rules in the city," Verhoeve continued. "To us, that means only one thing. The *moffen* want a bigger piece of the pie."

"What makes you think there's a connection between that and what happened in the club?" Riphagen asked.

"Black" Piet Verhoeve shrugged. "All I know is that the *moffen* are being difficult. And that's got us more than a little concerned."

Verhoeve sighed and stood up. As he put on his black felt hat, he saw the crestfallen look on Riphagen's usually arrogant face and for a moment felt sorry for him. He had known the lad for nearly 20 years and had been both mentor and guide to him during his glittering rise through the Amsterdam underworld.

"*De kogel is door de kerk*, Dries," Verhoeve said (literally "the bullet is through the church" -- what's done is done).

At the door, he turned and said, "Maybe it's time that we did a little favor for the *moffen*. Like finding the guys who hit the *Bevolkingsregister*. That would buy a little good will, eh, Dries?"

Riphagen nodded slowly.

"You've got good sources," said the crime boss. "Keep you ears open. Let me know if you hear anything about these ... these patriots. *Tot ziens,* Dries."

After he had left, Riphagen went to the mirror and looked at the still-puffy bruise under his eye. Admiring himself in the mirror used to be a favorite pastime but not now. Every time he saw his battered face, he felt his body go warm with humiliation at the memory of that horrible night. He had never been bested in a fight before, not even when he was a kid. Of course, he had always stacked the deck in his favor, either choosing a target smaller than himself or taking along a few friends.

Riphagen lusted for revenge. The target of that lust was not Major Werner Naumann but Monique Wolters.

Not that his hatred for Naumann was less intense. Riphagen would have murdered the SS man in a heartbeat if he thought he could get away with it. But that was the problem. The gangster would be at the top of the suspect list if anything untoward happened to the German officer, and then it would be a race to see who executed him first: the Gestapo or his own colleagues in the *penose* for endangering their delicate relationship with the Nazis.

Getting at Monique was also difficult. She was now under Naumann's protection and thus, off limits. But there *was* one way to exact his revenge. It wasn't as satisfying as he would have liked, but it would do. He decided to go after Monique's brother, Leo.

Leo had no protectors. No one was going to come gunning for him if something happened to the gangling, erstwhile art student. Only Monique would care. She would care a hell of a lot and that was the point of it all.

The only issue to be decided was whether he would kill Leo or just cripple him for life. Cogitating over the options occupied quite a bit of his free time during the last two days. On the one hand, killing Leo was preferable because it would cause Monique the maximum amount of grief. On the minus side was the fact that Leo still owed Riphagen about a thousand guilders from gambling debts. If he killed the little twerp, he would never see a cent of the money. And then he saw a solution. Riphagen would bring in some underworld muscle to beat the hell out of Leo and collect what money they could from him. Then he would have him killed.

The answer was so simple, he wondered why he hadn't seen it before. Riphagen smiled -- as much of a smile he could manage without moving his swollen cheekbone -- as he looked at himself in the mirror. It was the first time he had smiled since the fight.

In a suddenly buoyant mood, the Dutch Al Capone decided to go to his club that night. Not the fleeting visits he had been making lately, but to stalk the floors like the Riphagen of old, joking with the customers, keeping an eye on his dealers and fondling his waitresses. He went to his closet and picked out his clothes for the night, his trademark outfit of a sleek, double-breasted dove-gray suit, a black silk shirt, a white tie and a dark handkerchief for his vest pocket.

Yeah, he had been out of action too long. Those thieving employees of his would steal him blind if he wasn't there to keep an eye on them. And that Leo -- the little prick was going to wish he was never born.

Whistling an old Amsterdam drinking song, Riphagen picked out a clean towel and went into the bathroom to shave.

Chapter 14

There was a panel truck parked near the corner of the Beethovenstraat and the Schubertstraat as Leo Wolters walked home from the market. It was a dented, nondescript vehicle but it stood out in the neighborhood like a sore thumb. There were so few vehicles that were normally parked on the street that Leo knew the names and even the addresses of their owners. But he had never seen *that* truck before.

He tried to take a good look at it as he passed by on the other side of the street. It was painted red and resembled an ambulance. It might have been a delivery truck except that there were no markings on the side. Nobody was sitting in the cab. And then he saw it. A small, circular object protruding slightly from the open window on the passenger's door. Shit!

Leo walked rapidly home, carrying the day's shopping -- a small sack of potatoes, some turnips and onions, a couple of cans of beans and hash.

"Where's Herman?" Leo said to his sister, the moment the front door closed behind him.

"Where he always is. In his room. Why?"

"There are *moffen* on the street," he said excitedly. "Gestapo. They're looking for somebody. They have a signal-finding truck parked outside."

"Outside? Outside where?"

"At the corner of the Beethovenstraat and the Schubertstraat."

"Well, they can't be looking for you," Monique said calmly.

"If they start going house to house looking for *anybody*, they're going to find Herman," Leo whispered fiercely.

There was a noise in the hall and they both turned. Herman Meijer was standing there, his face thanatoid-white, his eyes large behind the lenses of his wire-rimmed glasses.

"What's happening?" he said. "Why are you whispering?"

Monique was about to tell him to mind his own business but Leo said, "*Moffen*. On the street. They're outside with a signal-finding truck."

Meijer blinked rapidly, looking back and forth between Leo and Monique.

"When is Maarten taking me out of here?" he asked.

"The sooner the better," Monique mumbled under her breath.

"What?"

"How should I know," said Monique, and she turned angrily and went into the kitchen.

"When am I getting out of here, Leo?"

"I don't know." It was clear that Leo and Herman were making each other nervous. Herman walked back to his room and shut the door and Leo went into the living room and peered out at the street below. He couldn't see the truck from his living room window. He couldn't see any Germans on the street at all.

Leo was still at the window twenty minutes later when Monique, all dolled up, walked into the living room.

"Are you going to stand there all night, Leo? You're worse than our *guest*. The Germans aren't looking for you."

Leo turned and looked at his sister. "Where are you going?"

"Out. I'm meeting Sylvia for a drink on the Leidseplein."

"You're not seeing Dries?" Leo had heard about the fight in the gangster's club from his sister.

"No. I think I better let Dries cool off for awhile. I'm taking the bicycle, okay."

"Sure. So where are you meeting Sylvia?"

"I told you. The Leidseplein."

"Where on the Leidseplein?"

"I don't remember the name of the bar. It's next to the American Hotel. Don't wait up. I'll probably be late. See you."

Before Leo could say anything else, his sister was out the door. She's been acting strangely, lately, Leo thought. Being evasive. Going out almost every night. But he was too preoccupied with his own situation at the moment to be overly concerned about his sister. He stayed at the window for another twenty minutes, until the last light of the afternoon faded away and the streetlight opposite his apartment came on.

He finally went into the kitchen to boil some potatoes for his dinner. When would Maarten take the little forger away? It was almost two weeks now that Herman Meijer had been under his roof. Every day he remained he became a greater liability. Leo couldn't keep his presence secret from the neighbors forever.

The day before Cees Spanjaard had stopped by with less-than-encouraging news.

"We can't move him yet, Leo," Spanjaard had said. "Thing's are too hot. The city is crawling with *moffen*. Maarten asks that you keep Herman under your roof for just a little while longer. He knows that it hasn't been easy for you and he appreciates everything you've done."

Leo nearly told Spanjaard to knock off the speech. Instead he asked how long he would have to keep Herman Meijer in his house.

"Until it quiets down. That's the best I can say. We're all hot right now, Leo. The raid has gotten to the *moffen* more than we thought it would. None of us is going out more than we have to.

Maarten sent me over here specially to tell you that we haven't forgotten about you and that we will move Herman as soon as it's safe."

The pressure of keeping the forger under his roof was indeed taking its toll on Leo. He was not sleeping well, he was smoking too much and he jumped at the sound of every passing car. Often his sister found him just peering out the window.

The headquarters of the Gestapo were only four blocks away. Four blocks! It was his worst nightmare that one day he would see the inside of that fearsome, red-brick building on the Euterpestraat. Just looking at the place from the outside was enough to terrify anybody. The barbed wire near the entrance way, the search lights, the sirens, the sentries and their guard dogs, the black flag of the SS with its two white lightning flashes fluttering from the pole in the front yard. Trucks pulling up at all hours of the day and night and the hapless prisoners being led inside. God, what did the cellar look like. Leo didn't want to know.

He knocked on Meijer's door. "Herman, dinner's ready. You want it in your room?"

"I'm not hungry," came a muffled voice from inside.

"Screw him," Leo said softly. He fixed up a plate of potatoes and hash and settled down in his living room to eat. I'm sure going to be glad when he's out of here, he thought.

On the other side of the bedroom door, Herman Meijer was a study of a soul in torment. He lay on his side in the bed, his head facing the wall, his legs curled up almost to his chest. He was trying to get some sleep but he couldn't stop the tremor that raced through his body. His head vibrated on the pillow like an idling motor. Sleep. Balm for a hurt mind. But there was no sleep in him. Too much to think about. He could not shake the feeling of doom that had settled over him.

Meijer's family had been living in Amsterdam since the 1700s, drawn to the city, like many Jews, by the relative religious tolerance that was practiced there. But the operative word was relative. Though there were no pogroms and Jews were not being murdered in their beds, they were still barred from a number of guilds in those early days and relegated to second-class citizen status. The Jewish dead, for example, could not be buried within the city walls, but had to be taken by boat down the Amstel River to a cemetery in the nearby town of Oudekerk-aan-de-Amstel. There they were buried in a sprawling cemetery that exists to this day. As a youth, Meijer had been taken to the cemetery by his parents a number of times and had gazed reverently upon the chipped and weathered headstones of his ancestors. It had given him a good feeling in a way he could not define as a boy. It made him feel like he belonged.

And the Jews did belong. As more and more arrived in the city, they began to break down the social barriers and take an active role in city affairs. They found success in business and helped finance the mighty Dutch East India Company in its far-flung commercial enterprises. The building of several large, ornate synagogues in the city proclaimed their rising influence and power. Yiddish and Hebrew words began to work their way into the local Amsterdam dialect. The slang word for the city itself -- Mokum -- is derived from the Hebrew word *makom* meaning place.

For more than two centuries, the Meijer family had found tranquility and prosperity in Amsterdam. It was definitely their *mokum* -- their place. And then the Nazis came.

In an effort to cool his over-heated brain, Meijer tried to sort out the causes of his torment.

It was complicated. Concern for Esther's welfare, of course, was a big part of it. Every time he closed his eyes, her face loomed before him. Where was she? Had she been raped? Was she still alive? Was she out of her mind with worry and fright?

Meijer was haunted by his last look at her and the alarm he saw in her eyes as he was led away by a guard at the Hollandsche

Schouwburg. Neither of them could have guessed that he was about to be released. She probably still didn't know.

That memory would start a merry-go-round of thoughts that spun crazily around in his head, each more horrible than the last. Meijer cringed at the possibility of some brain-dead SS thug prodding Esther with a rifle barrel, forcing her to undress, violating her, then passing her on to another guard. Please, God, if there is a god, please watch over and protect her. She's only known love and compassion in her life. She has no experience with sadists and killers. She's doesn't deserve to go through hell on earth. She doesn't deserve it.

But it was no good. Meijer had long ago lost his faith in prayers and the omnipotent benevolence of a higher authority. Prison had made him distrust religion. The Germans had made him an atheist. God would not save Esther from the murdering animals. Why should He? He wasn't saving anybody else. How could there even be a god when there were Nazis walking the earth.

But Esther accounted only partly for his anxiety. It masked an even greater dread -- a mortifying fear that the same or worse might happen to him. Even now, he was perhaps moments away from falling into the same vicious hands that now held his girlfriend. And he had far more to fear than Esther did. He was not an innocent girl with a clean record. He was a forger and an accomplice to crimes against the Third Reich. He had heard the stories. Everybody had heard the stories of the chamber of horrors on the Euterpestraat.

But even the possibility of imminent capture did not completely explain the angst that now gripped him. Something had been nagging at him practically since his arrival at Leo's home. And when he eventually identified the seed of his misery, it surprised him, because it was not fear or grief or anything like that. It was, of all things, disgust -- disgust with himself. He had made a mistake. A gross error in judgment. Error? It was the action of an idiot. How ironic it would be if, after all he had been through, he was finally brought down by his own foolishness. How could he have been so breathtakingly stupid?

Meijer dozed off, or he thought he did, because suddenly he was startled awake. There was some sort of commotion going on in the front of the apartment. He could hear the thuds of struggling bodies and the sound of a lamp breaking as it hit the floor.

He suddenly felt hot and cold at once, so filled with tension he could barely breathe. At any moment he expected the Gestapo to come storming through the door. He waited in bed, sick with fright, but nothing happened. The sounds of the struggle died away and he heard -- voices. The muted sounds of a conversation. Not loud, but it sounded angry. Then the struggle resumed. There was more rolling around and what sounded like somebody being slapped.

Meijer crept to the door and listened. There were more muffled words, then he made out Leo's voice. "I don't have it," he heard him scream. An angry voice said something back.

Curiosity got the better of Meijer and he opened the door a crack to take a look. What the little forger saw when he opened the door was three people looking back at him. It was impossible to tell who was more surprised.

Leo Wolters was on his stomach on the floor, his white face twisted in pain. A man wearing a leather jacket was on top of him with his knee placed squarely in Leo's back. The man had yanked Leo's head back by the hair, while at the same time, ratcheting Leo's right arm in a direction it was not meant to go. And there was another man standing there, looking directly into Meijer's eyes.
"Who the hell is that?" he said. Leo, who was in excruciating pain, only gasped, so the man on his back jacked his arm higher.

"Aaahhh. Aaaahhh! A friend! A friend," Leo screamed.

Meijer slammed the door and locked it. He heard someone yell, "I'll get him." But another voice said, "No! Come on." There was a thud and another scream from Leo, then the shuffle of feet and the slamming of the front door. Then silence.

Meijer didn't dare open the door again. He sat there on the floor, his body against the door, waiting. Waiting for somebody to take him away.

Monique had lied when she told her brother she was meeting a friend for a drink in the Leidseplein. She did have an appointment that night, but it was farther away at the Hotel Krasnapolsky.

The Krasnapolsky is an imposing building located on the other side of the Dam Square from the Royal Palace. Like the Doelen, the Victoria, the American and the city's other grand hotels, it was built around the turn of the century when ample numbers of well-heeled travelers were taking advantage of Europe's expanding rail network to visit Amsterdam. Over the years, the Krasnapolsky had played host to kings, dukes, dowagers, movie stars and international adventurers. It is rumored that a young merchant marine officer named Joseph Conrad began his writing career while sitting in the hotel bar, waiting for the winter ice to thaw so he could ship out.

Until last week, Monique had only been in the hotel one time, and that was to meet her father and mother for dinner in the crystal-chandeliered dining room. But during the last five days, she had visited the hotel four times, remaining the entire night on two of those occasions.

Monique didn't recognize the doorman on duty as she entered the hotel that night, but her attitude would have been the same if she had. She walked by him as if he didn't exist. She also avoided eye contact with the concierge, the desk clerks, the bellhops and all of the guests who crossed her path as she walked up the plushly carpeted stairs to the second floor room of Major Werner Naumann.

Monique knew that she was skating on dangerous ice and she had to be careful. Where once she flaunted her affair with a gangster, she told no one -- not her brother, not her best friend -- about Naumann.

She reached room number 207 and knocked lightly on the door.

"Come," came a voice from inside. She opened the door, waltzed into the room and greeted Naumann with a warm, open-mouthed kiss.

"That was worth waiting for," Naumann said, holding her in his arms.

"I'm sorry I'm late," she said. "But it's difficult getting across the city these days. Your countrymen are everywhere. I was stopped three times before I got here."

"That's because some of *your* countrymen have been setting fire to other people's property. It makes life tough for everybody. Some champagne?"

"Yes, please," Monique said, taking off her coat.

Naumann opened a bottle of Cristal, poured two glasses and handed her one. "*Prosit.*"

They drank the rich wine, not with delicate sips, but quaffing it as if they had just reached an oasis after a day's ride across the desert.

"Ummm. Where did you get this?"

"My private stock," Naumann said.

"It's delicious."

"Caviar?"

"Maybe later."

They put down their glasses and Naumann kissed her again. With the same right hand that he used to smash two men senseless, he tenderly stroked her neck and back, allowing his fingers to slide to the hollow of her spine, then over her tight rump to the declivity below. He held her so tightly she could smell the fibers of his uniform, the loathsome uniform of a feared and ruthless occupier. For an instant, Monique wondered why she was not repulsed. But the thought vanished as suddenly as it came as Naumann continued to arouse her with his hands and tongue. His strong fingers were everywhere, under her dress, gliding over her crotch, pushing aside her underwear and caressing the bone-hard pudendum. Monique closed her eyes and leaned her head back. She moaned as he inserted two fingers, probing as deeply as he could in the wet, turgid cavity. Nearly beside herself with lust, her tongue buried in his mouth, she rubbed herself against his hand as he maneuvered her against the wall. But when he started to unzip his fly, she gripped his hand.

"Not like this," Monique half-whispered, half-panted. She disengaged herself and with a coy smile, led him by the hand to the bed. Their lovemaking was intense and satisfying, if over a little too quickly.

Later, as Naumann lay on his stomach, Monique gave him a massage. Her fingers skimmed over his muscular torso, caressing again and again the ragged patchwork of pockmarks and scars on his back and shoulders. After their first night together, she had asked how he got them and his answer had been a flip, "I play hard."

Naumann had told Monique a few things about himself, but far from as much as she wanted to know. It's unlikely that she found out as much about him as war crimes investigators who spent months digging into Naumann's background.

He was born in Berlin in March 1917, making him 26 years old when they first met. The son of a prominent lawyer, Naumann was raised in affluent circumstances similar to her own. His family lived in a large house with servants and he was educated in private schools. Though only a mediocre student, he was a standout athlete and won laurels in boxing, wrestling and fencing; he later fenced for Germany during the 1936 Olympics where he met Adolf Hitler for the first time.

Like a lot of middle- and upper-class young German men in the 1930s, Naumann joined the strutting, black-uniformed SS shortly after finishing school in 1935. It was the thing to do at the time for a gentleman trying to get ahead in the world. His father, who was not a member of the Nazi party, was not displeased by the choice. The SS was a large organization and still growing and there was ample opportunity within its ranks for advancement. The senior Naumann knew his son would never be a lawyer or a doctor. So a military career -- even in the brutish SS -- seemed like a good choice.

Because of his athletic prowess, Naumann was posted to the organization's most elite unit, the *Leibstandarte*, Hitler's personal bodyguard troop. An appointment to the SS-*Leibstandarte* was highly prized; it was considered a ticket to fast promotion and prestigious assignments.

All of the *Leibstandarte* recruits were young and brawny and their physical condition was further honed through hours of running, marching, calisthenics and unarmed combat training.

Captured German records show that Naumann once again excelled in the physical side of his training, but produced only lackluster scores in the classroom. He found all those lectures about the "Master Race" and Himmler's batty *Weltanschauung* a bit boring. Still, he completed his officer training course and was assigned to duties at the unit's Lichterfelde barracks in Berlin. Those duties included serving as guard and aide to a number of top Nazis, contacts that would later prove helpful in Naumann's career.

At the outbreak of the war, the *Leibstandarte Adolf Hitler* was converted into a motorized panzer regiment and sent into battle, first in Poland and later in the Soviet Union. It was during fighting in Russia that Naumann proved himself to be an excellent combat officer, earning the respect of both his men and superior officers. In September 1942, he saved his company from annihilation by a Soviet tank detachment when he used a uniquely German weapon, a disposable one-shot bazooka called the *panzerfaust*, to knock out three of the Russian tanks. With the vehicles burning, he and his men were able to shoot their way out of what otherwise would have been a death trap. Not, however, before he was severely wounded by shrapnel from an exploding shell. The wounds turned septic before he could reach a field hospital and the festering infection had to be burned out with a heated iron.

Sent to Berlin to recuperate, he was awarded the Knight's Cross (with Oak Leaves) by Hitler himself, and promoted to major. His next posting was to Holland as a senior aide to SS-General Rauter.

Naumann was undoubtedly the most dangerous man Monique had ever known in her young life. For reasons that she didn't bother to examine, she always sought an element of risk in her sexual relationships. But Naumann was in a different league altogether from her other lovers, and not only because he wielded considerable power in the most fearsome Nazi organization in Holland.

The real danger was in associating with a German. Any German. Where once she might have been called a slut for going to bed with Riphagen, her affair with the SS officer could get her killed. She knew what had befallen other Dutch women who had shared their charms with the enemy. Sometimes they were beaten. Sometimes their heads were shaved. Every now and again, their young bodies were found floating in a canal. And the victims' neighbors would shake their heads, cluck their tongues and say what a pity it was. But they would always add, "It served her right."

Though only 19, Monique was well aware of the risks and she was frightened by them, but she could not find the will to break off the affair.

Events had moved so rapidly from their first meeting less than a week ago that she still hadn't had time to sort them out. She never expected to see the SS officer again after he took her home from Riphagen's club that first night and bid her a perfunctory good-bye. But the next day, he sent a small box of chocolates, together with a card asking her to meet him that evening in the bar of the Krasnapolsky.

"Chocolates!" Leo had said, looking incredulous. "Did Dries send you that?"

"Yes," Monique had lied, and later, in a state of considerable excitement, she had gone off to keep the appointment.

It seems beyond dispute that from the beginning there was an immediate and mutual attraction between Monique and the SS officer. Oblivious to the other customers, they talked for two hours in the hotel bar and the conversation passed so pleasantly that Monique no longer saw the uniform Naumann was wearing. What she did notice were his eyes, lustrous brown eyes so dark that she could not see where the irises ended and the pupils began. And they were shaded by long, delicate, almost feminine lashes. She discerned intelligence and sensitivity in those guarded, darkly tinted surfaces, eyes that others described as arrogant and cruel.

The following night, they again met for a drink, only this time it was in Naumann's room. It was two o'clock in the morning when Naumann roused a sleepy SS corporal to take her home. The lingering kiss he gave her in the doorway stayed with her until their next meeting.

She had gone home that morning, not feeling disgusted that she had slept with a Nazi soldier, but excited by the encounter with the man who had stood up for her against one of the most powerful hoodlums in Holland. She had not asked why he had done it, preferring to take on faith that it was a Galahadian act of chivalry.

If Monique was at all troubled by the fact that her brother was working for the Resistance while her lover was working to destroy the Resistance, she did not let it influence her actions. She had gone back to the Krasnapolsky the next night and the next. Naumann wanted to take her on the town -- dinner, dancing, maybe some gambling -- but she demurred. "You know it's very dangerous for me to be seen with you," she told him frankly. "Anyway, this is where I want to be at the moment."

And as she massaged his back, she reflected that *this* was where she wanted to be.

"Hmmm," Naumann said. "My back has not felt so good for a long time." He turned over, put an arm around her neck and pulled her down for another kiss.

In fairness to Monique, there is no evidence to suggest that she ever revealed any Resistance secrets in her pillow talk with Naumann. She was able to split her life into two: the time she spent with the SS officer and all the rest of her daily existence. She was careful to keep the two in separate, airtight compartments and in that she was successful most of the time. But the day would come when she would ruthlessly use her influence with Naumann to solve a personal problem, a deed that would end in tragedy and ruin more than one life before it spun itself out. But that was weeks in the future. At the moment she was content to lie in the arms of her lover and to experience the warm glow of love for the first time in her life.

"Stay the night," Naumann said, nibbling on her neck.

"I can't," she said, rubbing his chest. "My brother is getting suspicious."

"Stay," he said, as his lips clamped down on hers again.

"I want to," she said, breaking off. "You know I do." They kissed again.

"Would you ask Lemke to drive me home?"

A half-hour later, she was dressed and giving Naumann a good night kiss when the SS corporal knocked at the door.

"I want to see you tomorrow," Naumann said.

"I'll try." And with that, she kissed him again and went out the door.

Chapter 15

On the same night of Monique's tryst with SS Major Werner Naumann, Jeroen van Duin sat in his easy chair before a sputtering fire playing his violin. For an hour, he had run his bow aimlessly over the taut strings of his cherished Guarnerius, but producing little in the way of music. Sometimes his wife, who was reading on the couch, detected a few bars of Mozart or Brahms, but for the most part it was discordant gibberish, very annoying. For Josephine van Duin, a diplomat's daughter raised in the world of receptions and cultural events, it was like hearing the scrape of fingernails on a blackboard. Herself a well-respected novelist, she was on the verge of putting an end to the racket with Conrad's famous observation -- "That's not making music, it's murdering silence" -- but she changed her mind. Leave him alone. Let him work out his grief in his own way.

Both Van Duins had been thrown into a tailspin by the death of their only child the previous year. What an adorable boy Rogier had been -- so loving, so full of life, already playing duets with his father and he wasn't even ten years old. But he had become seriously ill and his healthy and active little body had wasted away in less than a month. And then he was gone. For weeks the Van

Duins had shut themselves off from their friends, keeping their grief confined within the walls of their Jordaan apartment. But after crying until she did not have a tear left, Mrs. Van Duin was ready to face the world again. Her husband was not. He was overcome with bitterness and hatred that nothing -- not the love of his wife, the support of his friends, his work for the Resistance -- could dissolve.

He focused his hatred on the Germans. They did not cause the boy to become ill, they did not kill him, but they were as responsible for his death as if they had put him against the wall and shot him dead. The Nazis had created a climate in which a lot of people were dying, and not necessarily from bullets. It they had not invaded Holland, if they had not occupied the country and stripped it bare to feed their war machine, there would be no food shortages, medicine shortages, fuel shortages, clothing shortages. They had brought filth and disease to Amsterdam as surly as vagabonds spread the plague in the Middle Ages.

Van Duin carefully laid the Guarnerius down in its case and covered it with a velvet cloth. The violin, which emerged from the Cremona workshop of Giuseppi Guarneri in 1732, had been in Van Duin's family for nearly sixty years and there was little about its pedigree that he did not already know. Its first owner was a Venetian musician and minor composer named Enrico Fermi. Van Duin's great grandfather purchased it in London in 1885 from a well-to-do Jewish family and took it with him on a world concert tour the following year, a tour that nearly ended in disaster when he left it in a San Francisco hotel. But owner and instrument were joyously reunited in Los Angeles after the conscientious hotel owner hired Wells Fargo to bring the violin to the City of Angels.

From the great grandfather, it was passed to the grandfather, Hendrik van Duin, a founding member of the Amsterdam Philharmonic Orchestra, and from him to Van Duin's father, who mortified his family by becoming a civil servant. But his father kept the violin in exquisite condition until Jeroen came of age and then presented it to him, along with a little speech about how he hoped Van Duin would one day give it to his son.

Van Duin never touched the instrument without feeling its rich history come alive under his fingertips.

"I think I'll go out for a bit," he said.

"Are you meeting Maarten?" Josephine van Duin asked.

"No. I just feel like taking a walk."

The rage had come upon him again. It had been building for a couple of days, finally reaching the point where he could sit still no longer.

With the streets thick with SS and SD men, Van Duin had followed Dijkstra's wishes and had not left his apartment since the attack on the *Bevolkingsregister*. He left the shopping and the other mundane tasks to his wife, and she had willingly done them, swelled with secret pride for what her husband had accomplished.

But Van Duin had to get outside now or go nuts. Like the irresistible primal urge that leads baby turtles to the sea, a bloodlust born of hate and frustration spurred Van Duin on. It would grow and grow until he couldn't sleep, couldn't sit still. The only catharsis was murder. The courtly musician was at times frightened of this fire that burned so fiercely within him. He no longer knew the limits of his evil side. What if for some reason he couldn't gratify this urge to kill Germans, would he harm his wife? Himself? He didn't know.

Van Duin buckled his heavy overcoat against his skeletal frame, put on a narrow-brimmed brown hat and took an umbrella from the rack near the door.

"I shouldn't be long," he said, giving his wife a kiss on the cheek.

"I'll have some tea ready when you come home," said Mrs. Van Duin. She let out a huge sigh as she closed the door after her husband. She wondered if life for them would ever get back to normal.

Josephine van Duin was very proud of her husband's Resistance exploits and someday she would tell everyone about how her husband risked his life to save others, how he was among the raiders who set fire to the *Bevolkingsregister.* But not now. There were too many informers about. She had to keep silent. And it wasn't so difficult, given her upbringing

As the daughter of a diplomat, she had schooled from a very young age not to boast, not to talk loudly, to comport herself at all times in a demure, low-key way. Bragging was gauche, something appropriate only for barroom louts.

Jeroen van Duin knew that he could rely on his wife's silence and often discussed his Resistance work with her. It helped ease the tension. That was not a liberty his colleagues took with their spouses. But he never told her what he did on those walks he took periodically in the heart of winter. There was no telling how she would have handled that news.

It was another icy night. Van Duin paused for moment on the porch of his apartment to adjust his gloves, then turned left, walking with purposeful steps along the dimly lit Egelantierstraat. When he reached the Prinsengracht, he again paused. Where to go? The Leidsestraat would be full of drunken Germans but it was getting dangerous there. The *moffen* had beefed up their military police patrols in the area following a spate of attacks on servicemen. Besides, it was some distance away, and Van Duin had told his wife that he would not be gone very long. There were a number of bars and nightclubs on the Rozengracht but the street was too close to his own home for comfort. The idea of committing a crime practically in his own backyard seemed absurdly rash. But after thinking about it for a moment, he concluded that the Rosengracht was not *that* close to his apartment. The chances of him running into anybody he knew were fifty-fifty, but if that happened, he would simply exchange a few pleasantries with the person and go home.

Van Duin started walking along the Prinsengracht, one of the principal canals of Amsterdam that ripple out in huge arcs from the city center. In those joyous days before the war, the canals and the bridges would be brilliantly illuminated with hundreds of lights, and the reflections of the 17th- and 18th-century townhouses would dance on the coruscating surface of the water. It gave the city almost a festive ambiance, even in the heart of winter. But not these days. Now the lighting was kept so dim one could barely see fifteen meters ahead. The canal water was ink-black.

Despite the turbid street lighting, Van Duin could see the jewel-encrusted golden crown atop the steeple of the Westerkerk, one of the city's most famous landmarks, but the sight of the monument only deepened his gloom. Van Duin had worshipped there every Sunday before the war. Always his eyes had searched the floor near the pulpit under which, it was said, Rembrandt van Rijn was buried near his son, Titus. How would Rembrandt feel if he knew the city had been overrun with *moffen*? Like shit, that's how.

There were only a few people on the street when he reached the large square in front of the Westerkerk. He saw a bicyclist or two pedaling along the Raadhuisstraat and a German military truck lumbered by. But he saw no military patrols, which was a good sign.

After a moment's rest, Van Duin turned right onto the Rozengracht to search for a German to kill. He went into the first bar he came to and took a table by the window. It was a typical "brown cafe," smoky, poorly lighted and roughly furnished with a few wooden stools and benches. Some old woolen blankets had been carelessly draped over the windows in an effort to comply with German blackout regulations.

The handful of customers inside, none of whom Van Duin recognized, paid no attention to him. Nobody was wearing a uniform.

Van Duin kept his coat on. When a waitress came over, he ordered a *vieux* and settled down to wait. It was 9 p.m. Still early yet.

Van Duin pushed aside an edge of the blanket and looked outside. Before the war, the Rozengracht would have been bustling with activity: the clangs and squeals of streetcars, the honking of cars, the squeaks of un-oiled bicycle chains, the talking, shouting and laughing of pedestrians. But now the street was practically deserted. The streetcars weren't allowed to run after 6 p.m. in a lame effort by the Germans to conserve power. The grave shortage of petrol kept cars home. And most people decided that the safest place to be on dark, cold wintry night was in their own living rooms.

When his drink arrived, Van Duin downed the fiery brandy in one go and ordered another.

As his eyes continued to adjust to the crepuscular light outside, he was able to make out a woman on the other side of the street. She was struggling with a crying child. The kid was throwing quite a tantrum but the woman ignored it. She yanked on the tike's arm and dragged him bawling down the street.

A bicyclist or two zipped by, a few pedestrians, a hungry dog scavenging for food. A couple of times he saw German soldiers but they were in pairs or threes.

And then he saw *him* in the muted light of a street lamp. A *mof*. Alone. He had come out of the bar across the street and was walking toward the Lijnbaansgracht, probably heading to the old warehouse that the *moffen* had converted into a *Wehrmacht* barracks.

Van Duin's pulse quickened. He stood up just as the waitress came over with his drink. With a wink, Van Duin took the *vieux* and drained the glass as he had done with the first.

"The misses is waiting," he said to the grinning girl. "I can't dilly-dally."

With a nod to the barman, Van Duin went out the door and crossed the street, looking left and right. Nobody. Perfect. His heart was racing. He had made a decision. He was going to do it. The street was virtually deserted. The *mof* was alone. He was wearing a heavy coat. He was moving slowly, a little unsteadily. He was 15 yards ahead, shoulders bent, hands in his pockets. Van Duin started to follow. His timing had to be perfect. He did not want to be near the *mof* until exactly the right moment. And the right moment was about two blocks away at the Lijnbaan Canal. There, the *mof* had to walk onto a bridge to cross the canal. Van Duin had been across that bridge a hundred times. There were guardrails on both sides. The rails were sturdily constructed, supported by stanchions that were connected to one another by a V-pattern of wrought iron. But the guardrails were barely higher than waist level. One good hard shove and bam!

Van Duin quickened his step. He no longer felt the terror that nearly paralyzed him the first time he had pushed a *mof* into the chilly, fetid canal water. On that occasion he was so petrified that he could barely breathe. But after nearly a dozen times, he had his emotions under control. His heart was racing but he was thinking clearly enough to warn himself to be careful. Don't fall in yourself.

The *mof* was nearing the bridge. He heard Van Duin approaching and he turned casually around. Van Duin began to weave a little as if inebriated. He started whistling. The German nonchalantly turned back and started to walk across the bridge. Van Duin had gotten just a glimpse of his face. It was a young face. A little fleshy. He couldn't be sure but he thought he saw a mustache.

He looked quickly around. Still nobody. He darted onto the bridge. Three fast steps brought him within striking distance.

It was then that something happened that had not occurred before. It caught Van Duin off guard. At the rapid approach of footsteps, the German's arm shot out and locked itself around the rail. One split-second later, Van Duin slammed the German sideways with such violence that even with the soldier's arm entwined around the iron, he nearly went into the canal. But he managed to hang on for dear life and began to yell, "*Hilfe! Hilfe!*"

Startled by the German's quick action, Van Duin continued to try to push him into the canal. When that failed, he started punching the man in the head. He hit him several times but with his reed-thin physique and under-developed musculature, the blows carried little impact. The German clung to the rail and continued to yell, "*Hilfe! Hilfe!*"

Van Duin -- now in a frenzy of frustration and rage -- sunk his teeth into the man's hand, chomping down with all the force he could bring. The German's hand was partially protected by a glove but Van Duin's teeth pierced the leather and bit painfully into the flesh.

With a scream, the soldier lashed out wildly with a fist. He then let go of the railing and grabbed Van Duin around the neck, all the while continuing to yell for help. As Van Duin struggled with the soldier, he saw out of the corner of his eye that people were coming onto the bridge. Whether they were Germans or not, he did not know. But in a single flash, he realized that his own chance of survival was virtually nil. He was a goner. Oddly, it was relief he felt, not panic or fear. So be it, he thought. But he was going to take this *mof* to hell with him if it was the last thing he did.

The German had released his hold on the railing to put a chokehold on Van Duin, which gave the Dutchman his chance. With one last desperate effort, he shoved the German's head and shoulders over the railing and pushed with all the strength he could summon. The two struggling figures teetered for a moment on the guardrail, then toppled over the side.

The shock from sudden submersion in the near-freezing water knocked all the wind out of Van Duin. He released his grip on the German and kicked wildly to bring his head to the surface, swallowing some of the dirty water as he did so. He began to cough and gag. His heavy overcoat was pulling him down.

Suddenly he was blinded by a powerful beam of light trained on his face. And then another. Van Duin turned around to get his face out of the glare but lights were on him now from both sides of the canal. Something was being shouted in German but he could not make his brain comprehend it. Then he remembered the *mof* he tried to kill. Where was he? He flailed around trying to locate the man. Maybe he still had time to drown him. But the soldier was not there.

The heavy coat, now saturated with water, was exhausting him. Van Duin could have taken it off but he decided to give up the struggle. He was just going to sink below the slimy surface. He raised his arms above his head and let his body sink. But something jabbed him in the side. He didn't know it then but it was the prow of a skiff. He heard more German words but he was too exhausted to care what was being said. Suddenly hands grabbed him by the water-logged coat. Hands were under his armpits and he was pulled roughly into the boat. He tried to focus his bleary eyes on his rescuers but that was impossible. A flashlight was shining directly into his face. Van Duin made a feeble movement to get out of the glare but something hard crashed down on his head.

Chapter 16

"My God. What happened to you?"

"Nothing."

"What happened to you, Leo?"

"I told you. Nothing. Leave me in peace, Mon. Please."

Monique Wolters had walked into the Schubertstraat apartment at three in the morning to find her brother lying on the living room couch. His face was a checkerboard of bruises and cuts. His lower lip was split and swelled to twice its normal size. He was lying on his back, arms crossed over his stomach, grimacing with pain.

"Answer me, Leo," Monique said sharply. "What happened here? Where's Herman?"

For an answer, Leo gave a low groan.

"Leo! I want an answer!"

"Leave me in peace, will you, Mon? Just turn off the light and go to bed. We'll talk about it in the morning."

With an oath of disgust, Monique said, "I am not going to bed until you tell me what happened here. This place looks like a hurricane hit it. Who was here, Leo? Tell me."

Leo moaned.

"Tell me!"

"Riphagen's goons."

"Riphagen's goons?" For a moment Monique was shaken. She thought the gangster had extracted his revenge for the beating he had taken on her brother.

"Why, Leo?"

"Do we have to talk about this now, I'm sick."

Monique looked at her brother for a moment, then walked into the kitchen to wet a cloth to clean his injuries.

When she returned, Leo was lying as before, moaning softly, staring at the ceiling.

With sensitive fingers, Monique gently applied the cloth to the injured areas of his face, cleaning away some of the dried blood, working as gently as possible around the spongy, liver-purple lumps. Only once did Leo wince. For the rest, he was soothed by the ministrations of his sister.

"Do you feel a little better?"

Leo nodded like a small child.

Monique continued to dab lightly at the caked blood under his swollen lip.

"Why did Dries have you beaten up?"

Leo hesitated for a moment. "I owe him some money."

Monique was almost relieved by the news. She was delighted that it was not because of her that Leo had been assaulted.

"From gambling?" she asked.

Leo nodded meekly.

"How much do you owe him?"

"A thousand guilders."

Monique suppressed a gasp.

"Leo! How could you be so foolish"

The erstwhile art student shook his head, miserably.

"What am I going to do, Mon? I can't go to pa for help."

That was true enough. The senior Wolters had already cleaned up his gambling debts once. He swore to his son that he would never do it again.

Monique went to the kitchen to rewet the cloth and returned. She applied the cold compress to the swelling under Leo's eye.

"That's not the worse of it," Leo blurted out.

"There's more?"

He nodded miserably. "The goons that beat me up. They saw Herman."

Monique thought about it for a second and said, "So what? So they saw Herman."

"They saw someone in the house that shouldn't be here."

"You're allowed to have friends over without getting Dries' permission," Monique said scornfully.

"You don't understand. It's not only that they saw him. But it's the *way* it happened, Mon. Herman peaked out at them from his room and when he saw them and they saw him, he ducked back into his room like a frightened rabbit."

He's not he only frightened rabbit around here, Monique thought.

"Where is Herman?"

"In his room."

"In his room? You mean he didn't come out to help you?"

Leo shook his head.

"Not even after they left?"

"No."

Monique turned and stared at the closed bedroom door with a look of disgust on her face.

"Where have you been all this time, Mon?"

"What?"

"I said -- Where have you been all this time?"

"Out."

"Out where?"

"Is that important right now, Leo? Just out."

Leo closed his eyes. "They're going to tell Dries about this guy they saw in the flat. Dries is going to know we are harboring an *onderduiker*."

Monique didn't say anything. Her brother was probably right. Everyone in the city had learned to spot the telltale signs of a secret sharer. The question was what would Riphagen do with the information. Monique, who knew the man fairly well, had a pretty good idea what Riphagen would do: blackmail.

"What are we going to do, Mon?"

Monique was suddenly too upset to answer. Riphagen was going to get his revenge on her one way or the other. If he didn't get the money he wanted, he would turn them both in to the Gestapo. Maybe he would get the money and *then* turn them in. He was more than capable of doing that. That bastard. That filthy bastard. And then what? What would happen after Riphagen informed on them. They would be arrested and shipped off to a concentration camp, that's what. And she couldn't turn to Werner Naumann for help. He wouldn't lift a finger for her if he knew she had been harboring a Jew.

"Mon?"

"Oh shut up, Leo!"

She sprang angrily off the couch and walked into the kitchen. She stood for a moment with her hands against the sink, in a rare mood of helplessness and despair. Shit! Why did she ever agree to allow that Jew in the house in the first place. It was her brother's flat but she could have thrown a tantrum that would have made Leo's head spin. That little Jewish twerp would have been gone the next day.

At the core of her anguish was a hazy concern that she did not recognize at once. But as it continued to gnaw at her, Monique realized what was really troubling her. She was distressed by what Werner Naumann would think once he found out that she had been sheltering a Jew. The thought made her wince.

Why should she be so concerned about Naumann. She had hardly known him a week. He might have a wife and three kids for all she knew. He was a soldier and could be transferred anywhere at any time. They were physically attracted to each other and she had enjoyed the fervid lovemaking but until that very moment, she had not realized that she had fallen in love with him. That's why she cared what he would think.

And that brought her mind around to the most serious problem she had at the moment: not the money her brother owed the gangster, but the Jew she was hiding in Leo's bedroom. The cowardly little Jew who had rewarded their charity by cowering in his bedroom while her brother was beaten up. He hadn't even opened his door to find out if Leo was still alive. That little coward.

There was a simple solution to their problem. Meijer would have to leave. Immediately. Once he was out of the apartment, Riphagen could say anything he wanted. It was the gangster's word against theirs. Naumann was sure to take her side. No doubt about it.

She went back to the living room.

"Leo," she said sharply. "I don't want any arguments. We have to get Herman out of here. As quickly as possible."

Leo, who was still lying on the couch, touching his battered face, said simply, "We will. Maarten said that --"

"We can't wait for Maarten!" Monique practically shouted. "We have to get him out of here now. Now! There's no time to wait for Maarten to move him. I know Dries. Once he finds out, he'll be over here like a shot to blackmail us."

"I know," Leo said unhappily. "You're right. But I can't just kick him out. Herman is a hell of a lot more valuable to the group than I am. If I throw him to the wolves, Maarten will have me flayed alive."

"He will not."

"He will, Mon. I know the guy. If he --"

"Stop it, Leo! I can't stand this whimpering. You're making me sick."

Leo immediately shut up under the hot glare of his sister. She, too, was quiet for a moment as she continued to dab at his cuts.

Then she said: "Maarten will understand. Trust me. He knows what a great risk you have been taking keeping Herman here." At the mention of the forger's name, she glanced at the bedroom door and then lowered her voice.

"If the Germans find Herman under our roof, we are going to be arrested," she continued. "That's a fact. And that's going to be very bad for Maarten. He knows that. The Germans have their ways of getting people to talk. If you tell them everything you know about Maarten and his group, he is going to be in big trouble. Now what do you think Maarten would prefer. Getting rid of Herman, or risking capture by allowing Herman to stay here?"

"But what would we tell him?"

"Tell him anything you want. Tell him that neighbors had been over here and saw Herman. Tell him that Herman hadn't obeyed the house rules." She looked at Leo's face and got an idea. "You can even say that Herman attacked you. He went crazy from the pressure and he attacked you one night and that's why you threw him out."

"But --"

"It's his word against ours, Leo. *Somebody* obviously attacked you and Maarten doesn't know who. If we tell him Herman did it, who's to say otherwise."

Monique's talent for scheming was coming through again, Leo thought. Like when she was a teen-ager and stole the key to her father's office to have a duplicate made. Leo thought the matter over. He could say that Herman went crazy from fear and duress. A convincing lie began to take shape in Leo's mind. Herman had become paranoid. He accused Leo and his sister of selling him out. He attacked Leo. There had been a fight in the apartment, with enough noise to wake the dead. They were forced to throw him out. No! Better yet. Herman had run away. He had run out the door of the apartment and had not come back.

Leo nodded slowly.

"You agree?" Monique asked, who had been watching him closely.

"I suppose so."   Leo pensively touched his swollen lip. "But how do we do it?"

"What do you mean how do we do it?"

"How do we get him to leave?"

Monique looked at her brother as if wondering if they really shared the same parents.

"Oh, come on, Leo. For Christ's sake. We just tell him to leave, that's all. We tell him he's no longer welcome under this roof. We tell him to get out. Period."

But Leo still didn't looked convinced

"What if he won't leave? I mean, where's he going to go?"

"He'll leave fast enough when we tell him that we're going to call the Gestapo. And as to where he goes, who cares? Just as long as he gets away from here. Good God! He must know somebody who will put him up for a little while."

"Who are you talking about?" It was more of an accusation than a question and the tense, high-pitched voice belonged to Herman Meijer. Leo and his sister were so absorbed in their conversation, they hadn't noticed that Meijer had come out of his room and was standing near the couch.

The newcomer's voice startled both of them but Monique recovered quickly.

"Is that how you get your kicks? Sneaking around. Eavesdropping on people."

"Who are you talking about?" Meijer demanded. His eyes were wide as saucers behind the wire frames of his glasses.

Monique refused to give him a direct answer, countering instead with questions of her own.

"Why didn't you help Leo when those men came into the flat?" she asked with genuine anger. "Why didn't you? Is this how you repay our hospitality and the risks we're taking hiding you? By cowering in your room when there's trouble. Look at his face!

Look at my brother's face. Look what they did to him. They might have killed him. And you didn't have enough guts to lift a finger to help."

Monique turned away from him in disgust and went into the kitchen to clean the cloth. If Meijer was stung by her words, he didn't show it.

"Were you talking about me, Leo?" he persisted. "Are you planning to throw me out?"

Leo gave a soft groan and shook his head. "We don't want to turn you out but now we have a big problem, Herman. Those men who beat me up are gangsters and they work for one of the biggest gangsters in Amsterdam. And when you opened the door, they saw you. They're probably reporting everything they saw to their boss right now. We're in big trouble, Herman."

Monique returned with the cloth and sat down beside her brother.

"Why don't you do everybody a favor and just leave," she said cruelly as she again gently dabbed her brother's cuts and bruises. "You have been nothing but trouble since you have been here. I want you out of here."

"Monique!"

"What?" said Monique, standing up. "He might as well know the truth, Leo. I am sick of him and I want him out."

But rather than looking hurt or humiliated by what Monique said, Herman Meijer was a picture of defiance. His glance shifted from Leo to Monique then back to Leo and when he spoke, he stared directly into Leo's eyes.

"I won't go down alone," he said quietly. "If the Germans arrest me, I am going to tell them about you. I will personally bring them to this doorstep, Leo. I promise you I will."

Leo's mouth fell open but Monique just stared at the little forger as if he had brought the plague into her home.

"I mean it," he said defiantly. "I swear to God I'll do it."

"You really are a disgusting little man," Monique said.

"I'm a Jew," Meijer blurted out. "Do you know what that means in times like these? Throwing me out of this apartment is the same as signing my death warrant. If the Germans pick me up, they will kill me, as sure as I'm standing here.

"You talk about the risks you've taken hiding me. What the hell do you think I've been doing for the last two years? I've been risking my life every day and not only because I'm a Jew. If the *moffen* knew only a tenth of what I have been up to, they would slice my balls off and make me eat them. Even while I have been under this roof, I have been risking my life to help save others. How can you even think of throwing me out, Leo?"

For a moment, Meijer looked like he would break down in tears. He took off his glasses, wiped his eyes and resumed speaking, this time in a calmer voice.

"If you are going to betray the cause we have both worked for, Leo, I don't think I can stop you," Meijer said. "But don't think you can do it and go unpunished. I mean what I said. If the Germans arrest me, it's as good as arresting you, too. I will bring them right to this door. I swear to God."

Meijer started to go back to his room but then stopped and turned slowly around. "And if the *moffen* don't get you, Maarten Dijkstra will. He doesn't like traitors any more than I do." And with that, the little forger went to the room and slammed the door.

"Jesus. Do you think he means all of that?" Leo asked.

"Of course he does," Monique snapped, "What does he have to lose?"

"He wouldn't dare," Leo said with finality.

Without answering, Monique went back to the kitchen, threw the rag in the sink and walked back through the living room on her way to her own bedroom.

"Where are you going?" her brother asked.

"To bed," said Monique. "It's four in the morning."

"What about Herman? What are we going to do about him?"

Monique didn't answer.

"Mon?"

"We'll worry about it in the morning, Leo. Good night."

She went to her room and shut the door, leaving Leo to stew on the couch.

Chapter 17

"You are a loathsome nuisance -- like a blister on my prick. I hope I can tell you this without hurting your feelings."

The speaker was *Befehlshaber* Willi Lages, the senior Gestapo commander in Amsterdam. He was sitting behind his desk in his third-floor office on the Euterpestraat, glaring at the man who stood at attention before him.

"You are nothing but a snoop and a spy," Lages continued. "You serve no function here whatsoever, except to tell tales to General Rauter."

"I am not a spy," Major Werner Naumann said stoutly.

"Then what are you, Naumann? What is your purpose here?"

Naumann remained silent.

"I asked you a question, Herr Major."

"I was assigned to be here by General Rauter," Naumann said, his voice wooden. "He could not be here personally so he sent me."

"To spy on us."

"To keep him informed on the progress of your search for the *Bevolkingregister* criminals."

"He might have sent someone less arrogant -- let's say, less conspicuous -- than yourself. If I may continue speaking forthrightly to you, Naumann, I find you an odious young man.

Your heavy-handed meddling in this affair has been burdensome to the point of suffocation."

Naumann stood respectfully at attention, trying to suppress a smirk at the corners of his mouth. Willi Lages enjoyed a formidable reputation in Berlin; Naumann had expected better from the man.

"I regret you feel that way, Herr Lages, but I have my orders and I intend to carry them out."

Since the April First meeting at General Rauter's headquarters, Major Naumann had become a frequent visitor to the Euterpestraat, dropping in unannounced on Lages, sitting in on interrogations, sometimes questioning suspects himself. Lages, who was accustomed to autonomy in running the office, had grown increasingly surly at having to explain his every move to this stooge of the general's.

"You're getting to be like a parrot on my shoulder, Naumann," he said after one of the major's impromptu visits. "Go away. I will call you when I have something to report."

But Naumann had not gone away, which led Lages to order the major to be in his office at nine that morning "to clear the air."

Lages got up from his chair and walked around the desk to where a chess game was set up on a small adjacent table. He walked with a slight limp, the result of a gun battle with a bank robber in Berlin in the 1920s when he was a young patrolman. A fragment of the robber's bullet was still lodged in his leg but he had fared better than the holdup man who was shot dead by another policeman.

Lages was playing long-distance chess with his brother, who worked at the Foreign Ministry in Berlin. The game had been going for weeks and several pieces from both sides already had been captured. The Gestapo commander eyed the board for a moment, then asked, "Do you play chess, Naumann?"

"No, Herr Lages."

"Pity. You're no help here, either." He continued to study the board.

"If you put the same energy into catching the *Bevolkingsregister* criminals that you put into your chess, Herr Lages, you would have caught them by now and I would be back in The Hague."

Lages kept his eyes locked on the board but his face looked bleached of color.

In the complex, murky world of the SS, it was often difficult to delineate the chain of command. Technically as head of the Gestapo-*Sicherheitsdienst* in Amsterdam, Lages was Naumann's superior. But Lages was also a civilian, an ex-policeman turned Gestapo enforcer, and as such, had no real authority over Naumann, who was an SS major and who took his orders directly from General Rauter. Lages' loathing for Naumann stemmed in part from his frustration at not being able to deal decisively with such a pain-in-the-rear subordinate.

"So, you are a critic as well as a snoop, Naumann," Lages said sardonically. "Is there no beginning to your talents?"

Naumann, stone-faced, stood in the center of the office, not so much staring at the Gestapo man as staring *past* him. Lages ignored him, focusing his attention on the antique wooden chessmen as if his life depended on the game's outcome. Finally he took one of his bishops and moved it to a spot directly in front of his queen.

"Thank you, Naumann, for helping me see through the fog of battle," he said. "I think defense is the wisest strategy at this point. Don't you?"

Naumann didn't respond. He wasn't expected to.

Lages resumed his seat behind the desk and began scribbling something on a sheet of paper. On the wall behind him, the glowering visages of Hitler and Himmler stared at his back in disapproving silence.

"If you have no further need of me, Herr Lages --," Naumann said, but he was interrupted by a knock at the door.

"Come," said Lages.

Capt. Ludwig Schenck, one of the senior SD examiners, came into the office and stood at attention before Lages' desk.

"What it is it, Schenck?" asked Lages.

"Good news, Herr Lages. I think we finally got the break we've been looking for."

"Continue," said Lages in a flat voice.

"Last night we arrested a man. Routine case. A local who pushed a soldier in a canal. We questioned him, of course, just to find out whether any of his friends have a fondness for the same hobby. It turns out he's an unemployed musician named Van Duin."

"Yes?"

"We have no information on him in our files. He's not a member of the Culture Chamber and there's no evidence that he has been performing illegally. In fact, we have no employment record on him at all.

"So?"

"So how has he been supporting himself and his family all these months?"

Lages nodded. "Resistance stipend?"

"That's what we thought. The fact that he refused to join the Culture Chamber made us think that he might be connected with Maarten Dijkstra's group. At first he denied any association, but now he's admitting it. In fact, he has been with the group since Dijkstra started it. The prisoner gave us some names and addresses. The names we already knew and the addresses no doubt are no longer good, if they ever were. More interesting, the prisoner seems to know something about the fire at the records building."

At that news, Lages' hard cop's eyes glittered and even Naumann, who had been listening to the conversation with a bored look on his face, perked up.

"Come on, Schenck, out with it," Lages said impatiently. He knew his man. Schenck was nettled by his well-deserved reputation for physical brutality and relished the opportunity to appear clever.

"We got lucky," Schenck said. "It had been a long interrogation. Haase was tired. I was tired. We were getting ready to wrap it up when I asked the prisoner -- very casually -- if he used gasoline or kerosene to start the fire at the records building. That's all it took. The prisoner began blubbering, 'Dijkstra. Dijkstra. Dijkstra. Not me. Dijkstra.' He said it over and over."

"Maarten Dijkstra," Lages said quietly. "Not exactly a surprise. What else did he say?"

"Nothing more, Herr Lages," answered the senior examiner. "He passed out. We thought it best to discontinue the interrogation for a little while. We took him back to his cell and I came here to tell you."

"When did you take him back to his cell?"

"About ten minutes ago."

"Good. Where's Haase?"

"Having a cup of coffee."

"Who else do we have?"

"Luther and Schmidt just came on duty."

"Ummm. No. I want Haase."

"He's been at it all night, Herr Lages. He's exhausted."

"We're not going to resume the interrogation immediately. Tell Haase to get some sleep and to report again to interrogation at noon. Tell Luther to be there, too."

"Yes, Herr Lages. And what about me?" Schenck asked. He had been up all night and was eager to go home.

Lages told Schenck to put his report in writing and take the rest of the day off.

After the SS captain left, Lages said to Naumann, "Well, Naumann, it looks like you soon might have something actually worth reporting to General Rauter. Do you care to observe the rest of the interrogation?"

Naumann nodded.

"Good. I will see you in interrogation at noon. Now if you will excuse me, I have to finish my own report to General Rauter. Good morning."

That's one first-rate son of a bitch Lages thought as Naumann walked out of the office.

It was no coincidence that the Gestapo cells and the interrogation rooms were in close proximity to each other in the basement of the building. Partly it was done for convenience. The SD guards did not want to be bothered dragging the nearly comatose prisoners up a flight of stairs after a wearying interrogation. But the real reason for the layout was to allow the examiners to benefit from the enormous psychological effect of having new prisoners hear the screams. It rarely failed to unnerve. Usually they started talking even before the examiners could get them strapped down.

That had not been the case with Jeroen van Duin, though. Van Duin had been a tough nut to crack. The examiners had to work him over for hours to get him to reveal so much as his name.

The man who once played second violin for the Amsterdam Philharmonic Orchestra had been fished out of the near-freezing water by the military police, clouted over the head with a flashlight and taken by boat to the nearby Lijnbaansgracht barracks of the Wehrmacht. There he was turned over to the SD and driven by truck to the Euterpestraat. (Technically the SD and the Gestapo were separate organizations, the SD having begun as the security arm of the SS, while the Gestapo -- short for *Geheime Staatspolizei* --was the secret police for the German state of Prussia. But under the direction of SS-Reichsfuhrer Heinrich Himmler, the Gestapo was eventually absorbed into the SS and its duties became inextricably linked with those of the SD, so much so that the names were, for all extents and purposes, interchangeable.)

The Germans did not dress the bloody gash on his head, nor did they provide a blanket or dry clothes. Instead, they took him to the fearsome basement and left him alone for several hours in a dark, bare cell.

Nauseous and blue with cold, Van Duin had curled into a shivering ball on the stone floor and prayed for a painless death. The blow to the head had caused a concussion and he quickly lost track of time as he drifted in an out of consciousness. For a while it seemed to him that it was surreally peaceful in the cellar. Every now and again he heard a voice or the faint clang of a door but mostly it was as quiet as a crypt. The only illumination came from a couple of ceiling lights in the corridor but his own cell was dusky and restful. His most vivid sensation, apart from his trembling muscles, was the effluent odor emanating from his sodden clothes. It reminded him of the mess in his apartment about a year ago when the plumbing backed up.

Van Duin had no idea how long he lay on the floor before he heard the first shrieks. Five minutes? Twenty? It didn't matter. The sounds of a fellow human being, perhaps even someone he knew, being put through living hell drove all other thoughts from his mind. The screams reverberated through the basement. Van Duin covered his ears but that did not block out the horrible noise.

Finally the shrieks ended and a short while later, Van Duin could hear the man being taken back to his cell. The guards walked right by his cell towing the nearly lifeless figure by the arms and shoulders. The prisoner was moaning but the sound that made the biggest impression on Van Duin was the scrape made by his shoes as they dragged along the stone floor.

Except for faint groans coming from somewhere in the cavernous basement, it was again silent. And then the guards came for him. He flinched with fright at the sound of a key turning in the lock. In another moment he was dragged roughly to his feet and led by the arms to an interrogation room.

Unlike his bare cell, the interrogation room had some furniture in it, if you count a wooden table and a high-backed metal chair bolted to the floor as furnishings. The guards pushed him into the chair and used padded leather straps to secure his arms, legs and chest to it.

Then two more men walked in, one carrying a canvas satchel like a plumber might own, which he placed solemnly on the table and unpacked with care. The sight of the man was more terrifying than the metal chair. He stood six feet three inches tall, barrel-chested, massive-skulled, with upper arms the size of oak logs. His thick neck swelled from the unbuttoned collar of his black jumpsuit and ended under a spiky pelt of crew cut blond hair. His name was Egon Haase and he was among the worst the Gestapo had to offer.

An Austrian-born grammar school dropout, Haase was famous among his colleagues for his prowess with pliers, scalpels, soldering irons and the like. His skill at inflicting pain with these implements impressed even the most hardened Gestapo examiners. One later told a war crimes investigator that the sub-literate Haase "had the hands of a surgeon but the brains of a sturgeon. He would do anything he was ordered to do -- *anything.* No questions asked."

Haase learned about murder and mayhem from experts -- the officers and men of the SS *Einsatzgruppen* (extermination squads) in the Ukraine with whom he served for nearly a year. It's estimated that Haase personally murdered a thousand men, women and children during that time. At some point during his service in the Soviet Union, Haase apparently suffered a mental breakdown. He was sent to a military hospital outside of Warsaw where he remained for two months, this despite the fact that there is nothing in his military record indicating he was physically hurt.

After his release, he was transferred to the Netherlands where he was assigned as an examiner at the SD bureau in Amsterdam.

Though his new duties rarely involved killing, they did allow him to exorcise his demons by inflicting the maximum amount of physical pain on other human beings. And in this, he became an expert. It's unlikely that he ever failed to break a suspect during the eighteen months he worked in Amsterdam.

The interrogation of Jeroen van Duin began as soon as Haase unpacked his tools. A hot, bright light hanging six feet above the metal chair was turned on, bathing the prisoner in its white glare. Van Duin clamped his eyes shut but opened them quickly enough when Haase hit him across the chest with a rubber truncheon.

"Eyes open," he barked. Haase had chosen the truncheon over some of his more fearsome tools because he didn't think Van Duin had much to reveal. Just another asshole who thought he could get away with shoving an innocent German soldier in the canal.

Haase played the bad cop to Capt. Ludwig Schenck's good cop in a routine that they had practiced many times.

"Come on, my friend," Schenck said in a soothing voice. "Nothing is worth the beating that my colleague is very capable of administering. Tell us your name. We will find it out sooner or later. You can save yourself a great deal of pain by making it sooner."

Getting the prisoner's rightful name was usually the first order of business. Names could be matched with dossiers already on file and those names might lead to other names. But for two hours, Van Duin refused to talk. He gasped, he grunted, he yelped and shrieked with pain as blows rained on him but he did not say one recognizable word.

Haase used the truncheon with pinpoint accuracy, hitting the prisoner across the bridge of the nose, under the ear, in the mouth, under the eye. One well-aimed blow broke his right wrist. Another opened a gash on his cheekbone.

Finally Schenck had stopped him. "Enough, Haase. Cool off. Go get a smoke."

Haase had left the room like a petulant schoolboy, glowering at Van Duin over his shoulder.

"I must say that you are a fool, my friend," Capt. Schenck said. "I should get a mirror and let you see your face. Nobody is going to offer you a role in the movies very soon, unless it's a role in a horror film. And all of this punishment was so unnecessary. What we are asking is not unreasonable. It's not strange that we want to know your name. You tried to kill a German serviceman last night. And it's through no fault of your own that you didn't succeed. I suppose you're lucky in a way. Had you killed that soldier, my friend's methods would have been far more severe. This I can assure you."

Van Duin's large head sagged to one side. His once-distinguished features had been battered and broken to the point where his whole face was a mask of red. No one was ever going to mistake him for David Niven again. He suddenly became aware of something small and grainy in his mouth. Van Duin located it with his tongue and identified the alien substance as a fragment of a tooth. He tried to spit it out but he could not get his dry, swollen, blood-caked lips to pucker.

"Do yourself a favor and cooperate," Schenck said reasonably. "In the end, you are going to tell us what we want to know. Everybody does. Why put yourself through this terrible pain. I will tell you something honestly. My colleague is crazy. Really crazy. He belongs in an institution. I have seen him torture children to get their fathers and mothers to talk. And enjoy it. He actually likes this work and -- unfortunately for you -- he is very persistent. He'll keep at it until you tell him what he wants to know. Oh-oh. He's coming back. Talk to me."

Van Duin's left eye was swollen shut but through the red mist in his right, he made out a fuzzy figure approaching him. He could not bring the figure into focus but he did not doubt that it was his other tormentor.

The other man did not come over at once, tinkering around instead on the table a few feet away. When he did approach, he was carrying something, something much smaller than a truncheon.

With one huge hand, Haase pressed down on the fingers of Van Duin's right hand, pinning his fingers to the armrest of the metal chair. With his other hand, the Gestapo man began to work a small sliver of wood under the nail of the prisoner's middle finger. Van Duin's entire body recoiled at the sickening sensation of the sharp, splintery object coming between his fingernail and the cutaneous surface underneath.

As groggy as he was, the musician jerked his head from side to side as the pain intensified. He tried not to scream but the agony was building to an intolerable level. He swung his head violently back and forth and his breath came in gasps. He wanted to tear his hand free but it was strapped to the chair and further immobilized by Haase's vice like grip.

Schenck's quiet, disembodied voice reached his ears. "It's a matchstick. Sharpened at one end."

At the point where Van Duin could stand the agony no longer, Haase stopped what he was doing and walked languidly to the table where he picked up other items and returned to the prisoner. His big hand again clamped down on Van Duin's fingers as he started to work another sliver of wood under a nail, this time on the index finger.

Van Duin closed his eyes and gritted his teeth; he was so out of his mind with pain and terror that he was unaware of what Haase did next.

What the big Gestapo man did next was to wrap a wad of cotton around the musician's right wrist. The odor of gasoline rose to Van Duin's nostrils. Then Haase struck a match. Five seconds later, the musician emitted a demonic scream that might have been heard a block away.

"What is your name?" Schenck demanded.

"My hand is burning!" Van Duin shrieked hysterically.

"What is your name?"

"Aaaaahhhhhh."

"Your name?"

"Van Duin! Van Duin! Dear God, help me!"

As the prisoner writhed and screamed and tried frantically to free his bound wrist, Schenck motioned to Haase who picked up a small pail of sand and dumped it on Van Duin's burning hand.

At noon, *Befehlshaber* Willi Lages and SS Major Werner Naumann walked downstairs to the interrogation unit where they were joined by a prim-looking female stenographer and a somewhat bleary-eyed Egon Haase. The fine blond hairs of Haase's eyelashes were crusted with sleep.

"Where's the prisoner?" Lages demanded.

"In his cell, Herr Lages."

"Have him brought to room one."

Though he would not have agreed, Van Duin had gotten off relatively lightly so far. He had been examined in a sort of all-purpose torture chamber that the Gestapo used for criminals, deserters and other troublemakers. His next session would take place in a room reserved for Resistance suspects, political prisoners and Jews. Interrogations in room number one generally did not last long.

Jeroen van Duin, his clothing soiled from repeated retching, his hair matted with blood from the very first blow with the flashlight, was dragged to room one by two burly guards. Again the chief item of furniture was a chair, only this time, it was a sturdy oaken chair secured to the floor with steel brackets. A circle of wood measuring about 9 inches in diameter had been removed from the seat.

Van Duin was roughly shorn of his clothes and pushed into the chair. His arms, legs and chest were secured with leather straps as before. The prisoner winced with shock and pain as the strap was cinched tight against his fire-blistered wrist.

And then a new twist was added. After the semi-conscious man was lashed in, Egon Haase went to a nearby table and returned uncoiling a length of black wire. He knelt down and ran the wire under the chair, using an alligator clip to secure it to the sensitive outer tissue of the prisoner's exposed anus. Haase went back to the table and returned with a second wire, this one thicker and with a bigger serrated clip. He clamped it to the tip of Van Duin's penis.

As before, a powerful light hanging above the prisoner's head was turned on and the interrogation began. With Naumann watching intently, Willi Lages did the questioning.

"We are not going to waste any more time with you," he told the prisoner. "Your choice is simple. Either answer my questions or face the consequences of your stupidity. Now then, what do you know about the fire at the records building?"

Van Duin slowly raised his head but he did not speak.

"Answer me," commanded Lages.

The Dutchman mumbled something but it was not coherent.

Lages nodded to Haase who was standing by the table with his hand resting on a knob of a small black box. At the gesture from the *Befehlshaber*, he gave the knob a twist and there was a faint hum of electricity. The effect on the prisoner was instantaneous. Van Duin's eyes bulged as if his head were about to explode. His body jerked upward in a violent paroxysm that for a moment appeared as if he were trying to tear the chair from the floor. His jaw opened despite his clenched facial muscles and a horrifying scream was torn from his throat.

Haase cut the current and Van Duin, drenched in sweat, sagged in the seat, his body limp. He was powerless to prevent his sphincter from opening and a watery ooze collected beneath his chair. He expelled a low, continuous moan.

The Germans waited a moment, then turned the juice on again. And again.

"What do you know about the fire at the records building?" Lages asked.

Van Duin talked. Rambled, really. For fifteen minutes he divested himself of everything he knew about the raid. It came out in a torrent of disjointed phrases and half-sentences, as if he were speaking while in throes of a terrible nightmare. Lages had to interrupt the grotesque monologue with pointed questions in order to make sense of it. And all the while, the stenographer took it all down as best she could. If she was at all disquieted by what she just witnessed, she did not show it. She sat near the table with her legs crossed, the pad on her knee, quietly taking down what the prisoner said. Occasionally she asked for something to be repeated.

Van Duin named Maarten Dijkstra as the mastermind of the raid and furnished the names of the other participants: Hugo de Jong, Cees Spanjaard, Jan Middelburg, Rob Groen and himself. He also told the Gestapo about the plumbing supply store on the Ceintuurbaan where the Artist Resistance Movement sometimes met, and the Admiraal de Ruyter bar on the Vijzelstraat where Dijkstra often met with colleagues. He also revealed the addresses of other safe houses and more importantly, he told the Germans where Dijkstra and Middelburg were living at the moment. He would have given the Germans all of the addresses but he did not know them.

When he had finished speaking, Van Duin collapsed. He was unstrapped and dragged naked back to his cell. Within two days he would be dead, shot by a firing squad in the coastal dunes on the outskirts of The Hague.

Lages and Major Naumann returned to Lages' office to await a typed transcript of the interrogation. A copy for each man arrived about thirty minutes later and thereafter, things moved quickly.

Lages called the commander of the Green Police in Amsterdam, Sturmbannfuhrer Rolf Guensche, and sketched out the manpower requirements he needed. Naumann called General Rauter in The Hague to let him know about the latest developments.

At 5 p.m. that afternoon, Guensche, Naumann, Lages and other Nazi enforcement officials gathered in the map room on the second floor of the Euterpestraat to plan their next move. The atmosphere was surprisingly cordial, given the intense rivalry that existed among the various organizations. Since everyone's dinner plans were canceled, sandwiches and coffee were brought in, along with a tray of foul-smelling Russian cigarettes, of which the supply in the city seemed inexhaustible. The map room was soon thick with smoke as the men got down to business.

Nobody objected when Lages said that a massive police action should be undertaken that very night. In less than an hour, with the aid of several detailed city maps, they put together an ambitious plan for doing just that. Six different addresses in Amsterdam would be raid simultaneously. A fleet of trucks would be mobilized to take the expected multitude of prisoners to the Euterpestraat or to a Green Police barracks near the Plantage Kerklaan. In one fell swoop, Lages planned to put the Artist Resistance Movement out of business once and for all. Zero Hour was set for 9 p.m.

As the meeting came to an end, Lages held up a hand and said: "One moment before you leave, gentlemen." The others remained respectfully in their chairs.

"We have been after Maarten Dijkstra for a long time," he said. "Now that we are close, I don't want anyone getting careless. Keep a tight rein on your men tonight. No gunplay if you can help it. These criminals are worth a lot more to us above the sod than dead. But no matter what happens, I want Maarten Dijkstra taken alive. Do you understand? If anything happens to him, those responsible will answer to me."

Chapter 18

Josephine van Duin at first was not concerned when her husband was late returning from his walk. She knew how claustrophobic it was sitting in the apartment and how it brought him some peace of mind to be outdoors, taking long walks in the city he loved.

But as midnight approached and he still had not returned home, Mrs. Van Duin began to worry. At one a.m., she did the one thing her husband warned her never to do, even if he vanished: she went to the home of a Resistance colleague looking for him.

More precisely, she went to the nearby flat of Coby Lauwers in the Jordaan where Coby's brother, Jan Middelburg, was sheltering.

"Jeroen went for a walk hours ago and hasn't come back," she calmly told Middelburg and the Lauwers.

"It's probably nothing to worry about," said Jan Middelburg. But everyone could see that in a blink, the young man had gone from yawning and sleepy-eyed to razor-sharp alert. Unlike his sister and her husband who were clad in dressing gowns, Middelburg had greeted Josephine van Duin fully dressed. He slept in his clothes in case he had to make another sudden escape in the middle of the night.

"Where does Jeroen usually go on his walks?" he asked.

"Oh, just around the neighborhood. Through the Jordaan. Sometimes over to the Westerkerk. He's usually back in an hour or so. This is the first time he has been so late."

It was clear to Middelburg that Mrs. Van Duin did not know what her husband sometimes did on his nocturnal rambles. Middelburg knew but kept quiet.

"I deplore being such a bother but it's gotten so late and I am really concerned about him," Mrs. Van Duin said. "It's not like Jeroen to stay out like this."

"If you have no urgent need of the bicycle, sis, I am going to borrow it," Middelburg said lightly.

Coby Lauwers, a tall buxom woman, said in feigned disgust, "Now why would I be needing my bicycle at 1:30 in the morning. None of your cheek. Off with you now, and don't ride into a canal."

"Not before I take a belt or two."

"Jenever? Now? You'll have your nip when you come back and not before," scolded his sister.

But her husband saw what the young man was up to and got the jenever from the cabinet in the living room.

"Piet Lauwers!"

"Hush, woman," he said, passing the bottle to Jan Middelburg, who unscrewed the cap and took a healthy pull.

"It'll help explain my presence on the street at one-thirty in the morning if I have some alcohol on my breath," he said to Mrs. Van Duin, lest she think he was a complete wastrel.

"Of course," said Mrs. Van Duin. She had first met the earnest young man a few months before when he showed up on their doorstep following his shootout with the police. Like most people, she had taken an instant liking to him.

Middelburg wiped his lips, screwed the cap back on and passed the bottle back to his brother-in-law.

"I shouldn't be long," he said, wheeling the bike out the door. And then he was gone.

"You make yourself comfortable, dear," Coby Lauwers said to Mrs. Van Duin. "I'm going to put the kettle on."

Jan Middelburg did not search for Jeroen van Duin, but rode instead as fast as he could toward the flat where Maarten Dijkstra was living. He had a good picture of what happened to his Resistance colleague and was fairly certain Van Duin was in the hands of the Germans, if he was not already dead. Given a choice between the two, Middelburg prayed for the latter. It was horrible and cruel to feel that way and maybe some day, when the war was over, he would have the luxury of grieving for his friend and repenting that such a dark thought had ever crossed his mind. But the reality was that if Van Duin were still alive and in the custody of the Gestapo, every man in their group was in grave danger.

Middelburg pedaled furiously, ignoring the stinging wind and the light rain that started to fall. He could have pedaled directly from his sister's flat in the Jordaan to Dijkstra's hideout by following the Herengracht, another of Amsterdam's major water arteries. But that would have left him too long in the open. The slight bit of liquor on his breath would only stand up to the most cursory inspection. If the Germans decided to do any checking at all, he would be in big trouble. Like his other Resistance colleagues, Middelburg carried a falsified identity card in another name but that, too, would not be enough. The Gestapo had its ways of finding out everything it wanted to about a person. The best way to minimize the risk was to stay out of view from German patrols, and to that end, Middelburg took a circuitous route through the alleys and narrow lanes, finally emerging near the Royal Palace, then quickly darting into another series of alleys behind the Vijzelstraat.

Finally he came to a tightly packed row of dingy buildings near the Mint tower that were so old and so dilapidated that one or two had tilted and were actually touching the gabled roofs of adjacent buildings, like drunks leaning on the shoulders of sober friends.

It was in the loft of one of these leaning buildings -- Vijzelstraat 246 -- that Maarten Dijkstra and his lover and former model, Saskia Hoogeboom, were being sheltered. To gain entrance to the building -- or to virtually any of the old buildings in Amsterdam, one had to have a skeleton key, known as a *loper*. There were only about a dozen different types of *lopers* in circulation at the time and if one collected them all, he could open practically every front door in the city.

After moving into the Vijzelstraat loft, Dijkstra had duplicates made of his *loper*, which he distributed to his closest followers so they could visit him at odd hours without rousing the neighborhood.

Middelburg took out the *loper*, opened the ancient front door and wheeled the bicycle into the small entranceway. The wooden floorboards creaked as he parked the bike under the stairwell. After locking the wheels, he went up the narrow rickety stairs to the fourth-floor loft where Dijkstra lived and knocked softly on the door.

"Who's there?" came a muffled voice.

"Jan."

The door swung open and Middelburg walked in. A sullen-faced Saskia, who was wearing a man's shirt as a nightgown, closed the door and without a word, went back to the tiny sleeping quarters. A moment later, Dijkstra emerged fully dressed.

"What's the matter, Jan," he said cheerfully. "Couldn't sleep, either?"

Middelburg quickly outlined what he heard from Josephine van Duin.

Dijkstra ran a hand through his bone-white hair. "What do you make of all that?"

"I think that despite your warnings, Jeroen was on the prowl for Germans again. And this time, his luck ran out."

"That's about how it sounds to me, too."

They stared at each other for a moment. Both men were in a state of controlled panic. If the worst-case scenario were true and Jeroen van Duin were indeed in the hands of the Gestapo, the consequences would be devastating. Van Duin didn't know everything but he knew enough to make his Nazi inquisitors very happy. He knew the names and addresses of sympathizers, the addresses of safe houses, codes and passwords. Beyond that, he knew where Dijkstra and his closest followers were living. That meant that the friends and family who had been sheltering them were also in extreme danger.

"Before I hit the alarm button, I have to find out what happened to Jeroen," Dijkstra said. He looked at his watch. "It's 2:45 a.m. now -- hmmm."

Dijkstra knew a man who lived a few blocks from the Van Duins. He might know what became of their missing colleague. But Dijkstra could not go there at three in the morning to ask questions without attracting a lot of unwanted attention. In a few hours it would be dawn. People would be going to work. It would be easier to move around.

The question was: could he afford to wait the extra few hours. If the Germans had indeed captured Van Duin, they might be interrogating him at that very minute. There was no telling how long it would take to break him. On the other hand, even if the Germans broke him quickly, it would still take time to organize a raid. For the raid to be effective, the Gestapo would have to hit a lot of addresses simultaneously. Otherwise, the alarm would be given and the Resistance men would disappear faster than rats up a drainpipe. The Germans would need time to plan such an operation, which meant that Dijkstra had the time to move prudently.

"It's probably better that you stay here for a bit, Jan," Dijkstra said. "I know your sister is going to worry but what I don't need right now is for you to get picked up."

Middelburg nodded his blond head.

"I think we have an extra blanket here somewhere," he said. "You should be comfortable enough for a few hours."

At 6 a.m., Dijkstra and Middelburg carried their bicycles downstairs and rode off together toward the maze of alleys and back streets that would take them to the Jordaan. At the Westerkerk, Dijkstra turned left on the Rosengracht and Middelburg continued on to his sister's flat.

Dijkstra rode directly to the apartment of a friend, an acquaintance really, an architect who, in deference to his own wishes, shall be referred to here only as Henk. Henk was in his mid-30s at the time, short, stocky with thinning blond hair and sharp blue eyes. He and Dijkstra had moved in the same social circles before the war and saw each other from time to time at parties. He "always liked Dijkstra but in no way would call him a bosom pal."

Henk was not a member of the Resistance but he knew that Dijkstra was. Over the past year, he had heard all sorts of rumors about the painter -- that he was hiding a dozen Jews at a warehouse near the harbor, that he was involved in the holdup of a German army payroll office, even that Dijkstra had masterminded the raid on the *Bevolkingsregister.* Henk knew the Germans wanted Dijkstra badly. They were offering a huge reward for his capture.

At the time of Dijkstra's visit, Henk's personal life was just getting back to normal after considerable upheaval the previous month (his wife suspected him of having an affair with his secretary and made him fire the young woman). After weeks of insults and recriminations, Henk longed for some peace and tranquility in his life.

All in all, he was not particularly happy to see Dijkstra on his front porch at 6:30 in the morning.

"Henk, I apologize for this untimely visit but I have to talk with you. It's very important. May I come in?"

Henk nervously looked up and down the street and seeing no one, opened the front door. Dijkstra wheeled his bike into the foyer.

"What's this all about, Maarten?" he asked sharply. "I'm not used to greeting visitors before seven o'clock in the morning."

"I said it was important, Henk, and it is." Dijkstra's words sounded like a rebuke and Henk was about to tell his visitor that he could turn his bike around and go back out the door again. Instead he asked, "What do you want?"

He didn't ask Dijkstra to sit down so the two men spoke in the foyer.

"I understand there may have been some sort of commotion in the neighborhood last night,"

Henk's eyes widened. "What's it to you?"

"Plenty. Was there a commotion?"

"I'll say there was."

"What happened?"

"Some fool tried to push a *mof* into the canal. It happened about a block from here at the Lijnbaan Canal."

"And?"

"And both he and the *mof* wound up in the water. The Germans came by in a boat and plucked them out. They took the fool away. I don't have a clue where."

"Did you get a look at him?"

"It just so happens that I did. At least, I think it was the same fellow. I was having a drink in a pub a couple of blocks away when this fellow walks in. I had never seen him before. Tall, distinguished-looking chap in a trench coat. He had a couple of drinks and then he left. Well, it was getting close to the time for me to go home, so I left a short time later. When I got to my apartment, I saw this big fuss on the bridge so I went over to take a look. I saw the *moffen* pulling this guy out of the water. They took him away in the boat, probably to the nearby military barracks. Somebody told me that the guy tried to push a *mof* into the canal.

"This guy they pulled out of the water," Dijkstra asked, "was it the same guy you saw in the bar?"

"To tell you the truth, Maarten, I don't know. The *moffen* had this big light on him and I could see his face but he was all wet and his hair was in his eyes and I couldn't tell you for sure if it was the same guy from the bar. But I think it was. He looked kind of similar.

"The guy in the bar. What did he look like?"

"Like I said, distinguished-looking. He had a little mustache."

"Like Errol Flynn?" Dijkstra asked helpfully.

"Yeah, sort of. Actually, I would say he looked more like David Niven. Yeah, he *did* look like David Niven, come to think of it."

"Thanks, Henk." Dijkstra turned to go.

"Oh. One other thing," he said. "I would appreciate it if you didn't tell anyone about my visit."

"I won't. But my wife's upstairs, probably with an ear at a keyhole. She'll want to know what you wanted."

"Can you trust her to keep quiet?"

"Are you kidding? She's the gossip queen of the neighborhood. She'll be blabbing about your visit the first chance she gets, which will probably be when her sister comes over for tea later this morning."

"Well then, tell her that if she talks, I will be back with some friends and we'll kill you both."

Henk's mouth fell open in surprise. He stared hard at Dijkstra, searching for some sign that the man with whom he had socialized for ten years was joking, but there wasn't any.

"You can't mean that!" was all he could think to say.

"Thanks again for your help, Henk," Dijkstra said. He carried his bike out the door and down the steps. The last time Henk saw him, Dijkstra was pedaling leisurely toward the Prinsengracht as if he had nothing but time.

Chapter 19

At 9:30 that night, a fleet of SS trucks moved out from the Euterpestraat and headed for the center of the city.

The streets were virtually deserted. Residents of Amsterdam had long since grown accustomed to the rumble of heavy trucks and took sanctuary in their apartments the moment they heard the drone of the engines. They watched the grim procession from behind curtained windows and gave silent thanks that the Germans were not coming for them.

The only illumination on the darkened thoroughfares came from the headlights of the conga line of trucks as they rolled past.

Some of the vehicles headed for the Vijzelstraat while others turned left and right, fanning out to a half-dozen points around the city: the Ceintuurbaan, the Jordaan, the Pipe. In all, the operation involved nearly 300 heavily armed security police and SS men, 30 trucks, a half-dozen attack-trained German shepherds and several large moving vans to cart away looted furniture from the homes of the suspects. With this small army, Willi Lages hoped to crush the Artists Resistance Movement in a single night. Lages decided against taking a personal role in the raid, preferring to let SS Major Werner Naumann be on on-site commander. That still allowed him to claim credit for any of the mission's successes, while giving him a scapegoat if things went wrong.

Naumann, apparently oblivious to Lages' motives, was delighted to be in charge of the operation and personally took charge of the arrest team sent to Maarten Dijkstra's hideout on the Vijzelstraat.

Armed with a Bergmann 9mm machine pistol, he led a squad of SS men up the stairs to the loft at 246 Vijzelstraat and kicked in the door. A German shepherd was unleashed into the apartment to locate the prey, but a minute later, the dog trotted out from the rear sleeping room. There was nobody there. Frustrated, the SS troops forced their way into other apartments and roughed up the neighbors in search of the missing Resistance leader. But it was to no avail. No one could tell them where Dijkstra had gone.

Gestapo agents sent to Jan Middelburg's hideout in the Jordaan met with similar results -- Middelburg and his sister's family had departed in a hurry, leaving most of their possessions behind.

At the nearby home of the Van Duins, the Gestapo finally struck it rich. They didn't nab Josephine van Duin as they had hoped to do, but they found a trove of antique furniture, silverware, china, art, rare books, a Persian carpet, a box full of jewelry and a strongbox stuffed with cash. All of these items were taken to a moving van for transport to an SD warehouse near the docks.

The one item that the Germans didn't get, never even knew about, was the Guarnerius violin. It was the one thing of value that Mrs. Van Duin took with her in her hasty and tearful departure from her flat.

As the Gestapo was cleaning out the Van Duin apartment, a squad of SS men under the command of Lt. Dieter Stahl raided the Admiraal de Ruyter bar on the Vijzelstraat, which often had been a meeting place for Dijkstra's group. Piet Kooij, the bar's owner, had fled, no one knew where. The Germans had to content themselves with ransacking the business and carting away all the beer and liquor.

A detachment of green-uniformed *Ordnungspolizei* had better luck when they smashed their way into Van Cuiper's Plumbing Supply store on the Ceintuurbaan, another meeting place of ARM. Somehow in all of the excitement, neither Dijkstra nor any of his men warned Van Cuiper of the impending trouble.

The Germans found him in his apartment above the shop and beat him mercilessly in front of his wife and two small children before throwing him into the back of a police truck. They then looted the shop, stealing virtually everything that could be carried -- faucets, pipes, plumbing tools, even the splintery wooden table where Dijkstra and his men had met a number of times before.

Van Cuiper was in for a rough time. He was taken to the Euterpestraat and brutally tortured by examiners who were convinced he knew where Dijkstra was hiding. He didn't and after two days of unspeakable savagery, the Gestapo finally believed him. After that, he was sent to Westerbork where he remained for about six months, then was shipped to Auschwitz. But the slight Dutchman proved to be more durable than he looked. He survived the war, was reunited with his family and after a couple of years, opened another plumbing supply business four doors from his old shop.

The Germans did not raid the homes of Hugo de Jong or Cees Spanjaard for the simple reason that Jeroen van Duin, physically broken and nearly out of his mind, did not know where they lived. Both men went into hiding anyway, De Jong taking refuge at his uncle's farm outside of Alkmaar and Spanjaard moving in with his brother on the Kerkstraat.

Also spared a visit from the Gestapo was the small printing plant set up in the harbor by Romke Dietvorst. Again, Van Duin did not know the address, nor did he know much about that aspect of ARM's activities. Dietvorst's operation would stay in business for another year, printing a myriad of documents that helped at least some of the condemned to stay alive.

As far as the Germans were concerned, the operation was a dismal failure. Despite good planning and the involvement of hundreds of troops, the series of raids failed to net one important Resistance fighter. The only man on their arrest list who was actually taken into custody was the unfortunate plumbing supply shop owner, Van Cuiper, who proved to be useless as a source of information. Van Cuiper knew nothing about ARM activities other than the fact that its members occasionally met at his business and that's only because he liked Dijkstra, who had been a customer of his before the war.

The fiasco led to the inevitable finger-pointing from the German commanders. Major Werner Naumann wasted little time firing off an angry report to General Rauter, excoriating Willi Lages for his foot-dragging methods and for wasting precious time "plotting and planning" when the situation called for immediate action.

"Herr Lages may be an able policeman, but he knows nothing about coordinating and directing a military operation such as the one we undertook last night," Naumann wrote. "His failings in this department was the main reason why the perpetrators of the Hall of Records outrage were allowed to slip through our fingers."

Lages was equally complimentary about Naumann, using adjectives like "slow," "bungling" and "dim-witted" to describe the SS major.

The Gestapo *Befehlshaber* tried to sweeten the failure by emphasizing the "cache" of valuables found at the home of the "criminal" Van Duin, property that had been "forfeited" to the Third Reich. The valuables included, according to Lages, original works of art by Degas and Bonnard, as well as more than one hundred woodblock Japanese prints that had been collected by Josephine van Duin's father during his years as a diplomat in Japan (Lages submitted to his SS bosses an inventory of the property seized at Van Duin's home, but omitted mention of a Ming vase and a set of antique silverware that later turned up in his Berlin home).

There's no record to General Rauter's reaction to the news that Maarten Dijkstra again had evaded capture. What is known is that the reward for the Resistance leader jumped from ten thousand guilders to fifteen thousand guilders. By late April that year, it reached twenty thousand guilders -- a fortune at the time. The lugubrious, beak-nosed SS general was said to have a picture of Dijkstra hanging in his office and told aides that he would shoot the Resistance leader on sight if their paths ever crossed on the street.

Leo Wolters did not hear about the raids for nearly two days and when he did, the bearer of the bad news was Cees Spanjaard.

Since taking Herman Meijer in, Leo had had very little contact with the Resistance. Maarten Dijkstra wanted it that way to minimize the risk of inadvertently leading the Germans to where the little forger was hiding. So Wolters had been left to fret and stew and worry on his own, virtually cut off from the group and not having any idea what was going on.

But now the secret was out. The gangster Riphagen knew, or at least suspected, that Leo was hiding a Jew under his roof and Leo was nearly petrified with fear. When Cees Spanjaard arrived unannounced at his door on a rainy Thursday morning, the first words out of Leo's mouth were, "Have you come for Herman?"

Spanjaard looked shrewdly at his old classmate. The tiniest hint of contempt showed at the corners of his mouth.

"No, Leo, I'm afraid there's been a change in plans."

"What do you mean?" Leo blurted out, unable to keep the panic out of his voice.

"I mean that the *moffen* got Jeroen van Duin."

"What? Got Van Duin! When?"

"The day before yesterday. The damn fool. They undoubtedly put the screws to him and they found out where Maarten was staying, where Jan was staying. Now the *moffen* are running around the city like a swarm of angry hornets. Kicking in doors. Making arrests."

"Maarten?" Leo asked weakly, his mouth agape.

"Maarten's well. He got away. Most of us got away. They picked up poor Van Cuiper. God knows what they're going to do with him. But the group is still intact and will be operational again real soon.

"But obviously, we can't move Herman at this time so he is going to have to stay here awhile longer," Spanjaard said. "I'm sorry, Leo. But that's the way Maarten wants it."

"But -- but if Jeroen blabbed, the *moffen* will come here, too. My sister and I are in great danger."

Spanjaard shook his head. "If the Germans knew about you, they would have been here already. We don't think Jeroen talked about you. He barely knew you and he didn't know that we hid Herman Meijer here. At least, neither Maarten nor I told him. You should be safe."

"I *should* be safe?" Leo repeated. "*Should* be?"

"There are no guarantees in this world, Leo. Nobody can promise you that you are going to get through this war untouched. You may not have noticed, but a lot of innocent people are already dead. I think you know that the *moffen* are no slouches when it comes to killing people."

Something suddenly occurred to Leo and the thought outraged him and brought the blood rushing to his face.

"How come nobody warned me that Van Duin had been captured, huh? How come? I thought you were my friend, Cees, but you just left me here to get grabbed by the *moffen* while you saved your own goddamn necks."

Now Spanjaard grew angry. "Knock off the whimpering. Nobody abandoned you. The fact is that we didn't want you to run away. The safest thing you could have done was to remain here.

And what did you plan to do with Herman? Just abandon him?" Cees looked around suspiciously.

"Where is Herman?" he asked.

"In his room, as usual."

"Why doesn't he come out?"

"Ask him."

But Spanjaard was now staring at Leo's battered face.

"What happened to you?" he asked, pointing at the damage.

"Aw, nothing." Leo didn't dare mention that he owed Amsterdam's most notorious gangster a large sum of money and the gangster was determined to collect it.

"It looks like you were run down by a street car."

"Personal matter. It's nothing."

Just then, Meijer came out of his room. He saw Spanjaard and his eyes lit up. "Are you here for me?"

Spanjaard shook his head. "It's too dangerous to move you, Herman. The *moffen* are all over the place. As soon as it settles down, we are going to put you in a home outside the city. You'll be a lot safer there."

But his words, rather than reassuring Meijer, seemed to have the opposite effect.

"I'm not leaving?" he asked, his eyes darting back and forth between the Spanjaard and Leo. "I'm staying here?"

"Get a grip on yourself, Herman," Spanjaard said. "What the devil's the matter with you? What's going on here?"

"He and his sister are going to kill me!" Meijer wailed, pointing a shaking finger at Leo. "The two of them are planning to betray me to the Germans. Ask him! Ask him! He admits it."

Spanjaard, stunned, bereft of words, looked questioningly at Leo. The young man he had known all his life was a dickhead, to be sure, but a traitor?

"Leo?"

"The man is out of his mind, Cees," Leo said angrily. "He's been acting nuts ever since you brought him here. Now he's accusing Monique and me of kicking him out or turning him in to the Germans. He's out of his mind."

"It's true!" Meijer insisted. "It's true. I've heard them talking. Always whispering when I come in and then looking at me as if I were dead already. They're going to kill me, Cees. You've got to get me out of here."

"Simmer down, Herman. Nobody is going to kill you. Nobody is going to turn you in to the *moffen*. Right, Leo?

Leo nodded.

"I am going to be meeting with Maarten soon and I will tell him that the arrangement here is not working out and that it's best for all concerned if we find a new place for you to stay. But in the meantime, it's imperative that you get a grip on yourself and don't make trouble. If the neighbors get wind of your presence, your life won't be worth a tin *stuiver*. Behave yourself and everything is going to work out. Okay?"

Meijer looked petulantly from one to the other, then went back to his room and closed and bolted the door.

"What's going on here, Leo? You better tell me."

"You can see for yourself. The man is nuts. He is shouting accusations at us. He's threatened me. He said that if he gets arrested, he's going to turn Monique and me in as well. You talked about the neighbors finding out, I be damned surprised if the entire block doesn't already know that I'm hiding a Jew here. The man's becoming a big security risk and the faster you get him out of here, the better."

"What happened to your face?" Spanjaard asked quietly.

Leo remained silent.

"I want an answer."

Leo looked like he was struggling with his conscience. He started to speak, then stopped, then asked: "What do you think happened?"

"I don't know. You tell me."

Again Leo was silent. "I told you I don't want to talk about it, Cees, and I mean it. It's nothing."

"Okay, Leo. I am going to be meeting with Maarten soon and I will bring him up to date about things here. Just try to keep calm for a couple of days and then we'll take Herman off your hands. Agreed?"

Leo smiled and the two men shook hands.

"You'll be hearing from us soon, Leo," Spanjaard said, wheeling the bike out the door. "*De mazzel.*"

The words brought an ironic twist to Leo's lips. Literally meaning "the luck," *de mazzel* is often said by Amsterdammers in bidding good-bye. The irony was that *mazzel* was another of the Yiddish words that had been absorbed into the Amsterdam dialect. It came from *mazel* -- luck.

As he watched Spanjaard pedal away, Leo wondered if the choice of words had been intentional. It would be just like Cees to subtly try to manipulate him. The bastard!

Chapter 20

April 18, 1943, began as the kind of morning Amsterdammers long for, especially after weeks of wind, freezing rain, hail and snow. It was still cold, to be sure, a few degrees above zero, but the wind had dropped to barely a breeze and the hard blue skies were crisp and clear.

It was the kind of early spring day that awakens the city's natural ebullience. Suddenly neighborhoods that only the day before looked bleak and deserted, were alive with activity. People were outside cleaning porches and windows, gossiping with neighbors, walking their pets, running errands, riding bicycles, reveling in the first real sunshine they had seen in months.

Dries Riphagen, the Dutch Al Capone, was not immune to the exuberance that swept the city. The gangster was in an upbeat mood on that bright, cloudless morning; he shaved with meticulous care and then put on one of his favorite outfits: a charcoal-gray, double-breasted gabardine suit. The creases in the pants looked sharp enough to split hairs, the shirt was crisp and snowy white. He carefully knotted a blood-red tie and deposited a silk handkerchief, the color of the tie, into the breast pocket.

As usual, Riphagen dressed in front of the mirror, only this time, he paid particular attention to his face. The swelling had nearly disappeared and there was only the faintest trace of blue under his eye. Maybe it was the weather, maybe it was the fact that his body had mended, but Dries Riphagen felt like a new man -- or more accurately -- like his old self again.

Only one thing marred the sleek image that stared back at him and the gangster -- with his eye for detail -- noticed it. A slight bulge near his left armpit where a big, loaded, well-oiled 7.65-mm Walther reposed in its leather holster. He patted the weapon as if to reassure it that it was far more important to him than a bulge in his suit.

He slapped on some cologne, smoothed his pomaded hair and then, with a final look in the mirror, picked up his hat and overcoat and headed for the door.

A sun almost platinum in color bathed the street in a harsh, white light.

Riphagen's Cadillac, with a driver at the wheel and another man beside him, was parked in front of his apartment. With the hulking Rutger still bedridden, Riphagen has asked his underworld patron, "Black" Piet Verhoeve, for a couple of experienced button men to help him maintain order in his domain, and Verhoeve had obliged. The young men who sat in his car were experienced toughs, expert bone-breakers who knew how to do their work without getting carried away.

"The Schubertstraat," Riphagen said, getting in. "And don't dent the machinery getting there."

The scowling driver pressed the starter and the Cadillac's V-12, 368-cubic-inch engine leaped to life. Riphagen loved the sound of the idling engine. He even knew a little bit about the technical side. One hundred and fifty horses; overhead valve fed by twin Detroit Libricator carburetors. It represented power, raw power.

The thug was indeed a good driver. He looked behind him before pulling out, drove carefully over the cobbles, stayed within the speed limit and checked the rearview mirror often for unwanted company.

Twenty minutes later, the Caddy, gunmetal-blue and gleaming, pulled to a halt in front the rundown, three-story building on the Schubertstraat where Leo Wolters lived.

"Curtain moved," the muscleman in the passenger seat said, looking up at the building.

"Won't do 'em no good," answered Riphagen. "They can't hide. C'mon."

Other windows whacked open. Nearby residents poked their heads outside and stared curiously at the big town car. What was such a fancy vehicle doing on this street?

Riphagen ignored the gawking neighbors as he led the way to the front door of the apartment building where Leo Wolters lived and rang the bell for the third floor. When it wasn't answered, he rang again and then motioned to one of the gunsels who kicked it open. A well-placed kick under the lock was just as effective as a *loper* in opening front doors. The door flew open with a crash that shook the building and brought more neighbors to their windows. Riphagen climbed the steps two at a time and stood for a moment on the third-floor landing outside Leo's door.

"Open the door, you little prick, or we'll kick it in," the gangster said loudly. He was about to signal one of the thugs to do just that when the lock slid back and the door slowly opened. Riphagen shoved his way into the apartment, throwing Leo into a wall. His two confederates followed.

The Dutch Al Capone looked around the apartment. "Where's Monique," he demanded.

"She's not here, Dries," Leo said, rubbing his shoulder.

"That's Mr. Riphagen to you, *klootzak*," he said. "Where's the fuckin' money you owe me. One thousand guilders."

Leo was about to answer, but he suddenly gave a yelp of fright and looked ready to bolt for the door; he recognized the other two hoodlums as the ones who assaulted him a few nights before.

Riphagen grinned venomously. "Relax," he said almost playfully. "They won't hurt you ... unless I tell 'em to. Where's my dough."

Leo was so cowed he couldn't get the words out.

"Where's my money?"

"I don't have it, Dries?"

Riphagen nodded slowly.

"You don't have it?" he asked quietly.

Leo slowly shook his head.

Riphagen raised his eyes ceilingward in mild exasperation, like a loving father at a loss to deal with a wayward child. It was a role he didn't play well, and he didn't play it very long. He rushed at the gangly young man like an enraged bull, put a hand to his pimply throat and thrust him down on the couch. In a blink, the Walther was out of its holster and clapped against Leo's skull.

"No more screwin' around, *klootzak*. You owe me a lot of money and the price has gone up. Way up."

Leo, despite his fear and the hand at his throat, blinked in surprise. "W-what do you mean?"

"You know damn well what I mean, you kike-loving bastard." Riphagen looked disgusted enough to spit in Leo's face, but instead, he pulled him roughly to his feet.

"I want five thousand guilders," the mobster said. "Pay up, nose-picker!"

"F-five thous ..." Leo couldn't finish the sentence.

"You heard me. Five thousand guilders. Pay up!"

"I don't have it," Leo said miserably.

"*I know you don't,*" the gangster said in a mocking voice. "You're not worth ten cents by yourself. But your daddy's got money coming out his ass. He'll pay to keep his stupid son from being arrested by the Gestapo for hiding a Jew. Don't lie, you little shit. Don't you dare lie to me."

Leo, who had been about to protest, closed his mouth. He could only stare helplessly at the Dutch Al Capone with fear-dilated eyes.

"Where's the kike?"

When Leo didn't answer, Riphagen slapped him in the face, an action he had seen often in American films. This role suited him better and he grinned with malevolent satisfaction as he beheld the fear of God in Leo's eyes.

"Where's the kike? In there?" And he indicated the closed door leading to Meijer's room.

For a moment, Riphagen looked as if he would have the door kicked down and Meijer dragged out.

"Listen," he said, continuing his Jimmy Cagney routine. "I know the kike's in there. I don't have to see him. Keep your face shut or so help me, I will really knock your pins out. I know he's in there, just like I know your daddy is going to come up with the scratch to keep you from going to a very bad place. You can take my word for it, a soft little shit like you ain't going to like it there one bit. Do you understand me?"

Leo nodded numbly.

"Good. The price is five thousand guilders. Do you hear me? Five thousand guilders. You have three days."

Riphagen glowered, Leo cowered. They understood each other perfectly.

The gangster released Leo and turned to stare at the closed bedroom door. "I know you can hear me, *vuile jood.* You can't hide. Nobody is going to shelter you after this. You're jinxed. You better stay right here with your good pal, Leo, and hope that his daddy comes up with enough money to save both your worthless asses."

Shoving Leo contemptuously aside, Riphagen made a motion and the two bone-breakers followed him out of the apartment. At the door, he turned around.

"When's Monique coming back?"

Leo could only shrug.

"Well, just be sure to tell her that I stopped by," he said, and he pointed to the angry red weal on Leo's white cheek. "And make sure you tell her whose fingerprints those are."

For five minutes after the hoodlums left, Leo leaned against the couch, not daring to move. His heart was beating so rapidly he thought he would have a seizure.

"Jesus," he said softly to himself. He took several deep breaths and expelled the air in nervous bursts. Slowly his eyes swiveled around to the closed door leading to Meijer's bedroom. Nothing. Not a sound.

Where was Monique? God dammit, he needed her. If Leo were in any way introspective, it might have irked him to realize how much he came to depend on the mental toughness of his younger sister. But he was not one who wasted time examining his own character. What he knew at the moment was that he was terribly frightened. He hadn't experienced a moment's peace mind since Meijer was placed under his roof.

When he felt steady enough to walk, he went to the kitchen and took down two drinking glasses. He filled one with tap water and into the other poured a generous slug of bathtub Russian vodka -- obtained through Riphagen in happier days -- to which he added a pinch of pepper and knocked back in one go, chased with water.

He poured himself another and like a sleepwalker, went to sit in the big chair in his living room. Some semblance of sanity returned as he slowly sipped his drink. God, what a mess.

In a rare mood of self-criticism, he put the blame for his troubles mostly on his shoulders. Yes, he had been a fool to gamble at Riphagen's club. Yes, he had been a fool to run up such losses. Yes, he had let Riphagen increase his credit. Several times. But he had been positive that his luck would improve sooner or later. And suddenly, he was a thousand guilders in debt. An incredible sum of money.

But the gambling debt was the least of his problems now that the hoodlum knew that he was sheltering a Jew. One word to the Gestapo and Leo would never wake up a free man again. Auschwitz. Treblinka. Rumors about these places had been circulating in the city for months. If even half of it were true... He couldn't bear thinking about it. That fate might even be preferable to a few hours in the cellars of the Euterpestraat. Despite the warm strength of the liquor, he felt his bones turning to jelly. Riphagen wanted five thousand guilders to keep his mouth shut. Five thousand guilders!

He thought: I have to contact Dijkstra. Dijkstra has to take Meijer away immediately. With the Jew gone, Riphagen could prove nothing. Leo would be safe. But he couldn't contact Dijkstra. He hadn't the faintest idea where the Resistance leader was. And even if he did, Dijkstra was in no position at the moment to help anybody.

What other alternatives did he have? He could turn Meijer over to the Gestapo himself. That would take all the wind out of Riphagen's sails. But he dismissed that idea the moment it popped into his head. The Resistance would hear about it and have him killed. Period.

He could kick Meijer out of the house. Evict him. Send him away. He could always claim to Dijkstra that the forger was not obeying "house rules." That he had become paranoid. That he was making threats, endangering everybody.

But there was a serious problem with that idea. Meijer had already said that if he were ever arrested, he would not go down alone. He would inform on Leo. And Leo believed him. Meijer on the loose was almost as big a threat as being an *onderduiker* under his roof.

Panic rising, Leo ran through it again and again in his mind, becoming more desperate with each passing minute. There seemed to be no way out, nothing he could do to extricate himself from the mess. He felt like there was a half-ton of weight on his chest. Dread and self-pity overwhelmed him.

When Monique came home two hours later, she found him still sitting in the chair, his face bleached of color, looking like a condemned man with only hours left to live.

Chapter 21

When he was a child, Herman Meijer loved to walk in Amsterdam's Vondel Park on a Saturday afternoon. In his young eyes the sprawling park with its tree-lined serpentine paths was the center of the universe. Everyone was there: young and old, men and women, the well-heeled strolling the same paths as the tatterdemalion.

On a warm summer day, a band would be playing and a huge crowd would gather to hear the music. Or there would be jugglers or acrobats or puppet shows. And little stalls selling food. His favorite snack was salted herring, with the fish cut into pieces and slathered in diced onions and pickles. He would hungrily eat the herring, using a toothpick to spear each piece right from the counter at the stall.

Sometimes Meijer went with his father but more often, it was his grandfather, Nahum Meijer, who took him on these glorious outings. The boy worshipped the older man, so tall and straight and all-knowing. He could identify every species of bird in the park and seemed to know a little story about each. Like the feisty lapwings that brooded in a meadow at the edge of the park, small birds but with the hearts of tigers, his grandfather used to tell him.

"But why is he flying in circles and making that pee-wee, pee-wee sound, grandpa?" Meijer asked.

"It's a she and she is trying to protect her eggs," said his grandfather. "See what she's doing? She's trying to lure that big crow away from her nest. She's saying, 'Why don't you pick on somebody your own size, you big bully.'"

Nahum Meijer solemnly explained to Meijer that spring did not officially begin in the Netherlands until the first lapwing egg was found and presented to the queen.

"Is that true, grandpa?"

"Would I lie to you, *boychek?*" said the old man with a big grin.

Nahum Meijer was an automobile mechanic by trade but one would not know it to look at him on those weekend walks in the park. He was very attentive about his clothes and personal hygiene and in his suit, he could have passed for a banker or a lawyer. His pink, fastidiously clean hands and fingernails looked like they had never been within twenty feet of a grease gun.

His grandfather had been the most intriguing figure in young Meijer's life; the old man seemed to know everything. He could ride horses and dance and there wasn't anything he couldn't fix. He even knew a thing or two about boxing and tried to give the awkward boy a lesson or two in the manly art of self defense ("Keep your left up, *boychek*, unless you want a big cabbage ear. Then the girls won't want to go out with you. That's it. Now jab, jab, jab and then -- powee!").

Mercifully, the old man never met a Nazi in his life. He passed away in 1935, five years before the invasion, dying peacefully in his bed at age 71, instead of in some godforsaken concentration camp.

For the past two days, Meijer had not eaten. He had barely stirred from his bed. He felt light-headed, dizzy, isolated. He spent the last two days in an almost hallucinatory state, midway between sleep and wakefulness. He daydreamed continually -- about his parents, his girlfriend, his beloved grandfather. Memories of his grandfather drifted into and out of focus. His grandfather represented the good days, the days before the Nazis, a time of peace and tranquility, when everything was innocent and new. Another lifetime ago.

Meijer had heard every word of the violent confrontation between Leo and the gangster, Riphagen. He heard the threats and the curses and the slurs. He heard the gangster calling him a kike and threatening to turn him over to the Gestapo if he were not paid five thousand guilders. That had been two days ago. Two days of nerve-wracking terror. He expected his door to be kicked in at any minute, and to be dragged away to die like so many before him.

Meijer had been out of his room only four times in the last two days -- each time to make a quick trip to the bathroom. He voided his bladder, drank a little water, then darted back to his room. He had stopped eating the food that was left outside his door, fearing that it was poisoned. It was *traif*, anyway. *Dreck*. Meijer had no stomach for such fare.

Leo had knocked on the door several times during the past two days and had called his name, but Meijer had not answered. He had long since stopped trusting Leo and his sister. How long had he been under the Wolters' roof? More than a month now. He was only supposed to stay a few days. Meijer had just about given up hope that Maarten Dijkstra would ever come to take him away. He was going to die an unwanted guest in a home he had come to detest.

Thank God neither of his parents had survived the world long enough to know what a *razzia* was. His father had died in 1938 of a heart attack. He was 48 years old and seemed to be in good health. His job as a mailman kept him fit. But one night after work, just after he turned in for the night, he was struck down by a massive attack and died. And just like that, Meijer's mother was a widow. The poor woman. She had witnessed the whole thing and never got over it. She died two years later and the doctors were never able to figure out why.

Meijer was the last of the line. The last of a family that had lived and prospered in the Netherlands for more than two centuries. He was the last of the line and he was hanging on by a thread. The thought filled him with ineffable gloom.

Meijer was lying on his back, arms folded behind his head, staring at the ceiling, when a soft voice startled him out of his reverie.

"Herman?"

At the sound of his name, Meijer sat bolt upright and listened.

"Herman?" It was Monique's voice.

"Herman, I don't mean to disturb you but I need your help. We have a problem. Can you hear me?"

Meijer heard every word but he didn't answer.

"I know you can hear me, Herman. Would you please open the door? I have to talk to you. It's very important."

When he still didn't answer, the voice came again. Quiet. Pleading.

"Herman. I know you're in there. I have a problem here and I need your help before it becomes a real emergency. It's in the bathroom."

In the bathroom? Meijer was intrigued but he remained still.

There was a soft knock ... and then that soft voice again. "Herman. Please answer me. This is a man's problem. I can't do it by myself."

Herman rolled off the bed as quietly as he could and slowly crawled to the door. He put his ear to the wood. Was there anybody else there? Leo? Where was he?

"Herman?"

"Leave me alone," Herman said, not bothering to keep the anguish out of his voice.

"Herman. Listen to me. This is serious. The plumbing has backed up in the sink. If it's backed up here, it's backed up all over the building. The superintendent will want to come up here to check the pipes. That's all we need right now."

"So what am I supposed to do?"

"You can help me clear the pipes so the super doesn't have to come up here. It's happened before. It's not difficult to fix. We have a wire we use. An old hanger. It'll take only a few minutes."

"So use it," Meijer said.

"I'm not strong enough to do it. Leo usually does it but he's not home."

Meijer continued to keep his ear pressed to the door, listening, straining for the slightest sign of a ploy, a trap.

"Herman." The voice was cajoling, insistent. "Is this any way to act? God damn it. It's not fair. We risked our lives hiding you for weeks and asked nothing in return. Now we are all in danger over something so stupid as a backed up sink and you won't lift a finger to help."

"What time is it?" Meijer asked.

"About 5 p.m."

"Where's Leo?"

"I told you, he's not here. He went out an hour ago. I don't know where."

"When's he coming back?"

"I don't know. If I thought he would be back soon, I wouldn't even have asked you to help. He knows how to fix it. He's done it before. But he's not here. I don't have a choice."

Meijer kept his ear glued to the door. He could hear Monique's breathing. He could hear the slight scrape of a ring as she nervously moved her hand back and forth on the panel. His senses were so alive, he thought he detected her pulse through the wood.

Meijer wanted to crawl back to his bed. He wanted to get under the sheet and pull the blanket over his head.

"Herman."

There it was again. If only she would shut up. Leave him alone. Go away.

"Herman. Can you hear me?"

"Go away, Monique! I can't help you. I'm sick. I haven't eaten for days. Just leave me alone. Please, leave me alone!"

Meijer waited for her answer, waited for her coaxing voice to continue, but there was only silence. He listened for the scrape of the ring on wood, for her breathing, anything, but there was nothing. Not a sound.

"Monique?" he called.

No answer.

Exhausted from lack of food and sleep, Meijer rested his head against the door and closed his eyes. God, when would this nightmare end?

As he leaned his head against the wood, he could hear faint sounds coming from the bathroom. Meijer listened intently. It did indeed sound like somebody was trying to clear the drain. He suddenly felt guilty.

Meijer kept his ear at the door. Yes. Somebody was working on the pipes. He could hear the metallic rattle of the hanger in the drain. He could even hear faint curses coming from the bathroom. Monique. Monique was cursing. What a piece of work that *shiksa* was.

She was right, of course. If the neighbors complained about the plumbing, and if the superintendent was sent up to Leo's flat, it could be disastrous for both himself and the Wolters. What was he afraid of? What could she do to him? Why was he so suspicious? They had trouble with the drain before and Leo had always cleared it. Meijer had watched as Leo used the wire coat hanger to do it. It certainly was not beyond the realm of probability that the drain was stuck again.

Meijer stood up slowly and -- still listening for any alien sounds-- carefully undid the lock on his door. The rasping noise coming from the bathroom stopped for a moment, then resumed.

He opened the door and peeked into the hall. The bathroom was right next door. He heard Monique muttering as she furiously worked the wire into the drain.

With the trepidation of a man walking on a minefield, Meijer stepped into the hall and tiptoed the few feet to the bathroom. The bathroom door was open and Meijer poked his head inside for a quick look.

Monique was alone in the bathroom. She was bent over the sink, trying to work the wire down the drain. She was clad in a bathrobe but the belt had loosened and one large, alluring breast had spilled out. Meijer gasped in surprise.

Monique looked up, caught Meijer's stare and looked down at her robe. With a shy smile, she adjusted the garment and tightened the belt.

"I didn't hear you come out of your room," she said. "You see. We *do* have a problem here. I was about to bathe when I saw that the drain was stopped again. Have you come to help me?"

Meijer looked ready to dart back to his room, but he nodded slowly.

"But you're sweating," Monique said. "Are you ill? Do you have a fever? Let me see."

"No, no," said Meijer, shying away as Monique approached. "I'm fine. I just feel a little warm."

"Don't be such a frightened rabbit," Monique said sternly, ignoring the protestations and putting her hand on Meijer's forehead. "No one is going to hurt your. But you do feel warm. Maybe you should go back to your bed and lie down. I'll make you some soup."

"No, no. I'm really not hungry," Meijer said. "I just came out to see if I can help you with the sink."

Monique took a towel and dabbed at the beads of sweat on Meijer's head. He could smell her perfume; the musky odor was making him dizzy.

"Stop fidgeting," Monique said. "I am not going to bite you."

She stood close to him as she mopped his brow, so close that he could just feel her soft, unhaltered breast against his pounding chest.

"There," she said. "That's all. Doesn't that make you feel a little better?"

Embarrassed by his mounting interest, he tried to back away but she had him closeted between herself and the wall.

"And you need a shave," she said, running her hand over the fuzzy stubble on his cheek. "You look horrible. Haven't you been sleeping?"

"I've slept," Meijer said. "A little."

"You are a very strange man," she said gently. "Why are you so afraid of me? What have I ever done to you?"

Meijer didn't answer. Alarm bells were ringing but he didn't know why.

"If you are so afraid of me, maybe you should go back to your bed and leave me to fix the sink. Ja?" Monique took a step back, clearing the way for Meijer to bolt from the bathroom.

"When's Leo coming back?" Meijer blurted out.

"I told you before that I don't know."

"Where did he go?"

"He didn't tell me. I'm not my brother's secretary. He doesn't tell me where he goes every time he leaves the house. Enough of these questions. Do you want to help me fix the sink? Yes or no?"

Meijer stood there, eyes wide.

"Yes or no?" Monique asked sternly.

She really is beautiful, Meijer thought, looking at the storm of yellow hair pinned neatly on her head. If she is the angel of death, she's a very beautiful angel. Meijer was trembling, but he did not know whether it was from fear or desire. It seemed like a lifetime ago that he had last made love. He felt a twinge as he thought about Esther. But thoughts of Esther dissipated in the face of the goddess who stood before him. He had never been with a woman as lovely as Monique. Never. Her scent, the closeness of her body, were turning his legs to water.

"I'll help you," he said weakly.

Monique touched his face and stared into his eyes.

"You really do need a shave," Monique said, again stroking his cheek. Then she giggled. "First we will clear the drain and then I will shave you. I will make you as smooth as a baby again. Soft and smooth as the day you were born. That is, if you trust me to shave you. Do you trust me with a razor?" she asked playfully. "Do you?"

Meijer was so addled he couldn't speak.

"Do you?"

"Yes." It was all he could do to get the word out.

"Yes?"

"Yes."

"Do you mean it?"

"Yes."

"Come," she said. "See the water in the sink. It won't go down."

The sink was indeed filled with water and some of it had slopped onto the floor. A little pool had collected on the floor between the sink on the left and the small bathtub -- shrouded by an old, mildewed bath curtain -- on the right.

"It will not be difficult to clear the drain," Monique said. "But it needs a man's strength. I can't push the wire far enough into the pipe. Take a look. See what you can do."

Monique still held his arm and she was directing him to look into the drain. Meijer bent over and peered into the basin. The sink was completely stopped up. Meijer saw limp strands of blond hair floating in the soapy water. That must be the problem. Monique usually washed her hair in the sink and the build-up of hair had clogged the drain. When he cleared the sink, he would tell her that it was more prudent to wash her hair in the bathtub. The drain there was larger.

Meijer was confident he could fix the problem. He had unstopped more than one sink while working as a handyman at the City Theatre and he knew a trick or two about bending the wire a certain way to get the best results.

"Where's the coat hanger?" he asked, but he got no answer.

"Monique?" he said, lifting his head. It was then he saw something that nearly stopped his heart.

As Meijer raised his head, his eyes coming level with a mirror, he saw Leo Wolters standing in the bathtub behind him. Leo looked petrified. His eyes were as wide as saucers. And in his raised right hand he held a hammer.

Meijer shrieked as Leo brought the hammer down.

Chapter 22

It's not clear to this day whether it was Leo or Monique who first suggested killing Herman Meijer. Not that it's a significant fact. What is important is that shortly after the disquieting visit from the Dutch Al Capone, both Leo and his sister began plotting the demise of their houseguest. To that end, each procured an item that later was linked to the crime.

Leo, under the pretext of doing some repair work in his flat, borrowed a number of tools from his landlord, including a large, rusty claw hammer. And Monique, accompanied by a female friend, made an unexpected visit to her father's home to retrieve an old, wooden clothing chest from her room. She told the friend, who was there to help lug the chest back to the Schubertstraat, that she planned to move out soon and needed the trunk to pack her clothes.

It was during this planning and conspiring stage that Leo let Monique in on a secret that he had been keeping since shortly after Meijer's arrival.

The little forger, it seems, had hidden away a couple of boxes of valuables -- virtually his entire personal estate -- and he told Leo where he cached it.

Meijer, like a lot of Dutch Jews, had put his most valuable worldly possessions in what he hoped was a safe spot with the intention of reclaiming them when the war was over. Some people left their treasures with trusted non-Jewish friends. Others buried their valuables in their back yards or in parks or forests.

With more foresight than most, Meijer had converted most of his cash -- which he considered a highly unstable commodity in time of war and occupation -- into gold and jewelry. These items, along with a couple of family heirlooms, he put in cigar boxes and hid in a spot that he thought would never be found -- behind a wall near the huge furnace in the cellar of the City Theatre on the Leidseplein. Meijer had worked as a handyman in the theatre off and on during the early part of the war, and was able to come and go pretty much as he pleased. Without attracting notice, he had knocked a small hole in the wall, placed the boxes inside and re-plastered and painted the spot. The cellar had been plastered and painted in so many spots over the years that one more patchwork job didn't stand out at all.

In a fit of panic and desperation, Meijer had told this to Leo shortly after he was brought to the Wolters home. Meijer believed re-arrest and death were close at hand. He was the only person who knew the location of the small golden horde and he didn't want the secret to die with him. He wanted Esther to have it if, by some chance, she survived the war. So he let Leo in on the secret.

Again it's only guesswork but it seems likely that the cache actually was not so little. Meijer had made a good living as a forger and art faker before the war and probably socked away quite a nest egg. It was certainly sizeable enough to inspire Leo Wolters to take a few risks. The fact of the matter was that Leo had been thinking about the jewelry quite a bit lately as his debts mounted. The cigar boxes with their precious contents amounted to one more reason Leo had to murder the forger.

With Riphagen breathing down their necks, threatening to denounce them to the Germans, Leo and Monique did not have the luxury of time to plan the perfect crime. The scheme they eventually came up with was a sloppy, slapdash effort, risky, difficult to execute, something they would never have considered under normal circumstances.

But these were not normal circumstances. In a Nazi-occupied country, harboring a Jew was a far graver offense than murdering one. The siblings correctly reasoned that they were far better off answering to the Dutch civil authorities for the homicide rather than the Gestapo for sheltering a "Jewish criminal."

Having decided to kill Meijer, the two wasted little time putting their plan into action. On April 20, 1943, two days after Riphagen's visit, Leo stopped up the bathroom sink drain with part of an old undershirt. Then he filled the basin with water, allowing some of it to slop onto the floor.

Monique undressed and slipped into her bathrobe, partly to lend veracity to her cover story and partly to distract Meijer as much as possible.

Then Leo, armed with the rusty hammer, got into the tub and hid behind the bath curtain. It was up to Monique to lure the jumpy forger out of his room and into the bathroom so Leo could kill him. And she did, using skills that would later serve her well on screen and stage.

She seems to have played her role convincingly, enticing the frightened and suspicious man into the bathroom and positioning him in such a way that he would be most vulnerable to a fatal attack -- with his back to his self-appointed executioner.

Now it was up to Leo to do his part -- and as usual, he nearly bungled the job.

Leo was scared out of his wits. He had never killed before. He had never so much as struck another human being in his entire life. Now he assigned himself the job of violating the most sacred of the commandments and he was not up to the task. Leo heard the exchanges between Meijer and his sister in the bathroom but their words barely registered. The throbbing of the blood racing around his head blotted out the reception. He knew they were talking but he hadn't a clue as to what they were saying.

And then, the unintelligible talking stopped and the bathroom was still for a moment. Leo peeked out from behind the curtain and saw Meijer peering into the sink. There was no sign of Monique. Leo steeled himself to do what must be done. How vulnerable the little Jew was. It would not be difficult. One good blow on the back of the head, that's all it would take. Leo braced himself for the pending violence, braced himself for the gout of blood and gore that surely would result from his deed.

Then he heard Meijer's voice. Meijer was asking for the coat hanger. It was now or never. Leo, a hot wire of tension and fright, raised the hammer and moved forward.

It was then that Meijer raised his head and caught sight of Leo's grotesquely terrified face in the mirror. He screamed. The scream had the effect of a rush of adrenalin on the panicking Leo. It gave speed and power to his arm. He had to silence the man before he roused the entire neighborhood.

Leo swung the hammer with tremendous force, but it was a wild swing and probably would not have disabled the forger, even if he had stood still. But Meijer did not stand still. He reacted like a startled rabbit, jerking his body sideways as the hammer descended. He barely felt the blow, which glanced off his upper back.

For one brief moment, the action stopped, as if both participants were frozen in a frame of suspended animation. The two men just stared at each other, too shocked and surprised to move. It was impossible to tell who was more frightened, the victim or his assailant. Meijer recovered first and tried to scurry for the door. Leo, who was still holding the hammer, climbed out of the tub and threw himself on top of the smaller man and a frantic, desperate wrestling match ensued.

Meijer was a small man and physically weak from two days without food, but he was also wiry and very slippery and when it came to protecting his life, he fought like a man possessed. He wiggled and twisted, he lashed out with his hands, he screamed for help, he tried to twist away, he kicked and hollered and he scratched at Leo's arms and wrists.

Leo fought with equal intensity. He still held the hammer but with Meijer struggling so fiercely, he never got a chance to swing it again. It was all he could do to hold on to the little forger. As the two grappled on the floor, the hammer was suddenly knocked from Leo's hand, leaving the men on more or less equal footing.

Meijer lashed out wildly, clawing at Leo's face, biting his arm, trying desperately to free himself.

It was then that Leo, who was trying to get his hands on Meijer's throat, looked up and saw Monique standing transfixed in the doorway. Her hand was at her mouth, the same gesture she made the night Major Naumann beat the devil out of Riphagen and his bodyguard.

"Go outside," Leo gasped, "Go. Keep the neighbors away."

Monique vanished.

Leo managed to straddle the little forger, putting most of his weight on Meijer's chest, pinning him to the floor. He got his hands around the forger's windpipe and squeezed with all his might. Meijer went blue in the face. His eyes swelled to the point of bursting and a smear of spittle appeared at the corner of his mouth. A sickly-sweet smell suddenly pervaded the small bathroom as Meijer, in mortal fear of his life, purged his bowels. But he still had plenty of fight in him. He continued to claw at Leo's fingers, trying to tear them away from his throat. He managed to grab the little finger of Leo's left hand and yank it sideways, breaking the grip and bringing tears of pain to his attacker's eyes.

Meijer tried to push the tall, gangly young man away but he didn't have the strength. He was wheezing, gasping for breath, unable to get sufficient air down his mangled windpipe.

Leo got his hands around Meijer's throat again and banged his head against the side of the tub. That did the trick. The blow knocked all of the fight out of Meijer. He groaned when his head hit the tub and his frantic fingers dropped from Leo's wrist. Leo felt the Jew's body go slack but he paid no heed to it. The desperate struggle had awakened a dormant bloodlust, sending him into a frenzy of desperation and rage. He knocked the forger's head again and again against the side of the tub; any one of the blows would have been sufficient to crack Meijer's skull. When at last he ceased to attack the inert man, Leo noticed for the first time that Meijer's eyes showed egg-shell white in their sockets under half-closed lids. There was no indication that Meijer was still breathing.

For several moments, Leo continued to sit on the forger's lifeless chest, too exhausted to move. Gradually he became aware of a growing red puddle on the floor but he was too exhausted and too sickened to do anything about it. He was in shock from what he had just done. He could not will his limbs to move. At a certain moment, he leaned over and started to retch, but since he had not eaten any lunch, nothing came out.

Leo did not know how long he sat there in the widening mess. A few seconds, a few minutes. He might have passed out. He wasn't sure. But he was brought back to alertness by a muffled scream. For one terrifying second, he thought it was Meijer, but the gasp had come from Monique. She was standing in the doorway with her hand to her mouth, looking as frightened as a lamb in a slaughterhouse.

"Help me up," Leo said weakly.

Monique just stood there.

"Help me up, Mon," he repeated. Slowly, Monique extended a hand and helped pull her brother to his feet.

Blood continued to pool under Meijer's head.

"It's all right, Mon," Leo said to his sister. "It's all right."

"The neighbors heard the fight?" Monique said in a shaky voice. "One of them came upstairs to investigate."

"What did you tell him?"

"What could I tell him? I told him you were rehearsing a play with a friend of yours. Hamlet. The big swordfight at the end. I apologized for the noise and said it would be over soon."

Leo nodded weakly. "You did fine," he said. "Just fine."

Eventually the siblings recovered enough strength to finish what they set out to do. They lifted the body of the little forger and put it in the bathtub, where the blood could drain without making a bigger mess.

They wiped the floor and fixtures with towels and put them in a burlap sack. They stripped off Meijer's shoes and soiled clothes, and Leo took off his own blood-stained garments as well. All of these things went into the sack, along with the few personal effects in Meijer's room. One incriminating item, however, was not disposed of: a thin volume of poetry that Meijer was using as a journal. He had neatly recorded his thoughts in the spaces between the lines. For whatever reason, Leo decided to keep it.

Leo weighted the sack with bricks and cobbles he had collected from the rubble of a damaged building, and the sack was placed in another burlap sack, which was then bound with a piece of clothesline.

Meijer was left in the tub for several hours. Presumably he was dead when they put him in. If not, he had certainly expired several hours later when they tried to get him into the clothing chest. It was a large, deep chest with lots of room, but rigor mortis had begun and the siblings strained and sweated for a half-hour to fold the body into a position so that the lid could be closed.

Around midnight, Leo and Monique lugged the chest and the sack down three flights of stairs and half carried it, half dragged it around the block to where a rented rowboat was moored in a small side canal. Monique was dressed in rough work clothes and she wore a cap. From a distance, she looked like a man.

Leo had rented the boat earlier that day from a nearby boatyard. They put the chest and the sack into the boat and shoved off. With Leo rowing, they headed out from the small, side canal to a major waterway -- the wide, deep Boerenwetering. And there, away (they thought) from the prying eyes of neighbors, they dropped the chest and burlap sack -- with their grisly contents -- into the turbid water. The burlap bag went straight to the bottom but the chest floated. Leo knew the wooden chest would not sink without added weight. But he also knew that the more weight he put in it, the harder it would be for them -- especially for Monique -- to get it down the stairs.

Having consigned their cargo to the waters of the canal, the Wolters rowed back to the side canal and re-moored the boat. The next day, after checking the little vessel for blood drops, Leo returned it to the boatyard. He then went home to prepare for the consequences that he knew would come.

Chapter 23

Adjutant-Detective Robert van Basten fidgeted in his chair in the squad room of the Criminal Investigation Division of the Amsterdam Police Department, housed in a dilapidated building on the Overtoom, not far from the Leidseplein.

Van Basten did not need the office clock to tell him that it was 11:10 a.m., ten minutes past his usual coffee time. Where was Irena with the coffee? A cup of fresh-brewed java was the highlight of his morning. Despite the scarcity of coffee in the city, and the tenfold increase in its price, CID always seemed to have an ample supply in the office. Sometimes small bags of coffee beans were offered to the detectives as bribes. Sometimes varying amounts of the precious commodity were confiscated from the homes of criminals they arrested. And six months before, the CID acquired ten kilos of the stuff following a raid on the warehouse of a black marketeer. The coffee was supposed to be turned over to the German-run Office of War Contraband but somehow or other it was misplaced on its way to the evidence room and never left the building.

It was now 11:15 and the young woman still had not arrived with her trolley of coffee and cookies. The so-called "coffee woman" -- Irena ter Steege -- was a favorite of Van Basten's. She was 20 years old, blond and pretty, the daughter of a police detective who had been killed in an automobile accident a number of years ago. Irena wanted to be a nurse and was working part-time as a nurse's aide in an Amsterdam hospital. To make ends meet, she also had a part-time job in the canteen of the Overtoom police building. The avuncular Van Basten and his wife had taken the young woman under their wing and had her over for dinner at least once a week. They loaned her money from time to time to help her cover her monthly rent. But at the moment, Van Basten was annoyed with her. It was 11:20 a.m. and he still had not had his late-morning cup of coffee.

In an effort to take his mind off the steaming brew, or the lack thereof, he focused his attention on the police report that lay before him. The first thing Van Basten did was to note the name of the reporting officer. Theodore Bakker, assigned to the 35th Precinct on the Stadionweg. Theodore Bakker? Van Basten ran through his mental catalogue of names and faces and decided he had never met the man. Pity. He always found it helpful when he knew the officer who wrote the report.

The document before him dealt with a body that had been found the night before inside a clothing chest, floating in a canal. From reading the lucid summary, Van Basten knew that Bakker was a thorough and competent officer and he felt better. He could use the report as a starting point for his investigation and move forward. It wasn't so simple with the reports of other officers he could name, officers who habitually turned in shoddy work, poorly written and incomplete, with names spelled wrong, times and places screwed up, important details left out. In such cases, Van Basten had to go out and redo the original reports so that he could begin his investigation on the firm ground of accuracy, rather than the quicksand of sloppy police work.

He read Bakker's report again. The nude body of a man found in a chest floating in the Boerenwetering. Murder had been an infrequent crime in those wonderful days before the occupation, but now, hardly a week went by without a few bodies turning up, often in a canal. The victims could be grouped in one of several categories: German servicemen; collaborators and informers; hoodlums; and miscellaneous. The latter group included those who fell victim to otherwise law-abiding people who used the fog of war to settle old scores: husbands killing their wives' lovers, for example. During the last three years, Van Basten had investigated more than a score of cases involving bodies fished from the canal.

The detective's first reaction on reading the report was that the victim belonged in the miscellaneous category. The nudity seemed to indicate an unlucky lover caught *in flagrante* by a violent husband. But there were other plausible explanations. He may have been stripped to make identification more difficult. Once a corpse was identified, it usually was a piece of cake to find the murderer.

Suddenly remembering the "criminal investigation guidelines" that had been issued to the CID last November by the German *Sicherheitsdienst,* Van Basten looked across at his sometime partner, Adjutant-Detective Leonard Hookstra, and asked, "Have the *moffen* been informed about the body?"

"I sent a messenger with the report to the Euterpestraat at 9 a.m.," Hookstra said. "One hour later, I got a call from a Lieutenant Rensmann of the SD. He wanted to know if we identified the victim."

"Have we?"

"No."

"Good," Van Basten grunted. It sickened him to have to cooperate with the Germans and he usually pulled every trick he could to avoid sharing information. He knew that he was on the shit list of Gestapo *Befehlshaber* Willi Lages, who had complained to Van Basten's boss that the detective had been "uncooperative" during a recent investigation involving the murder of a Gestapo informer.

Under pressure from Lages, Van Basten's superiors had docked him a week's pay and ordered him to be more "forthcoming" in the future.

"You can't screw around with the Gestapo, Rob," Deputy Chief Willem De Klerk, the head of CID, had said. "You are getting off pretty lightly this time. Next time, you might find yourself out of a job -- or worse."

Van Basten could only nod in agreement. He knew he would have to give the Gestapo whatever they wanted, but he couldn't tell them what he didn't know.

"Did this SD man -- Rensmann -- say why he was interested in this case?" Van Basten asked.

"He said it was routine."

"Routine, huh. Everything is 'routine' with those people. Did he say anything else?"

"Just to tell them the name of the victim when we find out."

Van Basten cracked an ironical smile. Sure. He would tell them. He would make it his number one priority.

"As killers go," Hookstra observed, without looking up from his paperwork, "this one is unusually considerate and generous."

"What do you mean?" asked Van Basten.

"Not every killer takes the time and trouble of this killer, who sent us a victim already encoffined and ready for burial. That reveals that this grisly business is the work of a truly considerate individual."

Van Basten smiled but did not offer a rejoinder. Educated at a Jesuit day school, he did not engage in the gallows humor his colleagues used to take the edge off their work. To him, death was not something one joked about.

Partly to change the subject and partly because he was keenly interested, Van Basten asked "Where's Irena with the coffee? It's 11:30."

"Irena's at home sick," said Hookstra.

"Anyone making coffee?"

"You want to volunteer?"

It was not turning out to be a good day. With a grimace of displeasure, Van Basten turned his attention back to the report. He took out a small, black leather notebook and jotted down the address of the informant, a plumber named Cornelius Kooij. His first order of business would be to interview Kooij and have a look around the neighborhood where the body was found.

Van Basten knew he had a reputation in the CID of being a plodder and he was not at all annoyed by it. If being a plodder meant going out and doing the legwork, knocking on doors and interviewing witnesses, then he was a plodder and proud of it. True, he was not known for brilliant hunches or for making flashy, headline-grabbing arrests. In his 18 years on the force, he had never fired a shot in the line of duty. His investigations tended to be painstaking and slow but in the end, they produced airtight cases that not only put criminals behind bars, but put the right criminal behind bars. Yes, Van Basten was deliberate, he plodded, and as his waistline expanded, he had to endure the jokes likening him to tortoises, snails and other dilatory creatures. But even his harshest critics, and there weren't many, had to concede that he was a dogged, competent, highly experienced detective. No one wanted him on the case if they committed a crime.

Since the time he was ten years old, all Van Basten ever wanted to be was a cop. His father, who was a civil engineer, tried to steer him toward the same vocation but the boy would not hear of it. At age 21, after service with the Dutch colonial army in Indonesia, Van Basten took the police examination and did well, but was not hired immediately. Because of the post-World War I depression in Europe, jobs were scarce and police work suddenly seemed like an attractive occupation. The Amsterdam Police Department was deluged with applicants, and Van Basten was placed on a waiting list. Finally in 1925, Van Basten was sworn in as a probationary policeman, issued a revolver, told that most of his training would be of the on-the-job variety and assigned to walk a beat with an older patrolman in the red light district. From that day onward, he never regretted his decision to become a cop. The job continually challenged him both physically and mentally and at the end of a shift, it usually left him with a pleasant glow -- like he had done a good deed that day.

Van Basten compiled a good if unsensational record during his nearly two decades with the force, a record that was unblemished by scandal or tainted by corruption. True, there were no instances of furious shootouts or of risking his life to save someone from a burning building, but Van Basten's career was not entirely devoid of dramatics. Five years before, his investigation of a jewel theft from an Amsterdam mansion led him to Belgium, France and Switzerland and ended with the arrest of seven people. Three years ago, Van Basten coolly arrested an accused cop killer as the suspect sat with a group of cohorts in an Amsterdam cafe. What made the arrest unusual was that Van Basten did it single-handedly and without drawing his gun.

"Henk Rappard," he said, laying a hand on the suspect's shoulder. "I'm Adjutant-Detective Van Basten. You're under arrest for murdering a colleague of mine." So confident, so self-assured was his manner, that Rappard offered no resistance and none of his colleagues interfered.

In April 1943, Van Basten was 40 years old, married for 15 years to the daughter of another policeman. He was of medium height, portly, with receding black hair and a pair of those lugubrious, basset hound eyes one sees on cops, priests, undertakers and life insurance salesmen. His one vanity: expensive dark suits that usually fitted him poorly and always looked rumpled. His one vice was a pipeful of industrial-strength tobacco. In the early days of his marriage, Van Basten's young bride -- the product of an abstemious family -- tried to discourage him from smoking, but after a year of gentle coaxing, she finally gave up. She had grown so used to the noxious aroma of his tobacco that their home would seem barren without it.

With a sigh of resignation that he would have to go into the field without his late-morning jolt of coffee, Van Basten clapped his hat on his head, shoved a notebook and pen in his pocket and said to his partner, "I am going to have a look at the scene of the crime. Want to come?"

Hookstra shook his head and pointed helplessly at the pile of papers and files on his desk. "It'll take a month to work through this lot. Goddamn *moffen* and their goddamn paperwork."

"Well, I guess I will have to conduct this investigation without your sage advice, then," said Van Basten.

Hookstra grinned. "I'll save a few files for you to deal with when you get back."

Van Basten signed out at the front desk, climbed on a police bicycle and pedaled down the Overtoom to the First Constantine Huygensstraat, which he followed for a couple of miles and several name changes until it intersected with the Boerenwetering Canal, where the body was found.

As he rode to South Amsterdam, Van Basten took note of the large number of uniformed Germans on the street. Ever since the raid on the *Bevolkingsregister*, the city was lousy with *moffen*. Green policemen on street corners, SS troopers manning checkpoints, soldiers patrolling neighborhoods, convoys of military trucks going back and forth. Van Basten was stopped twice by grim-faced SS men but each time he was allowed through after showing his police card.

His first stop was at 43 Hobbemastraat, the home of the informant, Cornelius Kooij.

The 46-year-old Kooij was a tall, balding man with an open, friendly, meat-and-potatoes face. He lived in a small, trim, single-story, red-brick home about a block from the Boerenwetering Canal.

The detective was pleased to discover that Kooij was a friendly, talkative man, only too eager to cooperate. Not all witnesses were like that.

"From my porch, you can see the spot where I first saw the chest in the water," he said, pointing to the canal. "I first saw it bobbing in the water yesterday morning. It was in the middle of the canal, too far away for me to tell what it was. I was curious about it but I didn't do anything about it. Doesn't pay to be too curious about things these days. But last night when I took the dog for a walk, it was still there, only now it was closer to the wall of the canal. It was close enough to touch. I was with my son, Hendrik, and together we managed to pull it from the water. It was heavy, very heavy, but I'm a plumber by trade and used to doing a lot of lifting, you know, carrying pipes up three flights of stares all day long. It's good for your muscles."

"Anyway, we got the chest out of the water but we couldn't open it. There was a padlock on it. I sent Hendrik back to the house to get a hacksaw from my tool bag and I sawed the lock off and I opened the lid."

Kooij paused and shook his head as he remembered the grisly contents of the chest.

"Terrible business," he said. "Hendrik is still in shock. He hasn't eaten anything since yesterday. Tch. Tch. No one deserves to end up like that poor bloke. What could he have done to deserve an end like that?"

"It says in the police report that you don't know who he was," Van Basten said in his quiet interviewing voice.

"Never saw him before in my life. I didn't get a good look at his face when he was in the trunk. I was still in shock then, of course, and anyway, his head was twisted around at a crazy angle and I couldn't get a good look at the face."

"But later when they got him out and put him down in the grass, I could see his face and I can say positively that I didn't know the man. Never saw him before in my life."

As they talked on Kooij's porch, two young pimply German soldiers walked by and gave them a wry grin.

"What are they grinning about?" Kooij mumbled under his breath after the troopers passed.

Van Basten shrugged and shook his head.

"*Vuile moffen,*" Kooij said. "Rotten krauts. Last week, I was riding my bicycle to a job when this *mof* came running up and grabbed the handlebars. He said, 'Army business. Army business,' and he pulled me off my bike so hard, he nearly threw me on the ground. And without a thank you or nothing, he got on my bike and rode away. A skinny little prick of a *mof.* Can you believe that. Needless to say, he never brought my bicycle back. I wish they would all go to hell. Or at least go home and leave us alone. *Vuile moffen.*"

Van Basten wanted to offer his whole-hearted agreement but he had learned to hold his tongue when talking to strangers.

"Do you know of anyone in the neighborhood who might know who he is?" the detective asked.

"No. Can't say that I do. I got to talking with some of the neighbors afterward," Kooij said. "You know how it goes. After the police left, we were standing around talking about it. Some of the neighbors had gone over to take a look at the man and some hadn't. Those who had, said they had never seen the guy before. 'Must not be from around here,' I remember somebody saying. 'Never saw him before in my life.'"

"What time was it when you first saw the chest in the water?"

"Well, it was yesterday morning, as I said. I'm a plumber by trade and I left the house to go on a job. That's when I saw something in the water. Must have been about 9 a.m."

"And you have no idea how long the chest had been there?"

"I didn't say that," said Kooij, suddenly looking cagey.

Van Basten looked at the plumber with flat, impassive cops' eyes.

"You do know how long the chest was in the water?"

"I didn't say that, either."

"Just tell me what you know or heard, Mijnheer Kooij?" Van Basten said patiently. He had learned a long time ago how self-defeating it was to be brusque or impatient with these yokels. If they felt slighted, they would clam up and a valuable source of information would be lost.

"There's a girl who lives in the neighborhood, actually she's not such a girl, anymore," Kooij said. "She must be about 25 now. Anyway, she lives a bit farther down the road on the Hobbemakade. The front window of her apartment is less than ten feet from the canal. I've known her since she was a little girl. Nice kid. Always says hello to everyone. Quite pretty, too. Her boyfriend works for the post office."

Van Basten listened to all this without interrupting. The only sign of impatience he displayed was to reach into his overcoat pocket and pull out his pipe and tobacco pouch.

"She works at the Fokker factory," Kooij continued. "I don't know what she does there. Putting in rivets on bombers for the *moffen*, I imagine. Well, we all have to make a living somehow, right. I'm not one to pass judgment on anybody. To each his own."

"Anyway, they have been working double shifts at the factory lately and she's been getting home late at night. Ten o'clock, eleven o'clock, sometimes midnight. She had just gotten home from the factory and was having a snack about one o'clock yesterday morning when she saw something."

The cagey yokel look returned to Kooij's face and he paused dramatically, waiting for the detective to ask him to continue.

Van Basten finished lighting his pipe before saying, "Yes?"

"As I was saying, she was sitting by the window, having a snack, when she saw a rowboat on the canal. There were two people in the boat. She couldn't see what they were doing but she thought it was damn unusual for two people to be rowing on the canal in the middle of winter in the middle of the night. She didn't stick her nose any further into it, of course. She just figured they were up to something they shouldn't be doing and left it at that."

"What's this young woman's name?" Van Basten asked.

"Anke Langerlaan."

"Do you know her address?'

"No, but if you walk from here, she lives in the first apartment building on the Hobbemakade. You can't miss it."

As Van Basten jotted the information down in his notebook, he asked, "How do you know all this?"

"Anke told me."

"When?'

"About eleven o'clock last night. She was just coming home from work on her bicycle when she saw a crowd of us neighbors standing around near the canal. The police had already left and we were talking about this terrible business. We told her about the body and she told us about what she saw from her apartment window."

"I see."

"Are you going to go talk to her?"

"Perhaps." Despite his reputation for thoroughness to the point of plodding, Van Basten did not place an interview with the woman high on his list of priorities. She probably would not be able to add much to Kooij's account, second-hand though it was. Something more pressing had occurred to him. The word "rowboat" had jogged his memory. Van Basten had been to South Amsterdam dozens of times on previous investigations and he knew that there was a man in the neighborhood who had a business renting rowboats. The detective was desperately trying to recall where the business was located. He couldn't remember.

"Do you know a man around here who rents rowboats?" he finally asked.

The incongruously shrewd and knowing look again crossed the plumber's face. "You think he's got something to do with this?"

"Just routine, mijnheer. Do you know someone who rents boats?"

"Can't say that I do. Don't do much fishing, myself."

"I see." Van Basten thanked the man for his help and climbed on his bicycle.

"A terrible tragedy," said Kooij, unwilling to let the interview end just yet. "Terrible thing to see. Hendrik's still not gotten over it. He didn't touch breakfast, he didn't touch his lunch. The boy hasn't even come out of his room. I've seen a few dead bodies in my time. Lots of them. I served in the French army in the last war and I was seeing death every day. But nothing like this. This was the work of a lunatic. Had to be. Who else could do such disgusting work of twisting the body to fit in the chest. We're all in danger with this lunatic running around."

Van Basten listened politely to some of this and when he had his fill, he pedaled away slowly, calling over his shoulder as he did, "With any luck, we'll catch him. Good day, mijnheer."

Chapter 24

"We Dutch had a lousy war!"

The booming voice belonged to Senior Police Constable Guus Emden. "*Lousy?* It was a disgrace! How long did it take the *moffen* to roll up the whole damn country, huh? How long?"

Adjutant-Detective Robert van Basten looked up from his paperwork and gave the constable a frosty stare. Emden was on his soapbox again. One would think the old fool was at least smart enough to keep his mouth shut.

Emden was a grizzled veteran who had been on the force longer than practically anyone. Some of the detectives had not even been born yet when he made his first arrest. No longer fit for street work, Emden helped out at CID, answering phones, getting files, taking statements. And when things were slow, he would corner some hapless soul and air his views on the issues of the day. His unfortunate victim in this case was Van Basten's partner, Adjutant-Detective Hookstra.

"Five days," Emden practically shouted. "*Five days!* Look at the poor Finns and the battle they put up against the Ruskies. Hell, look at those damn savages in Africa, throwing spears at the I-talians. Then look at us. A fat, smug, self-satisfied little tin pot monarchy with not a breath of fight in us. We're the laughing stock of the world. And where is our royal family right now. Huh?

Where are our so-called leaders? In England, that's where, having tea with the king. I'm happy for them. I can't wait for them to come home so I can tell them how proud I am of them."

Of course, nobody needed Emden to tell them what kind of war Holland had.

The Netherlands had remained neutral during the First World War, and desperately hoped to maintain that neutrality the second time around. But Hitler had other ideas.

German paratroopers landed in the peaceful Dutch countryside during the pre-dawn hours of May 10, 1940, seizing airfields and other key military installations with hardly a shot being fired. At Rotterdam's main airport, JU-52 transport planes touched down without resistance and disgorged the elite 16th Regiment of Airborne Infantry; its mission was to secure the bridges over the Nieuwe Maas River.

Soon, battle-tested panzer units were rumbling into the Netherlands. They swept aside a hastily assembled force of army troops and national guardsmen, many of whom had pedaled to the front on bicycles. The Dutch air force didn't stand a chance against the firepower of the Luftwaffe and could do nothing to prevent German bombers from demolishing downtown Rotterdam in a raid that left hundreds of civilians dead. When the Nazis threatened to do the same to Amsterdam, the Dutch capitulated and the royal family fled to England. They left behind a population of about 9 million people who would have to fend for themselves as best they could under Nazi rule.

As Emden began a fresh attack, Hookstra shot a pleading glance at Van Basten.

"Guus," Van Basten said. "Did you have any luck finding that file I asked for?"

Resentment and puzzlement competed for space on Emden's broad face; resentment that his disquisition was interrupted, puzzlement because he didn't know what Van Basten was talking about.

"File? What file? You didn't ask me to get a file."

"Didn't I? Well, I meant to. I worked on a suicide about a year ago. I think the victim was named Brinker or Bleeker. Somewhere in South Amsterdam. Any hope you can pull the file?"

Emden laughed harshly. "Wouldn't count on it. Not with the damned *moffen* pawing through the files. Grabbing this. Taking that. Leaving everything a damned pig sty."

"Well, would you take a look, please? It's important."

Van Basten outranked Emden, as did most of the detectives in the room, but they tended to treat the crusty constable deferentially. He had been one hell of a cop in his day.

Grumbling, Emden went off in search of the file.

Hookstra and Van Basten exchanged glances and shook their heads.

"You get the autopsy results yet?" Hookstra asked.

"I'm looking at them now."

"Anything useful?"

"Maybe." Van Basten did not like sharing information, especially in these troubled times. He liked Hookstra and the two worked well together, but aside from his wife and family, and a few colleagues from way back, Van Basten trusted no one. He knew the *moffen* had informers everywhere, and he behaved as if the police department was riddled with them, which it was. Still, he did not want to be rude, and there really wasn't anything of value in the coroner's report.

"Death seems to have been from a blow to the back of the skull," Van Basten said, beginning the ritual of cleaning and loading his pipe. "They have no idea what the murder weapon was. Just the usual 'blunt instrument.'"

"Have you got him I.D.ed?"

"Negative. There's nothing to help us there. No clothing. No tattoos. Nothing peculiar about the dental work. He's still a John Doe. The trunk was old but well-made. Expensive piece once, but nothing in it to help us identify its owner. The lab guys took photographs of Doe and I'm having copies made, but I haven't decided yet whether I'll have the beat cops show them around. The victim was pretty messed up. I don't think his own mother would recognize him from the photos we've got."

Van Basten was about to add that the victim apparently had put up a fierce struggle before he was killed, but a familiar voice interrupted.

"Do you mean Brinkman?" Emden boomed as he strode across the office.

"Pardon me?"

"You said you thought the guy who killed himself was named Brinker or Bleeker. Could it have been Brinkman?"

"Yes," Van Basten answered, and Emden slapped a file down on the desk.

"Helps when I get good information," Emden said severely.

"Still you found that file in record time," said Van Basten.

"Course I did," retorted Emden. "When you been around as long as I have, you know where to look. Well, I'll being seeing you. Have a report to type."

Hookstra chuckled as Emden walked away. "That should keep him busy for the rest of the day," he said. "Every time he hears the bell on his typewriter, he goes out for a beer."

"One of these days, he may actually learn how to type," said Van Basten generously.

"I think there's a better chance that the old beggar on the Kalverstraat will learn how to play his harmonica. By the way, the Gestapo dropped by while you were out."

"Oh."

"That young, snot-nosed twerp who acts as their liaison man."

"Lieutenant Rensmann?"

"The same."

"What did he want?"

"He wanted to know if we made any progress on the punk-in-the-trunk."

"And what did you tell him?" Van Basten tried to keep his tone normal.

"I told him it wasn't my case."

"Good work."

"He said he would call tomorrow."

"Tomorrow," Van Basten said wistfully, and thought, "Wouldn't it be nice if all the *moffen* were gone by tomorrow."

"Why is the Gestapo so interested in this case?" he asked, more to himself than anyone.

"You know how the *moffen* are. They're not happy unless they have a hair up their ass about something."

"Was he here specifically about the trunk victim?"

"I don't think so. He was in talking to the boss for awhile, then he came out and asked about several of the murder cases. And he very politely reminded us that we are to send copies of reports on any and all felonies to the Gestapo. Immediately."

For lack of anything better to say, Van Basten uttered a soft "hmmm." He turned his attention to the file Emden had brought and quickly found what he was looking for. Yes, he had been a little fuzzy about the victim's name but his memory was still sharp enough. There was a rowboat rental business in the neighborhood. He took out his little notebook and jotted down the name and address of Ton Verbeek on the Van der Postkade.

"I'm going out," he said to Hookstra. "If my wife calls, tell her I will be home for dinner. And on time, for a change."

"Rob," Hookstra said seriously. "Don't you think you should get that paperwork over to the Gestapo?"

"Later," Van Basten said, picking up his hat. "We can't catch bad guys sitting in the office, doing paperwork for the Gestapo. *Tot ziens.*"

He signed out at the desk, helped himself to a bicycle and again pedaled to South Amsterdam.

Van Basten rode to the Van der Postkade and once there, had no trouble finding the little rowboat rental shop. The business was located at the end of a narrow side canal that fed into the Boerenwetering. Several rowboats were tied up at a small dock and behind the dock was a windowless wooden building with a sign out front reading: "Verbeek's Boat Rental. Bait and Tackle Available."

Van Basten leaned his bike against the side of the building and went inside. There was a thin, leathery man of about 50 sitting at a desk, pipe in mouth, absorbed in a book. He did not look up when the detective walked in.

"Hallo, Mijnheer Verbeek," Van Basten said. "Do you remember me?"

Verbeek, white-haired and stubborn-jawed, took the pipe out of his mouth, studied his visitor, then pointed at him with the pipe. "Adjutant-Detective Van Basten," he said, breaking into a smile that revealed a number of missing teeth.

"You have a good memory," said the detective. "What are you reading?"

"Oh, just one of Hugo de Jong's sea stories. What brings you back to this humble neighborhood?"

"Unfortunately, the same sort of unpleasantness that brought me here last year,"

The "unpleasantness" last year involved a body that was found floating in the water right in front of Verbeek's little dock. He turned out to be an ailing, elderly neighbor of Verbeek's named Brinkman who had committed suicide.

"Ja?" Verbeek said. "Some new trouble?"

"A body was found in the Boerenwetering," Van Basten said. "Heard anything about it?"

"Me? No. This is the first I've heard."

Verbeek clucked his tongue and shook his head. "A *mof*?" he asked.

"Could be, but I doubt it."

Van Basten called up what little he remembered about Verbeek. He was retired, living on a pension from his many years as a tugboat hand in Amsterdam Harbor. He was married and his wife did some part-time work -- sewing or something like that. Verbeek's little boat rental business brought in some extra money and gave him an excuse to get out of his little house for awhile.

It was more than a hunch that brought Van Basten to Verbeek's door. Amsterdam had always been a sailors' city and on a sunny day before the war, the canals and rivers were crowded with boats of every size and variety: rowboats, skiffs, motorized launches, cabin cruisers, sailboats, tugs, barges and houseboats. People would be sunning themselves on deck, or drinking wine and calling out good-naturedly to those ashore watching the flotilla go by.

But during the occupation, relatively few people were allowed to own boats. The Germans saw to that. The Germans did not want to be bothered policing the many miles of waterways for Resistance fighters, criminals or others up to no good, so they confiscated most of the small craft. More often than not, the boats wound up as the property of German officers. The Nazis did allow some boat rental businesses to stay open, including Verbeek's, though they helped themselves to half of his ten rowboats.

As Van Basten saw it, the chance was better than fifty percent that the rowboat seen on the Boerenwetering by the young woman factory worker was rented.

"Been busy?" Van Basten asked casually.

Verbeek shrugged. "I've been busier. I have a couple of boats out now. Both fishermen. I sold one of them some bait."

"What about three days ago. April 20th?" Van Basten asked.

"Three days ago?" Verbeek repeatedly quizzically.

The portly cop nodded.

"I would have to check my register."

"Could you check, please?"

"Always happy to oblige the police," said the old salt with another pumpkin-toothed grin. He opened a drawer and extracted a torn and stained red ledger. "You can see for yourself," he said, turning to the correct page. Three days ago. April 20. There. Take a look."

Van Basten looked down at the ledger and saw three names, names that meant nothing to him. He noted when the boats were checked out, when they were returned and how much money was paid. One entry stood out from the rest.

"What do you remember about this customer?" he asked, pointing into the ledger.

Verbeek looked. "Leo Wolters? Not a lot. Hardly anything. He's rented boats here before. A few times. Takes his girlfriends out for picnics. Nothing special about him. Nice guy." A funny look crossed the older man's face. "Except the last time."

"What happened the last time?"

"Nothing important. Just that the last time, he didn't come with a girl. He usually always comes with a girl, but the last time, he was alone. That's all."

"Does he always keep the boats overnight?"

"Uh, that's a good question. Naw, I don't think he does. He usually brings them back the same day. But it's not unusual for customers to hang onto the boats overnight, especially if they plan to get up early to go fishing."

Van Basten nodded. But of the three customers who rented boats from Verbeek on April 20th, Leo Wolters was the only one who kept the craft overnight. Wolters returned it at nine o'clock the following morning, according to the ledger.

The detective pulled out his notebook and wrote down the customer's address, which was neatly printed in the ledger.

"What does Mijnheer Wolters look like?" asked the cop.

"What does he look like?" Verbeek rubbed his chin. "Nothing unusual. Ordinary. Young-looking. I would say he's about 20 years old or so. Kinda tall. I remember him tellin' me once that he was an art student. He wouldn't stand out in a crowd, if you know what I mean."

"Where is the boat Wolters rented?"

Verbeek checked the ledger. "License number L-1203. She's tied up outside."

"Which one is it?"

"The one closest to the office."

"Has anyone else had it out since Wolters rented it?"

Verbeek looked in the ledger and shook his head. "Naw. She's been here the last three days."

"Do you mind if I have a look at her?" asked the detective.

"Go ahead. Always happy to oblige the police."

Van Basten thanked the man and went outside. The rowboat in question was about twelve feet long and looked in poor repair. Most of its white paint had flaked away, giving the hull a repelling, scabrous appearance, as if it had contracted some hideous disease. The oarlocks were rusty and the oars themselves looked so weakened by rot that they would disintegrate with the first stroke.

The detective did not get into the boat. Instead, he kneeled on the dock and peered closely at the little craft, searching for marks and grooves that shouldn't be there. It didn't take his experienced eyes long to find them. Fresh-scored grooves on the thwart, small brown-black stains in the well. Here a gouge, there a scrape.

"I've seen enough," Van Basten said to himself, standing up.

"So, what's it all about, Detective Van Basten?" Verbeek had come outside and had been watching over Van Basten's shoulder.

"Just a little mystery that I hope to clear up very soon," said Van Basten. He walked over to his bicycle and got on. He debated whether to instruct Verbeek to keep their interview to himself, but decided against it. The more you give a person to talk about, the more likely he is to talk about it.

"Thank you, again, for your help, Mijnheer Verbeek," Van Basten said, pedaling away. "When the weather gets a little better, I'll be renting one of your boats myself."

Chapter 25

Viewed from a distance of decades, Leo Wolters' behavior in the days immediately after the murder of Herman Meijer seems cold-blooded and callous, almost grotesquely so. He spent most of his time, not in repentant prayer for having taken a life, but in taking care of some outstanding debts.

His first order of business -- after disposing of the body -- was to go to the City Theatre on the Leidseplein to dig up the small horde of gold and jewelry that Meijer had stashed away. He was able to do this without attracting any notice because, like Meijer, he worked in the building as a part-time handyman. Nobody raised an eyebrow when he went down to the cellar and knocked a hole in the wall near the huge furnace. And bingo. The cache was right where Meijer said it would be. Leo reached in and removed two cigar boxes containing all of Herman Meijer's worldly valuables. He replastered the hole, cleaned his tools and headed home with his newly acquired wealth.

It was shortly thereafter, the exact date is not known, that Leo showed up at the grocery store-cum-pawnshop of Jan-Wouter Schouw on the Beethovenstraat.

Despite a fearsome-looking scar under his left eye, Schouw was a jovial, outgoing young man and one of the most peaceable denizens of Amsterdam's *penose*. He was known in his South Amsterdam neighborhood as a good family man, a paragon of honesty and kindness who was scrupulously above board in all his business dealings -- shady though they were.

Schouw had an adoring wife (to whom he was steadfastly faithful), two fine daughters and a widowed mother who lived under his roof. Neighborhood children often brought stray dogs and cats to his home, knowing that Schouw loved animals and was willing to care for them. By April 1943, his menagerie included nearly a dozen dogs, cats and birds.

Jan-Wouter Schouw made a good living during the war from the black market. His clientele ran the gamut from the humblest street sweeper to upper-echelon Nazis. People came to him because they knew he had good connections and that he would not try to cheat them.

"Times were tough," he later recalled. "People didn't have a lot. I could have charged a fortune for a small sack of sugar but I didn't. Most of my clients were my friends and that's not how people are supposed to treat their friends."

Schouw, who passed away in 1990, was not ashamed of his wartime dealings and in his open, candid way, discussed the subject with anyone who took the trouble to ask (though he refused to reveal how he acquired the scar below his eye; that was a secret he took to the grave).

Schouw dealt in a wide variety of goods during the war but his specialty was converting jewelry and gold into cash or vice versa. In this, he operated somewhere between a pawnbroker and a fence. He never asked questions when buying or selling the merchandise. If a German officer wanted to unload some looted jewelry, Schouw obliged. If a client wanted to buy gold or jewelry, Schouw had a sizeable inventory from which to pick and choose.

"The key was to be discreet," he said. "I never talked about my customers, though some of them were pretty famous. I kept no records, except in my head. And I always paid a fair price. That's why I was allowed to stay in business."

But with the war over, Schouw broke his rule of confidentiality and on any number of occasions, talked with reporters about various clients. Some of his revelations caused embarrassment at lofty levels of the Dutch government, but despite his many statements to the press, he was sued only once -- by Leo Wolters.

The lawsuit stemmed from an interview on Dutch television that Schouw gave in 1960 as part of a documentary about the murky past of a distinguished Austrian diplomat. Wolters' name was mentioned only in passing, but it was enough to bring a lawsuit. The legal action cost Schouw ten thousand guilders, a considerable sum in 1960, more than enough to persuade him to never again publicly mention Wolters' name.

But the television documentary survives and with it, Schouw's clear recollection of a young, skinny, frightened Leo Wolters coming to his Beethovenstraat shop in 1943 with jewelry to sell.

Leo had dealt with Schouw before. He pawned a number of items -- mostly gifts from his father -- to cover gambling losses. Leo knew that Schouw was discreet, asked no questions and gave a good price for he merchandise.

Exactly what was in the boxes that he brought with him to Schouw's shop will never be known. What is known is that the black market dealer -- who knew his business and who carefully inspected each piece of jewelry with a powerful loupe -- found Hebrew inscriptions on several of the items, including a gold pocket watch. Schouw was not surprised by that. Throughout the war, Jews had sold jewelry to neighbors and the neighbors had pawned the jewelry with him. Nothing unusual about it. Anyway, Schouw's policy was to ask no questions. For him it was a routine transaction and he probably would not have remembered it, but for the amount and quality of the merchandise.

Schouw gave Wolters a considerable sum of folding money – three thousand guilders -- for the gold and jewelry, which he later remembered was "of superlative quality."

"I like to think that the money helped Wolters survive the war and go on to become a famous man," he said with a laugh during the 1960 documentary interview. "I paid a little more than I should have, but he looked so skinny and desperate. Like a starving young bird."

Though Schouw later retracted the story and apologized to Wolters as conditions of the legal settlement, there's no reason to disbelieve his account of their business transaction. He had no reason to lie and no one else ever challenged the veracity of his recollections.

For the next couple of days, Leo spent cash like a sailor in port. He forked over five hundred guilders to his landlord to cover several months of back rent. He restored his good name at a gambling club-cum-brothel on the Damrak by paying the seven hundred guilders he owed the owner. He cleaned up various other IOUs with shopkeepers, publicans and friends.

Rather than feeling depressed and unhappy by what he had done, Leo was in an ebullient mood as he paid off his many debts. It was a good feeling not to have so many creditors nipping at his heels. He was glad to be able to patronize the Damrak club again where he had developed a serious interest in one of the girls.

There were, however, two potentially troublesome clouds on the horizon. One was Maarten Dijkstra and his Resistance colleagues, who could be expected to react with anger and outrage when they learned about the killing. But Leo already had concocted what he hoped was a convincing, exculpating story that would clear him of wrongdoing in their eyes. It was the same story that he intended to tell the police, if and when they showed up at his doorstep.

Of more pressing concern was the reaction of Dries Riphagen to whom he still owed a one thousand guilder gambling debt -- a debt the gangster had increased fivefold through blackmail.

Leo was willing to pay the one thousand guilders but he knew Riphagen -- having demanded five thousand guilders -- would never be satisfied with the lesser amount. With Meijer dead, Riphagen could not blackmail Leo into giving him the money, but there were other options. Leo knew that with a phone call, Riphagen could have him killed. Or beaten up so badly that he would never walk straight again. Or have acid thrown in his face, as the Dutch Al Capone was rumored to have done with a petty hood who was making time with on of Riphagen's girlfriends.

Plainly put, Leo was scared to death of Riphagen. The Dutch Al Capone was violent and unstable, as dangerous as a vial of nitroglycerine. The Dutch had a word for someone like Riphagen -- *mafkees* -- a maniac, someone completely out of his mind. Leo did not dare to go to the Rembrandtsplein club to give the gangster the thousand guilders.

"You have to go there and give him the money, Leo," Monique said at dinner one night. "Otherwise he is going to come here looking for you. Or turn you in to the Germans."

Leo didn't answer but the apprehensive look on his face spoke volumes.

"Give me the money, Leo," she said. "I'll see that Dries gets it."

Leo looked up from his plate. "I thought you and Dries had called it quits."

"We have."

"So even if you give it to him, it's not going to do any good. He'll still want five thousand guilders."

"Don't get excited, Leo."

"I don't have five thousand guilders, Mon."

"I know. Leave it to me, Leo."

Again Leo looked curiously at his sister. "Leave it to *you*?"

"Yes. Leave it to me."

"What do you mean? What can you do that I can't?"

"I think I can convince Dries to be satisfied with the thousand guilders."

"How?"

Monique was silent.

"How, Mon?"

"Just leave it to me, Leo, and don't ask any questions."

"Mon?"

"I mean it, Leo. Just give the money to me and I will see that Dries gets it and that he doesn't bother you anymore."

Leo stared at his sister.

"Where's the money?" she asked.

Leo got up and went to the kitchen where he had stashed the money in an iron pot. He returned with a thousand guilders and gave it to his sister. Monique folded the wad of bills and nonchalantly deposited them inside her blouse.

"Now finish your dinner," she admonished. "And don't ask any more foolish questions."

Chapter 26

As Leo Wolters was going around town paying off debts and fretting about Dries Riphagen, Adjutant-Detective Robert van Basten was busy building a murder case against him.

Despite his reputation for plodding, or maybe because of it, Van Basten worked quickly and efficiently on the "punk-in-the-trunk" investigation, as the case came to be known at CID. Within days of starting his inquiry, the veteran detective had identified a possible suspect, and everything he had learned since then only strengthened his belief that Leo Wolters was the killer.

That Van Basten was able to assemble a strong case against Leo in so short a period is not surprising. The murder was clearly the work of an amateur, and not a very clever amateur at that. It was a hasty, sloppy affair with a neon-lit trail of incriminating evidence leading right to Leo's front door.

The address in the ledger at the boat rental dealer brought Van Basten to the three-story apartment house on the Schubertstraat, home to Leo and Monique Wolters. A more ham-handed, less-experienced investigator might have immediately put the "habeas grabus" on Leo and hauled him down to the station for a tough grilling, but not Van Basten. He knew that the more evidence one collected against a criminal, the easier it was to get him to confess during an interrogation.

So Van Basten began by interviewing the neighbors about what they knew of Leo Wolters. What kind of man was he? Anything suspicious going on there during the last couple of weeks? The detective hit pay dirt immediately. The entire apartment house was abuzz with talk about the recent doings at Chez Wolters. Neighbors said that for more than two years, the art student had lived quietly on the third floor, always respectful, always friendly, bothering nobody. Then, during the last week or so, there had been several big commotions in the Wolters apartment.

Everyone recalled that before one ruckus began, a large blue American town car pulled up in front of the building and people "dressed like gangsters" got out. They kicked in the front door of the building, damaging the door frame and breaking the lock (every tenant had to chip in two guilders to repair the damage). The thugs had gone upstairs and there had been a hell of a to-do in the Wolters apartment. Lots of shouting and threats and bumping around, as if someone were moving furniture.

The neighbors were still trying to figure out what *that* was all about when there had been another upheaval a few days ago. If anything, the second was worst than the first. It sounded like someone was getting murdered up there. Someone clearly screamed for help. Neighbors remembered it as a terrifying sound. One tenant said someone screamed, "Help! Help!" a number of times. Another heard a man begging, "Don't Kill Me!"

A couple of the more intrepid neighbors actually went upstairs to see what the fuss was about. And there they encountered Monique Wolters, white as chalk, standing on the landing outside the apartment, dressed in her bathrobe ("and she wasn't wearing much underneath," one informant said).

The neighbors had always liked the beautiful young woman. She was obviously well-bred, always polite and friendly, just like her brother.

When the neighbors asked what was going on in the apartment, Monique told them not to be concerned, that her brother was rehearsing for a play, that's all.

The neighbors were unconvinced. Rehearsing for a play? With all that racket?

"They're doing MacBeth," Monique told them with a nervous laugh but a straight face. "You know, full of sound and fury, and all that."

The apartment house residents looked skeptically at the young woman dressed only in her robe. They observed her nervous movements and frightened smile. Then they shrugged the matter off. Her brother *could* be rehearsing for a play. Nothing implausible about that. What else were they to think? That their polite, well-mannered young neighbor was busy murdering someone in his upstairs apartment. *Belachelijk* -- ridiculous.

There were some neighbors who still had misgivings about the noise but they did not attempt to intercede. In these uncertain times, only fools stick their nose in where it does not belong, they confided to Van Basten.

The detective looked sympathetic and nodded his head. He took a morgue photo of Herman Meijer out of his pocket and showed it to every tenant in the building. And to a person, they looked at it quickly, shuddered, and shook their heads no. No, they had never seen the young man before. Who was he?

"That's what I'm trying to find out," Van Basten said.

The detective uncovered more incriminating evidence when he interviewed the apartment manager, who had been the first to go upstairs to investigate the cries for help. The manager, a lanky, chain-smoking man of about forty, told Van Basten that a day or so after the ruckus, Leo had showed up at his door with a fistful of guilders and paid off three months of back rent.

"I was very pleased that he was settling his debt but also curious where he got the money," the manager said. "Considering that I had asked him for the back rent only last week and he said he didn't have it."

"And what did Mijnheer Wolters say when you asked him where he got the money?"

"He said he got loans from his father and from a friend."

"Did you believe him?"

"I didn't know what to believe. It's very possible he got a loan from his father. I hear he's a rich one. I wanted to believe Leo was telling the truth? He's a nice boy and he never caused any trouble. Until recently, that is."

"But didn't it strike you as odd that he suddenly had all this money?" Van Basten asked. "I mean, if getting a loan from his father was so easy, why did he fall three months behind in his rent in the first place?"

The manager gave an elaborate shrug. "How am I supposed to know what sort of relationship he has with his father? Maybe they were not on good terms for awhile and he refused to give him any money. How do I know? They could have patched things up last week and Leo could have hit him up for a loan. I don't know. What was I supposed to do? Refuse to take the money? The truth is I was delighted he paid his rent. I was considering kicking him out of the building and I told him that. He's a nice boy and all but I can't afford to have tenants who don't pay their rent."

"Why didn't you? Kick him out, I mean."

"If I had kicked him out, I might never have gotten the rent?" the manager said, looking smug. "I'm not that big of a fool. I figured in the end, he would be good for it."

Back at the detective bureau, Van Basten, in his methodical way, made a list of all the circumstantial evidence that he had collected linking Leo Wolters to the crime.

Wolters had a rented boat in his possession on the night that a woman had seen two people in a rowboat on the Boerenwetering during the early morning hours, a place near where the clothing chest with its grisly contents was eventually found.

Van Basten had inspected the boat and had found fresh scrapes and scuff marks that could have been made by a heavy object, like a body-laden clothing chest.

Neighbors at Wolters' apartment house had heard two commotions in the young man's flat in recent days. They were surprised because Wolters was usually such a quiet tenant. In the first incident, men dressed like gangsters had gotten out of a large, blue American-made car. Van Basten recognized the vehicle's description at once. The car was famous. It belonged to Dries Riphagen -- the Dutch Al Capone. What does he have to do with all this? Van Basten wondered.

During the second ruckus, neighbors clearly heard someone shouting for help. Someone even said he heard the terrified plea of a man begging for his life. Taken together, the evidence amounted to a near certainty that Leo Wolters was somehow involved in the killing of the John Doe.

On the other side of the ledger, Van Basten had found only one piece of evidence that was in any way exculpatory, the fact that none of the neighbors recognized the photo of the victim. Had any of the tenants declared that they had seen the man with Wolters in the past, that would have nailed the case shut right then and there. But nobody did that. They said they had never seen the victim before.

Van Basten took out another piece of paper and at the top wrote: "Possibilities." Underneath he made the following entries:

1. The victim did not live in the building, or if he did, he was an *onderduiker* (Worth pursuing?)

2. The victim never visited the building, or if he did, not often (Nosy tenants there would have noticed him).

3. Leo Wolters knows the victim from somewhere else (Where? What was their connection?)

4. Wolters did not know victim at all (Unlikely. He took a total stranger back to his flat and murdered him? Forget it!)

The detective decided to pay a visit to Leo's flat the next day. He would keep the interview low-key, at least to begin with. Just a few routine questions, he would say. Van Basten could show the morgue photo to Leo as he had done with other tenants and ask the young man if he knew the victim. Once he established some sort of rapport with the suspect (by that point Van Basten looked upon Leo as such), he could turn things up a notch. Ask about the fights. Ask about the boat. Ask about Dries Riphagen. This is going to be a piece of cake, the detective thought.

The interview actually went far better than Van Basten expected.

He arrived at the front door of the Schubertstraat apartment at 10 a.m. and rang the bell for Leo's apartment. The door was opened via a rope that ran from the door and along a wall, through small holes in the ceilings to every floor of the building. Tenants could open the front door by pulling a handle in the hallway on every floor.

The portly investigator huffed and puffed as he climbed the narrow stairs to Leo's apartment. He found the young man waiting for him on the landing with a puzzled look on his face.

"My name is Van Basten," the detective said, by way of introduction. "I'm with the police."

"Oh," said Leo. "Well, you better come in, then."

Van Basten found himself in the sitting room of a roomy apartment. The furniture was worn but expensive-looking. There were watercolors on the wall and a small piano in a corner. In another corner, a bookcase sagged under the weight of many volumes, and there were more books and papers stacked on the floor.

"Sit down, please," Leo said, indicating the couch. "What can I do for you?"

Van Basten later described Leo as a tall, skinny, ordinary-looking young man, nothing unusual, save for a mop of long hair.

A callow boy, was the policeman's snap opinion, but still with a certain *je ne sais quoi.* The policeman was impressed by the young man's demeanor. Leo was not at all rattled by the sudden appearance of a detective at his door. To the contrary, he was relaxed, cordial, hospitable, "quite the proper gentleman."

"I apologize for intruding on your day but we have a situation going on that I am trying to clear up as quickly as possible," Van Basten said. "I hope you understand."

"Of course. May I get you a cup of tea?"

"That's very kind but no thank you." Van Basten pulled his notebook from a pocket. "This shouldn't take long. I don't know if you've heard that a body was found in a canal not very far from here."

Leo nodded but didn't say anything.

Van Basten reached into his inside coat pocket and pulled out the photograph of Meijer.

"Did you ever see this man before?" he asked, passing the picture to Leo.

Leo glanced at it and handed it back. "Yes, I have."

"You have? Who was he?"

"His name was Herman Meijer," said Leo. "He was a Jewish *onderduiker* and I had been sheltering him here."

Van Basten scribbled in his notebook.

"He was living here?" he asked casually, still writing in his notebook.

"Yes."

"Was he a friend of yours?"

Leo shrugged.

"Was he or not?"

"To tell you the truth, I didn't like him very much. He was like a lot of Jews, if you know what I mean. Annoying. A bit *kapsones.*"

"You say you didn't like him very much, yet you were risking your life to shelter him. Does that make sense?"

Leo gave another limp shrug.

"You know, of course, that sheltering a Jew is against the law," said the detective. "As a public official, I am obligated by law to arrest you."

It was a diversion, meant to keep Leo off balance; he had no intention of arresting him for that. How many *onderduikers* had he come across during his investigations? More than a dozen and he had yet to turn one in to the Germans.

"You don't happen to know how this chap -- Meijer, you say -- wound up in the canal?" Van Basten asked.

"Yes. I killed him and dumped his body in the canal."

"I see," the detective said, making another notation.

"I don't think you do?" Leo said quietly.

"Pardon?"

"I don't mean to be disrespectful, but I don't think you have any idea of the circumstances you're dealing with here."

"Well, now, young man. I'm willing to listen. Why don't you just tell me what it is you think I should know."

Leo remained silent.

"I'm waiting."

When Leo continued to stare at him in silence, Van Basten said, "I'm a patient man, son, but I won't be manipulated. You can answer my questions here, or down at the station. You might even find yourself at the Euterpestraat if the Gestapo gets wind of the fact that you were hiding a Jew."

Leo stood up and melodramatically walked back and forth. Then he said, "What I am about to tell you stays in this room. Agreed?"

Van Basten thought: You young punk. Who are you to dictate terms to a police detective? Instead he said calmly, "I'm sure you realize that I can make no promises to you. I can offer this piece of advice, though. Your best chance is to be honest and straightforward with me. Anything less, and you are putting yourself at greater risk. Now tell me what you know about this business and be quick about it. I am tired of the games."

Leo sat back down in his chair, lit a cigarette, blew a stream of smoke ceilingward and said, "I had to kill Herman Meijer. It was a *Verzetsdaad* – a Resistance deed."

"Continue," said Van Basten, scribbling in his book.

"I don't know how much I can say about it."

"I suggest that you tell me everything you know."

"Very well." Leo told his story smoothly, tissue of lies though it was.

"Herman Meijer was a forger. He was placed under my roof by the Resistance while he forged documents for a raid. He was supposed to be taken away after he finished his work but due to some complications, he had to remain here."

"I think the pressure of being cooped up finally got to him and he snapped. He became paranoid. He accused me and my sister of plotting to turn him in to the Nazis. It was nonsense of course, but he believed it and we could not change his mind. He said that if ever he was arrested, he would denounce me to the Gestapo."

"A few days ago, everything came to a head. He started screaming at me, making a lot of noise, again accusing me of selling him out to the Germans. He made an awful racket. Herman's presence in the apartment was supposed to be a secret. The neighborhood is full of informers and here this idiot is screaming at the top of his lungs. I was terrified that the Gestapo was going to show up at my door at any moment. That would have been a disaster, not only for me, but for my group. I'm not a coward but who knows how long I could stand torture before they broke me."

"I told the fool to shut up, that he was putting us all in deadly danger, but he just kept yelling and screaming and carrying on. By that time, he had lost all reason. There was no talking to him. I grabbed him around the neck. My intention at that point, was not to kill him, but to get him to shut up. But he broke away from me and tried to get out the door. I went after him and we had a big fight. It started in the living room and ended in the bathroom. To make a long story short, I killed him by banging his head against the side of the bathtub."

Leo took a deep breath and exhaled forcefully, as if suddenly disencumbered of a terrible burden.

"Did you mean to kill him?" Van Basten asked.

"I honestly don't know. I was in such a frenzy that I can't tell you what was going through my head, other than I just wanted to end the noise."

The detective nodded in understanding. "By the way, where is your sister?"

"My sister?"

"Yes. You live here with your sister, right?"

"Yes. Yes I do. She's not home."

"Was she here on the night of the mur--, I mean, killing?"

"No."

"That's odd. Several of your fellow tenants told me that they saw her standing in the hallway outside your apartment the night Mijnheer Meijer was killed."

"She was not at home when the fight broke out. I guess she came back as we were struggling and stayed out of the apartment until it was over."

"I was told she was dressed only in her bathrobe," Van Basten said, keeping his voice neutral.

"In her bathrobe? Who told you that?"

"Was she dressed in a bathrobe?"

"Of course not. She had been out on the town with friends. Maybe she was wearing a gown or something. I don't know."

"How did you get the body out of the building?"

"You must know that we put the body in a clothing chest and carried it outside that way."

"Who's *we*?" the detective asked pointedly.

"A Resistance colleague."

"What's his name?"

"I'd rather not say."

"I told you that your best course was to come clean, Mijnheer Wolters. What's his name?"

"I won't tell you."

"It's your funeral, sir," Van Basten said, jotting something into his notebook. "I understand you had a rented rowboat at your disposal?"

Leo showed a flicker of surprise at the speed of Van Basten's investigation, but he gave a weary nod. "Yes, I had a boat. We put the chest in the boat, rowed out to the middle of the Boerenwetering and dumped the thing into the water. Then I rowed back."

Van Basten reviewed his notes, murmuring to himself as he did so. He seemed pleased at the way things were going and even gave Leo a little wink.

"Shouldn't be much longer, sir. Just a couple of more loose ends to tie up."

"Sure. Ask your questions."

"What does Dries Riphagen have to do with all this?"

Again surprise registered on Leo's face. "So you know about *that*, too, huh? The trouble with this building is that everybody has got his nose in somebody else's business."

"You were telling me about your connection to Riphagen?"

Leo sighed. "The killing of Meijer has nothing to do with Riphagen. I like to gamble. I dropped a bit of money at Riphagen's club. He got tired of waiting for me to pay it off so he came here to collect it. Period. End of story."

"Did you give him the money?"

"No."

"Why not?"

"Because I didn't have it."

"So you still owe him some money?"

"Yes."

"But if you're broke like you say you are, how is it that you gave three months of back rent to your landlord one day after the killing?"

Leo looked calmly at the detective.

"You have been busy, Detective Van Basten. I compliment you on your professionalism."

"So where did you get the money?"

"I got a loan. Enough to pay off the landlord, not enough to settle my gambling debt with Dries Riphagen."

"Who gave you the loan?"

"Does it make a difference?"

"I am not asking these questions to exercise my jaw muscles, son. Who gave you the loan?"

"A family friend."

"I need a name."

"Who said it was a he," Leo said, trying to sound playful and failing. "I don't want to involve this person in all this. It's not fair."

"It's not fair to take the law into your own hands and kill someone, Mijnheer Wolters, as you have just admitted that you've done. You are giving me little choice but to arrest you for murder."

"You can arrest me but you are only going to make a lot of trouble for yourself. I already told you that this was a *Verzetsdaad.* I have friends, powerful friends, who will support my account. And you will find that out soon enough if you arrest me."

Van Basten did not arrest Leo Wolters that day, despite the fact that there were more holes in his story than in a chunk of Leerdammer cheese. It seemed plausible that there was a Resistance connection to this business. What else would the Jew be doing under Leo's roof. The callow young man was definitely not the charitable type, the sort who would risk his life to save a Jew.

Van Basten did not want to endanger Resistance lives by blundering around in areas that were better left alone. He knew that Resistance groups occasionally had people killed. The victims were usually traitors or informers. Whenever he came across a

Resistance connection in a case, he backed off. In one instance, he went further than that, warning a Resistance hit man that fellow police detectives planned to arrest him for the murder of his girlfriend, whom the hit man believed was a Gestapo informer.

Van Basten decided not to take any further action in the Wolters case until he checked with his own Resistance sources.

Chapter 27

She felt warm-soft in his arms as they lay under a satin sheet, touching, caressing, exchanging slow, tender kisses. The capacious hotel bed in which they had spent the better part of three hours reeked of sex and their mingled scents. It was a warm, safe cocoon that both were unwilling to vacate.

"Don't you ever get enough?" Monique whispered.

"Never," said Major Werner Naumann. "Life's not long enough to ever get enough."

Naumann once confided in a letter to his brother that he had never known love in his life and probably never would. His attitude toward women was of the soldier's love-'em-and-leave-'em variety. He was as concupiscent as a rabbit and had bounced his way through the boudoirs of a bevy of young women in Germany, France, Denmark and Poland. At the time of his affair with Monique, Naumann was exchanging intimate letters with a young woman in Berlin and with the teen-age daughter of a professor in Warsaw, and he was carrying on an affair with a German secretary who worked in the office of the *Reichskommissar* for the Netherlands, Arthur Seyss-Inquart.

Naumann never admitted to loving Monique Wolters. The furthest he went was to describe her as "special."

"I was struck by her looks from the moment I first saw her in that bar," he wrote. "She was the most beautiful girl I had ever seen before ... (and) making love to her is like paradise on Earth."

The major knew himself well enough to recognize that he was not yet ready to abandon his freewheeling bachelor ways. He wanted to continue to sample and discard women as if he were at a smorgasbord. On the other hand, Monique was "worth keeping around to see how things develop."

A familiar thought flitted across Naumann's mind as he snuggled with Monique in the luxurious hotel bed. It came whenever he felt warm and safe. A year ago he was in Russia, slogging through knee-high slush, his socks soaked, his feet freezing. He was hungry, exhausted, burning with fever. And there were lots of people trying to kill him. There was no rest from the combat. Every day brought sniper attacks, mortar fire, the deadly bursts of dozens of machine guns. Friends were still there -- sick, starving, dying a little every day. Naumann closed his eyes. When he opened them, he said sternly: "We're spending too much time in this damn hotel room. Don't get me wrong. I've enjoyed every minute, but there's more to life than this. Much more. I want to take you out. Buy you things. Dinner and dancing. I don't like feeling like I am hiding --." But Naumann broke off when he saw a tear in the corner of Monique's eye.

Surprised and concerned, he asked, "What's the matter?"

"Oh, nothing. I'm being silly."

She pulled his head toward her lips and kissed him gently.

"Why were you crying, Monique?" Naumann asked.

"Nothing, I said," but she turned her head away from him.

Naumann rolled off her exquisite body and lay on his side, his head resting on his hand.

"If something is bothering you, you should tell me. We have no secrets, remember? Maybe I can help you."

After a few moments and with great reluctance, Monique said, "It's not me. It's my brother. He's in a lot of trouble and I am very worried about him."

At Naumann's emphatic insistence, Monique told her story. It was a more or less truthful account of Leo's troubles, with a few lies thrown in (and other details omitted) to get past the embarrassing bits.

She said that her brother had run up a large gambling debt -- one thousand guilders -- at the club of that gangster, Dries Riphagen (the name brought a scowl to Naumann's dark young face). In order to get the money to pay off his debt, Leo had done something really stupid. He had heard that a certain Jew was offering a lot of money to anyone who would shelter him. Leo, desperate for cash, agreed to do it. But after little while, he realized he was doing something very stupid and dangerous. He did not want to get arrested by the Gestapo for the sake of a Jew so he asked the man to leave. But the Jew, who like most Jews was very *kapsones,* refused to go, and so they had a terrible fight and her brother wound up accidentally killing the man. It was an accident, Monique assured Naumann. The stupid fool fell and hit his head against the bathtub. In a panic, her brother had put the body in a clothing chest and dumped it in a canal. Unfortunately, that was not the end of the business.

That gangster, Riphagen, had found out that her brother had been harboring a Jew and was now blackmailing him. The gangster wanted five thousand guilders or he would go to the Gestapo.

"But the Jew is now dead," Naumann said. "Riphagen's hold over your brother is gone."

"Oh, Werner," said Monique, stroking his hair. Her tone was that of a woman of the world speaking to a naive schoolboy. "You're a soldier and you know how to take care of yourself. My brother is weak, an easy target for someone like Riphagen. He won't let my brother off the hook, even if the Jew's now dead. He is going to demand five thousand guilders and if he doesn't get it --" Another tear rolled down Monique's cheek.

They lay quietly, Naumann staring at the ceiling.

"What was the Jew's name?" he finally asked.

"The Jew? Meijer. Herman Meijer." Monique sighed. "I know it's terrible to speak ill of the dead, but he was an odious little man. I know my brother did wrong bringing this man into our home but he was desperate for money. When this Meijer offered to pay him if he could hide in our apartment, my brother saw a way of getting out of hot water he was in."

"How did your brother happen to know this Jew?"

"At the City Theatre. They both worked there part-time as handymen. My brother told me that the Jew had been hiding out with another family -- I don't know their name -- but he got into a big argument with them and they kicked him out. He was scared out of his wits and he begged my brother to help him."

Naturally, Monique did not mention that Meijer was a forger, nor did she divulge his escape from the Hollandsche Schouwburg or his clandestine work for the Resistance. She would have had to have been an imbecile to reveal those things to an SS man, something Monique definitely was not.

"Does your brother have the thousand guilders?" Naumann asked.

"Yes, of course. He borrowed the money so that he could pay off the gambling debt."

"Give it to me."

"Give it to *you*?" Monique was genuinely surprised. "Of course, darling, but why? What are you going to do?"

"I think I can arrange things so Herr Riphagen never bothers your brother again."

"But --"

The SS major shushed her with a kiss on the cheek. "Trust me," he said. "Get the money to me as soon as possible."

Two days later, SS-Major Werner Naumann stood in the Euterpestraat office of Willi Lages and watched with a smirk as the Gestapo *Befehlshaber* read the report he had presented to him.

Lages read the document through with stoic calm before laying it on the desk and looking up at Naumann.

"What is this, Herr Sturmbannfuhrer?"

"It's a report about you that I intend to present to General Rauter today in The Hague."

"I see." Lages picked up the report and began to read it aloud. "To SS-Gruppenfuhrer Rauter, Commander of the Reich's Security Services in the Netherlands. Sir: It is my unpleasant duty to inform you that Willi Lages, the *Befehlshaber* for the *Geheime Staatspolizei* in Amsterdam, is unfit for command and should be recalled immediately to answer charges of incompetence, grand larceny and treason."

"Through his laziness and ineptitude, the perpetrators of the *Bevolkingsregister* fire still have not been apprehended, this despite the fact that considerable resources of men and equipment have been put under his command."

"Morale in the SS and the SD in Amsterdam is very low. It is known throughout the ranks that the *Befehlshaber* has devoted much of his energies to personal enrichment at the expense of serving the Reich. *Befehlshaber* Lages has taken over a warehouse on the Prins Hendrikskade, which he uses to store antique furniture, rugs, paintings, statues and other *objets d'art,* which by rights, should have been turned over to the Office of War Contraband. Items stored in this warehouse are secretly being transported to Germany via official vehicles and delivered to the Berlin home of the *Befehlshaber.*"

Lages put down the report and rubbed his eyes. "Why are you showing this to me, Herr Sturmbannfuhrer?"

"I have a second report I want you to see, Herr Lages." Naumann removed the document from a thin briefcase he held under his arm and passed it to the Gestapo chief who took it and began to read. He read the document with the same impassive expression as before and when he finished, he slid it across the desk to Naumann.

"What is the meaning of all this, Naumann?"

"I have written two reports to General Rauter: one charging you with grave dereliction of duty, the other complimenting your skill and competence and recommending that you be left in command of the Gestapo in Amsterdam, even though you have so far been unable to catch the criminals."

"You have not signed either report, Herr Sturmbannfuhrer," Lages said dryly.

"It will be up to you, Herr Lages, which report I sign and present to the general."

"Then I ask you again, what is it that you want?"

"A favor."

A favor! The words were like music to Lages' furry ears. He was now on familiar ground. Lages had been bargaining with crooks, stool pigeons, bureaucrats, judges, fellow cops and Gestapo colleagues his entire professional life. Nothing bad would happen to him now. Not when a little quid pro quo could be quietly arranged.

"What's the favor?" he asked, his voice tired, indifferent.

"I understand that the Gestapo has on its payroll a certain informer by the name of Riphagen."

"What of it?"

"He has been blackmailing a man. The man owes him a sum of money from a gambling debt but Riphagen also found out that the guy was sheltering a Jew and now he's blackmailing him."

Lages' eyebrows went up. "Continue."

"This man has since killed the Jew he was hiding but Riphagen is still trying to blackmail him. Riphagen is demanding five thousand guilders. What I want of you is this: I want you to contact this informer of yours and order him never to bother this man or his family again. Period."

Naumann counted out five hundred guilders and put it on Lages' desk. "This is the money that this Riphagen is owed from the gambling debt. Tell him to take it and be satisfied with it. And make sure he gets the message never to bother this man or his family again."

Lages kept his face as blank as a plank when he asked, "What is this to you, Naumann? Why are you involving yourself in this trivial nonsense?"

"Personal matter."

"I see." There was not a hint in Lages' expression that he already knew the major and a young Dutch woman were "screwing their brains out" nightly at the Hotel Krasnapolsky. Lages correctly guessed that the guy in question was a brother or some other relative of the woman's.

"You surprise me, Naumann," Lages said, leaning back in his big chair. "I didn't know you were such a skilled hand at these sort of games. Quite frankly, I put you down as -- if you will forgive my bluntness -- as a stupid brute. All brawn and no brain. And now I come to find out that you have currents of guile and cunning I never detected. These hidden talents of yours indeed come as quite a shock. And a reminder of the dangers of underestimating one's colleagues. Now tell me a little bit about this killing you mentioned."

Naumann looked surprised. "Is that relevant."

"If it weren't relevant, I wouldn't ask, Herr Sturmbannfuhrer."

"You have yet to tell me which report you want me to submit to General Rauter," Naumann said.

"I think we can dispense with the games, Naumann. The terms you proposed are acceptable. I will arrange to have a word with the gangster -- Riphagen. I think we can convince him to cooperate."

"Today, Herr Lages. I want you to get him in here today."

"That's a bit quick, Naumann, but let's see if it can be arranged." Lages picked up a phone and said to his secretary, "Connect me with Capt. Schmidt. Karl Schmidt in *Judenreferat* IV-B-4."

A moment later, Lages was talking to the SD captain, who worked out of a cramped office on the second floor of the Gestapo building.

"Karl, I urgently need to speak to one of your informants -- Dries Riphagen. Send a couple of men around to his club. I want him in my office by two o'clock this afternoon. Understood? Good."

Lages hung up the phone and said, "Satisfied?"

Naumann nodded.

"Now tell me about this killing of the Jew."

"Frankly, I don't have many details. This man I was talking about who's being blackmailed by Riphagen -- "

"What's his name?"

Naumann stared at the Gestapo commander.

"I don't think it is wise to operate with my head in a bag, Naumann," Lages said soothingly. "If I am going to stick out my neck, I need to know some basic facts. Now what is this man's name?"

"Leo Wolters."

"And what's the name of the Jew he killed?"

"Meijer. Herman Meijer."

"Now tell me about the killing."

"There's not much to tell, Herr Lages," Naumann said. "Wolters was in debt to this gangster. He needed money quickly. The Jew offered to pay him some money to hide him. Wolters accepted. They later got into a fight and Wolters killed him."

"What did he do with the body?"

"He put it in a clothing chest and dumped it into a canal."

The clothing chest rang a bell in Lages' cop memory. He had seen a report on the killing a few days before.

"What canal?" he asked.

"The Boerenwetering."

Yes, that fit. That was the name of the canal that Lages had seen in the report. He nearly smiled at the irony. The Boerenwetering was a stone's throw from the Gestapo headquarters on the Euterpestraat.

"Very Good, Naumann," Lages said. "Now that I have a few details, I can help you with a clear conscience. It is, of course, a grave crime to shelter a Jew. But this man seems to have atoned for his misdeed by killing the criminal. I don't think we have to pursue it any further. As for this business with Riphagen, leave it to me." Lages pointed to the money on the desk. "I think we can persuade Mr. Riphagen to be satisfied with five hundred guilders. When are you going to The Hague?"

"Tomorrow morning."

"Well, I wish you a good trip, Herr Sturmbannfuhrer. Please give my regards to the general."

Lages stood up and extended his hand across the desk. Naumann shook it, clicked his heels and left the office.

The Gestapo commander took a cigar from the humidor on his desk and lit it. A most informative interview, he thought, blowing a lazy smoke ring toward the ceiling. He now had enough on Naumann to put that son of a bitch away for good. Attempted blackmail of a Party official, obstruction of justice, interfering with an official investigation, an accessory after the fact to murder, not to mention the security implications. Naumann was fraternizing with a woman whose brother was sheltering a Jew. Maybe he even used his position with the SS to aid and abet the crime. Yes, it was dynamite, but Lages was not prepared to light the fuse just yet. Let the son of a bitch present his report extolling Lages' investigative skills to General Rauter. Now that he had the dynamite, he could detonate it whenever he wished.

"Did you hear all of that, Lt. Rensmann?" he called out.

A door behind his desk opened and a young man wearing the black uniform of the SD emerged from the small inner office.

"Every word, sir," said Lt. Karl-Dietrich Rensmann. Rensmann, a blond, freckled-faced young man of twenty-two, served Lages' as an aide and general factotum. Among his non-official duties was arranging the shipment of the *Befehlshaber*'s war booty back to Germany.

"What did you make out of all of that, Rensmann?"

"I think the major has gotten himself in over his head with that Dutch girl he's been screwing, pardon my language, sir."

"Never mind. Your assessment is spot on. But that's a story for another day. In the meantime, it looks like our SS friend has inadvertently helped us close the books on a murder case."

"You mean the corpse, in the chest, sir?"

"Indeed I do. Bring me the file, Rensmann, and let's have a look."

The lieutenant disappeared into the inner office and returned with a thin dossier which he opened and placed on Lages' desk.

The file contained only a copy of the first police report and a cursory follow-up report written by the investigator on the case, Detective-Adjutant Rob van Basten.

"Hmmm, I see my old friend Van Basten has been assigned to the case. And as usual, he has been less than forthcoming with the Gestapo. He tells us virtually nothing in this follow-up report. The victim is still called a John Doe. No suspect is mentioned. He said he interviewed a number of people but he does not provide their names. He's been investigating this case for nearly a week. Is it possible that after five minutes, we know more about it than he does?"

"That hardly seems possible sir," said Rensmann.

"I share that opinion, lieutenant. It hardly seems possible."

Lages closed the file, leaned back in his chair and blew another smoke ring.

"We can not be played for fools, Rensmann," Lages said. "And that's what Detective Van Basten -- and some of his colleagues -- is doing. They're treating us as if we're fools. And we're letting them do it because it's politic to maintain good relations with the local constabulary."

"Can they really think that we don't know what they're all about? Hiding information, protecting the Resistance, dealing in the black market whenever they feel like it. In general, just thumbing their noses at us?"

Lages was quiet for a moment as he stared into the blue-white haze above his desk.

"You know, Rensmann," he finally said. "I think it's about time that we teach these fellows a lesson. A lesson they're never going to forget."

Chapter 28

The meeting was arranged quickly and in the utmost secrecy.

Through his Resistance contacts, Adjutant-Detective Rob van Basten learned that Leo Wolters was a sometimes errand boy for Maarten Dijkstra's Artists Resistance Movement. Those same sources -- when told of the urgency of the matter -- were able to set up an interview with the infamous Dijkstra, at that time the most wanted man in the Netherlands. Recognition signals were agreed upon. Van Basten said he would wear a trilby hat, have a pipe in his mouth and would be carrying a straw shopping bag. Nothing about Dijkstra's appearance was relayed to the policeman. The Resistance leader would make the contact if and when he thought it safe to do so.

The meeting took place on a bright, cold morning amid the hustle and bustle of the Albert Cuyp street market. Carrying his straw basket, Van Basten walked slowly past the stalls which, before the war, overflowed with produce, meat, fish, grains, spices, pasta, coffee and tea, honey and jam and canned delicacies from around the world. The market still attracted big crowds even though there was a lot less around to buy. A lot less.

The detective walked to the end of the street, turned around and walked slowly back, pausing to gaze at the wares of one stall, then another. He was eyeballing a meager selection of apples, braving the frantic elbows and umbrellas of housewives fighting for food for the dinner table, when a man spoke softly into his ear.

"Mijnheer Van Basten?"

"Yes."

"Would you like to get out of this cold?"

"That would be nice."

"Follow me, then. I know a nice spot."

The stout detective fell into step beside a slight, keen-looking, middle-aged man wearing a sturdy overcoat, thick gray scarf and a woolen cap. In profile, the only features that stood out were the taut lines around his mouth and a sharp, beaklike nose.

They walked in silence for a couple of minutes, pushing their way through the throng of bickering shoppers. After they cleared most of the crush, Dijkstra, staring straight ahead, said quietly, "I owe you a debt of thanks, detective, for the Olthof business." Jan Olthof was a notorious Gestapo informer who was liquidated by the Resistance earlier in the year. Though Dijkstra was not personally involved in the assassination, which was handled by another group, he was among the Resistance leaders who voted by secret ballot to have Olthof -- a prominent newspaper publisher before the war -- killed.

"I hear your effort to, ah-- short-circuit the police investigation got you into some trouble with your bosses -- and the Gestapo," Dijkstra said.

"Nothing I couldn't handle," said Van Basten.

As they reached the corner of the Ferdinand Bolstraat, Van Basten paused casually in front of a large store window and peered into the glass.

"You needn't worry," Dijkstra said. "Our backs are being watched."

The Resistance leader led the way to a small cafe on the Ferdinand Bolstraat where they seated themselves at a table at the rear. Dijkstra loosened his gray scarf, leaving the material draped over his shoulder. He kept his coat and cap on.

"That was a brilliant piece of work at the *Bevolkingsregister*," Van Basten said jovially, settling into his chair. "That was your handiwork, right?"

Dijktra's thin lips spread in an enigmatic smile. "Why have you asked for this meeting, Adjutant-Detective Van Basten?"

Well, if that's the way he wants to play it, Van Basten thought.

"How well do you know Leo Wolters?" asked the policeman.

"Why do you want to know?" came the reply.

Van Basten looked directly into the guarded brown eyes of the most wanted man in the Netherlands. He admired the man more than he could articulate but this was business. Van Basten gave his best I'm-the-copper-and-I'll-ask-the-questions stare. Dijkstra got the message.

"I must apologize for being what must seem to you as evasive and uncooperative, detective, but unfortunately that's the way it's going to be until I'm satisfied about you and your reasons for seeking this interview. Now why do you want to know about Leo Wolters and how well I know him?"

"I'm investigating a homicide involving Leo Wolters," Van Basten said.

If Maarten Dijkstra was surprised by the news, he did not show it. "Who is Leo supposed to have killed?" he asked.

"It's not a matter of *supposed to have*, sir," the detective said. "Mijnheer Wolters *admitted* the killing. He killed a Jewish man who had been hiding under his roof."

Dijkstra tried to keep his face expressionless, but to Van Basten's experienced eyes, the Resistance leader's reaction was as easy to read as a road map. The slight furrow above the brow, the intense stare. Dijkstra might as well have leaped from his chair in shock and outrage.

"The victim's name was Meijer," Van Basten went on. "Did you know him."

Dijkstra nodded slowly.

"Who was he?"

"One of my men," said Dijkstra.

"Is Leo Wolters also a member of your group?"

Dijkstra considered his words carefully. "Not exactly. He does a little work for us occasionally."

After a moment, Dijkstra said, "I'm too old to be playing games, detective. I'm sure you know or can guess that the killing you mentioned is of considerable interest to me. I hope you will share with me what details you can and I will give you what background I can."

Van Basten nodded. "Agreed. Perhaps we can start by you telling me how Meijer came to be living under Wolters' roof."

"Herman Meijer was doing work for us. He was a very able forger, but you probably already knew that."

Van Basten did know it. Wolters had told him. And he had subsequently unearthed Meijer's extensive rap sheet from CID files.

"He was doing important work for us when he was picked up by the Germans during a routine roundup of Jews. They put him in the Schouwburg," Dijkstra continued. "We were able to arrange his release and we put him in with Leo Wolters while he finished his work for us."

"Mijnheer Wolters described the killing of Meijer as a *Verzetsdaad*?"

"A *Vetzetsdaad*?" Dijkstra blurted out, astonished.

"Yes. A Resistance act. Do you know anything about that?"

"Nothing. I don't know what the hell he's talking about."

"You didn't sanction the killing?"

"Of course not! Meijer was an important member of my group. He was far more valuable to me than Leo Wolters."

"Wolters said that Meijer had become paranoid. That he thought Wolters was planning to turn him in to the Germans. Further, he said that Meijer was yelling and making a big fuss in Wolters' apartment. Do you know anything about that?"

"Nothing."

"He also said a member of the Resistance helped him dispose of the body."

Dijkstra shook his head. "This is incredible," he said. "Simply incredible."

"How well do you know Leo Wolters?" asked the detective.

Dijkstra again took his time before answering. "I've known him several years. He was a student of mine before the war. He's been at parties at my house with other students. I've known him awhile but I can't say that I know him well. If someone asked me if I thought him capable of murder, I would have laughed at the idea. Leo killing somebody? Ridiculous. He was a soft, idle rich man's son when I first met him and I'm afraid that's how I still see him. I would have said he didn't have the backbone to kill another human being. But as you can see, I may not be the keenest judge of character."

"What do you know about Leo's sister?"

"Monqiue? Next to nothing. I met her once or twice. Very beautiful. A bit on the wild side, I've heard."

"Do you think that she's capable of murder?"

"I honestly haven't a clue. Was she somehow involved in this business?"

Van Basten nodded.

"I would very much appreciate it, detective, if you told me what you know about this murder. The loss of Herman Meijer is a severe one for us. We will be looking into it ourselves."

The policeman gave the Resistance leader a severe look. "I caution you against taking the law into your own hands, Mijnheer Dijkstra."

Dijkstra gave a bark of laughter. It came out involuntarily, like a sudden burp, a harsh, scornful laugh that took Van Basten by surprise.

"*Law?*" Dijkstra mocked. "*What law?* There is no law in Holland today. The world has been turned upside down. The lunatics are running the asylum."

"There is still the rule of law in this country, Mijnheer Dijkstra," the cop admonished. "You would be well advised to remember that."

"Don't threaten me, detective," Dijkstra said quietly. "As for the rule of law, *we* are the law in this country. Not the Nazis and not you."

The men glared at each other, but just for an instant. Neither wanted the meeting to turn unpleasant.

"I apologize for my intemperate remarks, detective," Dijkstra said. "I think the pressure of all these months on the lam has taken its toll on my manners."

"Quite understandable. Consider it forgotten."

Van Basten went on to share with Dijkstra most of what he knew about the case. He said that the motive for the killing appeared to be money; that Leo Wolters had fallen behind in his rent and probably owed money to a gangster named Riphagen. Shortly after the murder, Leo had paid of his landlord in full. Conclusion: Meijer had some money and Leo murdered him for it.

The detective went on to give Leo's side of the story. That Meijer had become troublesome, paranoid, that he had threatened to give Leo's name to the Germans if he were ever captured. Leo said he had become concerned for his own safety, as well as the security of his Resistance colleagues, so he killed Meijer.

Dijkstra listened to it all in grim silence and then asked a question.

"Have the *moffen* shown any interest in this case?"

"I'm afraid so," Van Basten answered. "An SD man named Rensmann has been calling me every day for an update. I've told him very little. I have not given him the name of the victim or the name of the suspect but I can't stonewall the Gestapo forever."

"Of course not. But now I have to ask a very big favor of you and I know that you're not going to like it."

"What is it?"

"I am asking you not to arrest Leo Wolters."

"That is indeed a remarkable request," Van Basten said dryly.

"If you arrest Leo Wolters, the Gestapo may show up at your jail and take him off your hands," Dijkstra said. "You've already told me that they are showing an interest in this case. And they won't have to do much to get Leo to talk. If they yell at him once, he will begin to babble like an Amazon parrot. Leo doesn't know a great deal about our organization, at least, I think he doesn't, but he just might know something that the Gestapo will find useful."

"So what do you suggest?"

"Leave him to us."

"I see."

Van Basten had become so absorbed in the conversation that he had neglected to keep an eye on the comings and goings of the bar. He suddenly looked up and swept the premises with his eyes. To his surprise, they were the only two people in the establishment. Even he barman had vanished.

Dijkstra smiled. "I wanted this meeting to be private," he explained.

Van Basten nodded. "You seem to have quite a bit of *protectie* in this town," the cop said with genuine admiration.

"I can get things done. What about my request, adjutant-detective?"

"Consider it granted, at least for the time being. Now that I have spoken to you and ascertained that Wolters was telling the truth, at least with respect to his Resistance connections, I see no pressing reason to arrest him at this time."

Dijkstra offered his hand. As Van Basten shook it, he said, "But I meant what I said about taking the law into your own hand, mijnheer."

"I know you did," Dijkstra said with another of his enigmatic smiles. "*Fiat justitia.*"

"*Et ruant coeli,*" Van Basten responded.

The detective caught the surprise in the other man's eyes.

"It was a favorite saying of one of the priests at school," said Van Basten. "Let justice be served, though the heavens fall."

Dijkstra grinned and clapped him on the back. "Hopefully we will meet again some day -- under less stressful circumstances. Have a few beers and tell some tall tales."

"I would like that."

"For the time being, then, *tot ziens*. I think it's better that we leave separately. You can go out the front door."

"And you?"

"I'll see myself out later."

Van Basten gave a curt nod and left. They would never see each other again.

That afternoon, Dries Riphagen found himself playing host to some unwanted guests, a couple of murderous-looking bruisers from the Gestapo.

The German enforcers were led into Riphagen's office by a terrified dealer who said, "The Gestapo's here to see you, Dries," then he scampered back to his card table.

An alarm went off in Riphagen's head. He did not know these Germans, which meant that the visit had nothing to do with his ongoing business dealings with the Gestapo. What else could they be there for? He offered them a seat, but the Germans declined. Cigars were also waved away.

"Then what do you want?" the Dutch Al Capone asked gruffly in German.

"We want you, Herr Riphagen," said the smaller of the two, Capt. Ludwig Schenck. "*Befehlshaber* Willi Lages would like to see you immediately at the Euterpestraat."

"About what?"

"He did not give a reason, Herr Riphagen. My suggestion is that you don't waste time with a lot of pointless questions and you come with us. Now!"

Through sheer willpower, the Dutch Al Capone retained the look of mild annoyance on his face. Every instinct in his body was yelling, "Danger! Get away!" but he dared not show fear. Though his bowels were turning to water, his mind was racing, skimming possibilities, ways and means. If he could get out of the office, he had a better than even chance of getting away. There were lots of people who would hide him. To the end of the war, if necessary. But why push the panic button? He honestly had no clue why the Gestapo wanted with him.

After glaring at the Germans for a moment, Riphagen said, "Very well. I suppose we shouldn't keep the *Befehlshaber* waiting. I'll call my driver."

He was reaching for his phone when the other enforcer, a towering brute with crew cut blond hair, yelled, "*Nein.*" The menacing look on the German's face alone was enough to stay Riphagen's hand.

"You won't need your driver, Herr Riphagen," said Capt. Schenck. "We have a car. Egon, get Mr. Riphagen's coat."

Egon Haase was once described by a colleague as a "concrete block with lips." Willi Lages had purposely sent the fearsome Gestapo examiner to minimize the chance of any resistance from the gangster. Haase grabbed Riphagen's overcoat from a rack and thrust it into his arms.

Riphagen put on his coat and glumly accompanied the Gestapo men to their car. He tried to question Schenck during the ride to the Euterpestraat but the captain dismissed his inquiries with a curt, "You'll know soon enough."

Haase parked the car across the street from the graceful, three-story red-brick building with its dainty, white-trimmed windows that housed the Gestapo. Even a hard case like Riphagen, who had been in the building a number of times, was struck by the grotesque contrast between the elegant exterior and the horrors that went on inside.

With Schenck on one side and Haase on the other, Riphagen was led up the stairs to the third-floor office of *Befehlshaber* Willi Lages.

"Herr Riphagen," Lages said cordially, coming out from behind his desk and limping over to the gangster to offer a handshake. "It's indeed a pleasure to finally meet you. I have heard only good things about your work for us. Capt. Schmidt has been particularly complimentary of your efforts on our behalf. Please sit down."

Riphagen hesitated for a moment before sitting down in a chair near Lages' desk. Lages nodded to the other Gestapo men and they left the office.

"I suppose you are wondering why I asked for this meeting," the *Befehlshaber* said, resuming his seat behind the desk.

"I was wondering that, yeah."

"Well, let me fill you in, then," Lages said pleasantly. "I hope you were not alarmed by this unexpected request for a meeting. I assure you, it's strictly routine. We're both busy men so I'll cut to the chase. "

"I understand you are familiar with a young good-for-nothing named Leo Wolters? I can see by your expression that you are. Good."

"I also understand that this Wolters owes you a sum of money with regard to some imprudent wagering in your club. Further, that you are trying to collect an additional sum from him, let's call it interest on the money he already owes you. Yes?"

Riphagen sat in his chair in dumbfounded silence, stunned by Lages' detailed knowledge of the affair and mystified by the Gestapo man's interest in it.

"I'll make it brief," Lages said. "For reasons that I needn't go into, I would very much like it if you discontinued your efforts to collect any money from Herr Wolters. I must further request that you do not go near him or his family again. Is all of that agreeable to you?"

Riphagen blinked a couple of times but said nothing, so Lages coaxed him on with a gentle, "Yes?"

The gangster nodded slowly.

"Excellent. I knew we could come to some sort of understanding without a lot of fuss. Now that I've told you the bad news, I have a bit of good news for you."

Riphagen sat up, intrigued.

"We've managed to collect the money Herr Wolters owes you from the original gambling debt, so we can square that account right now." Lages opened a desk drawer and pulled out a thin wad of bills bound by a rubber band and placed it on the desk in front of Riphagen. "It's all there but you may count it if you wish."

With a scowl on his face, Riphagen did count it.

"There's only fifty guilders here," he said angrily. "The punk owes me one thousand guilders."

"Really. I had heard the debt was considerably smaller. In fact, I remember feeling puzzled as to why you were so concerned about such a trifling sum."

"What about the rest of my money?" asked the Dutch Al Capone.

"Yes, that is a problem," said Lages. "I'm afraid I can't do much about it at this time, Herr Riphagen. I won't bore you with a long-winded explanation but my hands are indeed tied at the moment. I'm afraid you will have to be satisfied with the fifty guilders, at least for the time being. I apologize for the inconvenience and everything but that's the way it has to be. I hope you understand."

When Riphagen didn't say anything, Lages said, "Well, I guess that covers everything. Sorry again for the inconvenience." Lages pushed a button with his foot and a moment later, a glowering Egon Haase came into the office.

"Sergeant, would you escort Herr Riphagen back to the street? I'm afraid you are going to have to arrange for your own transport back to your club, Herr Riphagen. We are a little understaffed at the moment."

Under Haase's baleful stare, Riphagen stood up and walked toward the door.

"Oh, Herr Riphagen," Lages called out. "I cannot emphasize enough how displeased I would be if I were to learn that anything untoward happed to Herr Wolters or his family. Good afternoon, sir."

Chapter 29

Had Adjutant-Detective Van Basten observed the behavior of Leo Wolters in the days immediately after their meeting, it might have put him in mind of another of the Latin proverbs he learned in school: *Qui male agit odit lucem* – a sinner hates the light.

For several days after that interview, Leo did not leave his flat. Monique did whatever shopping was necessary before disappearing on her own mysterious errands.

Leo was in a terrible state, eating little, sleeping less. He had behaved with poise, almost nonchalance, in front of the detective, but now, for the first time since killing Meijer, he seemed to understand the gravity of his situation. There were powerful forces that wanted his hide, each for different reasons. It would be a race to see who got him first: Maarten Dijkstra, the police or -- God forbid -- the Gestapo or Dries Riphagen.

He hadn't ventured outside for days, terrified that a hit man was lurking nearby, waiting to put a bullet in his head. His apartment, of course, was no sanctuary, either. Riphagen and his thugs had proved that. But at least inside, he would have some warning before he was attacked. He kept a heavy armoire in front of the door, which had to be laboriously moved every time Monique entered and left the flat. He did not own a gun, but there were kitchen knives about, and he made a crude cash by putting an iron padlock in a sock, which he kept with him at all times.

Leo believed that the best way of dealing with the crisis was to let things cool down. He had convinced himself that if he could just stay out of sight awhile, his enemies would lose interest in him. For the first time since leaving his father's home, he considered moving back to the family estate outside of Amsterdam. If an intruder came near the main house, he would be easily spotted, and there were several burly servants around to handle matters. And of course, there were firearms on the property, including shotguns his father used for hunting.

Leo went as far as to call his father and make arrangements to stay there a few weeks, but before that could happen, a messenger of doom *did* arrive at Leo's door in the unlikely form of Saskia Hoogeboom.

On a clear, cold afternoon in late April, Saskia, wearing a scarf and a bulky brown overcoat, walked up to the porch of the Schubertstraat apartment building and rang the bell. And when nobody answered, she rang again. And again.

Finally, somebody pulled on the rope controlling the latch, and the large green entrance door swung open. As she had been directed, Saskia climbed the stairs to the third floor and found Leo standing in the doorway of his apartment, waiting for her.

The two had met a few times before, in those halcyon days before the Occupation, but she had not paid much attention to him. She had seen him at those sherry parties Maarten liked to throw for colleagues and students, but remembered little about him, other than some vague gossip that his father was rich.

"Saskia! Well, this is a pleasant surprise," Leo beamed in his best hail-fellow-well-met voice.

"Gosh, it's been a long time. You're looking well. Come in! Come in! If I knew you were coming, I would've cleaned up the place a bit. No matter. Come in! I'll put the tea on," but Saskia just stood there. The wan, willowy young woman didn't know what to make of this effusive greeting. She had no memory of ever speaking to Leo before, or he to her. But her orders were specific. Don't engage in small talk. Don't dally. Just deliver the message.

"Maarten wants to talk to you," she said quietly.

"What? Now? But I can't. I'm expecting an important call. From my father."

"Keep your voice down," Saskia said sternly. "Yes, now. Maarten says it's urgent."

Suddenly, the joviality disappeared from Leo's face. He just stared at the young woman. Saskia couldn't be sure, but she thought he was on the verge of tears.

"We're wasting time," she said.

Leo nodded slowly. "Just let me get my coat."

He put on his worn sailor's pea jacket, locked the apartment and followed Saskia down the stairs.

"Where are we going?" he asked, falling into step beside her, but she didn't answer.

"You can't tell me where we're going?" he persisted.

"I'm taking you to Maarten," she said.

Leo tried a couple of more times to engage her in conversation but she did not respond. They crossed the Boerenwetering and walked to the Ceintuurbaan, which they followed until it intersected with the Ferdinand Bolstraat. There, they stood at the corner while Saskia looked first in one direction, then another.

"Where's Maarten?" Leo asked, but she didn't answer. A minute ticked away with agonizing slowness, and Leo became more agitated. He was just working up the nerve to walk away when a battered black taxi pulled to the curb.

"You are to get in the taxi," Saskia said.

"What about you?" Leo asked, panic rising, but Saskia had already turned and was walking back along the Ceintuurbaan.

Leo hesitated. He looked into the taxi. There was only the driver inside, a dark-haired young man he didn't recognize. His eyes darted back to Saskia, who was quickly walking away.

"Saskia," he yelled, but she ignored him.

"Get in!" barked the driver.

Leo looked back into the cab. The driver had an automatic leveled at his chest. "Get in, you fool."

"You're going to kill me," Leo blurted out.

"I will kill you if you don't get in. Now, get in!"

Leo meekly got into the back seat and the driver put the car in gear and sped away.

Leo did not dare ask where they were going. The fact they were going anywhere was actually a good sign. If the man had orders to kill him, he could have shot him down in the street and driven off. That was the Resistance way. No doubt about it.

From the Ferdinand Bolstraat, the driver skillfully guided the taxi to the Stadhouderskade, made a left and drove in the direction of the Overtoom. The once-picturesque Stadshouderskade looked barren and eerie. There were no strollers about. No cars. The last of the evergreen trees had been cut down for firewood months ago. They passed the Vondel Park, which remained popular with Amsterdammers despite the heavy presence of German troops, and turned right toward the Leidseplein.

The cab pulled up in front of the Hotel American and Leo was ordered to get out.

"Go into the dining room," the driver said. "You will be met there."

Leo wanted to ask by whom, but a look from the driver shut him up. He got out of the cab and walked into the hotel.

Despite the wartime privations, the hotel managed to retain the raffish elegance from the days when Gertrud Margarete Zelle -- the infamous Mata Hari -- danced there. The dining room was full of men in business suits chatting quietly among themselves. Red-jacketed waiters and white-aproned busboys flitted from table to table. There were also small clusters of mid-level German officers enjoying a late lunch. The rattle of cutlery and the buzz of conversation spoke of a normalness that for a moment eased Leo's fears. He was looking around for Dijkstra when a voice at his ear said, "Don't turn around. Go to the kitchen. To the right."

Leo did what he was told. He found his way to the kitchen, where a dozen men and women were engaged in one task or another. He looked around but there was still no sign of Dijkstra. Waiters picked up plates of food and went, cooks cut up vegetables and a man who seemed to be the head chef went around tasting sauces and nodding approvingly. But still no Dijkstra.

Finally the "head chef," or whoever he was, walked over to him. "Go into the office. That way," he said quietly.

Leo went into the small office adjacent to the kitchen and saw Maarten Dijkstra sitting alone at a desk, reading *De Telegraaf.* Like most of the patrons in the dining room, the Resistance leader was wearing a business suit, and even had a crisply folded white handkerchief in his breast pocket. The last time Leo had seen Dijkstra wearing a suit was before the war. It took him a split-second to recognize him.

"You must be hard up for reading material to be looking at that collaborationist rag," Leo said, with a disastrous stab at flippancy.

Dijkstra did not smile or even offer to shake hands. He stared coldly at his former pupil. "Sit down, Leo."

Leo, his brittle smile disintegrating, tried to hide his fright with a rush of words.

"Look, Maarten. I know why you sent for me. I --"

"Shut up, Leo."

Leo's next words died on his lips and he sat down at the desk, looking as forlorn as a puppy that had just been whacked with a newspaper.

Dijkstra stood up and closed the office door. He put a cigarette to his lips, lit it and watched the smoke drift toward the ceiling. He seemed in no hurry to speak, and when he finally did, the words came out in a tired monotone.

"Why did you kill Herman, Leo?"

Leo was petrified. The gravity of those words had hit him like a blow to the heart. In desperation, he was about to blurt out something when Dijkstra again stopped him.

"I suggest you think over very carefully what you are about to tell me, Leo. You are going to get only one chance to tell your story."

By now tears were rolling down Leo's cheeks.

"I *had* to kill him, Maarten. Please believe me. I *had* to. Herman was going crazy. He thought I was about to denounce him to the Gestapo. He said if he was arrested, he'd bring the Gestapo back to my door. Those were his very words. It's the truth, Maarten. I swear it's the truth. You can ask Cees. He saw some of it. Herman was cracking up. He was becoming a security risk. For me, for you, for the whole group. I had to do it. It's the truth. I swear it."

Leo broke down. "It's the truth, Maarten," he sobbed. "It's the truth."

Dijkstra stood by the door smoking, watching Leo, saying nothing. Leo covered his face and blabbered on, trying to fill the void of Dijkstra's silence. "I had to do it. I swear. I had to do it."

The Resistance leader smoked leisurely while continuing to watch his former student. And when the butt had all but disappeared between his fingers, he flicked away the final threads of tobacco and walked to the desk where his overcoat, shawl and snap-brim hat lay.

"It's too dangerous for you to go back to your flat, Leo," he said, wrapping the thick woolen shawl around his neck. "If the police arrest you, there's a good chance the Gestapo will get hold of you, and obviously we can't have that. For your protection as well as ours, you're going to have to disappear for a while."

What did he mean? Leo lifted his head and scanned Dijkstra's face. Was he going to live or die? But Dijstra betrayed nothing.

"I want you to walk out through the dining room ahead of me," Dijkstra said. "The taxi is waiting outside. Just get in and wait for me."

Leo stood up on leaden legs. "Please, Maarten --," he started to say, but Dijkstra again held up a hand.

"Just do what I say, Leo. Everything is going to be okay."

Leo nodded numbly. He opened the office door and walked out. He kept his eyes down, not looking at anybody as he passed through the kitchen on the way to the dining room. He had no idea if Dijkstra was following behind him or not.

In the dining room, the lunchtime crowd had thinned, but there were still plenty of *moffen* about the place. Then he thought: now is the time to make a run for it. Dijkstra wouldn't dare try to stop him under these circumstances. But the idea came into his mind stillborn. Leo knew he didn't have the spine for that sort of adventure.

He crossed the dining room and had almost reached the hotel lobby when he came face to face with the last person he expected to see. Both stopped and gaped.

"Leo!" said a flustered Monique. "I thought you were home."

Leo was about to reply when he noticed that his sister was not alone. A tall young man in a dark German uniform was at her side. Leo was so surprised he couldn't speak. What was Monique doing with the *mof.* His eyes shifted from the German to Monique, then back to the German.

The German smiled and nodded, but his eyes did not remain long on Leo. A slightly puzzled look appeared on the German's face as he noticed, then focused on the man in the fedora who was walking behind Leo. Their eyes met and locked and for one brief instant, time seemed to stand still. Witnesses would later recall in graphic detail what transpired in the next few moments, as if they had watched a slow-motion film sequence. There were, of course, many conflicting statements, which is normal in cases when people going about their business suddenly witness dramatic events. But there was also general agreement on a number of points.

To this day, there are those who swear that the German in the SS uniform uttered a single word -- "Dijkstra!" -- before all hell broke loose.

The hat-clad man so identified sprang forward, knocked Leo violently aside and bolted for the doorway, but the German was too quick for him. He lunged at the Resistance leader and managed to grab his coat. For a moment, the two men grappled violently, both trying to draw their pistols. Dijkstra's weapon was in his overcoat pocket and he was faster on the draw. He brought the gun down hard on the German's skull and pushed him away, then continued his dash for the lobby.

The stunned German got his service pistol out and snapped off one shot. Dijkstra staggered but kept going. The German took aim and three more shots rang out -- *but they did not come from his gun.*

A young waiter, later identified as Jan Middelburg, had pulled a revolver from under his red jacket and fired three bullets into the back of the German's head from near point-blank range. Monique screamed as her lover --Werner Naumann -- collapsed in a bloody heap near her feet. He was probably dead by the time he hit the floor.

Though badly wounded himself, Dijkstra managed to get out of the hotel and into the waiting cab. From outside, witnesses heard shouting, the screech of tires and more gunshots.

Back in the dining room, Jan Middelburg was frantically trying to get out of the building. He pushed aside several people as he ran toward the kitchen. Since there was no rear door there, he apparently intended to climb out the kitchen office window.

He barreled into the kitchen at full tilt, throwing down carts of dishes in an effort to slow up his pursuers. As the kitchen staff scurried out of the way, Middelburg looked wildly around, trying to remember where the office was. Several soldiers stormed in and Middelburg fired once, sending the Germans ducking for cover.

"Get out of the way," he shouted at a big, fat cook who stood between him and the office. Middelburg tried to fling the man aside, but it was too late. Arms were around him now. He shook off one attacker but another tackled him at the legs and brought him to the floor. He tried to get to his feet but another German had jumped on his back and was pulling on his right arm.

Middelburg still had the revolver in his right hand. With strength borne of desperation, he managed to pull his arm free and bring the gun to his face. Someone -- possibly one of the cooks -- screamed, "No," just as the young freedom fighter pulled the trigger.

There was bedlam in the dining room. Women were screaming. Germans with weapons drawn rushed back and forth. A waiter who stooped to help the fallen SS man was kicked aside by a civilian who yelled in German, "Stay back or you will be shot!" Sirens could be heard outside and somebody said an ambulance had been called.

In all the confusion at the front and rear of the hotel, no one noticed when Leo slipped an arm around his shaking sister and led her away.

Chapter 30

At the time of the gun battle at the Hotel American, Adjutant-Detective Rob van Basten was at home. It was his day off and he was ensconced in a spare bedroom-turned-office, which he fondly referred to as his *plekkie* -- his spot. The office was Van Basten's refuge from the world. He went there to read, or ruminate, or just relax and smoke. The furnishings were Spartan: a turn-of-the-century desk picked up at a flea market, a shelf full of *roman policiers,* which he devoured, and a well-worn green sofa. The walls, too, were bare, save for an up-to-date calendar above his desk, and a decent copy of an 18th century print showing the sinking of the Dutch East Indiaman *Woestduijn.*

On that day, Van Basten was reading on the sofa, but it was not one of his French mysteries. He was absorbed in a top secret police dossier labeled *The Culture Chamber.*

Like records from his own cases, this file was not kept at CID. The detective who assembled the data was officially assigned to the burglary detail, but his unofficial duties were far more sensitive: he was a liaison between the police department and the Resistance. This fact was known to very few officers, and if he and Van Basten had not been old drinking buddies, it would not have been known to Van Basten.

Until then, Van Basten knew little about the Nazi-controlled Culture Chamber. He read how the hated bureau was the springboard for Maarten Dijkstra's Artists' Resistance Movement, and how Dijkstra stormed out of the emergency meeting of artists guilds at the City Theatre in 1942 with the strongbox of members' dues under his arm.

"*How much is in there?*" Dijkstra had asked the treasurer, after his blistering speech to his fellow artists.

"*About five thousand guilders,*" the treasurer replied.

Dijkstra had picked up the chest and walked out of the theatre, followed by Cees Spanjaard, Hugo de Jong, Jeroen van Duin and others. Nobody tried to stop them.

Shortly thereafter, the raids began: the holdup of the German army payroll office in Amsterdam, the theft of food ration coupons from a Nazi warehouse in The Hague, the liberation of two Resistance men from the Utrecht municipal jail. And, of course, the attack on the *Bevolkingsregister* in Amsterdam.

All of this information was in the file Van Basten had in front of him. But there was more. Much more (to be caught by the Germans with such information meant certain death).

There was a list of Dijkstra's closest associates and their known addresses. There were many details about his operations, details that would not become public until after the war. It was from the file, for example, that Van Basten first learned of the clandestine printing plant Dijkstra had set up in the harbor with help from his printer-friend Romke Dietvorst. The plant that churned out thousands of identity cards, food coupons, residency permits, work permits and other documents, which were distributed to *onderduikers* all over the country.

The detective was so engrossed in the dossier, he did not hear his wife come in.

"I've been calling you, Rob. You have a phone call."

"Jesus, Sylvia! Don't sneak up on a man like that." He had tried for years to discourage his wife from coming into the office when he was there, but for the life of him, he could not get her to comply.

"I didn't sneak up on you, Rob," she said indignantly. "And I told you fifteen minutes ago your dinner was ready."

With a sigh, Van Basten put down the file and went to the living room to take the call.

"Van Basten," he said.

"Rob, it's Hookstra."

"Yeah, Len?" It had to be urgent for his partner to be calling him on his day off.

"The shit's hit the fan, Rob. There's been some kind of shootout at the Hotel American. A real OK Corral. An SS major was killed. So was a Resistance man. The *moffen* are in an uproar. They think Maarten Dijkstra is responsible. There's a report Dijkstra was wounded, but he apparently got away. The Gestapo's been on the blower to the chief, and the chief has called for all hands on deck. Even guys who are off."

"Why."

"I don't know. Maybe the Gestapo is going to draft us to look for Dijkstra. I don't know but the chief wants everybody here."

Van Basten tried to concentrate, but so many thoughts were competing for attention. The mention of Dijkstra immediately brought another name to mind: that punk Leo Wolters. It was just a hunch, but the detective was sure Wolters was somehow mixed up in this.

"Rob! Did you hear me?"

"I heard you. I heard you. Listen, Len. Do me a favor. Tell the chief I'll be in but I have to do something first."

"This is urgent business, Rob. That means drop everything and get over here."

"What I have to do is also urgent."

"What's that?"

"Arrest a murderer."

Van Basten hung up. When he turned around, he saw his wife standing there.

"What are you looking so grim about? he asked.

"Because you are. What's going on?"

"Did you hear any of that?"

"I heard you say you have to arrest a murderer."

"And I do." He gave his wife a peck on the cheek before hurrying back to his office for the file. He made sure all of the papers were together, then put the file with his own secreted records. From a desk drawer he took out a small automatic and slipped it into his pocket. He also took out a rumpled tie (Van Basten had his "standards" when making arrests, and they included wearing a tie).

As her husband hurried around, Sylvia van Basten took his untouched plate and put it in the oven. Not for the first time would a meal have to be held over.

"When will you be home?"

"I don't know, Sylvia. Everything's a mess at the moment. I hope to be home in a few hours, but no promises."

No promises. It had been said so often, it had become a joke between them.

But Van Basten wasn't smiling as he took his hat and coat and kissed his wife good-bye.

"I'll give you a call," he said. He opened the front door, then stopped short.

"Herr Van Basten?"

There were two men on the stoop -- one tall and massive, the other smaller, older. They both wore trench coats.

"Who the devil are you?" Van Basten demanded.

The smaller man reached under his coat and produced a dog tag-like piece of metal that he wore on a chain around his neck. He held it out for Van Basten, but the detective barely glanced at it. He knew what it was.

"What do you want?"

"It's not what we want," said the man. Van Basten hated Dutch words coming from a German's mouth. "Herr Lages would like to see you at the Euterpestraat. At once."

Before Van Basten could protest, the man's mountainous companion stepped forward, pushed the detective's arms in the air and roughly patted him down.

"Don't resist him, Herr Van Basten," said the other. "He's not a gentle man."

Van Basten's small automatic was quickly found and removed, as were his wallet, keys and pocket watch.

Sylvia van Basten, who had watched the scene with mounting terror from inside the doorway, couldn't stand it any longer. "Leave him alone! Leave him alone! He's done nothing wrong!"

She tried to get outside. She wanted to physically push the Germans off her property, but her husband, who was still standing just outside the doorway, blocked her.

"Get back in the house, Sylvia," he said. "Stay in the house."

"I suggest you do what your husband says," the smaller German said calmly. "It's just routine. He'll be home in a couple of hours."

But by that time, Sylvia van Basten was near hysteria. Later, she did not remember the frenzy of tiny punches she landed on her husband's shoulder as she tried to get by him and at the Germans. She continued to scream, "You get away from here! Get away! Now!"

Van Basten grabbed his wife and pinned her flailing arms to her side. "It's not going to do us any good if you get arrested, too," he said into her ear. "I have to go with these men. There're no two ways about it. You go back in the house. When we leave, go to your mother's and stay there. When I get out, I'll meet you there. Don't argue. Do exactly as I say."

He kissed the top of her head, pushed her firmly back in the house and closed the door.

Sylvia van Basten watched numbly from a window as her husband and the Gestapo agents got into a car and drove away. Her eyes told her something horrible had happened, but her brain refused to believe it. The house reeked of normalness. Her husband's tobacco was still in the air. His dinner was in the stove.

She cringed as the first frightful stories came to mind. She shut her eyes to blot them out, but the ghastly things she heard about the Gestapo filled her head.

"Dear God, please return him to me," she wailed aloud. "*Please* return him to me. So many years together can't end like this!"

Chapter 31

Most of what happened to Maarten Dijkstra during his last days is a mystery. It *is* known that following the shootout at the Hotel American, he was brought to a Resistance safe house on the Singel and that a doctor was summoned. Dijkstra then ordered the "taxi driver" -- the journalist-turned-partisan Rob Groen -- to go to the home where he and Saskia had been sheltering and "get her out of there" as fast as possible. This, too, was done.

Dijkstra had been shot on the right side of his upper back, about two inches below the shoulder blade. The wound was serious (though not mortal) and he had lost a lot of blood. The doctor arrived, examined the injury, but refused to perform surgery. He said that the slug had fragmented and that removing the lead should be done in a hospital. The doctor left to make arrangements. When he returned two hours later, Dijkstra was gone.

The Gestapo had little difficulty tracing the wounded Resistance leader to the safe house, where they found him alone, lying on a blood-soaked mattress. Dijkstra was brought to the dreaded building on the Euterpestraat where he remained for several days. There is no record of his interrogation but it must have been unspeakably brutal. Willi Lages gleefully wrote his superiors that "this criminal is finally in our hands."

Plans were soon in the works to rescue Maarten Dijkstra but they were abandoned as foolhardy. The building was ringed with an electrified fence and patrolled day and night by guards and attack-trained dogs. There were search lights, sirens and barbed wire (later that year, a couple of Resistance men were killed when they tried to plant a bomb in the building).

Sometime during the early hours of April 27, Dijkstra was carried to a Gestapo truck and driven to the huge SD prison outside The Hague where he was kept in an isolation cell for a couple of days. A Dutch orderly who caught a brief glimpse of the Resistance leader described him as "unrecognizable."

On April 29, Dijkstra, who couldn't walk, was put in another truck and driven to the dunes outside the city. There were several prisoners with him on that last ride and they carried him from the truck to the killing grounds in the dunes. There were no last cigarettes, no blindfolds. The prisoners weren't even tied to poles. After they had walked a short distance from the road, their SD guards simply shot them in the back.

The Germans made no public announcement about Dijkstra's execution, but word of his death leaked out and was published in Resistance newspapers across the country. It was a terrible and disheartening blow for the Netherlands, struggling through its fourth year of occupation. Dijkstra's family asked the Germans to return his body but the request was denied. There was no body to return. After the prisoners were killed, their bodies were doused with petrol and burned. What was left of the remains was shoveled over with sand and dirt. Even the exact place of execution is not known.

Maarten Dijkstra's death did not put an end to the Resistance group he founded. The printing plant he set up continued to function for nearly a year. The roguish printer Romke Dietvorst and his crew put in 16-hour days in an effort to save as many as they could from Holland's dwindling Jewish population. It's estimated that more than a thousand people survived the war, thanks to the fact that Dietvorst kept the operation going after Dijkstra's execution.

The plant might have continued operating to the end of the war, but for the efforts of the incorrigibly flagitious Dries Riphagen. Riphagen was told by his crime bosses that he could bring luster back to his tarnished image in the *penose* by helping the Germans track down the perpetrators of the *Bevolkingsregister* fire. Though he failed in that effort, he did find out the location of the Underground's printing plant near the harbor and passed the intelligence on to his SD contact, Capt. Schmidt.

On June 19, 1944, the Germans raided the plant. They arrested seven people, including Dietvorst, and confiscated a huge amount of stolen and forged documents. The Germans put explosives in the building and blew it to smithereens. Dietvorst was taken to the Euterpestraat and never seen again.

Chapter 32

Westerbork, May 1, 1943

Dear Rinus:

I can't believe I'm still here! When I was first brought to this hellhole six weeks ago, I thought my "visit" would be a short one. I figured that I would either be shipped to Auschwitz or Sobibor or I would be dead. In fact, one and/or the other have been the fate of most of the people who were with us when we first arrived.

I do not know what has become of Cohen, our dear friend and my former law partner. As I have written previously, he was immediately taken and put in the dreaded "S" section of the camp - - "S" for *Straffe* (punishment). We never saw him again. I've tried again and again to find out something, anything, about his fate but have gotten nowhere. The "S" section is tightly controlled by the Germans. Prisoners sent there are beyond the reach of civilized law and human decency. They might as well have been dropped off the end of the Earth.

As for us, Heddy and I are still alive and still kicking. As awful as this place is, we know there are even worse places.

The *moffen* have been sending Jews by the boxcarful to Sobibor. We here rumors from time to time about what's going on at Sobibor and Auschwitz and if one-tenth of it is true, they will go down in history as the most evil, godforsaken places the world has ever seen. Some of the rumors are so appalling, so ghastly, it's hard to credit them, but this much seems to be true. Inmates are forced to work there around the clock on practically no food. When they die, and they die like flies, their bodies are brought to huge crematoria and burned. A pall of vaporized human flesh perennially hangs over the camps and the stink of death is everywhere.

Every Monday, the *moffen* send a huge train to Westerbork to pick up Jews. The tracks run right through the middle of camp so that the Jews can be herded into the cattle cars without ever setting foot outside the perimeter. It's surreal to witness this "loading" of human cargo, so surreal that I sometimes get the feeling that I've died and gone to hell. Some of the cars are painted with the words: *Huit Chevaux/Quarante Hommes.* It's obvious that the *moffen* can't read French. I've seen them cram as many as eighty people into a car before shutting and locking the door.

More rumors. I heard that the trip to Poland takes three days. The inmates have to stand the entire way, packed together like sardines, no ventilation, no food, no water, no sanitation. Half of them are dead by the time they arrive at Sobibor or Auschwitz.

The trains leave from camp every Tuesday, early in the morning, for Poland. Sometimes there are a thousand Jews on board, sometimes more.

I expect that eventually, we will find out firsthand about Sobibor and Auschwitz but for the time being, we seem to have found something of a place for ourselves here at Westerbork. Heddy's culinary skills are being put to good use in the kitchen and I am working in the registration hall, taking down the names and addresses of each new batch of inmates who are brought here. It's because of my job that I have access to pencil and paper to write these letters. Who knows, maybe one of these days, I will be able to deliver them to you in person!

If you are wondering why we were assigned "permanent" jobs here instead of being deported like most of the others. The answer is simple. We became friendly with a German Jew named Baum who is a supervisor in the registration hall. He got us the jobs. Actually what he said was, "I'm saving your lives." He emphatically assured us that our chances of surviving the war are a lot better at Westerbork than anywhere else under German occupation -- and we believe him.

But to tell you the truth, Rinus, my job is eating me up alive inside. Every week brings more people to the camp. My job is to "book them in." I can barely look at their faces, knowing what I do. Some of these people come here actually believing the nonsense the Germans have told them -- that they will be settled in a Jewish colony in the south of Holland, where they will be safe and out of harm's way. They haven't the faintest idea what's in store for them and I am not the one to tell them. They'll find out by themselves soon enough.

A little good news. You may find it difficult to believe, I certainly do, but living conditions have actually improved since we were first brought to the camp. The food has certainly gotten better. We eat at least twice a day and sometimes get a snack or two. There's not a lot of food but it's enough to keep us going. The *moffen* have even allowed us to get some packages from home. Last week, Heddy's brother sent us a thick wedge of cheese, some bouillon, some pancakes (we ate them so quickly I could not even tell you if they were stale or not), biscuits, tea and even some fresh fruit.

And the inmates are getting reasonable medical care now. There's medicine in the infirmary and doctors and nurses (all Jewish, of course) on hand to take care of the sick and injured. The *moffen* even brought in the injured crew members of a downed American plane for medical treatment before sending them off to a prisoner of war camp.

As I said, things could be a lot worse for us than they have been (so far).

The commandant of the camp is a chap named Gemmeker, and I would say that like the camp, we could have done a lot worse. Gemmeker doesn't seem to like it here very much. I think he would be happy if he never had to set foot in the place. He leaves the internal running of the camp to the German Jews who were here when the Nazis invaded. He looks after security around the camp and makes sure the Jews are ready to go when the trains roll in. Gemmeker believes that the big enemy at the camp is boredom, so he has arranged boxing matches and cabarets and "music night" and the like. And if you want to work, you can work. Some people have jobs pounding old batteries into scrap or doing other make-work tasks. And every day, large details of inmates are sent outside the camp under heavy guard to dig trenches and bunkers. The *moffen* are obsessed with the idea that an Allied invasion is imminent. They are digging holes in the ground all over the place. It's really quite funny to watch and I am looking forward to the day when I can laugh about it all. But things are far too depressing around here at the moment for much laughter.

And now, Rinus, I must tell you a remarkable story.

Last week, while I was at my table in the registration hall, "booking in" the latest batch of Jews, I looked up and caught one of the new arrivals staring at me. Usually when one looks at a person who is staring, the other person averts his eyes, but this man continued to stare at me. The funny thing was that he looked familiar. In all my weeks here, and with all the faces I have seen, I had not come across anyone I knew, and I was grateful for that. But this chap looked familiar to me -- vaguely so, anyway.

When he reached my table, I asked him his name and he said it was Van Basten. Rob van Basten. Again the name rang a bell but I could not for the life of me remember from where. He was obviously experiencing something similar. He continued to stare at me, as if racking his brains trying to figure out where he had seen me before.

I continued asking the routine questions -- how old he was, where did he live, how many members of his family were with him (he was alone). When I asked him what his occupation was, he said he was a police detective. And then I knew. I had met him before. A number of years ago during a murder trial. I was defending a man named Pohl who was accused of murdering his wife -- one of my less illustrious clients. Van Basten was the detective who investigated the case. I had cross-examined him at length and I remember that our exchanges were for the most part, civil and professional, though he appeared annoyed at the duration of my examination.

After the trial was over (and Pohl was convicted) I did not see the detective again until last week when he turned up here, of all places. I wanted to ask him what he was doing there, how he became an inmate, but there was no opportunity to do so. After he answered the routine questions, he was moved along to the next station.

The next day, I inquired about him and learned that he had been assigned to barracks number 67, but before I could go over to see him, he came to see *me*. He came to my barracks and walked among the rows of bunks until he spotted me.

"Mijnheer Vanderman?" he said.

"Vanderwal," I corrected, as we shook hands.

"Excuse me. I have a better memory for faces than for names. My name is Van Basten. I don't know if you remember me or not."

"Of course, I do. The Pohl murder trial."

"Correct," he said, and then his face broke into a wide grin. "We have now met twice, neither time under particularly congenial circumstances."

"Are you still on the force?" I asked.

"I *was* still on the force until a couple of days ago."

I wanted to know what he was doing here, what he had done to warrant such a fate. But I thought that it was better if this information came from his lips without any prompting from me.

There were not many inmates in the barracks at that time of day. Most were working outside the camp digging trenches. But we still spoke to each other *sotto voce*. Like Amsterdam, Westerbork is full of stool pigeons.

"How did you wind up here?" Van Basten asked.

"I sheltered a Jew and the *moffen* found out about it. More precisely, an informer told them about it."

"How do you know you were turned in by an informer?" he asked. Once a cop, always a cop, I thought.

"Because the informer tried to blackmail me before he turned me in."

"Tch. Tch." Van Basten gave a little sad shake of the head. "There are always a lot of rats around but it's after the flood that they really come out. What's the traitor's name?"

"Riphagen."

"*Riphagen*. Dries Riphagen?"

"That's him. I suppose as a cop, you've had your fair share of dealings with him?"

"I never met. Only heard about him. But I didn't know he was doing a little informing on the side."

"Oh, yes. And don't forget blackmail. But you seemed surprised when I mentioned his name."

"Only because his name came up on the last case I was working on. A coincidence, I suppose."

I figured it was the right time to ask a few questions of my own.

"What case were you working on?"

"Another murder investigation. Like you, someone was hiding a Jew in his home. Unlike you, he wound up killing the man and dumping his body in a canal."

Now it was my turn to express surprise. "But *why*?" I blurted out.

Van Basten shrugged. "I was still sorting all that out when the *moffen* arrested me. In all probability, it was nothing more complicated than greed. The Jew had some money and the other man wanted it. Simple as that. With a war going on and the *moffen* not very interested in Jew-killers, he thought he could get away with it."

"What happened to the killer?"

"What happened to the killer? Nothing. He's going about his business in Amsterdam. Free as a bird."

"Why didn't you arrest him?"

Van Basten looked troubled. "I was on my way to arrest him when ..." He hesitated for a moment, then changed the subject. "So, what's in store for me here? What do I have to look forward to?"

"I really don't know," I said and it was the truth. The Germans could do anything they wanted with him. They could give him a job in the camp. Or they could ship him out on the next train. Or they could put him in the "S" section. Or they could shoot him. Or they could even release him and send him back home.

"It usually depends on what you've done or what your religion is." I hesitated before asking, "Are you Jewish?"

"No."

"Well, that's a big mark in your favor. If you were Jewish, the chances are you would be on the next train for Sobibor. Another plus for you is the fact you have been put in a regular barracks. If the Germans considered you a troublemaker, you would already have been placed in the punishment compound."

"But the unfortunate truth of the matter is that your fate is entirely in the Germans' hands. They can do anything they want with you. My best advice to you is to prepare yourself for anything. And I mean anything."

Van Basten nodded slowly as if to say, "that thought *has* occurred to me, too, mijnheer."

Frankly, I was impressed at how well the police detective had handled himself thus far. He appeared composed and self-assured to the point of even joking about his predicament.

He had an unsettling way of looking at me when he asked questions. He looked right into my eye, sizing me up, weighing the quality of my information.

"So why are you here?" I finally asked him.

"I ran afoul of the Gestapo," he said.

"What did you do?"

"That's a story for another time. We'll speak again." Without another word, he walked out of the barracks.

The story of the murdered Jewish man disturbed me, Rinus, in a way that is difficult to explain. Having experienced firsthand both the gratification and the burden of sheltering a hunted, frightened human being, I was utterly appalled by what Van Basten told me. Who could be so cruel as to give refuge to a wanted man, then murder him. How could anyone betray such a sacred trust? And for what? Money. I tried to visualize the killing in my mind and was sickened by what I conjured up. Thoughts of the faceless victim and his horrible demise kept me awake most of the night.

The next day, after my stint at the registration hall, I sought out Van Basten and was pleased to find him sitting outside his barracks with an unlit pipe in his mouth.

"They let me keep my pipe," he said, taking the thing from his mouth. "But they took my tobacco away."

"I think I can get you some," I said.

"That would be greatly appreciated."

I told Van Basten that his story of the murder of the Jewish man was troubling to me and had kept me awake most of the night.

"Yes. That's an occupational hazard of my profession," he said. "That's why I learned a long time ago not to get emotionally involved in a case. Keep it strictly on a business level and you'll sleep better."

He wound up telling me rather a lot about the horrible business. It seems that the murderer was a young art student named Wolters and the victim was an escapee from the Hollandsche Schouwburg named Meijer. Meijer was an expert forger and he was sprung from the Schouwburg by the Resistance and placed under Wolters' roof while he finished some work.

But Wolters, it seems, had gotten himself into trouble with a gangster. Yes, it was my old friend, Dries Riphagen. Wolters apparently owed Riphagen quite a bit of money, so he killed Meijer and stole his money to pay off the gangster.

As depressing as all this was, the story got even worse. It seems that before Detective Van Basten could finish his investigation, he was arrested by the Gestapo and brought to the Euterpestraat.

What amazed me was how calm and philosophical he was about it. He said he was not even surprised when the Gestapo suddenly showed up at his home.

"I rather expected to have a visit from those boys, one day," Van Basten said. "To be honest, I haven't exactly been cooperating with them, as I was ordered to do. CID has received a number of directives from the Gestapo ordering us to send them copies of every report we write on every investigation we do, right down to shoplifting and conspiracy to commit jaywalking. God only knows why they want to see all of that paperwork but they do."

"So we send them the reports. But some of us are keeping two sets of books, so to speak. There are the reports we write for the office file -- with a copy going to the Gestapo. And then there are the *real* reports, which we write at home and keep hidden away."

"I got into trouble with the Gestapo earlier in the year when I investigated the killing of one of their informers. They suspected that I was holding back information and, to be honest about it, that's exactly what I was doing. They complained to my boss and I suppose that since that time, I've been on somebody's shit list. Anyway, I knew that it was only a matter of time before they would come around to arrest me. I warned my wife to expect it but when the time actually came --." Van Basten broke off as he thought about it. "-- My wife is a good woman. She promised me she would be brave. But when those goons from the Gestapo showed up on our doorstep to arrest me, well -- she didn't take it very well."

He paused again, then said with a bitter laugh, "The ironic thing was that *I* was arrested just as I was walking out the door to arrest Leo Wolters."

Van Basten told me that was taken to the Euterpestraat and put in a cell, where he spent the night, and the next day, he was interrogated by the Gestapo's head man in Amsterdam.

"This man, Lages, has a well-deserved reputation for nastiness," Van Basten said. "But with me, he was on his best behavior. He didn't rant. He didn't have me beaten. There was no spotlight in my eyes. He hardly asked me any questions at all. It was more a lecture than an interrogation. He told me that because of my lack of candor -- that was the word he used -- candor. Because of my lack of candor with the Gestapo, I had obstructed and damaged several important Gestapo investigations. He said that as much as he regretted doing it (because he heard I was a good cop), he was sending me away for the rest of the war. He said that within a day, I would be transported to Westerbork and after that, would probably wind up working in an armaments factory in Germany. And true to his word, I was taken to the train station that night and shipped out. And now I find myself here, wondering what the hell is going to happen to me."

Van Basten did not have to wonder for long. When the early morning train for Poland rolled out of camp Tuesday, he was on it. I expect he will never investigate another case again and as for his last case, well, it looks like somebody has indeed gotten away with murder.

Well, Rinus, that's the latest from this end. I hate to end this epistle on a depressing note but I have to turn in soon. I have to be up early tomorrow because another train of doomed souls is scheduled to arrive in camp at 3 a.m. and I'm expected to be at my desk to "book them in."

I hope things are well with you and Anna. Best wishes and may Liberation Day come in our lifetimes. *Tot ziens,*

Ruud Vanderwal

P.S. -- Stay out of trouble.

Chapter 33

By the time the war ended in the Netherlands on May 5, 1945, Hitler was dead, Soviet troops were in Berlin and most of Europe had been liberated. Amsterdam and the northern Dutch provinces, considered by the Allies strategically unimportant, remained firmly under German control until the bitter end. Liberation Day in the Netherlands preceded the total capitulation of the Third Reich by two days.

A tidal wave of revenge swept the country in the months following Liberation Day. People who for five years lived under the thumb of a ruthless occupier demanded retribution for their suffering. A wide net was cast and anyone who had any dealings with the Germans whatsoever was subject to arrest, including one poor man whose only crime was to have tended the rose garden of a Gestapo officer.

Records kept to this day in the *Centraal Archief Bijzondere Rechtspraak* show that one out of every ten of the Netherlands' wartime population of 9.3 million citizens was suspected at one time or another of collaborating with the enemy. Of those, more than 100,000 people were subsequently arrested, including hundreds of so-called *moffenmeiden* -- women accused of fraternizing with Germans -- many of whom were tarred or had their heads shaved or were subjected to other forms of public humiliation.

Men arrested for collaboration were treated far worse. Put in internment camps while awaiting trial, they were beaten senseless by guards, forced to clean floors with their tongues and had their heads shoved into their slop buckets. The treatment was too much for one Nazi official, a former Dutch parliament member named Meinoud Rost van Tonningen. Driven nearly insane by the guards' brutality, Rost van Tonningen threw himself from a third-floor cell block to the concourse below. He died on the spot.

One Dutch historian said the brutal treatment served as a "relief valve for so much pent-up misery."

Thousands of volunteer constables were sworn in to help overworked police arrest suspected collaborators and war criminals, and special courts were set up to try war-related cases. But with so many cases to be investigated, the authorities had to release thousands of prisoners without trial while they concentrated on prosecuting "the real bad guys."

The Nazi *Reichskommissar* for the Netherlands, Arthur Seyss-Inquart, was arrested, as were such top henchmen as SS General Hanns Rauter and Gestapo *Befehlshaber* Willi Lages.

Dries Riphagen, who had continued his lucrative criminal career throughout the war (all the while continuing to inform on Jews), went into hiding after Liberation Day but was eventually tracked down and arrested in Amsterdam. Before he could be brought to trial, however, he escaped from police custody and -- with the aid of friends -- was smuggled out of the country (according to one story, he was put in a coffin and driven to Belgium in a hearse). After a brief disappearance, Riphagen resurfaced in Spain where he was soon arrested again. But while awaiting extradition to the Netherlands, this amazing man got away again, and with a fake passport (obtained for him by a Jesuit priest), he flew to Argentina where he used his ill-gotten gains -- safely banked in Switzerland -- to buy a large home on the outskirts of Buenos Aires. There he played host to local politicos, Nazi fugitives, old mobster pals, and of course, plenty of young women. It was not long before he counted Juan and Eva Peron among his friends.

Leo Wolters and his sister, Monique, came through the war without a scratch, due largely to their insignificance. The Gestapo had bigger fish to fry, Dries Riphagen didn't dare risk Willi Lages' animosity over the likes of the Wolters, and the remnants of Maarten Dijkstra's Resistance group were too busy trying to stay alive themselves to seek revenge.

War's end found Leo and Monique still living in the Schubertstraat apartment.

With Dijkstra's capture, Leo's flirtation with the Resistance came to an end. He sweated out a couple of weeks in great fear that the Gestapo would come for him next, and when that didn't happen, he hunkered down for the duration of the war. He continued to work as a handyman at the City Theatre but to that, he added occasional work as a stage manager and assistant director, eventually becoming a director himself -- directing his first play in March 1945, two months before the war ended. Appropriately enough, it was a murder story based on an Agatha Christie novel.

Shortly after Liberation Day, Monique Wolters moved out of the Schubertstraat flat and in with a rising young actor named Ivan Voorster, with whom she lived on and off for several years. Whatever grief she felt over Naumann's death remained locked within a cool, stern facade.

In April 1946, practically three years to the day of Herman Meijer's killing, as Leo was preparing to direct his third play at the City Theatre, two special constables showed up at his door and arrested him. The charge was murder.

He was taken to an internment camp at Levantkade outside of Amsterdam where he spent the next three months at hard labor, building latrines and carrying hay from surrounding farms to be used as mattresses. Whether he was ever subjected to some of the more sadistic practices of the guards is not known.

Then on a rainy summer day in July, Leo was put on a truck and taken to The Hague to stand trial. It was not until he was actually seated in the courtroom for a pre-trial hearing that he found out who his accuser was -- none other than the indomitable policeman, Adjutant-Detective Robert van Basten.

Leo was badly shaken to see the detective sitting in the courtroom. He starred at Van Basten as if he were seeing a ghost, and in some respects, he was. More than a year after his liberation from Auschwitz, Van Basten still looked like a walking corpse. There was a dead-white tinge to his skin, particularly around his eyes and shrunken cheeks, and though he had started to put back weight -- thanks to Sylvia van Basten's nourishing cooking -- the once-corpulent detective liked to joke he still looked more like Count Dracula than Fatty Arbuckle.

What he went through at Auschwitz and how he survived are stories for another day, but seven months after his liberation, when Van Basten was fit enough to return to work, he was given his old job back with the Amsterdam Police Department. There were a mountain of cases awaiting attention but Van Basten had his own agenda, and at the top was Leo Wolters. Through discreet inquiries, he discovered Leo, too, had survived and still living at his old address.

"I swear to you, Len," Van Basten said to his partner, Leonard Hookstra, as they once again sat across from each other at CID. "That bastard is not going to get away with murder."

Van Basten still had his most important files, thanks to the fact they were hidden in his home throughout the war. He organized his case, presented it to a judge and personally saw to it that the jurist immediately signed an arrest warrant for Leo Wolters, rather than just adding the case file to the overflowing slush pile of criminal matters awaiting attention. The detective then hand-picked the two constables who served the warrant, and he watched from a car as Leo was led away in handcuffs.

On that rainy July day in 1946, as Van Basten sat at the prosecution table, he paid scant attention to the defendant. Looking up once and catching Leo's eye, Van Basten gave him a curt nod, then turned his attention back to his paperwork.

When the trial began, Van Basten told his story well to the three presiding judges, and he submitted the police reports he had risked his life to preserve. He told of his interview with Leo Wolters and how Leo *admitted* killing Herman Meijer, though claiming it was a *verzetsdaad* -- a Resistance act.

The detective then described his meeting with Maarten Dijkstra shortly before the Resistance leader was shot and captured, and how Dijkstra had been shocked to learn of Meijer's death. Dijkstra emphatically had denied ordering Leo Wolters to kill Meijer, Van Basten told the court.

"*Herman Meijer was an important member of my group,*" the detective testified that Dijkstra told him. "*He was far more valuable to me than Leo Wolters.*"

Then there was the matter of money, and how Leo had run up debts all over town, including a large gambling IOU to Dries Riphagen -- a debt the hoodlum tried to collect by sending a pair of his bone-breakers to Wolters' apartment.

"But within a day or two of Herman Meijer's death, Mijnheer Wolters was suddenly flush with cash," Van Basten testified. "He gave several months back rent to his apartment manager, and we know he paid off other debts. When I asked Mijnheer Wolters about the money, he refused to say where he got it from."

Staring hard at the defendant in the dock, Van Basten told the judges he was "one hundred percent convinced Mijnheer Wolters killed the victim for *profit,* not patriotism."

The judges complimented Van Basten for his bravery and resilience and for presenting a compelling case. The prosecutor clapped him on the back when he sat down and whispered that a conviction "seems a certainty."

But Leo's father had hired two of the best lawyers his money could buy and they soon proved they were worth every guilder. They did what attorneys do when faced with convincing evidence against their client -- they attacked the credibility of the policeman who collected it.

The attorneys alleged that Van Basten's own hands were not clean, that he had dealt in the black market throughout the war. To back up the allegations, they produced affidavits from two people. One was an underworld informer whose testimony carried little weight, but the other was from a junior police detective named Jos Zijl.

Zijl was seriously ill (he would die within weeks of the trial's conclusion) and could not attend the proceedings. But the thrust of his affidavit was clear: Van Basten was a crooked cop. Zijl swore that "time and again," he saw Van Basten being bribed "with coffee, or money or sometimes, sexual favors."

When read in court, Zijl's statement had a devastating impact. Why would he say such things against a colleague if they were not true?

Within a day of the affidavits being read in court, Van Basten was removed from the Wolters case and assigned a desk job at CID. A week later, he was notified he was the subject of an internal police investigation.

Stunned by the turn of events, Van Basten found himself powerless to do anything about it.

His first thought was to go to Zijl's home and "beat the damned truth out of him," but wound up sending flowers instead after learning how sick he was.

"You may want to do the same for me," Van Basten wrote bitterly on the card, "since my career is dead thanks to you." Zijl did not respond.

It seems clear that Zijl perjured himself -- and betrayed a fellow cop -- in order to insure that his family was taken care of after his death. His son later admitted that for many years, the family received monthly checks from an insurance company co-owned by none other than Leo's father, Michiel Wolters.

With the credibility of the state's lead investigator ruined, Wolters' attorneys called their young client to the witness stand.

Wolters, soberly attired and as serious as a judge, freely admitted killing Herman Meijer, but maintained it was a Resistance act. He told the story of being forced to kill the forger because the Gestapo was close to finding Meijer's hiding place; and if Meijer had been arrested, it would have put Dijkstra's entire network in grave danger.

"Herman knew Dijkstra's operations intimately," Leo testified. "He knew about the printing plant in the harbor. He knew about the safe houses. He knew the phony names Jews were using and where they were living. He knew those things because he was forging the documents. The Gestapo would have had a field day if they ever got their hands on him."

And without ever saying so directly, Wolters implied that it was Maarten Dijkstra himself who gave the order to kill Meijer.

"I loved Maarten," Leo said in a barely audible voice, tears welling in his eyes. "In many ways, he was like a father to me. He was my teacher in peace, and my leader in war. I will never say anything that will in any way bring dishonor to his memory. But I will say with a clear conscience that if he were able to do so, Maarten Dijkstra would be in court today and would be sitting by my side at this table. And when called, he would tell this court that I was a soldier, not a murderer. Anything I did, I did for my country."

It is probably for the best that Van Basten was no longer in court when Leo testified. There's no telling how he would have reacted to that testimony. How the court reacted is a matter of record. With a staggering number of cases still to be heard, the judges did not want to "waste precious court time trying to repair a flawed prosecution." By day's end, the murder charge was dismissed.

Following his release from custody, Leo returned to Amsterdam and was soon hard at work directing another play at the City Theatre, but his father was still troubled. He was concerned that idle theatre gossip might hurt the family's good name at some point in the future. So, the senior Wolters used his friendship with two prominent newspaper publishers to get favorable articles written about his son's "exoneration."

Both papers subsequently ran lengthy profiles of Leo, articles that greatly embellished his Resistance work while emphasizing that he was cleared of wrongdoing in the killing of the Jewish *onderduiker*, Herman Meijer.

In the articles, Leo again described the killing as a *verzetsdaad* -- a horrific thing he was forced to do in order to protect his Resistance colleagues from arrest and torture.

"I will have nightmares about it for the rest of my life," he was quoted as saying in one article. "A day doesn't go by that I don't think about it. I am as much a victim as the young man I killed."

Those first two articles proved invaluable to Leo in another respect: they led to his big break in the Dutch film industry. A film producer read them and asked Leo if he would like to direct a documentary about Holland's underground fight against the Nazis. *Would he?* Leo jumped at the opportunity. Six months later, he finished his first film, a documentary called *Shadow War* that became a huge hit in the Netherlands. Over the next two decades, he would make ten documentaries and feature films about the war, many of them focusing on the careers of collaborators and criminals.

With each passing year, as Leo's reputation as a filmmaker grew, he became bolder in what he said about his wartime "exploits." By the 1950s, he was hinting that the raid on the

Bevolkingsregister would not have succeeded without his behind-the-scenes help. A couple of years later, he boasted that he was at Maarten Dijkstra's side that eventful evening in 1942 when Dijkstra stormed out of a meeting of the artists guilds with the guilds' treasury under his arm. People who were there disputed it but who listened? The Dutch wanted to believe that their crusading filmmaker was a genuine war hero.

In 1952, Leo made a documentary about the wartime trade in stolen art, in which Leo named a sitting member of parliament as one of the major art dealers who did business with Nazi officials.

The film nearly undid Leo's own career. It led to a huge backlash from people who knew Leo during the war and were fed up with his boasting. Leo was nearly unmasked as the murderer and liar he was, but then the Wolters' legal machinery went into high gear. The same two attorneys threatened and harassed Leo's accusers -- with everything neatly couched in polite, impeccable legal terms -- and ultimately silenced them. Leo dodged the bullet again.

Leo continued making films -- some modest hits, a couple gems -- and with the success came the usual trappings: the *finca* on Ibiza, the apartment in New York. He flirted with Eastern religions, experimented with drugs, earned a black belt in karate, traveled widely, built up an art collection and enjoyed a Don Juanish reputation with the fast set.

In the early 1970s, Leo's career as a filmmaker reached its peak when he won the Palme d'Or in Cannes for *The Culture Chamber,* a gritty, violent, fictional account of the Dutch Resistance.

The Culture Chamber caused a sensation in the Netherlands, on the way to becoming a box office smash in Europe.

In Cannes, the tall filmmaker was mobbed by journalists when he took a stroll with his sister, Monique, along the beachfront promenade known as La Croisette the morning after he won the award. He walked in regal silence amid the frenzy of photographers and reporters, finally pausing beneath a huge poster advertising his own film and raising a languid hand for order.

"Gentlemen. Ladies. It's impossible to conduct a meaningful interview under such circumstances," he said in clipped English. "I am going back to my room at the Carlton. I will be happy to talk to a half-dozen of you there. Let's see. Ummmm. You, you, you, you, you, you. Give me your press passes and follow me back."

Twenty minutes later, the journalists were seated comfortably in his suite at the Carlton, sipping coffee and waiting for the interview to begin.

Leo was then approaching 50 years old, tanned, mustachioed, handsome, with long, thick gray hair he slicked back, and a pair of sharp blue eyes. He was dressed in jeans and a denim shirt and he wore a large peace symbol that depended from a chain around his neck to his thickening waistline.

Monique Wolters had a small part in *The Culture Chamber* -- she played a cronish SS guard -- but had the reporters not known that, they would not have made the connection with the elegant woman who re-filled coffee cups and acted as hostess for her brother. She was a couple of years younger than Wolters -- slim, expensively dressed; her well-coifed blonde hair did not seem to be dyed.

The room was already overflowing with flowers when the journalists arrived, and more were brought to the door during the course of the interview. If the sender was well known, Monique would read the card out loud in a breathless voice.

"It's from Vincent Price," she said, taking from a bellboy an elaborate arrangement of red, white and blue tulips.

"My old art chum," said Leo. "What did he say?"

"He says, 'If I knew you were going to be this successful, I would never have outbid you for that Oller landscape. Well done. Congratulations. See you at the next auction. P.S. -- is there a part in your next war flick for a slightly-over-the-hill vampire?'"

Leo chuckled and shook his head. "If there isn't, I'll write one."

One reporter placed a small tape recorder on the coffee table. "Do you mind if I use this. For accurate quotes."

"A little accuracy would be nice for a change," Leo answered affably. In fact, he was friendly and courteous through the entire interview, never ducking a question, never trying to make the journalists feel small for asking it.

Yet, there was an arrogance about him that a thin veneer of civility could not hide. Its clearest manifestation was in the answers he gave during the interview -- smug, windy replies that seemed to make whatever he said a boast. This unpleasant characteristic surfaced with the first question someone asked.

"You have been very outspoken about American involvement in Vietnam," said a British reporter. "Do you think that will hurt your chances of a nomination for an Academy Award?"

Leo did not answer immediately, busying himself instead with lighting a Dannemann.

"There are," he finally confided, "a number of very important experiences in my life. My birth was certainly one of them. And the first time I got laid, of course. And my LSD experiments. And the time I lay flat on my back in the Sahara and gave my hand to God. And the first time I killed a man." He paused for effect. "He was a German and I strangled him. I can still see his face. That's not a pleasant memory to carry around all these years but I can soothe my conscience by telling myself that he was an invader in my country and an instrument of a terrible regime."

"But I don't know why American soldiers are in Vietnam killing Vietnamese peasants. I have thought about it a lot and I cannot find an explanation for it. Maybe you know the answer. If you do, would you please explain it to me."

Nobody attempted an explanation. Instead, a wire service reporter said: "Your film has raked up a lot of unpleasant history in your country. What do you say to those who charge that you are just trying to settle old scores with some of your fellow artists in the Netherlands?"

Leo fixed his attention on the cigarillo that he held lightly between two fingers. "I suppose it is a good idea to clear up some misconceptions. This film has been widely misinterpreted. It was not done as an act of revenge against those who shamed my country but as a tribute to a man whom I loved and admired very much."

"Maarten Dijkstra?" asked a woman from *Paris Match*.

"Correct."

"Maarten is one of the great war heroes," Leo said. "As far as Holland is concerned, he may be the greatest. He was one of those willing to stick his neck out at a time when most people were -- uh, how shall I put it -- were interested in keeping a low profile. Very few people outside the Netherlands know about what went on in my country during the Nazi occupation. The total of their knowledge is the Anne Frank story and they don't even have their facts straight about that. What happened to the Jews in Holland was a national disgrace. Eighty percent of the Jewish population -- one hundred thousand people -- was wiped out. Percentage-wise, we lost more Jews than the Russians. That's how bad it was in Holland."

"But in your film, you made it seem like some of Dijkstra's associates were traitors," said the Brit.

"Some of them were," Leo responded neatly.

"How do you know?"

"Because I looked it up."

That took everyone by surprise. "You looked it up? Where?"

Wolters laughed derisively. "Where! In archives, where do you think? At the federal archives in Bonn. At the National Archives in Washington D.C. And in Holland, at the Center for War Documentation in Amsterdam. They all have file rooms full of information on people who collaborated with the Germans during the war. It's not difficult to look up a name, if you know a few tricks."

"But *why*?" asked the British journalist.

"Over the years, I have looked up a lot of names. I looked up the name of every person I served with in the Resistance. I looked up the name of practically every person I ever knew."

The stunned silence that followed those words made its own statement.

"Leo, really," Monique said with a nervous laugh. "You have to be careful around the press. They'll believe everything you say."

"Brave people died during the war," Leo said in a steely voice. "Some of them were friends of mine. They died patriots, fighting unspeakable evil. When I think about them, I get crazy. Crazy with rage against those who did wrong during the war. The traitors. The collaborators. The informers. The people who sold their neighbors to the Germans for seven guilders and fifty cents per head."

Someone changed the subject and the interview continued for another 45 minutes with Leo talking about the film, the recent break-up of his second marriage, a rumored affair with a lusty Italian actress (he denied it), his art collection, World War II, the Academy Awards, his next project (another documentary about the war) and his plans for a long-delayed holiday in Jamaica.

The journalists bought every word of it and cranked out routine puff pieces that ran in leading newspapers and magazines around Europe. So thoroughly had Leo managed to bury his true wartime past that the subject of Herman Meijer's murder never even came up.

Chapter 34

He lunched alone on March 20, 1972 -- his fiftieth birthday -- by choice, not necessity. Invitations by the score lay in a neglected pile on his desk. His phone had not stopped ringing since *The Culture Chamber* was nominated for an Academy Award.

The last few months had been unbelievable, a whirlwind of interviews and parties and business deals and applause. First the Palme d'Or, then an Oscar nomination. The following morning, he was flying first class to Los Angeles, courtesy of the Hollywood studio offering big bucks for his next picture. There would be more parties, more interviews, more applause. He felt exhilarated by all the attention, but also burned out. He was tired of answering questions and dizzy of offers flying at him from all directions. He craved time alone and spent his last morning in Amsterdam walking aimlessly along the canals. At about noon, he stopped at the Night Watch Cafe for a beer and a sandwich, graciously autographing a menu for his waitress. After exchanging polite nods with the diners, he buried his head in a newspaper until his meal came.

He was sipping his beer and reading the paper when a portly gentleman wearing a dark suit and a trilby hat approached his table.

"Mijnheer Wolters?"

Leo looked up. The face was at once familiar and unfamiliar. Then with a start, he recognized the man.

Leo recovered quickly and slipped easily into his urbane patter. "Detective Van Basten? Is that you?" He stood up with a wide smile and outstretched hand. Van Basten held a briefcase, which he put down beside the table to shake Leo's hand.

"I didn't think you would still recognize me," Van Basten said affably.

"Of course I recognize you," Leo beamed, pumping the detective's hand. "Our previous meetings were not such that they would be easy to forget. How long has it been?"

"More than 25 years," said Van Basten. "Seems like a lifetime ago."

"I must say that you look much better than the last time we met," said Leo.

Van Basten smiled and patted his stomach. "The last time we met was not long after I was liberated from the camps. Yes, I managed to put some weight back on. Now, the doctors have me on a diet. They say I have to lose 30 pounds."

They stood looking at each other, Leo with his smile locked on his face, Van Basten poker-faced, but not unfriendly.

"Would you mind terribly if I sat down at your table for a moment," Van Basten said. "These old legs don't hold me up the way they used to."

"Yes, of course! Sit down. Do you want a beer? Something to eat? Oh, that was stupid of me. You're on a diet."

"It's okay," Van Basten said, sitting down and removing his hat. "Actually, I could use a snack. Just don't tell my wife."

Leo beckoned the waitress, and Van Basten ordered a beer and a portion of *satay*.

"Do you come here often?" he asked.

"Every now and again," answered Leo. Van Basten nodded and looked around. The Night Watch Cafe was next door to the American Hotel. If Van Basten thought it an odd place for Leo to be lunching, he didn't show it. The men stared at each other and grinned.

"So how have you been?" Leo asked. "What are you doing these days?"

"Keeping busy. I retired from the police force some years ago, but I'm still in the business. I have my own agency here in Amsterdam.

"Private detective agency?"

Van Basten nodded.

"Yes, I seem to remember reading something about you a couple of years ago."

"Really? Hmm, let's see. Perhaps, in connection with the Van Vliet kidnapping?"

"Yes, that was it! You helped the police find him."

"Too late to do him much good, I'm afraid," Van Basten said and Leo nodded in sympathy. Van Vliet was the scion of a newspaper millionaire. He was kidnapped, shot in the head and buried by the kidnapper, who let the family believe for weeks he was still alive. The kidnapper was eventually arrested and imprisoned and most of the ransom was recovered.

Van Basten's beer materialized and he took a healthy pull.

"And there's no need to ask what you've been up to," Van Basten said, wiping his mustache. "Belated congratulations, by the way."

"Thank you."

"I suppose you will be going to America pretty soon."

"Yes, indeed. I fly to Los Angeles tomorrow. My American hosts tell me to come prepared for good food, good wine, company and good business."

"It must be very exciting. My wife and I saw *The Culture Chamber* a few evenings ago. She said it was the best movie she had seen -- ever. For what it's worth, she thinks you'll win the Academy Award, hands down."

"Thank you. That's very kind of you to say. I'm trying not to get my hopes up. I've won the Palme d'Or, and that's already a lot. An Oscar would be icing on the cake."

Van Basten's food came and he started to eat.

Leo watched him a moment, then asked: "So what brings you to this neighborhood, Detective Van Basten? I guess I should say Mijnheer Van Basten."

"You do," answered Van Basten, wiping a dab of peanut sauce from the corner of his mouth.

"*Me*? Why do you want to see me after all these years?"

Van Basten cleared his mouth with a swig of beer, ran a napkin over his lips again, and said, "I'm afraid to say that this is a business call. Excuse me a moment." He reached down and started to fiddle with his briefcase.

"So it is not a coincidence, our meeting here?" Leo asked.

"'Fraid not," said Van Basten, still rooting around in the briefcase.

"How did you know where to find me?"

"I followed you from your home. I've been keeping tabs on you for a few days now."

"*Really*? I must compliment you on your professionalism, then. I had no inkling."

Van Basten, absorbed longer with his briefcase than one might expect, nodded absently.

"And why have you been doing that, pray? Keeping tabs on me, as you put it?"

"Ah, here it is." Van Basten pulled an envelope from his briefcase.

"You haven't answered my question, Mijnheer Van Basten. Why have you been following me?"

"I was hired to," said Van Basten.

"Hired? By whom?"

"By the person who asked me to give you this," and he handed the envelope to Leo. The filmmaker took it gingerly, as if it had been dipped in poison. His name had been typed on the front, but nothing else. He could feel there was a piece of paper inside."

"What *is* this?" he asked.

"See for yourself. I could have just knocked on your door and given it to you, but there was a stipulation from my client that I give the letter to you in a public place."

The mask of urbanity slipped, and for just a moment, the old hunted look returned to Leo's eyes. Then he chuckled.

"I must say this is all very peculiar. 'Corny' is a better word, if you're familiar with the Americanism. I wouldn't dare put it in a film."

Van Basten smiled in agreement and shrugged his arms. "I'm just the messenger," he said, and resumed eating.

Leo stared at the detective for a moment, then tore open the envelope and removed two folded sheets of paper. He unfolded them, looked at one, then the other, and went as white as the pages he was holding.

"What is the meaning of this?" he blurted out. "Where did you get this?"

"I guess you recognize the handwriting."

"Answer me! Where did you get this?"

"That's your handwriting, isn't it, mijnheer? That's *your* handwriting on *your* membership application for the Culture Chamber. I am, of course, speaking of the real Culture Chamber, not the fantasy you put on film."

Leo was too taken aback to speak. He stared at the photo-copies as if he were looking at his own death warrant.

"That's your name on the top," Van Basten continued. "and you signed at the bottom of both pages."

"My German probably isn't as good as yours," Van Basten went on smoothly. "But from what I made of it, that's the application you submitted to the German authorities in Amsterdam on May 13, 1944, in order to be allowed to work as an assistant director at the City Theatre. They even gave you a little stamp because you paid the two guilder fee in full. I guess you still had a little of Herman Meijer's money lying around. And look. You even signed under that oath on the back of page 2 to faithfully obey the rules of the Culture Chamber. If I recall, that means you agreed to turn over to the Nazis any Jewish artist you knew about."

Leo shook his head and stared out the window in disbelief. Van Basten sipped his beer and watched him. A full two minutes passed before Leo spoke again. "You still haven't told me where you got this."

"Yes, I guess that is something of a mystery to you, since your father's lawyers did a very thorough job sanitizing the records -- both German and Dutch. Unfortunately for you, they restricted their efforts to *this* country. And you know how fanatical the *moffen* were about record-keeping. Everything in triplicate. This piece of evidence of *your* wartime collaboration turned up in Bonn."

"I can't believe this," Leo said. "This is crazy. This is a joke of some kind. You had somebody forge this. I remember you, *Detective* Van Basten. I remember you like to play games with people. Take the mickey out of them. What do you intend to do with this?"

"Me? Not a thing. I've accomplished my assignment. But I believe my client has made some plans. If I'm not mistaken, copies have already been distributed to every major newspaper, television and radio station in the country."

"You're lying," Leo almost shouted. "He wouldn't dare. I'll sue him for every cent he's got."

"I think she would welcome it," said Van Basten pleasantly. "At least, that's what she told me."

"*She?*"

"Yes, she."

Leo tried to regroup, to find some way of proceeding. He wasn't going to bluff his way out and he knew it. In many ways, Dutch society is a forgiving one. But not for liars. And not for frauds.

"Why?" he asked pitiably. "Why now?"

"I'm really not an expert on all the background," Van Basten said. "My understanding is that certain records only recently have become readily available to the public. There was a small item on the back page of my newspaper about six months ago. I didn't pay much attention to it, but my client did. It seems the Germans generated an outcry when they announced they were going to destroy certain rarely consulted wartime files to make room in their archives for more recent documents.

"To pacify the public, the Germans agreed to give interested parties from around the world a ninety-day period to claim what files they wanted. They published a complete list of what they intended to destroy, and lo and behold, there was a listing for the Dutch Culture Chamber."

"My client decided to go to Bonn and have a look. She spent a few days in the archives, found an index for the Culture Chamber files and looked up your name. And, yes, you were registered. She made a few copies, then arranged to have the file transferred to our own World War II documentation center in Amsterdam. And now you know what I know."

"Except for one thing," Leo said softly.

"Oh, yes, the name of my client. Ordinarily, I would keep a client's name confidential, but I will make an exception in this case. My client is Saskia Hoogeboom.

"*Saskia Hoogeboom*?" Leo looked nonplussed. After a moment, he sputtered, "*Maarten's girlfriend*?"

"Yes. If I may be candid, she has never forgiven you for what happened to Maarten Dijkstra. She believes that Maarten might be alive today if he did not have to come out of hiding to clean up the mess you made by murdering Herman Meijer."

The two men again stared at each other, then Van Basten continued: "Saskia went into hiding after Maarten's death and somehow, she managed to survive the war. And she's watched in amazement your rise to fame and fortune."

"Six months ago, Saskia saw this article about the German records. She made a few phone calls, and then she went to Bonn and rummaged around in the old records until she hit pay dirt. Quite a lady."

"Is your client here?" Leo asked softly.

"Yes, she's standing behind you."

The filmmaker turned around.

"Hello, Mijnheer Wolters." Leo saw a petite, gray-haired lady, neatly made up, not a hair out of place.

"I just came by to congratulate you on the success of *The Culture Chamber*," she said. Leo started to speak but before the first word came out, she slapped him across the face with surprising energy. Her hand must have swiped his nose because it started to bleed. She then picked up Van Basten's glass and dashed some beer in Leo's face.

A hush came over the bar. Then from somewhere came the flash of a camera. Leo became aware that blood was trickling from his nose. He slowly picked up a napkin and dabbed at it.

He again started to speak, but Saskia Hoogeboom put the glass down, turned her back on him and walked out of the bar.

Leo was acutely aware that every eye was on him. For a moment, he seemed not to know what to do. He looked pleadingly at Van Basten, who had stood up and was picking up his briefcase.

"I did the things I had to do to survive," Leo said quietly. "You were there. You knew how it was. All I wanted to do was survive. What did I do wrong? Huh? Tell me. What did I do wrong?"

Van Basten drained the last of the beer and put the glass down. "I did not know she was going to do that. I don't think she knew it herself. Still, I disagree with her only on a small point of procedure. It's a pity to waste good beer."

He put his hat on and started to leave, then turned around.

"You are not going to go to prison for your crimes, Mijnheer Wolters. I doubt if this little episode is even enough to ruin you professionally. I understand a lot of artists and writers joined the

Culture Chamber in the war. They had to if they wanted to work. But at least they had the good manners *not* to point fingers at anybody else.

"No, I'm afraid that whatever humiliation we can inflict on you over this is the only punishment you're going to receive," Van Basten said. "And that's a pity. By the way, that camera flash you may have noticed was from one of my operatives. I'll send you a copy. Good day."

Leo remained at the bar several minutes after the detective left, too dumbfounded and embarrassed to move. Finally, he laid some money on the table and walked out. How he spent the rest of the day is unknown. But at 8:30 a.m. the next the next day, he took his first-class seat on a KLM jetliner and flew to Los Angeles.

Afterword

Of those whose fates have not been mentioned:

Nazi Reichskommissar Arthur Seyss-Inquart was tried at Nuremberg and hanged.

SS General Hanns Rauter was tried by a special tribunal in the Netherlands and also executed. Gestapo Befehlshaber Willi Lages also was condemned to die but the sentence was commuted to life imprisonment.

Egon Haase, the dreaded Gestapo examiner, escaped to Argentina where he was killed under suspicious circumstances in 1956.

Dries Riphagen returned to Europe after a lengthy sojourn in Argentina and settled on the Costa Del Sol from where he successfully resisted Dutch attempts to have him extradited. He died peacefully at a Swiss clinic in 1973.

Ruud Vanderwal and his wife survived their ordeal at Westerbork and returned to Amsterdam where he resumed his law practice. Ruud died in 1969, followed a year later by his wife.

Saskia Hoogeboom never married but lived for many years with a globe-trotting Canadian businessman whom she met in Amsterdam. In the early 1980s, she emigrated to Canada.

Monique Wolters became one of the Netherlands' leading actresses. In addition to stage work and parts in a number of international films, Monique starred in a long-running Dutch TV comedy series about a lawyer and his wife. But in the mid-80s, she suddenly retired. As of this writing, she lives as a virtual recluse on the family estate outside Amsterdam, cared for by a couple of devoted retainers. Monique has never spoken publicly about the murder of Herman Meijer.

Leo Wolters did not win an Academy Award for Best Foreign Film for *The Culture Chamber*, but his disgrace could not have been greater if he had won. When his Culture Chamber membership was revealed in the Dutch press, Leo found himself a pariah, ridiculed on television, shunned by society and an object of scorn wherever he went. The social invitations dried up and couldn't raise 100 guilders to make a movie.

Desperate to reestablish himself in the Dutch cultural world, Leo threw himself head first into the waters of expiation. He wrote an autobiography that read like Rousseau's *Confessions*. In it, he recorded the gory details of Herman Meijer's killing and even published extracts from the diary Meijer kept. But he still insisted the murder was a *verzetsdaad* -- a Resistance act. Nothing could shake him from that lie. The book was a bestseller in Holland, and just like that, Leo was back on the TV chat show circuit to talk about it.

In the end, he weathered that storm like he weathered others. Over the next two decades, he made more movies and opened an art gallery on Amsterdam's trendy Prinsengracht. The only noticeable effect from all the negative publicity was that he never made another movie about the war.

On the night before his 70th birthday, while sitting alone in his study, Wolters shot himself in the head with a .38-caliber revolver. He did not leave a note.

On Nov. 26, 1944, the Royal Air Force bombed the Gestapo headquarters on the Euterpestraat in Amsterdam, damaging the building but not destroying it. The air raid was but a minor disruption for the dreaded terror organization, which simply moved its operations to the Apollolaan. After the war, the elegant red-brick building was again used as a school. The name of the street has since been changed.

The so-called Bevolkingsregister -- the municipal Hall of Records -- was torn down after the war. Likewise, the apartment on the Schubertstraat where Wolters and his sister lived is gone, turned into a shiny shopping center.

Of the Hollandsche Schouwburg, through which 60,000 Dutch Jews passed on their way to almost-certain death in a concentration camp, not much remains. At the end of the war, it was briefly used again as a theatre, but this outraged many Amsterdammers who believed that the site of so much misery should not be a place of entertainment. Most of the once-sprawling structure was torn down and the huge stage was uprooted and destroyed.

Inside the truncated building today, a visitor will find a marble monument with the surname of every Dutch Jew who perished in the war. The name of Meijer is represented in the small white letters, as is the name of Frank, and thousands of others.

The city erected a statue of Maarten Dijkstra near the site of the old Bevolkingsregister but later moved it to a park in the town of Abcoude where he was born. Robert van Basten visited the park once but never went back.

"I don't think Maarten would have liked the statue," the octogenarian told a journalist on a brilliant, bustling summer day in Amsterdam in 1990, a year before his own death.

They were having lunch at an outdoor table on the Leidseplein. Van Basten, who had retired from the private eye business long ago, had requested the interview "to talk about a few things" while he still had breath to do so.

"I only met Dijkstra once, as I told you," Van Basten said. "But from what I heard about him, he did not like hero-worshipping, putting people on pedestals. That was not his style."

He pointed to a street filled with shoppers and pedestrians. "That's Maarten's monument!" Van Basten said. "A city free of occupation. A happy city. Laughter instead of terror! If you don't mind an old copper quoting Latin, I saw an inscription once that seems to fit. *Si monumentum requiris, circumspice*. If you seek his monument, look around you."

ABOUT THE AUTHOR

Jeffrey D. Stalk is a journalist and writer living in Los Angeles. He has worked for newspapers and wire services and has lived many years abroad. During his time in The Netherlands he learned about the the 1943 raid on the Amsterdam Hall of Records, which inspired this novel.

65720247R00190

Made in the USA
Middletown, DE
03 March 2018